it! Raunchy with a good storyline too!

Gemgem, Amazon

sex scenes are smoking, and surprising!

Rose, Good Reads

! Spicy, sexy and a super fun read. […] I found
ory gripping and the sex scenes so hot! […] Would
tely recommend!

Leana, Amazon

sexy with a great story that has lots of twists and
tur I read it in less than a week, such a page turner!

IzzyW, Amazon

t read, I didn't want it to end!

Facebook comment

ove, LOVED it! […] I just wish I'd saved it for my
er holiday […] Sequel please!

Miss R., Amazon

Th oughly enjoyed reading this, some may say a little too
m ! It's sexy, sassy and sensational! I really hope there's
to come from Annabelle Knight, a very talented author!

Amazon Customer

as a great storyline which is well written, certainly
predictable and I'm curious to see if we find out future
loits of Autumn!!

Lynne Robertson, Amazon

ABOUT THE AUTHOR

(Photo: Jennifer Gosling Photography)

Annabelle Knight is a sex and relationship expert. She's appeared on many TV programmes such as *This Morning*, *The O'Brien Show* and *Big Brother's Bit on the Side*. She's featured regularly in magazines and newspapers and can often be found frequenting the nation's airwaves offering sex advice and discussing hot topics.

ANNABELLE KNIGHT

The Endless Autumn

AUSTIN MACAULEY PUBLISHERS™
LONDON • CAMBRIDGE • NEW YORK • SHARJAH

A CIP catalogue record for this title is available from the British Library.

ISBN 978-1-78693-960-9 (Paperback)
ISBN 978-1-78693-961-6 (eBook)

www.austinmacauley.com

Revised Second Edition (2017)
First Published (2017)
Austin Macauley Publishers™ Ltd.
25 Canada Square
Canary Wharf
London
E14 5LQ

DEDICATION

I split this dedication two ways.

Firstly I dedicate this book to my sister. Without you I would have twice the inheritance but my life would only be half as good.

My dedication goes secondly to my husband, whose constant love, support and cups of tea saw this book, and my sanity, through to the end. I love you.

ACKNOWLEDGEMENTS

My Amazing Family

Danny and Andrew
(Blacksheep Management)

Lovehoney

Schmidt #nonewfriends

Kate Thompson

The Perverse Vegan

Jules Stenson

Lily, Lee and Jen

Pornhub

CHAPTER 1

'SHIT!' AUTUMN THOUGHT TO HERSELF AS SHE hastily cleaned her teeth. *'I swear I had more time than this!'* She stole a look at the clock adorning her vintage dresser; the minute hand ticked over to show the time had just gone eight in the morning.

It was the middle of the summer and already the day promised to be beautiful. Autumn Carter would have noticed this if she'd had time to open the curtains. Scrabbling around madly for clean clothes and still slightly groggy from the night before, Autumn tried in vain to get herself together before heading off to work. She was noticeably more hung-over than she should have been and this was seriously hindering her ability to perform even the most basic of tasks. She spat out her toothpaste, managed not to gag on the powerful taste and wiped her mouth on the corner of her boyfriend's towel, which had been neatly folded up and placed over the rail.

Returning to her bedroom and opening her chest of drawers for clean underwear, she re-checked the time, hopeful that the more she looked the slower time would go; sadly no such luck. She was now way beyond running late for work. She rummaged for a second trying to find a matching set, but her haste in putting clothes away meant that everything had been stuffed into the drawers awkwardly, making it impossible to find anything quickly. Resigning herself to the fact that she just wasn't one of those women who wore matching underwear, she pulled out a black bra and the first pair of knickers her fingers closed around.

"Why did I drink on a school night?" she muttered as she hastily pulled up the girlish pink pants fate had selected. She turned to her disorganised wardrobe now in an effort to find something half decent to wear. She chose an outfit speedily, opting for a green satin top and a high-waisted skirt combo. Autumn felt that the outfit was both professional and comfortable. Turning up hung-over for work was bad enough – but on a Friday? It screamed 'immaturity', and no matter how professional her outfit was it couldn't cover up her attitude! Thursday drinking was like a huge beacon to her colleagues. It cast a spotlight on the fact that she didn't take her job seriously enough and that she just couldn't wait for the weekend.

Autumn was undoubtedly irritated, but the worst thing about it was that she was irritated at herself. Clocking the time once more, her mind sprang into action. *'I need a good excuse,'* she thought. Bad traffic? Perhaps an accident had delayed my arrival? Or, she smiled to herself, perhaps just good old-fashioned women's problems? Yup, that's the one. Her boss, although a successful businessman and not afraid of anyone or anything, would definitely shy away from anything period related. Plus, it would be fun to watch the ever suave and always collected Jack Thorne squirm a bit under the pressure of having to discuss her time of the month. Autumn chuckled to herself and turned her attention back to the task in hand. Feeling annoyed and a bit hot and sticky, she tried to think of a way to do everything she needed to do in the time she had left.

She looked at her watch again, hoping that maybe, just maybe, she'd got it wrong. A further realisation set in. She should have left already. Real panic started to set in now as it dawned on her that not only would she be late, she'd also go hungry. This was due to the fact that there was absolutely no way she had time to grab even the quickest slice of toast, let alone time to sort out her lunch for the day.

"Uggghhhh," Autumn groaned aloud, a combination of annoyance and resignation lacing her voice. The dull, throbbing, wine-induced headache was creeping back. It seemed like only five minutes had passed since her boyfriend Ben had woken her up with a soft kiss on the forehead and her must-have cup of morning coffee, but unfortunately for Autumn, it had been more than an hour ago! She glanced in the mirror for a last-minute once-over before leaving the house. Autumn stopped dead in her tracks.

"What the…?" She trailed off, staring at her mid-section in the mirror. There, on her favourite Karen Millen satin top, was a horrible, oily-looking stain. It was the kind of stain that instinct told you would never truly be gone, and she knew that no matter how much she washed that top there would always be a small, dark, discoloured patch like a ghost of this terrible morning haunting her. Angrily she scrubbed at the stain with a half-used face-wipe that she had grabbed out of the bin, annoyed with herself for not getting up on time, being so messy and just generally bowling around from one disaster to the next. How the hell had Ben got the time or energy to get to the gym while she was still snoring in bed?

Autumn had got her morning routine down to a fine art and over the last six months whilst working at Thorne PR had slashed the time she needed to get ready for work by almost half. Now it took her a mere 30 minutes to shower, eat breakfast, slap on a bit of makeup, throw on one of her many black pencil skirt/satin top combos and get herself en route to the office. She dabbed at the stain with a dry cotton pad and threw it in the bin when she was sufficiently satisfied that it was no longer glaringly obvious. Finally, Autumn felt ready to leave. She grabbed for her bag, totally missed it and knocked the contents all over her bedroom floor.

"FUCK!" she scolded herself harshly. This was the final straw. She squatted down to retrieve her belongings. Her pencil skirt was way too tight nowadays and the waistband dug in uncomfortably. Autumn made a mental note to politely decline any treats that might be offered to her during the day. Which, with the best will in the world, would be hard as it was nearly impossible to resist any of June's home-baked goods. She may not have been the greatest admin assistant ever born, but her chocolate chunk flapjacks were to die for! Mouth salivating slightly, Autumn shook the idea from her head and scooped her belongings back into her bag, zipped it and slung it over her shoulder as she stood up. Nimbly as she hopped downstairs Autumn tried to remember where she'd kicked off her shoes the previous evening, and, for the tenth time that morning, cursed herself for not being more organised. She stopped at the foot of the stairs and surveyed the living room, hoping to catch a glimpse of her work heels.

Autumn's living room, although homely, echoed the chaos of her wardrobe. In the middle of the spacious open plan room was a coffee table, which boasted a few used mugs, a couple of empty takeaway boxes and one empty bottle of Malbec that she'd polished off the night before. However, underneath all the clutter, the table itself was beautiful. It was cream, elegant and seemed to be everything she wanted to be. It had previously belonged to her parents and she loved it. Either side of the coffee table and facing each other were two sofas. They were in the same state of disarray, both of them littered with study books, notebooks, half-written articles, or magazines of a less intellectual persuasion.

Again, she cursed herself. "Why didn't I finish that bloody essay?" she said aloud. "Why did I get a takeaway and drink a bottle of red?" Autumn inwardly called herself a moron and decided that once again she needed to sort herself out. Autumn needed get her shit together and become a fully functioning, well-rounded young woman.

Autumn wasn't just late for work. It seemed like she was late for everything nowadays especially since her academic workload had started piling up. Even though she only worked part-time at Thorne Public Relations, it seemed like a full-time position; she was definitely taking on a bit more than she could handle. Initially she had been hired as an admin assistant; however, she'd soon taken on the role of receptionist as well. She took a minute to vow to herself that she'd make a special effort from now on, that she'd sort out her life and be one of those super-polished professional power types that only drank champagne and teetered around in nothing less than Christian Louboutin skyscraper heels. She headed to the kitchen to grab something, anything, out of the fridge and noticed her shoes haphazardly left in front of the hall mirror on her way.

In the kitchen, the sight that met her eyes stopped her in her tracks. Autumn smiled to herself: the kitchen was spotless, washing up done and put away, kitchen counter sparkling and not even so much as a toast crumb on the side! Opening the fridge, she grinned as in it was a lunch box with some Paracetamol and a little note written on a pink heart Post-it taped on top.

'What a guy,' she thought. *'He always knows what to do to make things just that little bit better.'*

Ben Wood was a reasonably new to the industry actor and he had done well during his short time trying to make it. He had recently secured himself a small role in *The Edge*, a wonderfully gritty crime drama on Sky. It wasn't a big role but it had started to transform his life. Before, he'd do the odd advert, be an extra in a period drama or just wait tables at a restaurant in town, but now, with his new role secured, he had a lot more freedom. He spent a lot of time at the gym and when he wasn't perfecting his physique he was learning lines on set. Autumn was lucky. He was gorgeous, funny, caring and best of all he was hers. They'd been together for almost two years, and since they met had barely spent any time apart, well aside from when he was at the gym. Which at the moment seemed like every waking second. Since he'd gained a little bit of profile he'd become very image-conscious. He more than made up for his absence in thoughtful little ways, though, and Autumn couldn't hold it against him. She knew Ben had worked hard for this and given up a stable and well paid job as an estate agent to chase his dream, and after all, he was an actor; his looks mattered!

'Not like me,' she thought as she caught a glimpse of her reflection in the gold shabby-chic, full-length mirror in their hallway. Autumn was below average height – 'petite', Ben liked to call it, but who was he kidding? She was tiny! She surveyed herself: her blonde hair had gone a bit flat, not a look she cared for. *'If only people knew the secret battle girls with thin hair went through every day,'* she mused as she tried to give her hair do a bit of a lift.

"So much for the Brigitte Bardot bouffant I was aiming for," she muttered to herself as she continued her attempt to up the volume. She re-pinned a stray piece of hair and scrunched her fingers through the roots. Settling down hadn't been kind to her figure. Autumn did scrub up well and wasn't about to fall into the morbidly obese category any time soon but she was still struggling to adjust to her curves. At college Autumn had been on the netball team, the hockey team and had run cross-country. Her athletic figure had been lost at university. It was hard to keep a trim tum when you replaced going for a run in the park with going for a rum in the pub. She blamed a combination of factors: her workload, of course the cheap drinks and not forgetting buy-one get-one-free pizza at Pizza King on the way home from a night out. Now, between studying and working like a crazy person, her dress size was slowly on the up.

'Still,' she thought, *'I've always got my health!'* Doing an exercise her best friend David had suggested, she quickly listed five things she liked about herself: "Good skin, nice nails, long eyelashes…" She trailed off, wondering why she could only ever get to three.

"Really, that's all I've got, and one of these aren't even real!" she uttered, staring at her long, French-manicured nails. Giving up on the last two she made one last-ditch attempt to look presentable. Autumn smoothed down her skirt, 'jujjed' up her hair, applied a nice clear lip balm and slipped on her shoes before heading out the door. She flicked off the light switch as she went and heard a loud pop. *'I'll fix that later,'* she thought to herself, knowing deep down that Ben would do it when he got in. The door closed behind her, the Yale lock offering a satisfying clunk as she went, protecting her little home.

It was a beautiful day. Her little red Fiesta was thick and stuffy but the sun felt nice on her skin, her wine-induced headache was fading, the Paracetamol was starting to take effect and the dulcet tones of Ed Sheeran playing on the radio soothed her further. The song was like an aural massage, and a much needed one at that. It looked like she wasn't going to have to make up an excuse about why she was late for work. The traffic was dense with commuters, who, Autumn suspected, were in the same boat as her. Even so she was moving steadily and she felt herself drift into autopilot as she navigated the same road she'd driven down almost every day for the last year. The office was on the outskirts of town, and the drive was pleasant enough; although a brief stint on the motorway was needed, she enjoyed it nonetheless. Especially on days like today when the sky was clear with only a few billowing clouds lazily floating by. The fields, which were to either side, were dotted with cows lazing happily in the sunshine and occasionally bending down to dine on the lush grass beneath. It was around a twenty-minute drive from her house to Thorne Public Relations, give or take five or ten minutes if a coffee and cake stop were needed. The conveniently positioned service station had a great little café and Autumn was partial to pretty much all of their offerings. Today, however, was a different story, and no such pit stop could be made. She barely had time to indicate, let alone stop for her usual pep-me-up double-shot coffee and white chocolate and raspberry muffin. Mourning the loss of her sweet treats momentarily, Autumn almost missed the turning.

"Shit!" she muttered under her breath as she did a spot of evasive driving, weaving in front of the car slightly behind her. The car beeped and Autumn saw in the rear-view mirror a solitary finger sticking up at her.

'Wanker,' she thought, even though she knew that she was in the wrong. It didn't stop her being mad at the man behind her; she felt herself going red as she put her foot down in an attempt to get away from the guy. Pulling down the sun visor, Autumn checked that her complexion wasn't beetroot. A few minutes later she was pulling up beside the offices of Thorne Public Relations. She parked and hastily unbuckled her seatbelt, keen to get into the office before anyone could notice her late arrival. She grabbed her bag from the passenger seat and got out of the car before slamming the car door behind

her with a bit too much force. Autumn rushed up to the gate and pushed at the heavy iron rail expecting its usual metallic creak as it opened, but nothing. It was locked. Usually some early hours worker would leave it propped open so that other colleagues could just slip in without having to mess around with their key fobs. Giving the mirrored entry system the evil eye, she unzipped her bag and stuck her hand in, trying to locate her keys with minimal effort. After a quick rummage, she was still keyless.

"Hmmm, where are you?" she said out loud as she delved deeper; the keys were still somehow managing to evade her grasp. Sighing at her seemingly endless parade of bad luck she plonked her bag on the wall, unzipped it fully and wiped her forehead as she began to take things out one by one. First came her purse, a dark green one that her mum had bought for her several years ago. It was a bit frayed at the edges and the clasp didn't really work but it was a firm favourite and wouldn't be getting replaced anytime soon. Next was her copy of *Wow* magazine, and finally her makeup bag, which was considerably slimmer than it used to be. The shoulder strap of her top fell down, and Autumn could feel herself getting irritated. She wiped the new layer of sweat that had formed away from her forehead. The sun that had been such a blessing earlier was now beginning to get on her nerves. The bag was now practically empty apart from a few receipts that had been hastily stuffed in on one of the many other occasions where she was running late and her lack of time didn't permit her to put them away properly. Her keys weren't there. Autumn cursed and realised they must have fallen out earlier when she knocked the contents of her bag all over the bedroom floor. She looked at her watch and cursed again; God knows how many phone calls she'd have missed. Jack would be pissed but thankfully he wasn't in until lunchtime so there was some time for damage limitation.

"Ahem."

There was a deep clearing of a throat from behind her. Autumn spun round on her heel, almost knocking the array of her belongings off the wall. Her heart sank as she realised who it was behind her.

'Fuuuuuuck!' she thought desperately. What was he doing here so early? He wasn't meant to be here until later, 'Goddamn!' Trying to look even just the tiniest bit collected, she straightened up and looked him in the eye before immediately lowering her gaze in a mixture of frustration and embarrassment at being both late *and* caught trapped outside by her boss.

"Umm, hi Ja…" she managed before being cut off.

"Mr Thorne," he said abruptly. Autumn knew she was in trouble; he never made her call him Mr Thorne. That term was reserved for people he was at odds with or anyone he felt 'below' him.

"I, err, I left my keys…" She began mumbling apologetically, trying to offer a half-decent explanation for her tardiness. She could feel his gaze boring into her; she felt like a naughty schoolchild caught stealing sweets and knew that her cheeks would be flushed pink with embarrassment. Without saying anything, Jack leaned over Autumn, his hand resting on her shoulder, and gently but firmly moved her out of the way. As he moved past her she inhaled his scent; he actually smelt really good. Her senses filled with a clean but musky aroma. The smell made Autumn's stomach flip slightly. 'It must be the same fragrance Ben has, or had, or wore once,' she reasoned.

Jack swiped his fob and the gate clicked open loudly and offered a rusty scraping noise as it was pushed open. The harsh, grating sound snapped Autumn back to her senses. Jack walked through leaving her in his wake, her hand replacing his on her shoulder. She brushed away at the hot patch she now felt on there and hurriedly collected up her belongings, not for the first time that day. Autumn scurried in after him, the hot feeling of embarrassment still colouring her cheeks.

CHAPTER 2

AS AUTUMN WALKED THROUGH THE RECEPTION area and to her desk, the phone went and the familiar ringing forced her pace to quicken. Slightly out of breath she snatched up the receiver.

"Good morning, Thorne Public Relations, how may I direct your call?" Autumn's voice oozed professional calm; if only the person on the other end of the phone could see her. If there was one thing that could be said about Autumn Carter it was that when the time really called for it she could put on a show. Inside she was a drowning moron, on the outside she was an uber-calm, cool and collected young professional who held down studying for a journalism degree along with a very happy relationship and a full-time, part-time job. On the end of the phone was Chris Lambert. Chris was a major client of the firm, in his fifties and insisted on everyone calling him 'C', although Autumn knew what she thought the initial should actually stand for. Autumn took great pleasure in making a point of calling him 'Chris' at every opportunity. I mean, what did he think he was, a member of an American boy band? He was pretty average looking with a bit of stubble and never quite wearing the right tie with his suits. Standing at almost six foot tall, and greying at the temples slightly, it was clear that an indulgent lifestyle had taken its toll on him. His midsection always pushed uncomfortably against his shirt, which left the buttons constantly fighting a battle to hold on. Autumn could see he'd been quite attractive in his younger days, but as it stood now not so much.

Chris Lambert was a wealthy sports media type who had used Thorne PR for years. He was also amid a messy divorce and in his own words wanted to financially flay his soon to be ex wife. Although in Autumn's mind it was he who owed her. He'd put her through hell by the sounds of it with a string of affairs with women who gradually became younger and younger. To her it was his poor wife who'd be leaving this relationship with the battle wounds, not him. Chris was there to discuss his company's PR strategies; still, that little fact didn't stop 'C' from telling absolutely everyone who would give him the time of day how his divorce was going. Autumn knew it wasn't her job to have an opinion on the clients at Thorne PR, but she couldn't help feeling a bit weirded out by Chris Lambert. Instead of dwelling on these feelings she switched on pro mode and did her best to answer the seemingly millions of questions Chris was firing at her. When was Jack back in? Did she know if provisions had been made for their meeting? Was Jack pencilled in for anything else that afternoon? She smiled internally. She'd spent almost a year answering these questions from him and had come to know that they were all code for: I'm going to be a bit late; I want some free food and whatever booze is going, even if it is only 1 p.m. Also, I plan on staying for a while, so cancel or move anything else scheduled in for that day.

Chris Lambert was such a strange man, expecting everyone else to take him and his life so seriously but not doing so himself. Autumn wondered whether the divorce really was his idea, but he seemed to be adamant that he wanted rid of his wife. Autumn thought she sensed sadness within Chris whenever the topic of his divorce was brought up: his eyes flashed, crestfallen for just a minute, every time it was mentioned. If Autumn was a betting girl, she'd have put money on the divorce not being entirely his idea. Her information had been acquired using a variety of tactics. Chris wasn't exactly backward at coming forward and it seemed like he wanted to get his side of the story out first. It didn't really matter who he was talking to, as long as he was the one doing the talking. In his desperate attempt to appear to be the one in the driving seat divorce-wise, he often over-shared information. The extra lines that had appeared around his eyes over the last few months were obvious signs, Autumn thought, that the divorce was taking its toll on him. But then again, she reasoned that could be down a variety of factors: they were talking about Chris Lambert, after all, and it could be the abundance of alcohol or maybe another twenty-two year-old keeping him up at night. Autumn shuddered at the thought of Chris and a twenty-two year-old doing anything, let alone staying up to the early hours fumbling about.

Returning her attention to the phone call, she almost second-naturedly answered Chris's questions. "Yes Chris, everything's in place. No, Jack hasn't got anything else today. Actually, Jack's already in the building." The last answer wasn't quite what Chris had hoped to hear. Jack, although accommodating for all his clients, didn't like to be kept waiting and was never afraid to make it known. It had been made quite clear on more than one occasion that Jack Thorne was possibly one of the only people on the planet who could intimidate Chris Lambert.

She replaced the receiver and opened up her emails. The little red light on the answering machine was flashing manically. Autumn stopped for a second, took a deep breath and stuck a Post-it note over the flashing light.

"That's better," she said to herself. Autumn scanned her inbox and selected the most important one to deal with first. She clicked on one from D. Davies. So what if D. Davies happened to be her closest friends from her course? David was currently halfway around the world on a whistle-stop tour of America and Autumn missed him tremendously. He was due home next week and she couldn't wait for her partner in crime to return. A day without his funny texts, emails and calls seemed like an entire year. David was tall, very tall in fact: he towered over Autumn which, by the end of any time spent together left her with a very sore neck. He was also incredibly funny, generous to a fault and really intelligent. Autumn had often found herself favouring the help of David rather than her tutor. No disrespect to their lecturer, but when someone regularly confused the overhead projector's remote control for a whiteboard eraser then they kind of lost all academic authority.

The only thing that could be improved upon when it came to David was his dress sense. He loved bright clothing and never cared if his outfit went together well. Autumn's favourite outfit of David's had to be, hands down, the bright green chinos that he always paired with a lovely lilac jumper.

Double clicking on the email, it opened up into full view. Autumn began reading, feeling only ever so slightly guilty that there were at least a dozen 'work' emails to get through and God knows how many phone calls to return. Still, that didn't stop her from poring over David's email first.

Dearest Darling Autumn,

Whaddup home girl? This will be the last email I send you until I'm home. I'm doing another few days travelling, then we're renting a car and driving part of the Pacific Coast Highway before getting our flight back. I expect I'm going to be super jet-lagged so I'm going to have to insist you stay up all night with us drinking Jack & Coke and playing Texas hold 'em! (I'm so Americanized!) By the way, you may be wondering who 'we/us' is… Well, brace yourself. I've met someone! He's coming back with me. You know me, super impulsive and never think a thing through. Well, we met, hit it off and the rest as they say is history! I've invited him to stay with me. His 'mom' lives down south near Surrey so he's going to visit her while he's over. You'll love him. His name's Gregg, he's a fitness freak, a little bit older than me, he's really nice, well actually he's pretty perfect. Can't wait for you to meet him! Anyway, gotta dash sweets. Be good and give that big hunk of a man of yours a kiss from me.

Love always D x

The phone next to her burst into life. Its ring was almost sarcastically loud; the sound tore into Autumn's brain and clawed at the receding headache, daring it to return to full force. She had barely finished reading David's email and scouring through some of the pictures he'd sent. She was so jealous. He looked tanned, happy and relaxed in every single picture. He was right, his new boyfriend was lovely looking! Gregg was a bit shorter than David and had dark eyes and a warm, dark, chocolatey-smooth skin tone similar to an old school friend of hers, leading Autumn to believe that, just like her friend Asser Bailey, David's new man could be of Jamaican descent. He had a mop of curly hair with a few sun-kissed blond streaks running through the tips. Autumn sat back in her chair, still gazing at the photos David had sent. He'd been gone for barely a month and already he'd found someone willing to fly halfway around the world for him. She knew that David wouldn't struggle to catch up with the work he'd missed out on doing over the summer break. If Autumn had decided to go travelling over the summer, then that would have meant the final nail in her coffin. Her academic career would have been over and she would have almost certainly received a big fat 'F' on her final exam paper.

The telephone on her desk rang; the interruption brought her back to the real world with a thud.

"Okay, okay!" Autumn grumbled as she snatched up the receiver once again. "Good Morning, Thorne Public Relations, how may I direct your call?" Her voice took on that smooth professional tone that she reserved for Thorne Public Relations calls. It was 'C' again, informing her that he was going to be just the teeniest bit late.

'No surprise there then,' she thought to herself.

"So how long do you think you'll be, Chris?" she cut him off mid-excuse, eager to get off the phone and back to David's pictures. Chris assured her that he was, as they spoke, literally in the car and on his way. She hung up the phone convinced she'd heard the ping of a microwave in the background and that 'C' wouldn't be with them anytime soon. Jack wasn't going to be thrilled about being kept waiting but the money brought in by this client would mean that he'd have to bite his tongue, or at least try to.

Autumn reached down and pulled on a light cardigan; even though the weather was warm the old stone part of the building that her desk sat in always seemed to feel cool. She returned to her emails, thinking better of continuing with David's online scrapbook and opting to open what seemed to be the most important work-related one. She typed her replies furiously in an effort to get as much work done as swiftly as possible. She didn't fancy telling Jack that not only would he be waiting a while for his meeting, she hadn't done anything she was meant to do. She didn't think a blow-by-blow account of David's trip, tan and handsome new man would be appreciated at all.

It was a full hour before Chris walked through the door, red-faced and sweaty like a teenage boy being caught with a bottle of lotion in one hand and a dodgy magazine in the other. After the obligatory excuses, consisting of roadworks, traffic jams and lost keys – *'Hold on, I thought you were in the car, on your way when you called?'* Autumn mused – she settled him down in the boardroom and bought him a glass of water which he gulped at noisily, making Autumn's stomach turn. She returned to her desk, picked up the phone and punched in Jack's extension number. It rang several times before he picked up.

"Yes?" A curt voice barked down the phone.

"Err, Mr Lambert's here to see you. He's waiting in the meeting room," Autumn replied, her tone cool bordering on frosty. There was no word from Jack, just a grunt of acknowledgement, then the phone went dead.

'Twat,' she fumed to herself. Okay, she'd been late and missed a few calls but he was behaving like a snotty little brat, totally unprofessional and just downright rude. After all it wasn't her fault he'd been early, nor was she to blame for Chris being about a decade late! She could feel herself bubbling inside, a mixture of anger and frustration. She knew she'd get the blame for anything else that went wrong in Jack's precious little world today.

'I mean, really! Who does he think he is, speaking to me like something he stepped in, putting the phone down on me, touching my shoulder like that... ugh!'

The door of the boardroom opened then slammed shut. Autumn could hear muffled but raised voices; the rough deep baritone of Jack versus the slightly Northern, much more softly-spoken, stutterings of Chris Lambert. Autumn returned to her desk, secure in the knowledge that neither one of them would be causing her any more problems for some time now. She sank back in her chair, and even though she'd not exactly been employee of the month this morning, she felt like she'd done a full day's work already. She slipped off her shoes underneath her desk and rubbed her foot: aching feet already and it wasn't even lunch time. As she considered this her hand slid from her bare foot and into her bag. A quick text to Ben would be okay, surely? No one was around and he'd be back home by now after his gym session. She reasoned that she needed to at least send a message to thank him for the flawlessly clean kitchen, the thoughtful food and the lifesaving Paracetamol. In reality, though, she just wanted a friendly word from her boyfriend. She knew just hearing from Ben would comfort her and make her feel a bit better about everything. She tapped at her keypad quickly, keeping one eye on the doorway just in case. When the message was sent she shoved her phone back in the side pocket of her bag and reluctantly turned her attention back to her emails. For Autumn, getting stuck into work today was going to be easier said than done.

CHAPTER 3

AUTUMN STARED AT THE TOP RIGHT HAND CORNER of her computer screen: the clock seemed to have been stuck at two minutes to five for the last hour. She knew clock-watching wasn't going to help matters, and it certainly hadn't made the day go faster, but she couldn't help it. As her mum always said, "A watched pot never boils, darling." The day's monotony of replying to emails had been broken up slightly by a visit from one of her colleagues. Although she was young, Rosa was a project manager. Her intelligence and savvy ability had ensured she'd climbed the career ladder in record time. Rosa had become one of Autumn's closest friends at the firm. She was tall, toned and very attractive. To top it all off she was really kind and had a wicked sense of humour. Autumn felt genuinely lucky to have found such a good friend in Rosa. She had visited Autumn at least a couple of times during the day, under the guise of needing something posting, or some other menial office task that no one else seemed willing to do. Whilst at the reception she'd hung out with Autumn for a bit. They'd had a good old gossip, caught up on the latest office politics, talked shopping and chatted about one of Rosa's many men. Mid-conversation Autumn's eyes dropped: she immediately noticed something glistening around Rosa's wrist.

"What is that?" Autumn exclaimed and held out her hand.

"What?" asked Rosa, a coy grin spreading across her olive face.

"That!" Autumn returned, pointing to Rosa's wrist.

Wrapped around Rosa's delicate tanned wrist was a beautiful diamond tennis bracelet. It glistened in the sunlight, which cascaded through the full-length windows positioned behind Autumn's desk. Rosa looked at her, and then at the bracelet. She rolled it around in her delicate fingers, inspecting the glint of each diamond.

"A friend bought it for me," she offered without taking her eyes off it.

"A friend?" Autumn asked incredulously. "You mean a man friend?"

"Maybe..." Rosa blushed slightly. "It's from that really expensive jewellers in town, you know the one by Franco's Bar? You know, what's it called?" she asked, still staring at her bracelet and not meeting Autumn's eyes.

"It's called John Cusson and you know that perfectly well – don't change the subject, Rosa! Is that or is that not from a male admirer?"

Rosa blushed further, pink flushing her tanned face. Autumn was not used to seeing her friend embarrassed.

"He's just a good friend," Rosa said. Autumn didn't reply but instead left that unsatisfactory answer hanging in the air like the bad lie that it was. "Fine, you win," Rosa said, breaking the silence. "Yes. A male admirer bought it for me. A really nice male admirer, that I might have started dating."

"You've been dating someone? Since when?" Autumn asked.

She could barely believe what she was hearing. Rosa was a serial dater who never seemed to let anyone get close to her; most men barely saw a third date. She was, without a doubt, an expert on dating. Rosa was forever being asked out and accepting and it was easy to see why. Rosa was stunning inside and out and her natural beauty teamed with her sparkling personality meant that she was never short of admirers. Men seemed to be instantly drawn to her.

It was the end of the working week; Rosa had already been out with two different guys and apparently had a secret someone that deemed her worthy enough of such a fantastic piece of jewellery. Autumn had her suspicions. She knew there was one guy Rosa had been out with whom she must have really liked. When Autumn had asked her if she was going to see him again, Rosa had answered with a coy smile and shrug of her shoulders rather than her standard, dismissive reply of "Nah." Autumn recalled thinking that Rosa must have had a bit of a thing for him, but whenever Autumn had pressed her on the subject all Rosa had said was that he was good looking and had a great body. Autumn suspected Rosa liked him for more than that but she'd always been one to keep her cards close to her chest and Autumn knew that this time would be no different. There had been no mention or even slight indication that they were at the 'diamond bracelet' stage of the relationship yet, so it was little wonder Autumn had found it difficult to contain her surprise.

Rosa was the type of woman who felt that if you didn't let them get close then you'd never get hurt. Autumn understood where she was coming from but still found it an ideal hard to get on board with. After all, in Autumn's humble opinion, what was worth more of a risk than love?

"Why don't you just give him a proper chance?" Autumn had asked her friend; she remembered jumping at the sound of an old-fashioned bike horn that sounded from Rosa's bag.

'Saved by the bell,' Autumn thought to herself, wincing slightly as Rosa pulled the phone from her bag. The loud bike

horn text tone sounded for a second and third time in quick succession. *'Someone's keen,'* she mused to herself.

"Because I don't know if I really want to yet, so I'm taking it slowly for now," Rosa said, scrabbling to silence her phone. "I'm young, I like dating and when I do decide to settle down then I will." She looked at the screen of her phone with the faintest smile.

"But what happens if he's 'the one' and you just don't give him a proper chance?" Autumn had questioned.

"Oh, come on!" Rosa had answered incredulously. "I know you're all pro-love and all that but you don't seriously think there's only one person for everyone, do you?"

Autumn hadn't really known what to say to this. So she avoided giving an answer, instead changing the subject entirely. When Rosa left to continue with her working day Autumn had begun to give the notion some thought. She had never truly considered it before. She knew that she'd met Ben, she'd fallen in love with him faster than a rate of knots and that she wanted to be with him and only him. It wasn't really a conscious decision, it just *was*. He was a constant support to her; he looked after her, loved her and was the best thing about her. He made her want to do better in life and to be a better person. Thinking about this made her grin, a big grin that took over her entire face. She must have looked ridiculous, sat there by herself, smiling like a loon and staring off into space. A fellow employee walked past and stared at her like it was Angelina Jolie and not Autumn Carter that was sat at reception. Sometimes even Autumn made herself feel sick at how slushy she was.

Five p.m. on the dot. *'Yes!'* Autumn thought, *'home time.'* She gathered up her bag and slung it over her arm and rummaged for her car keys. She stopped dead in her tracks by

Jack's deep voice: "Autumn, can I see you for a moment in my office please?"

Jack's words rumbled through the nearly deserted hallway, down the stone staircase and into the reception. Most of the employees had left early: it was a Friday, after all, and there had to be some perks to the job. Dumping her bag back down onto her chair, Autumn exhaled loudly and apprehensively tiptoed her way up the large staircase, a little uncertain of why exactly she was trying to be quiet. She turned down the hall and made the short walk to Jack's office. Autumn reached out to Jack's door and as soon as her fingers brushed the cold metal of the antique steel door handle, she realised she was still shoeless. Turning on her heel she began back down the corridor: she couldn't have a meeting about being unprofessional with no shoes on.

There were still a couple of people milling about in the offices to the side of the hallway. The cleaner was dragging an ancient-looking Hoover into the boardroom; Autumn nodded towards her and managed a half-smile. Her stomach was doing somersaults. Was Jack going to yell? Was she going to have to stay late? Was she about to be fired? She got back to her desk and bent down; with as much grace as a baby elephant she reached down for her shoes and slipped them on. Running back into the hallway she decided to opt for the lift instead; procrastination was not her friend right now and she was going to do everything in her power to get this meeting over and done with as soon as possible.

Inevitably Autumn reached Jack's office. The door was now ajar, so she hesitated, her knuckle hovering just an inch from the solid oak door and just below the silver-plated plaque that bore Jack's full name, 'Jack Thomas Thorne' and the position which he held at the company, 'CEO'. Taking a deep breath and preparing for the worst she knocked. She was beckoned in from the inner depths of Jack's sanctum. She pushed the door open fully and stepped inside.

Jack's office was impressive, to say the least. It had once been two rooms but with the building's refurbishment a few years ago had since been knocked into one, very grand, space. Jack's décor was masculine and modern; the room was a monochrome masterpiece that oozed importance and elegance in equal measure. It smelt good: the musky odour from earlier was stronger in here, and on his desk were a top of the range design computer, a box of cigars and his diary. This was a black leather-bound book with solid silver corner protectors and his name embossed in gold leaf on the front. Obviously, Autumn had never been inside the diary but she was certainly familiar with it; he was barely seen without it. For someone who ran a PR and design business which was essentially built on the latest technology, it seemed odd to her that the CEO would rely solely on an old-fashioned diary to track all his comings and goings.

All in all, Jack's office certainly wasn't your run of the mill boss's office. A floor to ceiling circular fireplace stood proudly in the centre of the room, Jack's huge chrome and glass desk imposed itself in front of the back wall and in front of it sat two black leather armchairs, ensuring that Jack's guests were as comfortable as he was. Large black bookshelves lined the walls either side, packed with an array of books, which from what Autumn could tell, covered every topic from exotic travel to interior design and everything else in between. In the far corner of the room rested a couple of white canvas sofas, and a state of the art television hung on the wall scrolling through images of the company's most successful and well known campaigns. The French doors, which were painted in a beautiful dove grey, overlooked the veranda where, when the weather permitted, Jack would entertain clients and hold meetings with other members of staff. The room was finished off with expensive looking furnishings and, to top it all off, a drinks cabinet boasting a very expensive collection of high-priced spirits all set out behind what was again an expensive selection of cut crystal glasses.

Autumn relaxed a little when she saw Jack: his eyebrows weren't knotted together and his forehead wasn't a jumble of stress lines. He didn't look like a person who was about to fire someone. He was reclining slightly and coming from some invisible source was soft jazz music – not exactly to Autumn's taste but then again there was over a decade between them.

"You wanted to see me?" she said.

"Sit down," answered Jack, gesturing to the black leather chair in front of his desk without lifting his eyes from the papers in front of him. Autumn perched; she didn't want to stay for long as she had a tonne of course work to get through and besides, Ben would be back at home, waiting for her.

"Drink?" Jack offered, which Autumn politely declined.

"So, I want to talk to you about today, Autumn." Jack stared at her, Autumn felt uncomfortable under his gaze. She could feel his eyes boring into her and shifted in her seat.

"It won't happen again..." she started to defend herself when he raised his hand to silence her.

"That's not what I've asked you here for, I mean what happened at the gate." Autumn stared, mouth slightly open, she felt her face redden slightly and shifted in her seat once more. Jack cleared his throat and went on, "I apologise if I was inappropriate in any way. To tell the truth I was a bit embarrassed by the whole thing. I've not been the easiest boss in the world today, and I just wanted to apologise in person."

Autumn's mind flashed back to his warm breath on the nape of her neck, to his hand on her shoulder, her bare flesh burning at his touch. She was getting hot again:

embarrassment flushing her cheeks, she shrugged off her cardigan and bundled it up before placing it on her lap. His eyes followed the cardigan and rested there for a few seconds longer than they should have. Autumn began to feel uncomfortable all over again. What was happening here? Did she have a crush on Jack? Did he have a crush on her? Were they flirting?

'Oh God,' she thought, *'this is just awful.'* Her mouth was dry, she shifted in her seat uncomfortably. She had never once thought of Jack in this way. In fact, she'd never thought about anyone else other than Ben in that way.

"Actually, I will have that drink, if it's still going?"

As soon as the words were out of her mouth Autumn regretted them. What was she doing? Was she reading too much into this? He's brought me up here to apologise, not make a move on me. She felt silly and chided herself for behaving in such a way, like an awkward teenager with a crush on their teacher. Her embarrassment was apparent because Jack was grinning slightly.

"What's up?" His tone was more jovial now, almost mocking.

"Nothing," Autumn muttered. "I'm just..." she trailed off and smiled. "I'm just being silly."

Jack poured her a small whiskey, and as if guessing she'd question the stingy amount explained it away with the fact that he knew she would have to drive home. Autumn sipped at the whiskey: it felt good, and it slipped down her throat easily. She was surprised at how much she enjoyed it, especially considering she'd spent a great deal of her day feeling hung-over. The golden liquor was deep and comforting, it warmed her chest and began to burn at the back of her throat. She stifled a small cough. Jack glanced up at her; apparently her whiskey-induced splutter had stolen his attention from something important. He returned his gaze and knitted his eyebrows together, a look of mild annoyance settling on his features.

Several minutes went by. Not a word was uttered and Autumn began to feel uncomfortable again. She now felt as if the tension was actually visible, and that Jack hadn't even noticed. She didn't know what she was doing there. He'd apologised and she'd prolonged the meeting by asking for a drink. Now he wanted to get back to his work and she was sat there like a lemon, choking down whiskey that probably cost more than she could earn in a month. He flipped over the page of the document that he was concentrating on so fiercely. She sat there, fiddling with the ring on her index finger; she stole a glance at Jack, he was still fixated on his paperwork; she wriggled in her seat, pulling at her blouse, and tried to smooth her skirt down, anything to make this feel even just the tiniest bit less awkward.

She glanced up again. Jack's eyes were no longer averted they were locked onto her. He fixed her with an intensity that seemed to gnaw away at the last bit of comfort in the room. Feeling awkward, she scolded herself for being so childlike. Autumn couldn't fathom why was she behaving so oddly. She'd been in Jack's company plenty of times and had never had this sort of reaction to him looking at her. She told herself, once again, that he'd bought her here to make amends, to apologise, and here she was, sat in his office feeling like he'd just propositioned her. After all, he couldn't exactly help how he looked at a person.

She drained the rest of her glass and went to set it down on his desk. Already condensation had formed on the outside and it slipped from her hand and fell the last inch with an audible clunk. The noise made her jump. Standing up quickly she smoothed down her skirt, more out of habit than anything else and thanked him for the drink. Autumn began to gather up her belongings wishing to leave whilst she still had a modicum of dignity left.

"Sure I can't tempt you with another?" he asked, almost more out of politeness than anything else. Autumn could tell that he just wanted to get on with his work and the time for socialising with the boss had passed.

"Small?" he asked.

Maybe she'd read the situation wrongly, maybe the uncomfortable silences and intense stares were just how Jack had a nice time? Even if that were the case it wasn't exactly how Autumn chose to enjoy herself. She wanted to go, but some part of her wanted to stay, just to see what would happen in the following minutes or hours she spent in his company. Against her better judgement, she sat back down, nodding to another glass. She really shouldn't. The rose gold face of the watch her great grandmother had left her reassured her, though. It told her that the time was twenty past five: it felt like she'd been there much longer. Autumn decided, perhaps against her better judgement, that she could afford another ten minutes or so.

"Just a very small one," she concluded, an air of defeat to her voice. "I do still need to drive home, after all."

CHAPTER 4

AUTUMN CLIMBED OUT OF THE TAXI, ONE HAND steadying her as she ducked out of the passenger door, a little tipsier than she should have been. She was regretting having that second, and third, drink. Jack had insisted on paying for a taxi to get her home safely; she'd protested, insisting that she didn't have time to wait for a cab, as she needed to get home quickly. He'd pressed the matter, insisting on her getting home safely. He even offered to pay for a return journey to collect her car the following day and gave her his company login details for the taxi firm they used so she could retrieve her car easily, and for free. Autumn again left out the fact that the reason she was keen to get home was her doting boyfriend, waiting patiently for her. Autumn couldn't believe the 'ten minutes or so' she had intended to stay for had turned into another hour. Jack's words still echoed in her head.

"It's better to be late in this life than early to the next, Autumn. You're waiting for a taxi and that, my dear, is that," Jack had said, so wait she did. She'd already dropped Ben a text to let him know she was coming home later than she'd intended and with the whiskey and conversation getting her a little hot under the collar she had followed up with a slightly racier text, outlining exactly what she wanted to happen when she eventually did return home. As she sat there, mere feet from her boss typing out the illicit words, she felt a sudden feeling of power wash over her. Jack had no idea the kind of filth she was sending to Ben and that fed her ego like lighter fluid fuels a flame.

The time in Jack's office had begun with polite conversation. He was friendly enough; the exchange between them had begun with office chat. Autumn had commented on the new coffee machine in the staff lounge and Jack had countered by asking her what she thought about the new seating arrangement in there. The conversation had been stiff to begin with but gradually warmed into something a little looser. In the time Autumn had been in his office, they'd gone from seating to sex. Although not quite as bluntly as that: Jack had offered up a few personal details about himself, including the fact that he was married. His wife had started a new business, party planning, and by all accounts was very successful in her field, especially for someone who had barely been in the business a year. Autumn felt a tiny twinge of envy at this; she couldn't help feeling jealous of this other woman's success and apparent ease in life. Autumn worked hard, studied and constantly felt like she was swimming upstream. It didn't seem fair somehow that this woman had everything so good with little or no struggle to be spoken of. Autumn had never seen a ring on Jack's finger so had always assumed he was a career-focused singleton but, with Jack confirming his marital status in person, Autumn had to reason that perhaps he just didn't like wearing jewellery. In fact now she came to think of it, she didn't think she'd ever seen Jack wear so much as a watch.

He went on to enquire into her own personal life. For some reason, Autumn didn't really want her boss knowing absolutely everything about her so she decided to let a few things slide, namely her boyfriend. Her wonderfully kind, and drop-dead gorgeous boyfriend. She felt guilty; the feeling clawed at her heart and made her chest feel heavy, or was it the whiskey? Pushing that thought to the back of her mind she fumbled for her house keys. After a few minutes the dawning realisation hit her, she'd forgotten them this morning.

'Duhh,' she mocked herself: that's how this whole thing with Jack had started. If she'd just remembered her keys in the first place then he wouldn't have caught her delving into her bag's abyss at the office gate, he wouldn't have had to let her in, touch her shoulder and then later apologise for it over whiskey and jazz. Suddenly the whole event seemed so cringe-worthy, seedy and just plain sad.

She hoped Ben had left the door open and was still up. His long days and gruelling schedule had seen his bedtime get earlier and earlier. She was now lucky if they managed to grab a couple of hours in the evening before he yawned, stretched and headed off up the stairs to bed. She knocked lightly and listened for a minute. No answer. She tried the door handle; it was her own home, after all. It turned easily and the door opened. She stepped inside into darkness and reached out for the light switch. Flicking it she gingerly prepared for the dazzling glare. Nothing. She was still stood in darkness; she tried the light a couple more times; still nothing. Puzzled, she called out for Ben and took out her phone, turning the torch on to find out the extent of the problem. The white light shone illuminating her home in an eerie glow, there was nothing out of the ordinary. Everything was in its place, she shone the torch up to the light: *'Ahhhhh,'* she remembered now, the bulb had blown. She gently bent down to remove her shoes, leaving them where she had stood and by the torchlight of her phone crept upstairs to bed.

Not only was Ben was up, he was in the shower. She could hear the water beating down and smiled as she heard a contented little moan escape Ben's lips. *'He must be loving that shower,'* she mused. Maybe it was the alcohol's influence but suddenly Autumn felt very sexy. She wanted to be with Ben, in the shower, she wanted to press up against him and taste him as the hot water ran over their entwined naked bodies. Stripping as she entered their bathroom, she stopped in her tracks: he was facing away from her. Partially hunched over, her view was obscured by the steamed up enclosure but there was no mistaking what he was doing. His muscular right arm moved up and down in strong, purposeful strokes, the pace quickening with every move, his muscles tensing with each quiet moan. His left hand was supporting his weight and was resting on the wall of the shower high over his head. Autumn just stood there, she didn't really know what to do; she was stumped. She knew Ben masturbated – of course he did, all men did regardless of what their other halves might believe. But why was he doing it now? She'd told him she was on her way home and even sent the dirtiest text message she could manage.

'Maybe he didn't get the message?' she reasoned. She stood there for a moment or two, not sure whether she should join in or not. Autumn Carter was dumbfounded. The time had passed for action, so now it was all a bit awkward. She felt like a Peeping Tom, so hastily backed out of the bathroom as quietly as she could. She went over to his bedside table and picked up his phone. She pressed the menu button and the phone asked her for a passcode.

"A passcode?" Autumn said out loud, bemusement lacing her tone. Ben had never had a passcode in all the time she'd known him, so why on earth would he need one now? Her messages were still there on his screen, unopened. So at least that was that explained. She decided to wait it out. Ben didn't appear to be finishing up any time soon and maybe he'd be up for round two.

Autumn decided to light a candle and set the mood: she chose a sugared vanilla candle from her drawer. Ever since she was a little girl she'd always enjoyed scented candles. The heavenly aromas relaxed her and after a hard day at work they were perfect, especially if that hard day was finished with a steamy session at night. As Autumn lit a match and held it to the candle's wick she could hear Ben finishing up in the shower. The torrent of water had dried up, and the room was strangely still now. Knowing she had little time Autumn blew out the match, set it aside and climbed onto their king-sized bed. After a few minutes of waiting, she sat upright: Autumn decided that she needed to relax a little bit. She adjusted herself into a more comfortable position, shimmying down the bed a little further and laying back, using the plump pillows to prop herself up. She placed her hands over her stomach and smoothed her hands downwards, slowly tracing a light line over her skin, her fingertips barely making contact.

'Not as easy to smooth out my tummy as it is my blouse,' she noted. Looking down at her naked body Autumn wasn't too displeased. She had good skin, smooth skin, she was pale but her tone was almost flawless, aside from a few freckles and the odd mole on her thighs. She trailed her fingertips lazily over her midsection, slowly. She drew circles around her belly button and stroked her hips up and down, letting a little moan escape her lips. Autumn relaxed further, allowing herself to enjoy the soft and sensual stimulation she was experiencing. Eventually she allowed her hands to trail upward. They grazed over her breasts and brushed over her nipples, which soon stiffened to small pink buds, standing prominently to attention as if awaiting another's touch. It felt so good; the tension of the day eased away and she lowered her hands slowly but purposefully downwards once again, trailing

them down, past her navel. She kept going. Autumn parted her thighs marginally and began teasing herself, only ever so slightly. She wanted to be ready for Ben when he finally emerged from the bathroom.

After what seemed like an eternity, albeit an enjoyable one, Ben pushed the door open and walked into the bedroom. His hair dripping with water, falling carelessly over his eyes, he brushed it backward with the tips of his fingers. Autumn took a moment to admire her boyfriend. He looked almost god-like; his body was the best it had ever been and she found herself drawn to him even more. Right then and there, in that moment, she wanted him more than she ever had in her life. The luxurious fluffy white towel he had wrapped around his waist was a stark contrast against his tanned skin. The faint trace of dark hair which started just below his bellybutton and trailed down underneath the towel invitingly was speckled with water droplets, only adding to the appeal. He looked up and seemed startled by her presence.

"Babe!" Ben sounded uncertain. "I thought you'd been held up at work. How long have you been here?" he questioned.

"Long enough," Autumn's voice was husky and thick from her relaxed yet aroused state. She parted her legs a little bit more and said, "I had to come home. I couldn't wait to see you." She gave Ben a cheeky wink which she hoped came off more flirty than cheesy. Ben didn't say a word for a moment, as if weighing up his options. He raised his hand to his head and massaged his temples contemplatively.

"Oh Babe," he said, "I would but I'm knackered. I've been on set, to the gym, done the shopping and washed and polished my car." He reeled. "Plus, my head is absolutely pounding."

'Well there's nothing better to kill the mood than talking about Tesco and T Cut,' she thought. Feeling slightly self-conscious Autumn reached down for her nightclothes and pulled

them on over her head. The mood had taken a nose-dive and now felt flat. The atmosphere had, for Autumn at least, been a highly sexualised one, electric with possibility and potential. This headache of his seemed to have come on rather quickly: *'He didn't seem to have much of an issue with a pounding head while he was pounding himself.'* Although she was profoundly irritated at his flat-out refusal she couldn't help but grin to herself. *'Why am I only ever only this funny in my own head?'*

"No worries, hon. I've had a long day too." Feeling unattractive and rejected she rolled over and blew out the candle. They were in darkness with just the iridescent glow of a neighbouring street light intruding through the bedroom curtains. Ben reached out for her and stroked the small of her back. His phone vibrated against the surface of the bedside table. This jogged her memory somewhat.

"Why do you have a passcode on your phone now?" she asked, hoping her tone was casual and not accusatory.

"Work," he answered distractedly. She turned over and could see he was reading whatever super-important message had come through; that meant he couldn't answer her properly.

"Work?" she pressed. "What do you mean?"

"Well, I've got some other actors' details now, and important emails. If I lost my phone I don't want anyone being able to get into it." He added cheekily, "Plus there's all those photos of you on there." He poked at her in the side and wiggled his finger playfully. He didn't need to say any more. Autumn reasoned that she would add a passcode to her phone tomorrow too. She may not have a celebrity-filled phone book and an inbox full of loads of important telly emails from directors and the like, but she did have one or two pictures of Ben on there that she wouldn't want anyone else to see. They were for her eyes only.

She rolled over and snuggled closer to him. He was facing away from her but reached behind to hold her, albeit rather awkwardly. He was still reading his emails and not paying Autumn anywhere near what she would deem as enough attention.

"Come on babe," she said, trying not to sound too whiny. "Turn that off and turn over please. I don't like being the big spoon." He was already putting the phone down. He dropped it on the floor and turned over taking her in his arms. He gave her a soft, long kiss on the forehead and squeezed her tight.

"I love you," she said, stifling a yawn. Despite the night still being young she had begun to feel rather sleepy.

"You too," he replied. He gave her one last squeeze before releasing her and turning back over onto his other side. Autumn barely noticed as she scrubbed the day away with a face wipe. Ben's hectic routine meant that he indulged in many early nights so Autumn decided to cut her losses.

'If you can't beat them, join them.' She thought. Autumn was asleep within minutes; Jack's whiskey without a doubt helped her on her way. She slept soundly and didn't stir once throughout the entire night.

CHAPTER 5

"OH GOD," AUTUMN CROAKED. *'YOU'VE GOT TO BE kidding me,'* she thought to herself, *'day two with a hangover.'* At least she didn't have to be up for work this time. She rolled over and reached out for Ben, her hand outstretched, fingertips searching for his warm skin. All she felt were cold sheets. She cracked an eye open and squinted over to Ben's side of the bed. He wasn't there. He couldn't possibly have gone to the gym. Not again. Not on a Saturday morning. What kind of crazy person does that? Autumn turned her thoughts to her own day ahead. She'd got university work to get on with and this fuzzy head was nothing that a bacon sandwich and a cup of coffee wouldn't fix. She glanced at the clock: 8:45am. She could afford another hour in bed. She'd work twice as well with a bit more sleep under her belt, so she rolled back over and pulled the covers up around her, enjoying the comforting warmth that they provided. Squeezing her eyes shut against the world, she tried to get back to sleep. She rolled over again and altered the position of her legs, trying to get comfortable. But, sadly, for Autumn the time for re-joining the world of slumber had passed. She was well and truly awake now. Nothing for it then, she reasoned. Time to get up, get dressed and get on with some work. She dragged the duvet with her and went downstairs rubbing the sleep out of her eyes and stretching as she went. She dumped the duvet on the sofa and decided that maybe a bit of Saturday morning telly wouldn't be the end of the world. Finding the remote control was easier said than done: it took her several moments of searching under clutter to find it. The TV blared into life. Autumn turned it down instinctively. For some reason Ben always watched TV with the volume turned all the way up.

Autumn found herself watching a clip from Ben's show. Feeling a sense of pride she settled herself on the arm of the sofa. The screen flashed from clip to poster to the presenter. He was joined by two of the women from the programme: they were all the sitting on retro designer sofas in a light and airy looking studio dressed up to look like the viewer had accidentally stumbled into their private living room. It was soon apparent that one of the women, the youngest – and in Autumn's opinion the better looking of the two – was the star of the show. Unforgivably Autumn had never actually watched a single episode. Ben insisted that paying for the package that the channel aired on was a waste of money and reasoned that since they had never watched the show before, why would they watch it now? Autumn had initially felt guilty about this; she wanted to be supportive but honestly, overly glossy crime dramas weren't really her thing and if Ben wasn't bothered, then neither was she.

"So dish the dirt then," one of the presenters cooed at the fabulously polished guests. "Anything juicy going to happen on the show?"

The leggy beauty coyly shook her head by way of an answer. "I couldn't even if I wanted to, we're all sworn to secrecy," she replied carefully, all the time smiling through perfect Hollywood teeth.

Autumn walked over to the kitchen and opened the fridge. She inspected its offerings and took out a packet of her favourite oak smoked bacon. She set to work making herself some breakfast, enjoying the satisfying sizzling sound the bacon made the second it hit the pan. Leaving it to cook she returned to the living room and settled herself on the arm of the sofa.

"All I will say," she continued, "is that there's going to be a massive love triangle at some point."

Autumn strained to hear what she was saying over the sound of the bacon. The actress finished with a smug smile and gave a knowing look down the camera. Autumn felt like the woman was staring straight at her.

'If that's Ben she's talking about, then she can think again! Not in my lifetime,' she thought in a commanding tone.

After watching a little bit longer the women on the screen went on to disclose pretty much every plot twist and turn imaginable.

'So much for "sworn to secrecy",' Autumn thought, as the actress went on to reveal that the love triangle didn't involve her but played her cards close to her chest when pressed for more information from the presenter. Eventually, the actress, who Autumn was beginning to dislike, disclosed that the love triangle would involve a strong female character who was not yet in the show and two of the leading men.

"Phew," Autumn breathed out a sigh of relief. Not that she was the jealous type but seriously, who would want their boyfriend cavorting around with *her*? It didn't matter if it wasn't real life, it wasn't happening.

Wandering back into the kitchen Autumn assembled her bacon sandwich, accessorising it with a drizzle of ketchup and a mug of tea. She devoured it in record time, even for her. The flavour of smoked bacon did nothing to quell the sour taste that the show had left. So she ate her food with the TV turned off. It was probably for the best anyway. She really needed to get on with her work and she'd skived enough in recent times.

Opening her course book and grabbing her notepad and a pen, Autumn set to work and soon she was lost in her work. The hangover subsided and she found herself really enjoying being productive. *'Maybe I'll join Ben at the gym one day?'* She considered this for a moment or two then dismissed it. *'One step at a time,'* she reasoned. Maybe it'd be good for them: working up a sweat in the gym might lead to working up a sweat in the bedroom. Autumn had felt a little hot under the collar since the previous night, although she did carry a little guilt about enjoying herself with Jack. She didn't feel too bad about it; in fact, her not-so-dangerous liaison had actually made her think. She needed to spend more time on Ben, make sure their relationship was the best it could be. She knew she'd been taking him for granted recently, in fact she couldn't even remember if she'd taken him out for a celebratory meal when he'd got the part on *The Edge*. She also knew that their sex life could do with a bit of a shake-up. It wasn't bad – far from it – but it could be better.

'I guess sometimes life just gets in the way,' she pondered. Ben was after all crazily busy now and all the time he spent away working on his craft had allowed her to get on with a few things of her own. She knew this wasn't how it should be; she should be strong enough, independent enough and determined enough to sort out her own life even with Ben there. But whenever he was present all she wanted to do was to be with him, do things with him and do things for him. Her own needs took a backseat. So, perhaps these recent events had, if anything, allowed her to identify that there was a problem: a small one, but it needed to be tackled, unless she wanted it to turn into a big one. It was right there and then that she decided to make the following weekend one to

remember! Opening her laptop she typed into Google, 'sexy lingerie'. Around a million results came back to her. Feeling slightly overwhelmed she hesitantly clicked on one of the top results. The choice was absolutely staggering. There was just so much to look at. Did she want fishnet? Mesh? Crotchless? Not wanting to push the boat out too far, she decided that she wanted sexy but top priority was that she wanted to be comfortable – what was the point in looking amazing if you didn't feel it as well? She settled a lacy red thong set: she was going to make Ben's weekend one he wasn't going to forget in a hurry!

Autumn felt confident she'd made the right choice, and glowed at the thought of his reaction to her in it. Ben had always liked her bum, he was forever giving it a pinch or a playful pat, and it was with this in mind that she decided to flaunt her best asset. She had a clear vision in her head of how she wanted to look. She was going to go big with the hair, smoky with the eyes and nude with the lips, team all that with the new underwear and a pair of heels and she just knew that the spark would be back – not that it had diminished entirely, she could just feel it waning and it was a feeling that she distinctly didn't like.

Once it was ordered she closed her laptop gently, and her mind wandered to the night she had in store for them when her new purchase arrived. She could feel the warmth between her legs already, the anticipation was such a turn on. *'Really?'* she asked herself. What had happened to her in the last twenty-four hours? She hadn't always been a sexual person, but as with a lot of women as she'd matured and become more confident in herself, her sexual urges had become more prominent. She'd still only had sex with three people in her entire life. Her first boyfriend, Bradley, had been great and had worshipped the ground she'd walked on. Unfortunately, he'd also worshipped the ground that a lot of other girls had walked on too. Autumn had broken up with him after his fifth and final indiscretion; she didn't need that kind of stress in her life. After that she'd had a one-night stand with university course mate in her second year. She'd known Simon Brown for a while. He was kind of gangly looking with thick glasses and a mop of mousy brown hair that always looked as though it could do with a good brush. She'd never really fancied him but did find him hilariously funny. On one particular evening Autumn had been high on alcohol and low on self-esteem, she'd ended up taking him back to her house after ill-advised encouragement from a girl on the netball team that she barely knew. Sex with Simon had been a bit clumsy and a bit awkward and had pretty much ended their friendship the following day. After those two, she'd concentrated on her studies: while her friends went out all night she was either spending cosy nights in with David or hunched over her laptop agonising over every word she typed. *'And look where that's got me…'* she internalised, *'still studying three years later and working as a receptionist. Oh yeah, I'm really living the dream!'*

Once she'd graduated and decided on a further qualification to make her extra employable in the writing world, she'd met Ben. She'd decided to write some sample articles to send off to various magazines and newspapers. She dreamed of writing for her favourite women's magazine, *Wow*. It was a perfect balance of interesting articles, advice and lifestyle pieces and peppered with a few snippets of only the juiciest celebrity gossip. More than anything she dreamt of writing for Melissa Abbott, editor-in-chief at *Wow*; she'd spoken at Autumn's university on the ins and outs of working in the world of journalism. She'd been all over, worked for loads of papers and magazines and really knew her stuff. Autumn had known that she wanted to be like her from the second she started talking; her broad Scottish accent echoed through the auditorium and was like music to Autumn's ears. Melissa Abbott was a tall, commanding woman with a relaxed style and quirky oversized glasses. She was a creative through and through and had somehow managed to conquer all odds to become the youngest editor of a great magazine. Autumn knew she had exacting standards so understood that her sample articles needed to be perfect.

Autumn cast her mind back to when she had first met Ben. Laptop in hand she had entered a cool-looking coffee shop with purple velvet sofas and dark wooden walls. The walls were adorned with an array of old fashioned pictures and cool artefacts. Behind the sofa where she had chosen to sit hung a beautiful bike from the 'fifties, a shelf filled with odds and ends and a painting of some dogs playing cards. All in all it was very eclectic and Autumn found the place fascinating. Ben had been her waiter. She'd ordered a large cappuccino with extra vanilla shot and a muffin before opening her laptop, setting it on the table in front of her and starting on her soon-to-be masterpiece. Ben had asked her out as she was paying. He hadn't been backwards in coming forwards and told her outright just how beautiful he thought she was. They became instantly inseparable and from their first date until now Autumn hadn't even so much glanced at another guy. Flirting with her boss, or any other man for that matter, was something totally new. There was nothing wrong with a harmless bit of flirting, she told herself, especially if it were to some way benefit her sex life with Ben. Although she couldn't shake that nagging feeling that if she had to keep reassuring herself over it, then maybe it wasn't as 'okay' as she was making out. She decided that she needed the opinion of someone on the outside of the situation, someone totally neutral. After all, it was extremely difficult to be objective about something like this. She needed a different outlook on the whole situation and who better to talk about relationships than her multi-dating man-expert of a friend, Rosa Dawson? Autumn picked up her phone – the crack in the screen made her shudder and she vowed to get it fixed asap. It definitely did not look like the type of phone of someone who had their life together. *'What's the point in spending all that money on a phone if you're not going to fix it when it's broken?'* she concluded to herself. Autumn scrolled down to Rosa's name and pressed call.

"Hi there, you've reached the voice-mail of Rosa. I can't answer right now, leave me a message and I'll get back to you…" Autumn hung up and tried again. Same thing. She left it a few more minutes and on her third and final failed attempt to get through to her friend she decided to do the unthinkable: call her house phone.

"Hello?" Rosa's voice answered the phone, sounding uncertain.

"Hey hon, it's Autumn. You okay?" Autumn began.

"Why are you calling my house phone? I thought you were going to be one of those 'have you had an accident in the last 8,000 years?' people!" Rosa said, putting on a dramatic American voice.

"Your mobile's going straight to voice-mail," Autumn explained. "Do you want to come over later? I could do with a chat."

"Mmmmm, let me just check." There was a pause for a second as Rosa checked, Autumn could just imagine Rosa's perfectly manicured nails flipping through her diary just to make sure she didn't have a fabulous date lined up with her mystery guy. "Yeh, should be fine. See you at six?" Rosa asked. "But, only for an hour or two, okay? I've got a load of stuff to do at home."

"Perfect," Autumn replied. "Bye lovely."

"See you later. Can't believe you don't get enough of me at work!" Rosa added cheekily before hanging up.

Autumn placed her phone on the coffee table and turned her mind back to her work. She furrowed her brow: it practically took all of her concentration just to read the title of the next chapter, 'Writing for Success in a Dog Eat Dog World'.

'Right,' Autumn thought to herself, mentally rolling up her sleeves, *'let's get stuck in.'*

It had seemed like mere minutes ago when she'd spoken to Rosa. In fact it had been hours. The quick-paced knock at the door startled her, as she had been so deep in thought that she'd lost track of the time. Autumn sighed, folded down the corner of her textbook and shoved it under the sofa along with her laptop. Autumn trudged to the door and opened it. She suddenly felt lighter at Rosa's mere presence. When she opened the door she was greeted by Rosa, complete with wide smile and her outstretched arms.

"Go on then, tell me what's up," Rosa said, engulfing Autumn in a comforting hug.

"Nothing, not really anyway, just could do with some company," she replied, wriggling out of the familiar embrace and stepping aside to let Rosa in.

Rosa gave Autumn a look that said *'I know that's not entirely true but I'll let it slide for now'* and produced a bottle of Autumn's favourite wine out of her oversized bag, a knowing smile etched across her features.

"Ahhh, thanks," Autumn began gratefully, "but I really don't think I can. I drank Thursday and Friday…" Rosa cut her off mid-sentence, her knowing smile giving way to pseudo-indignation.

"You went out on Friday without me?" she exclaimed, her eyes wide with mock-horror. She broke off laughing and said, "Screw you, I had a date anyway!"

They walked through the living room and towards the kitchen. Rosa stopped to place her shoes and bag ever so neatly next to the sofa. She hesitated, then collected Autumn's shoes, which were haphazardly lying at odd angles and popped them right next to hers, in a neat little line. Autumn looked at her reproachfully, she couldn't help but feel offended by the action.

"Sorry," Rosa said when she saw Autumn looking at her, one eyebrow raised. "OCD and all that," she explained.

It took Rosa all of five minutes to convince Autumn to have a glass of red: Autumn rarely said no to Malbec. They clinked glasses and sipped at the crisp wine. Autumn let the cool liquid slide down her throat; that familiar warming sensation followed it. She made a mental note that from now on she would not drink on school nights or Sundays. Three days in a row was a bit excessive. Her liver hadn't seen this much alcohol action since her student days and she definitely didn't want to start down the path of the everyday drinker. No, this was a one-off – and after all, she had had an eventful few days.

Autumn and Rosa chatted aimlessly for a while, Rosa dishing the dirt on her date from the previous evening. It hasn't been with the mystery guy at all, but instead someone else. However, this guy was a no, and a flat one at that. The idiot had bragged about how much he earned a year, the car he drove and had even hinted that he was very well endowed. All of this had turned Rosa's stomach and within the first hour she had found herself making her excuses and leaving. He didn't seem to mind though; Rosa afforded him once last glance as she left and noticed he'd immediately moved on to the pretty waitress who had served them.

"It wouldn't have been so bad if he hadn't been five foot nothing and had a widow's peak," she laughed. "I could have happily put up with the dickish behaviour for one night if he'd looked a bit more George Clooney and a little less George Osborne."

There was a brief pause in the conversation and the two women looked at each other somewhat awkwardly. Autumn wanted to ask why Rosa was bothering with other guys when she had a man she liked who thought so much of her he'd showered her with gifts. Autumn hadn't failed to notice the brand new designer bag and sunglasses Rosa had accessorised herself with; she thought better of it. Even though she was traditional in the fact that once you were with someone, you were with them, Autumn knew that not everyone felt that same way. We're all different after all, and perhaps Rosa had some sort of 'agreement' with this guy. The thought of that made her shudder: Rosa was so much better than that, so Autumn decided that she was better off not knowing the detailed ins and outs of the situation.

"I know what you're thinking." Rosa said bluntly, "I'm not two-timing. I agreed to a date with Mr Mustang ages ago, thought it better I got it out of the way early on." Autumn still couldn't see why Rosa hadn't just told him where to go. But that was Rosa all over: she was just too nice.

"You don't need to justify anything to me," Autumn said reassuringly. Rosa sat there for a moment, gazing down and rolling her bracelet between her thumb and forefinger idly.

"Well that's all my news," she said with a start, flipping her glossy hair over her shoulder in one equally effortless and glamorous movement. Her tone softened. "Come on, babe,

I know you didn't ask me over to just hear about my awful date, so go on then. What's wrong?"

"Nothing's wrong," Autumn began, tucking a stray piece of her blonde hair behind her ear as she instinctively defended her position. "It's just..." She trailed off before taking another sip of wine. "I think Jack fancies me."

"Jack who?" Rosa asked, her voice squeaking a bit at the end.

"Thorne," Autumn replied seriously, looking directly at Rosa with an earnest expression. Rosa held her gaze for a split second before bursting into laughter.

"Sorry, sorry," she spluttered. "Why on earth do you think that? I mean, have you seen his wife?"

Autumn looked offended.

"I mean I just don't think you're quite his type, that's all," Rosa finished carefully, avoiding eye contact with Autumn for the first time that evening.

Autumn relayed the entire story, making sure to put special emphasis on the brushing of her shoulder and the way she'd been summoned to his office after hours for whiskey. When she was done, she took a long sip of wine; her eyes were wide and for some reason she felt a bit shaky. Rosa was quiet for a moment, mulling all this over in her head. Autumn knew what she was going to say: she was going to ask her what on earth she was thinking, say that she was playing with fire and have serious words about how Ben would feel about all this. Autumn waited, nervously turning the stem of the wine glass in her fingers. After what seemed like an age Rosa opened her mouth to speak.

"Are you kidding? He can't fancy you. He's married!" Rosa repeated her earlier sentiment. "I mean, you have seen his wife, haven't you?" She scoffed.

Autumn shook her head feeling belittled. Up until that evening she hadn't even known he was married. She knew Rosa wouldn't mean any harm and would only be trying to help but there was something in her tone and delivery that made Autumn feel badly.

'It's not like I'm a troll or anything,' she thought defiantly to herself.

"Well," Rosa carried on, blissfully unaware of the atmosphere change in the room. "She's gorgeous, really cool and super successful. Her family are from Brazil originally but she grew up in America, I think. You want to see her, Autumn, she's incredible," continued Rosa, "but to be honest babe, even if she wasn't all those things, Jack's still married and he's still your boss. He's really professional and wouldn't go there, even at client events I've never seen him flirt with another woman. He's just not the type to stray – and besides, he's like a decade older than you. All you've got to go on is he accidentally touched your shoulder then he apologised for it and offered you a 'peace whiskey'!" Rosa stopped, short of breath after her rant.

Autumn blushed suddenly, feeling like that same old silly schoolgirl again. Now that she had said it out loud she realised how ridiculous it sounded. "Oh my God. You're right, aren't you," she said. "Ugh, I kind of liked it as well," she admitted – stopping short. Autumn hadn't meant to say that. She hadn't liked it, it had been creepy and inappropriate. The only attention she wanted was from Ben.

"Of course you liked it. Your boyfriend's never here. He's always off working out or just plain working," Rosa countered.

Autumn hadn't seen it from this point of view. Maybe she had liked it – only a bit, though. She paused and thought about it further; the more she thought the more sense it made. Ben's career was going from strength to strength and here she was, stuck in her everyday life, doing everyday things; nothing exciting ever really happened to her. Maybe she'd just liked the excitement of another man's attention, whether it had been real or not. That was it, light bulb moment. She and Rosa reached the same conclusion at the same time. Rosa took a step toward her and put her hand on Autumn's arm.

"Autumn, I think you just liked the attention. You're not getting enough from Ben at the moment and you hadn't realised it. Perhaps you should just keep this to yourself. Ben's got a lot on now, you know, filming and trying to get noticed for bigger jobs. He really needs all the support you can give, right? This would just stress him out and as long as you're not actually doing anything or have bad intentions then there's no harm done." She went on, "Not saying he does but if for whatever reason Jack, or any man for that matter, shows you some attention, my advice would be to just lap it up. As long as you're not physically acting on it, I think it's fine."

"What?" Autumn was visibly shocked by this. "I couldn't do that, it doesn't matter if I don't physically do anything, just accepting drinks and attention off someone else is basically cheating." She paused. "Isn't it?"

"Don't be mental. Of course it isn't. Ben can't give you what you need right now." Rosa gave Autumn's arm a gentle pat. "You're not doing anything wrong Autumn."

She withdrew her hand and picked up her wine glass from the counter, she tipped her head back and downed the last of her wine. Rosa broke out into a huge Cheshire cat kind of smile: her perfectly white teeth gleamed like a Hollywood A-lister on the red carpet of the latest blockbuster première. "Right, well I'm off." Rosa gave Autumn another hug and kissed her on her cheek. "Don't get yourself worked up over this, you've done nothing wrong."

With that she gave her friend a kiss on the cheek, swept out of the door and strutted to her car. Autumn watched her go then quietly shut the door and returned to the sofa. She sat staring at the blank TV. The empty wine glass lazily lolled about in her hands. Rosa's reaction had confused her. At first, she'd seemed incredulous, almost mocking. This had made Autumn feel unattractive and frumpy. She knew she wasn't going to be on the cover of *Vogue* any time soon, but she wasn't flat out ugly. Rosa's reaction had made her feel this way. She felt sad now, deflated even. And when Rosa had suggested lapping up any attention, she managed to get because Ben wasn't there, well that had been the final nail in the coffin.

Rosa wouldn't have said anything to intentionally upset Autumn. Maybe it was just the stark truth: was Ben going to move onto bigger and better things? This time a few days ago, she had been happy, meandering along, grateful for the notes he left her and thoughtful little things he did. But now all those actions felt hollow, as if he was doing them to try and paste over the cracks that now suddenly seemed so glaringly obvious. She mulled over these new feelings, trying to pinpoint exactly what was making her feel so uncomfortable.

After a few minutes sitting in the dead silence of their home, Autumn decided to quit moping. She was reading too much into this. The more she thought about it the less sense she could make of her feelings. So, what would be the best course of action? She could sit here feeling sorry for herself, or, she could leap into action and spend some quality time with her boyfriend, and that's what she decided to do. Autumn looked at the clock. It was just before eight in the evening, and Ben would be home within the next hour or so. She sprang up from the sofa, went into the kitchen, put the radio on, turned it up and set to work. She didn't have any time to waste.

CHAPTER 6

BEN TURNED HIS KEY IN THE DOOR AND WENT inside. The house was eerily quiet.

"Babe?" he called out. He knew she was there somewhere. Her car, having been collected from outside the offices of Thorne PR, was now outside and he was sure he'd seen the bedroom light suddenly go off as he walked up the drive.

"Autumn?" he called again, a playful tone to his voice. The house seemed different to how it normally did; he could smell something sweet in the air. He dropped his gym bag down onto the floor and flipped the light switch.

"Bastard," he muttered. He'd been meaning to change that bulb and had totally forgotten. It was dark in the living room but not pitch black. The outside street light cast enough light inside for him to see a little. It took barely two minutes to change the bulb: Ben always made sure a store of supplies was kept in the kitchen corner cupboard for such emergencies. He was knackered. Today had been long. He'd been on set most of the day. He had intended to go to the gym straight from work, but some of the cast members were going for drinks and he'd been invited. He went, had a mineral water with his fellow actors and stayed for a while to talk shop. Afterwards he had managed to squeeze in a quick workout but had cut it short when he realised the time. It was an all-new experience and Ben was loving every second. The perks that came with the job were great and now he was earning a regular wage he could start thinking about things that he'd only dreamt of before. His list was extensive and included a new car, a new house and something extra special for the girl that he loved, a little reward for putting up with his shit and being so very patient with him.

Ben walked up the stairs. He had seen Autumn's pile of work protruding from under the sofa and assumed she'd be asleep – '*probably shattered*,' thought Ben as a wry smile crossed his lips. He pushed open the bedroom door and did a double take. Lying on the bed was Autumn.

She looked incredible, laying there in nothing but a red, lacy thong and high heels. Autumn had done her hair and makeup to perfection and on her feet she wore black stilettos that she knew would set Ben's pulse racing. Several candles lit the room, creating a sumptuous glow, which Autumn radiated in. The delicious sweet smell he had noticed downstairs was much deeper up here. He walked over to the bed, not saying a word, and with purpose took her in his arms. They shared a deep passionate kiss: his tongue probed hers and she returned by gently biting his lower lip. She inhaled his scent; he hadn't showered and his musky odour was truly heaven to her senses. He smelt raw, animal-like and it turned her on an incredible amount.

Autumn unbuttoned Ben's shirt and slid the smooth material over his shoulders. The shirt fell to the floor and Ben took a step back and began unbuttoning his jeans. He slid them down with ease and stepped out of them. Standing there in just his underwear was a sight to behold. He was muscular – he'd had a great body before, but now, with all the extra time at the gym, he was looking unbelievably chiselled. His smooth, sculpted abs flexed as he leaned in towards her. Autumn reached out eagerly and took him by the hips. He lifted her up with ease and held her tight as she wrapped her legs around his waist, their mouths barely parting for more than the briefest of moments. He sat her on top of the dresser and knelt down, his face level at hip level. Ben carefully pulled her thong to one side and gasped. She was totally shaven. He felt himself stiffen in an instant, fighting his own urges in order to satisfy hers. Ben leaned in and nuzzled between her legs, gently licking around her most sensitive spot. He stroked her inner thighs and lightly traced his tongue over her smooth skin; she became wetter and began arching her back as undulating waves of pleasure began to course through her. She ran her fingers through his hair, pulling him closer, desperate for that moment of sweet release.

Ben kept her waiting, prolonging her gratification and building delectable intensity with each gentle caress of his tongue. Once he was satisfied she could take no more, he moved in and concentrated on her sweetest spot. He kissed between her legs, taking her sensitive bud in his mouth, applying just a small amount of pressure. It was enough to make her gasp loudly. Autumn leaned back in bliss, a bead of sweat trickled between her breasts. She arched her hips, offering herself to him fully. He obliged willingly and parted her thighs further with a determined grip. She wriggled under his attention, luxuriating in the warm rays of pleasure that cascaded over her. She let her head fall back as she moaned over and over again, the strength of her orgasm shaking her to the very core. Ben didn't let up. He continued flicking his tongue over her clitoris, applying a steady pressure, ensuring he prolonged her ecstasy for as long as possible. She bucked hard against him, her body shaking, racked with divine delight.

Autumn uncrossed her legs from behind his head. He responded to her hint and came up so the two could share a deep kiss, his tongue searching. She could taste herself on his lips. Without breaking their kiss, he took two fingers and placed them at the entrance of her femininity. He gently parted her smooth lips and revealed the glistening wetness within. Ben inserted his fingers inside her, keen to explore her warm wetness further. He curved his fingers upwards, creating a delectable arch that made Autumn moan throatily. He moved his fingers purposefully as if he wanted to beckon another orgasm from her, caressing her internal sweet spot over and over again, the intensity building with each stroke. Ben began to feel a change in her body: he pressed harder and quickened his pace, the warm wetness of her convulsed as she clamped down hard against his fingers. He pulled away from her so he could watch her climax but kept his fingers moving diligently within her, again wanting to prolong her desire for as long as he could. She called his name amongst cries of pleasure and, once the orgasmic waves had washed over her, he withdrew.

Autumn took his fingers, covered with her essence, and sucked on them greedily. He drew her forward to the edge of the dresser and stood up fully. He was hard and hungry for his own release. He began to push himself inside her, pausing to enjoy the feeling of her tightness around his throbbing cock, then in one swift movement he entered her. He held her hips steadily so that Autumn was all but pinned down and thrust into her slowly, savouring the experience and enjoying how wet he'd made her. He pressed his thumb against her clitoris and moved it in small circles. Ben kept the pressure firm and the movement constant. Autumn cried out, enveloped in the waves of another orgasm. This tipped Ben over the edge and he came hard, his body shuddering with the force of the powerful orgasm. Autumn looked at him, he returned her gaze and pulled her closer towards him. Ben lifted her up and effortlessly carried her over to the bed where they lay in a post-orgasmic stupor.

“That was incredible,” Autumn said, her voice hoarse. Ben agreed and kissed her lovingly. Autumn could feel that their connection had been restored and contentedly stroked his hair as he drifted off. Ben fell asleep quickly, clearly exhausted not only from his day but also from the energetic and frantic session they had just had. Autumn stayed awake a little while longer, undressing herself and taking care to remove her makeup and brush out her hair. That had felt good. She’d felt wanted, needed even, and unbelievably sexy.

‘I’ll definitely be doing that again,’ she thought to herself, as she tied her long blonde hair up in a messy bun. Initiating had felt good; it had made her feel confident and in control. She felt united with Ben, a connection she hadn’t felt in quite some time. She nestled up to him, enjoying the warmth of his body next to hers and closed her eyes. Turning her thoughts to the next day, she decided that as that evening had been so successful perhaps they could spend the day together. She still had a load of coursework to get done but sometimes you just needed to put your relationship first. This was Autumn’s last thought before she joined Ben in slumber.

CHAPTER 7

THROUGH THE SLIT OF ONE CRACKED EYE AUTUMN tried to make out the time: she was pleasantly surprised to see that it hadn't even gone 8 a.m. Swinging her legs out of the bed she sat up, stretched and yawned. She felt good: last night had been incredible, everything she'd hoped for and more besides. She glanced over at Ben, still fast asleep and snoring ever so slightly. Autumn turned her attention to the bedroom. It looked like a scene from a film that if you were staying in a hotel, you'd have to pay for. Her red thong sat in the middle of the floor, to the side of that her heels. She smiled as she remembered kicking them off last night as Ben went down on her. Ben's clothes were also on the floor, strewn about in the order he'd taken them off. She went to the dresser and got out an old T-shirt and a pair of faded jogging bottoms. Pulling them on she trudged into the bathroom.

Autumn looked at herself in the mirror as she brushed her teeth. Her reflection showed the image of a person who was refreshed: her head was clear, her cheeks flushed and her complexion bright. Her hair was still in the bun she'd put it in the previous night, although a fair bit messier now. Rinsing her mouth out she decided to do a bit of housework whilst Ben was asleep so that she could spend the rest of the day making a fuss of him.

She padded back into the bedroom taking extra care not to wake Ben. He'd been rushed off his feet recently so he really did deserve a long lie in. After all, it was a Sunday. Autumn scooped up the clothes from the bedroom floor and collected the rest from the wash basket. *'Washing first, then a quick tidy round and then I'll make us some breakfast.'* The doting girlfriend routine actually felt rather nice and she made an internal note to try and make this a regular Sunday morning routine. Putting the clothes in the washing machine she patted each item down as her mother had done when she was younger – "Just to make sure there's nothing in the pockets," she could hear her mother explaining. Good job she did: Ben's phone was nestled nice and neatly in his back pocket.

'He would have killed me if that had gone through the wash,' she thought to herself. Taking it out, she instinctively pressed the menu button: it had 2% battery left and a message displayed on the screen from an unknown number. Autumn scanned the number trying to recognise it. She didn't. Nope, she had absolutely no idea who it could be from. The message consisted of just three words: "Are you alone?" Autumn's stomach flipped as she slumped back on the washing machine and read the message again.

"Are you alone?" she slowly read aloud. Who wanted to know if Ben was alone and why? She swiped at his screen to open the phone. Bloody passcode! Why did he have a passcode? He'd never had one before, she was always using his phone when she forgot to charge her own. Or when she needed to contact someone and couldn't be bothered to try and find her own phone, which was no doubt located somewhere in the murky depths of her bag. She tried his PIN number and then his birthday. The phone arrogantly taunted her with an obnoxious buzz and the words 'try again.' She knew a third incorrect attempt would lock it, and then he'd know she'd been trying to snoop, but she needed to know more. Who was the message from and why had they texted him so late at night to find out if he was on his own? All these questions whirled round in her head. Was she reading too much into this? She didn't think Ben was the cheating type. He'd been cheated on in the past and had often spoken about how terrible it was. But, then again, he might not be cheating. Someone might be pursuing him? The actresses on *The Edge* were all good looking, and thin. Or maybe it was a fan – maybe? Was Ben well known enough to even have fans? Autumn suddenly felt very frumpy. She looked down at her greying ensemble, threadbare and baggy. There was no trace of the sex appeal and confidence she'd exuded the previous night: all that was left now was a chubby, frumpy girl who had no career to speak of and was all but failing her course.

Autumn pressed the menu button once more. She wanted to look at the message again, as if by some miracle she hadn't spotted something obvious the first time, a blatant explanation to quell her suspicion. No such look, just those three little words that made her question the person she loved: "Are you alone?" Yes, she thought, I'm very alone right now. The phone flashed once and then went dead. *'The battery's gone,'* she thought. Placing the phone on the side she went into autopilot, stuffed the washing in the machine, added detergent and turned it on, all the while wondering what her next course of action should be. It was then and there that Autumn decided that more than anything, she wanted her mum.

Ben bustling into the kitchen interrupted this thought. He was showered and dressed and had on the aftershave that Autumn absolutely adored. He planted a big wet kiss on her forehead and followed it with,

"Ahhhhh. I've been looking for that."

He snatched the phone up and tried to turn it on. "Ugh, no battery," he said, his tone laced with annoyance. "So, what do you want to do today?" He stuffed the phone into his pocket.

"I think I'm going to go see my mum," Autumn replied, her voice dry and thin. Ben gave a half smile in acknowledgement then turned to leave the room.

"Aren't you going to put it on charge?" she asked, gesturing at the phone charger plugged in by the microwave.

"I'll do it upstairs," he said, barely glancing back to her as he bolted back to their bedroom. Once Ben was out of sight Autumn picked up her bag, slipped on a pair of ballet pumps that had been left by the door and made her way to her car. Her red Fiesta seemed to be miles away, her legs felt heavy with every step and she struggled to place one foot in front of the other. She opened the door and climbed in, wincing at the heat that escaped and blasted in her face. Autumn drove off to her mum's house, the music turned up loud in an attempt to drown out the destructive thoughts swirling around in her head.

It wasn't a long drive to her parents' house but the locations of their respective homes couldn't be further apart. The Carters' family home was situated in a beautiful spot, surrounded by well-kept gardens tended to by their family gardener, Miguel. Autumn had known Miguel all her life and he was pretty much a part and parcel of their home. She'd seen him twice a week, every week for the entire time she'd lived at The Barings. The house was a large five-bedroomed affair set back from the road down a large winding drive. There were trees planted either side of the driveway, giving the home a very stately manor feel. They had neighbours of course, but each house was built in the middle of their own horseshoe of land, giving each of the residents of 'Hilltop Lane' the feeling of exclusivity and importance.

"Darling, well don't you just look beautiful?" Sarah Carter exclaimed excitedly as she swung the door open enthusiastically and their pet cat, Jasper, bolted for freedom when the door opened. Autumn tried to give him a quick stroke as he ran past, but the black and white blur was too quick for her. He shot past her at seemingly the speed of light and without looking back. Autumn looked up at her mum as she walked towards the house. Sarah Carter was a small, bubbly woman, who always wore a big smile and exuded warmth and comfort. She was petite, standing at just over five feet tall and although small in stature she was larger than life, personality-wise. Autumn had inherited her mum's honey blonde hair and pale blue eyes, the only difference being that Sarah Carter's hair had always, for as long as Autumn could remember, been cut into a neat, chin-length bob. She was a librarian, which everyone always found so funny because she was definitely not the shy and retiring type. Telling other people to be quiet when she was the exact opposite seemed to tickle a lot of people. Everything about her was loud, from the volume of her voice to the colour of her clothes. She was outspoken and enjoyed every second of everything she ever seemed to do. Autumn had never known such a positive person before: her mum never seemed to have a bad day. Her dad on the other hand was a different story. Autumn's parents were like chalk and cheese. Her father, Richard Carter, was the head teacher at a local secondary school and was quite shy and retiring, but in Autumn's opinion they balanced each other out perfectly. She had often thought that it was their stark differences that meant they worked so well together.

"No I don't," Autumn counteracted bluntly. She didn't believe her mum for a second. She had after all seen her reflection this morning: not a pretty sight, especially when teamed with a red and blotchy face from shedding tears. She looked a mess and she knew it.

"You do, sweetheart," her dad chimed in, appearing over her mum's shoulder. A loving smile graced his lips. He leaned over and gave her and his wife an all-encompassing hug, clearly delighted to have the company of his two favourite ladies.

"No, Dad," she reiterated, "I definitely don't."

On the drive to her parents' house she'd shed a fair few tears, more out of frustration than anything else. She'd spent the last week in some state of confusion or frustration. She was starting to feel a little out of control, like she didn't know if she was coming or going. Had she been flailing for a while and not realised? Happily plodding away in a job that wasn't what she wanted but rather something that she needed, and struggling with her workload – all the time becoming increasingly concerned that maybe a career in journalism was just a pipe dream. It was an almost impossible industry to succeed in, with so many people wanting to work for so few publications. Her parents had offered on more than one occasion to fund her whilst she studied, but being an independent sort of girl, she'd politely declined, instead preferring to pay her own way, even if it did mean a lot more work. She'd also allowed herself to become distracted from her friends. She hadn't socialised with any of her course mates since goodness knows when; in fact, the only friendships she maintained were with David and Rosa.

Autumn knew that the confusion and frustration she was now feeling had put a knotted crease between her brows, that the tears had made her eyes glazed and puffy and that her face was probably still a ghastly shade of blotchy red. But still her lovely, kind and supportive parents thought she looked perfect. Her heart swelled and she felt an enormous amount of love for them.

"Mums always think their daughter are beautiful, no matter how hungover, upset or tired they are," her mum said.

"How about two out of three?" Autumn managed a wry smile.

"I'm your mum darling; I know when something's up," Sarah said knowingly. She took her daughter by the arm and encouraged her inside. "Go and put the kettle on, Richard." She nodded her head towards the kitchen and Autumn's dad, knowing when he wasn't wanted, dutifully floated off to make them both a cup of tea.

Autumn felt instantly more relaxed. She loved their family home. It had been where she had grown up, she had so many fond memories of this house: family Christmases, neighbourhood get-togethers, her first glass of wine at 16 and when she had become older rolling in drunkenly with her friends. Trying to stealthily navigate their way to Autumn's bedroom at 2 a.m. without being detected had never gone down well. She'd also had her first kiss on the porch steps and even though she would never admit it to her parents had also experienced her first ever sexual encounter there too. His name had been Bobby Phillips. He had been her first kiss and first love. Well maybe not, but it sure felt like that at the time. They had been fifteen and had kissed and fumbled on those steps until the early hours of the morning one Friday night, neither one of them really knowing what to do but enjoying it anyway. Their 'relationship' had lasted about the same amount of time as every other teenage romance: it had fizzled out in a matter of weeks. Bobby found a new flame with a classmate of hers and she of course had fallen in love with Justin Timberlake, much like every other teenage girl at that point in time.

"So, are you going to tell me what's up or do I have to guess?" Sarah asked, taking the two cups of tea from Richard and setting them down on the coffee table in their well-appointed lounge. Autumn looked up, checking her dad was well and truly out of the room before confiding in her mum. Some conversations were meant for women's ears only.

"It's nothing really. I saw something I don't think I should have." She went on, "It was a text message on his phone... it was from a girl... well actually I don't know who it was from... he didn't have the number saved but they sent it late last night, or at least I think they did and it just said 'are you alone?' I'm pretty sure whoever texted him is a gorgeous girl who's after him, probably a fan or, oh God, one of the actresses!" Autumn wailed to her mum, the words fell out of her mouth in one big jumble of emotional distress. She felt sick at the thought of someone pursuing her boyfriend and sicker at the thought of Ben welcoming it.

"Well," said her mum, "I could have guessed it was something to do with Ben, it's always been boy trouble. Whenever you've felt the need for an impromptu 'Mum only' visit in the past, it's usually had something to do with a boy."

Autumn nodded and sipped at her tea. She'd begun to wish she hadn't bothered starting down this road. She had zero evidence that he'd done anything untoward and dwelling on it was only making her feel worse. She needed to shake these feelings of insecurity and mistrust. It was amazing to Autumn how one seemingly little thing had knocked her so badly.

"Look. Just talk to him. What's the point in all this silliness when you could just speak to him and have whatever this is all about sorted in moments?" Sarah was one of these straight-talking kind of mums, she told you how it was even if it wasn't exactly what you wanted to hear. Autumn had started sniffling. She drained the last of her tea and wiped at her eye with the corner of her hoodie.

"Mum," Autumn started, but Sarah cut her off.

"I know you came here for a bit of tea and sympathy and I'm happy to provide one of those, but you don't need the other. Don't overreact darling. You've not been betrayed or hurt in any way and until you have a bit more than a three-worded text message then it's simply not worth giving yourself a headache over."

Sarah knew her daughter well: crying had always given her a pounding headache, ever since she was a little girl. She went in her bag and took out two Paracetamol tablets before handing them over. Autumn inspected them, letting them roll around in her palm without purpose.

"Here, take these and let's have another cup of tea," her mum said unreservedly. "We should sit in the garden; I've a got new water feature to show you." Autumn smiled, her mum definitely was one of a kind. There had been no discussion as such, no tantrums and no speculation: just good, sensible advice.

'Good old Mum,' she thought to herself as they went outside and into the sunshine. The sun almost immediately lifted Autumn's mood. It was hard to remain blue when the weather was just so beautiful. August was her favourite month. It was nearing the end and the weather was cooler than it had been earlier on but the skies were still clear and the sun still shone. She lowered herself into her parents' wrought iron garden furniture: the chairs had been strategically placed so that whoever was sat in them could enjoy a view of the long manicured mature garden and the substantial pond. Autumn noted the new spherical water feature that had been placed in one corner, the trickle of the water providing a perfect soundtrack to the beautiful weather. Autumn turned around to look back

at the house. She could see her mum busying herself through the kitchen window: she was rummaging through an overhead cupboard and Autumn had a sneaking suspicion that with this round of tea there would also be some ginger snap biscuits. Ginger snaps were a firm favourite of both her and her parents and what apparently had initially bonded them on their first date.

Her stomach rumbled. With everything that had happened this morning she'd forgotten to eat. *'How unlike me,'* she mused. *'Maybe a bit of heartbreak wouldn't be so bad for me after all.'*

Sarah reappeared and, as Autumn had guessed, the tray had a plate of biscuits right in the centre. Autumn and her mum chatted for a while: they covered everything from work to the Carters' new neighbours. Eventually Sarah began to encourage her daughter to return home. The sun had begun to dip and the air had grown cooler. Autumn shuddered and pulled her sleeves down.

"Isn't it time you went back home and sorted things out with your boyfriend, darling? Poor Ben will be sitting there wondering what's happened to you."

Autumn nodded, rose out of her seat and hugged her mum hard.

"Thanks Mum, I really needed this. It's been nice," Autumn smiled and Sarah agreed.

"Yes darling, we really must do this more often, and not only when you're having a crisis."

Her mum gave her a warm smile and put her arm around her shoulder. The two walked back inside and into the warm, homely atmosphere of the house. Autumn waved her goodbyes through the doorway as she walked to her car, looking back to see both of her parents smiling broadly, her dad's arm protectively around her mum. Autumn took a deep breath and exhaled, feeling miles better than she had when she'd arrived. She climbed into her car and started the engine. *'Time to sort this out, no more silliness, just honesty,'* she decided resolutely.

"I do hope they sort this out," Sarah said to Richard as she snuggled in closer to him.

"They will," Richard responded. "They're a good couple, just like us." He winked at his wife and as he closed the door to the outside world gave her a long and loving kiss on the top of her head.

CHAPTER 8

BEN LOOKED UP AS SHE ENTERED THEIR HOME. HE wore a look of utter annoyance and infuriation.

What the actual fuck?" he demanded. "If I just upped and left you like that you'd be fuming. We were supposed to spend the day together. Where the fuck have you been?"

Autumn was taken aback, Ben only ever swore like this in extreme circumstance. She wasn't expecting such an aggressive onslaught the second she walked in. She dropped her bag on the floor and found herself transfixed on it. All of a sudden it was very difficult to make eye contact with him.

"I told you, I needed to talk to my mum," Autumn said and lifted her gaze from the floor. Ben was angry, she could see it on his face, a knitted brow and wide staring eyes had replaced his usually warm and relaxed expression. He sat there, not saying a word, just looking at her clearly expecting something more than she had offered so far. She could tell he wanted a real explanation but she felt silly, she'd been so angry – but at what? Her mum was right, she should just talk to him. Easier said than done, especially at times like these. Autumn went on to explain to Ben about finding the phone, seeing the message and panicking. Her words came out in a garbled nonsensical mess, much like they had earlier when she was talking to her mum. Ben looked at her, then his phone, then back to her.

"You've been through my phone?" he asked. His voice was barely above a whisper and laced with disbelief.

"No, you've got that passcode on it now, but now I know why," Autumn said, surveying her boyfriend.

Ben slumped back down, his head gazing down at the phone in his lap, he lifted his head and looked at her. "Autumn, I am not cheating on you. I told you why I've got the passcode and that message you're on about wasn't even for me. I don't know who it was from, but I don't have the number. I don't know what else you want me to say."

She didn't reply. Did this even make sense? Was this plausible? She looked at Ben and saw sadness in his eyes.

"How could you think I'd do something like that to you?" he asked. "Even just for a second!"

Autumn sat down beside him, she rested her head on his shoulder and felt him flinch. She didn't move, just stayed right there for a few minutes.

"I'm sorry, but you've just been so busy recently that I feel like I'm playing second fiddle a lot of the time. You need to make more time for me, more time for us," she said. Her tone was compassionate, her voice pleading with him.

"More time?" he asked incredulously. "Babe, I don't have any more time. So let me get this straight. Because I'm busy and you see a misdirected message, you just assume I'm cheating. I'm working, babe, working hard in a really shitty industry that chews people up and spits them out if they're not good enough. I'm trying to make myself good enough so I last, so I can build us a comfortable life."

Autumn felt terrible. He was doing all those things and more besides, and here she was, suspicious, snooping and only making things harder for him. She apologised profusely again, this time trying to give him a hug: she felt as though she needed some sort of physical interaction with him now.

He didn't stop her but he didn't return the gesture either. The two of them sat there for the rest of the evening, most of it spent in silence. When they did talk, it was wooden and forced. As the night grew colder so did the atmosphere surrounding them. Eventually they resigned themselves to bed.

They didn't make love that night. In fact, they barely made eye contact.

CHAPTER 9

AUTUMN AWOKE THE NEXT MORNING FEELING AS IF she'd been run over. She looked at the alarm clock: there was plenty of time before she needed to get up. She turned around determined to make amends with Ben and put this whole sorry state of affairs behind them. She couldn't believe her over-reaction and insecurities had ruined their one free day together. The drama of yesterday seemed so petty and pointless now. She'd come to the realisation that things were going to be different especially now Ben was experiencing some success. His priorities might change and his time become less readily available but he loved her and she loved him so that had to count for something. Turning over to Ben she was surprised to find him wide awake, bolt upright and on his phone. When he noticed her he put the phone face down on his bedside table and turned to her.

"Want to start over?" he asked.

"More than anything. I'm so sorry. You know I trust you, right?"

"You should do, I've done nothing wrong," he admonished. Autumn looked hurt again. "Look. We're just going to need to give each other a bit more space and learn to trust each other a bit more if we're going to make this work." Ben tilted her head towards his, he moved towards her and took her in his arms, kissing her deeply. He snaked his hands around her back and one fluid motion pulled off her top and began to caress the naked skin beneath.

"Mmmm," she purred, "I like where this is going."

Ben continued to work on her breasts, gently rolling her nipples between his thumb and forefinger, squeezing slightly to inflict a delicate pinch. The soft pink buds hardened against his touch. He rolled her onto her back and climbed on top of her, sucking on his index and middle finger. His legs each side of hers, he pulled her pyjama shorts to one side and slipped his deliciously wet fingers inside her, teasing a moan from her lips. They kissed again, their tongues intertwined. She probed the inside of his mouth with her tongue, extending it hungrily, desperate for the warmth within. He returned the gesture. He ended their long and passionate kiss by biting her bottom lip; she withdrew at the sharp, harsh feeling. Leaning over her, Ben shifted his weight – he was, after all, supporting himself using just one arm. His muscular bicep bulged and Autumn instinctively reached up to grab hold of it. She squeezed his arm and let out a little moan of pleasure as Ben teased her inner recesses. Autumn could feel herself aching for him to be inside her. She wriggled against him, bucking hard against the delicious sensations his fingertips exacted. He needed no more encouragement; he withdrew his fingers and slid his firm shaft inside her, easily and with vigour. She gasped, opening her legs wider to allow him into her fully. She raised her hips up and down rhythmically, meeting him perfectly each time. The pair became more frantic, each drive of his hips resulted in a loud cry from Autumn. She could feel the passionate build-up of pleasure and awaited its release. It came not long after, her body convulsing as the orgasm swept through her, she bucked against the heavy swell of her orgasm, but still Ben continued. He was staring at her now, drinking in the sight before him. Autumn's face flushed and her eyes rolled back. Soon it was Ben's turn: he came. It was short, sharp and severe; he braced himself and climaxed loudly, beads of sweat dripped from the ends of his dishevelled hair and down his chest. When the post-orgasmic haze had subsided, the two uncoupled and Ben left their bed in favour of the bathroom.

"What do you want to do today?" she called through to him. The water from the shower overshadowed her voice thick with content. She cleared her throat and repeated herself, this time a little louder.

"Don't you have work? Besides I've got a busy one today," he replied. "I'm running lines with the guys from work, then I want to go for a run and if I get time do some weights at the gym."

Autumn was disappointed. She'd thought that maybe they could spend the day together; she wasn't back at work until the following day and although she should be getting on with course work she figured that seeing as the day had already gotten off to a great start it would be a shame to waste it studying.

'Let's face it,' she thought, *'a bit of time together would be good for us.'* Especially seeing as they'd had a little blip, she really did think that some TLC for their relationship would do them both wonders.

"Oh, okay," she said, trying to hide the disappointment in her voice. "I thought we might spend the day together. You know, have a little break from the world?" she trailed off. Ben's head appeared in the bathroom doorway. He was grinning.

"Gotcha!" he exclaimed cheekily. "I'm all yours today gorgeous, I've got the day off..."

Autumn sat up a little and grabbed at the pillow behind her. Laughing, she threw it at him as he ducked back into their bathroom.

"Why don't you come and join me in the shower?" he suggested with some force. "Let me treat you to round two."

Autumn rose from their bed and practically sprinted to the shower. She didn't need to be asked twice. She pulled down her shorts as she went, discarding them next to the wash-basket and hopped into the shower alongside Ben. Once more he took her in his arms, lifting her up and lowering her onto his still impressive erection. He bent at the knees to accommodate her petite size and supported her with his strong arms. Their shower session didn't last long. It was wet and warm and with the previous morning's activities still buzzing in their heads neither one of them could contain themselves for long.

They spent the rest of the morning in and out of the bedroom. They made love once more after the shower, on the floor of the bedroom. Again, it had been heady and passionate. All of Ben's attention had been lavished upon her and it felt utterly amazing. She felt alive with passion. Autumn couldn't remember the last time they'd both decided to play truant from life and just enjoy one another; the prospect of the day together was both exciting and exhilarating. She felt good, the sex had been incredible; it felt fresh and new, as if Ben had taken a refresher course. Orgasms before lunchtime: she really was a very lucky girl.

The day passed in a blur. Ben took her for an indulgent, champagne-fuelled lunch at Leonard's, a gorgeous bistro restaurant and bar in town. Once a dilapidated old theatre, it had been bought and renovated a couple of years ago. Now it stood proudly in the centre of town, its imposing opulence oozing both elegance and class. The prices were for most of the diners for special occasions only, but today, nothing was too much. Ben pulled out all the stops for her: there was even a bottle of champagne on the table awaiting their arrival. As the waitress popped the cork Autumn looked at Ben, her eyes shone and she took a moment to reflect on just how good they'd got it. She couldn't remember a time when she'd felt this contented. The air had well and truly been cleared now and the tough time they had had seemed like a distant memory. When the waitress came over again to refill their glasses, Autumn asked if she would mind taking a picture of the two of them. She dutifully obliged, taking a step back to get them both in. Autumn felt a pure, genuine smile erupt on her lips: the restaurant, the champagne but most of all the company was perfect. Over the course of the meal they chatted openly about pretty much everything. She had delved into his work life, an area that had, unimaginably, not really been touched on, or at least not in any great depth. As she sat there with Ben chatting excitedly about other acting possibilities, it dawned on her that she really wasn't in the loop when it came to anything he did outside of the house. Autumn felt the teeniest pang of guilt at this, and vowed to take more of an interest in Ben's work. *'No more distractedly asking how his day was and not really listening to the answer,'* she vowed. From now on that would be a thing of the past. She was determined to make their relationship stronger.

The waitress brought over the bill and Ben paid.

"Why don't you ever use that lovely leather wallet I bought for you?" she asked, casting a disapproving glance towards the khaki green fabric wallet he used instead. "I even paid extra to have it personalised," she added.

"I just like this one," Ben said defensively. "I've had it for years," he finished sulkily.

"All the more reason to get rid of it!" Autumn joked. She knew Ben would probably have that old wallet until his dying day. He loved it so much. It had been a gift from his mother many birthdays ago and, for some inexplicable reason, he thought it was the nicest wallet in the world.

Afterwards they took a leisurely stroll through the park. Waterhigh Park was a vast expanse of land; there were no swings or slides in this particular park, but instead endless beautiful gardens stretched out before them and eventually gave way to extensive woodlands. As they walked along, Ben's arm draped around Autumn's shoulders and they chatted, joked and laughed. Autumn felt incredibly happy and very content. If she could change anything it would be the amount of time Ben spent checking his phone, responding to work emails and taking calls from his agent. He wasn't staring at the screen all the time but every now and then, mid-chat, she'd feel as though he'd checked out of the conversation for a moment. It was annoying more than anything when she had to repeat herself so often. Still, she couldn't complain: Ben was starting to get a bit more attention in the acting world and Autumn knew he wanted to make the most of it, so it was only natural that he'd want to stay on top of it all.

"Sorry babe, I'll just be two seconds, I need to send this email," Ben said, his fingers manically typing away at a rate of knots.

"It's fine," Autumn said distractedly, her eyes taking in the absolute beauty of her surroundings. The tall trees had given way and she realised they were now atop a small hill. The view was incredible: in the distance she could see the houses of neighbouring towns and villages. Further along she could just about make out the tall spire of the church near her parents' house. Eventually the houses, churches and other buildings she could see gave way to the horizon. The sun's rays were intense and beat down heavily on her bare shoulders. Autumn took off her sunglasses, closed her eyes and raised her head to the heavens, enjoying every last inch of sunlight that fell on her face. She could feel droplets of perspiration beginning to form. Autumn turned to Ben and asked him what he wanted to do for the rest of the day. There was only silence that met her. She turned around to see him still frantically tapping away at the screen of his phone.

"Ben?" she said a little louder, interrupting his flow.

"Sorry," he said again. "One second, gorgeous." He looked up briefly and gave her a cheeky smile. Autumn found it hard to be annoyed with him when he was so damn cute. After a few more moments, he returned his phone to his back pocket, took her by the arm and pulled her in for a long kiss. His hands grabbed at her, pulling her into him further. He snaked his arms around her and slid his hands under the waistband of her skirt. She sniggered awkwardly and pulled away from him; something about the certainty of his touch had made her uneasy.

"What are you doing?" she said, looking around them wildly.

"Come on, babe," Ben said encouragingly, "no one's around."

"I just don't feel like it right this second," Autumn said defiantly. "Anyone could walk past and I really don't want to." Ben considered this for a moment then, as if deciding against himself, released her. As he stepped back Autumn noticed a very impressive erection bulging from beneath his jeans. His penis pressed against the fabric urgently, leaving very little to the imagination. Ben looked at her, his eyes steely and resolute.

"Oh come on!" he said again, exasperatedly. "It'd be a shame to waste *this*." He nodded to his crotch then looked back at his girlfriend, his eyes pleading with her to reconsider. Autumn shook her head and mumbled an apology of sorts.

Ben was making her feel like a prude and she didn't care for it one bit. Feeling as though their perfect day might be ruined if they carried on down this path, she reluctantly reached out, grabbed his arm and pulled him back down the hill towards the cover of the trees. Within minutes they were enjoying each other under the concealment of the thickly blanketed trees, bushes and shrubs of Waterhigh Park. Ben pushed her up against a nearby tree. Autumn gasped as the rough bark rubbed against her skin abrasively. Ben quickly put one hand firmly over her mouth.

"Shh," he hissed. "You don't want to be discovered now, do you?" he said mockingly in her ear.

Ben pulled her skirt up and moved her knickers to the side. He pushed two of his fingers into her mouth, coating them in saliva and then purposefully pushed them inside of her, moving them in and out, curving them round and pressing against her inner hot spot firmly. Autumn gasped again, only this time with pleasure. She was beginning to enjoy herself now: she felt exposed and unprotected. Initially this had worried her but now, well now it seemed to be the main factor for her arousal. After a few moments of intense foreplay Ben moved backwards slightly, unzipping his jeans as he did so. He pulled out his erection: it was swollen and throbbing hungrily. His veins bulged and a droplet of pre-cum glistened at the tip invitingly. He bent down at the knees and came upwards suddenly, taking her with more force than she'd expected. She banged up against the tree, a sharp exhalation of breath left her lips. Ben's hand was still clamped over her mouth, preventing any further sound from escaping. He thrust his hips urgently, eager for his own release; he didn't seem to be concerned with Autumn's pleasure at all which silenced any romantic notion Autumn had. She continually banged against the rough surface of the tree trunk that was supporting them.

Ben's pace quickened: he'd released his hand over her mouth and was now gripping the tree firmly, using it to thrust into her as deeply as he possibly could. She leant forward to kiss him, trying to incite some romance. He pushed her back, pulling up her top as he did so and exposing her breast. He bent forward, taking her nipple into his mouth. It instinctively hardened at the attention being lavished upon it. He sucked on the hardening bead greedily and moments later, he came. His knees buckled as his body jerked. Ben found himself going into spasm with the delectable sensations he was experiencing; he gripped the tree harder, his knuckles whitening as he clung on in a fit of ecstasy.

Once the intensity of his orgasm had subsided he let himself slide out of Autumn, pulling a tissue out of his back pocket and handing it to her. She took it hesitantly and began to wipe herself, in no way feeling satisfied. As she mopped up the product of his pleasure, it dawned on Autumn that she was feeling uncomfortable. She had enjoyed their outdoor activities, had felt desired and wanted but also felt a little like she'd missed out. Although, she reasoned, the longer they were at it the more likely they were to be discovered. Once she'd mulled this over in her head a few times she felt better and it was with this thought that she came to the conclusion that it was probably for the best that it had been over and done with quickly.

Autumn rearranged her clothing to cover her modesty as Ben leaned over and kissed her on the cheek. He lingered there for a moment and inhaled deeply, enjoying the aroma of her. He could smell her sweet sweat, a musky sexy smell that enveloped his senses. This, teamed with the smell of raw sex and the lingering scent of her perfume, was almost too much. His stomach did a flip. Those scents combined made him feel on top of the world. Ben puffed his chest out, feeling caveman-like, his animal urges now satisfactorily quashed. Autumn looked at him: he obviously felt very happy with himself.

"That was awesome," he said in a self-congratulatory fashion as he led her back down the hill, "and exactly what we needed, don't you think?"

Autumn nodded in agreement, without really agreeing at all.

CHAPTER 10

AUTUMN LOOKED UP FROM THE MAGAZINE: THE bell above the door tinkled signifying the arrival of another customer. She inhaled deeply, the comforting smell of the coffee shop filling her senses. She glanced down at the watch she'd inherited from her grandma. The rose gold face confirmed what she thought. David was, in true David fashion, late. She looked back to her magazine, not really taking in what was in front of her. The article entitled 'Seven Ways to Better Orgasms' was sloppily written and wasn't capturing or keeping Autumn's attention, no matter how hard she tried to read it.

'I could do so much better than this,' she thought to herself. Annoyance laced with jealousy bubbled inside her. It was so unfair that someone with far less journalistic talent than she had, had her dream job. She glanced again at her watch and sighed loudly when she realised that barely a minute had passed since the last time she looked. A nearby waitress glanced over at the sound, a nervous look etched on her face: she was clearly concerned at the idea of having to deal with an annoyed customer. The waitress relaxed a little when she saw Autumn's sheepish grin.

"Sorry," Autumn said apologetically, "I'm just fed up of waiting for my friend."

"It's okay," the pretty waitress replied, her short blonde ponytail whipping round as she turned to face Autumn. "Free top up while you wait?" she suggested, brandishing an American-style coffee pot at Autumn.

"Oh go on then," Autumn smiled. 'It'd be rude not to."

The waitress wandered over to her, coffee pot in hand and topped her up. She dropped a little plate of flapjacks on the table in front of Autumn.

"These should help pass the time," the waitress said. "They're on the house of course," she concluded with a smile.

Autumn took them gratefully and tucked in, not realising quite how hungry she was. The sweetness of the flapjack tantalised her taste buds and her mouth filled with saliva as she popped another piece into her mouth. She closed the magazine and dropped it into her bag.

Autumn was so excited to see David; the anticipation was building up inside her, threatening to overflow at any moment. He'd been away for what seemed like an entire lifetime and she'd missed him terribly. Getting used to not hearing from him every day had been tough. She couldn't blame him, though. He had decided that he needed a break from the world and had packed himself off to America. She would never have had the guts to do something like that. Autumn liked the safety and security of planning and preparation. David was the antithesis of her in this respect; in fact, as Autumn pondered David's free nature, she realised with some envy that ever since she'd known him he'd been able to be spontaneous without it having any negative effect on his life. If Autumn had decided to just up and leave for the summer, she'd likely come back to no job, a tonne of coursework and a bank balance in need of some serious TLC. There was no doubt about it: to Autumn, David was so brave. Nevertheless it had been hard on her, even though it was only a few weeks without him. Not having him immediately by her side when she needed him was tough. She always had Ben and Rosa, but David always offered a balanced, sensible view on any situation. He was a total rock and Autumn was only now realising just how much she relied on him for everyday support. He'd had still been in touch, of course: she'd received emails, but only when he wasn't enjoying himself too much and was able to visit an internet café. Autumn had been surprised that internet cafés still existed, but David had assured her that in the good old US of A there were plenty.

She chewed happily on her freebie flapjack and relaxed in her chair, enjoying the soft velvet against her skin. She sank into the armchair and, with the boredom of waiting for David reached down for her magazine. She flicked through the pages again, still unimpressed. She wished the newsagent hadn't been out of *Wow* magazine and hoped against hope that the one she'd ended up with would improve as the page numbers increased. A few minutes ticked by, the background noise of the coffee shop buzzed around her. She went into autopilot, lazily scanning articles about diets and pictures of celebrities on nights out. She sipped at her coffee and flipped the pages of the magazine systematically, not really taking anything in, when she heard a familiar voice.

"AUTUMN!" the voice exclaimed. "My darling, how are you?"

Autumn jerked her head upwards and a wide grin spread across her face. It was David, her lovely David, in all his tanned glory, wearing what looked to be some kind of bright blue tie-dye poncho with crisp white jeans. Autumn smiled widely and got up. She didn't say anything but stretched out her arms and enveloped him in a huge bear-like hug, burying her face into his shoulder.

"I've missed you so much!" she exclaimed excitedly. She waved at the waitress who nodded and started to wander over, pad and pen in hand.

"Coffee?" the waitress asked, eyeing David approvingly. David was tall and had a messy mop of light brown hair that was just begging for someone to run their fingers through it. While not conventionally handsome, David had a charm about him that meant that people warmed to him instantly.

"Two cappuccinos, please," David ordered after a brief pause whilst inspecting the menu.

Autumn interjected quickly. "Just one please, I'm fine with what I've got," she said, gesturing to her cup.

"It's not for you," David said coyly. "I might have bought someone with me," he added mysteriously. There was a short silence before Autumn put two and two together.

"Your new man!" Autumn said, clapping a hand to her forehead. "Oh God, I'm so dumb, sorry David! Of course, where is he?" she asked, the words tumbling out of her mouth with mild embarrassment.

Autumn couldn't help feeling a little miffed that she wasn't going to get David all to herself, but those feelings of dissatisfaction and annoyance quickly gave way when she saw the look of utter delight on David's face as Gregg entered the coffee shop. Autumn was speechless for a moment. She knew that Gregg was good looking, she'd seen photos of him after all. Nothing could have prepared her for what he was like in the flesh. It was easy to see why David had fallen head over heels for him so quickly. He was possibly the most handsome man Autumn had ever seen. He was well built, with flawless, smooth dark skin. He had mesmerising brown eyes, which were framed by beautiful, long eyelashes that any girl would have been envious of. His hair was now shaved short and he wore a plain white T-shirt and dark denim jeans, which showcased his physique perfectly. It took Autumn a moment to collect herself; the sharp finger she felt poking her side brought her back around into reality.

"Autumn? Are you alright?" joked David as he prodded her with some force, his finger digging into her side uncomfortably.

"Oh God," she muttered. "Sorry, I'm Autumn." She extended her hand in a business-like fashion. Gregg laughed and shook it jovially.

"It's a pleasure to meet you," he said, his accent much milder that Autumn had expected. He sounded very gentle and warm. Gregg had a southern American drawl that was soft and mellow. His voice was like music, instantly relaxing all who heard it.

"Likewise," Autumn returned. "I didn't know you were here," she explained, going on to say that in his last email David had said that Gregg would be going down to Surrey to visit his mother.

"Well I had to meet the most important lady in David's life, before he met the most important one in mine," he explained.

It was with that comment that Autumn was sold. Gregg was as charming as David; they bounced off one another and seemed to Autumn to be a perfect fit. They had fabulous chemistry and it was plain to see that they were both mad about one another. Their meeting lasted hours, and they chatted happily whilst getting to know one another.

"So how did you guys meet?" Autumn asked midway through their conversation.

"You tell it Gregg," David insisted. "He's way better at telling stories than me."

Gregg looked flattered and began to tell Autumn the story of how they had first met. It had been a really hot day, and Gregg, who owned a small chain of gyms, was looking at a retail space in downtown LA. David was staying in the hotel opposite. It was a 'happy accident' kind of story. David had gone for breakfast late that morning and Gregg, after viewing his potential new space, had decided on a late breakfast as well. They'd happened to choose the same café. Gregg was only moments behind David. He queued for a table behind him, placed his order behind him and had paid just behind him. They hadn't noticed one another until they came to leave, David had held the door open for Gregg, as, once again, he was just behind. Gregg had thanked David, David had replied and the rest, as they say, is history. They walked down the street, making polite but easy conversation when they realised that they were both heading to the same place.

"We ended up having our first date, literally the instant we met each other," laughed David in conclusion.

It was such a lovely story and Autumn felt so glad for her friend. David seemed happier and more content than he'd ever been and it was lovely to see. As the conversation began to run dry, David interjected to say that they really must be going as they had early dinner plans and were then going to see a film. They drained the last of their coffees, said a fond farewell and left. Autumn turned around and watched her dearest friend walking away, arm in arm with the man whom Autumn knew would make David very happy.

Autumn's working week began and continued with all the excitement of being stuck in the house, during a power cut with no battery on your phone or films on your laptop. The commonplace routine was becoming dull; her work at Thorne PR was, to put it mildly, boring as fuck. Answering the phone and posting letters wasn't exactly her idea of a dream job and it stifled her creativity. At least that's what she told herself, which was why she was finding it so difficult to get on with her coursework. Autumn couldn't believe she'd had the entire summer to do her final assignments and revise and yet she was still going to have to pull at least one all-nighter to ensure she didn't fail spectacularly. David on the other hand had done the majority of his work before he went away and would finish the rest with comparative ease before they sat their exams.

"Autumn, a word please." Jack's voice crackled over the intercom on her desk. There was a familiar click as he hung up his phone, not even waiting for Autumn's answer.

'I could be really busy,' she simmered. Jack was throwing his weight around, yet again. He'd been particularly difficult recently. Even though he was her boss there was a right way and a wrong way to speak to people. *'Maybe he's just not getting any,'* Autumn mused meanly. She slipped her feet out of the comfy slippers that were kept hidden behind her desk and slid her feet into her marginally less comfortable work heels.

As she trudged up to Jack's office she passed the staff coffee room. *'Surely I have time to pour myself one small cup of coffee,'* she reasoned.

Autumn detoured into the staff lounge. The sun streamed in through the floor to ceiling windows and lit the room beautifully, highlighting its exceptionally polished decor. The chrome surfaces dazzled brightly and the crystal light fittings twinkled prettily. Autumn poured herself a coffee and realised there was no other way to put this off. Sighing, she headed upstairs to Jack's office.

"Come in," Jack's voice said in a commanding tone after she'd knocked twice. Autumn entered, and paused for a second. Jack wasn't sat at his desk but was, instead, on the veranda outside. Autumn looked out through the French doors and caught a hint of his shadow on the sheer curtains as they danced in the breeze.

"Jack?" she quizzed. There was no answer; she hesitated before pushing through the billowing material. It was strangely still on the veranda: the breeze seemed to be deadened in the quiet space. Jack was stood at the edge, a small wall protecting him from the sheer drop the other side. Autumn walked towards him and stood by his side, her gaze following his. They were high up and had a spectacular view of the surrounding areas, which stretched out for miles in front of them. They stood there for a moment, before Jack spoke.

"It hasn't escaped my attention that you're wasted on reception, Autumn," he began. "How would you like a promotion?"

Autumn didn't know what to say. The job, although monotonous and stifled, suited her in terms of hours and flexibility. It afforded her the luxury of a regular pay packet with time to spend on her studies and her social life. Surely a promotion would mean more dedication on her part? More work in a job that she didn't intend on keeping once she had all the relevant qualifications to go into journalism fully?

"You wouldn't need to work any extra hours, plus you'd get a pay rise," he added, taking off his suit jacket and laying it over the wall in front of him.

"Well, that's very flattering Jack, and thank you, of course, but I…" Autumn was cut off abruptly.

"You'd be working more closely with me. We're getting busier by the day, Autumn, and I need someone to help me more," Jack said. He continued by outlining her new duties and offered her a small bump in pay. "So, what do you say?" he asked.

"Well, I…" Autumn took a sip of her coffee, vying for time. She didn't want to agree to anything without speaking to Ben first.

"Fabulous," Jack smiled. "You start effective immediately. We have an important client meeting first thing tomorrow morning. You'll have seen it in the diary. I'll need you to sort out the boardroom this evening, arrange for provisions and the pitch is in here." He handed her a thick folder, which she took and almost dropped from its weight. "Familiarise yourself with the 'ins and outs', will you? I'll also need you to charm the client, and also, how's your shorthand?" Autumn took a breath to answer but Jack continued regardless. "Well, I'll need you to keep a record of the meeting. Any personal information, everything we discuss and anything else that may be of value to us later."

Jack finished and turned to her, looking her in the eye for the first time since she'd joined him on the veranda. He placed a hand on her shoulder. The breeze caught Autumn's hair and blew it around her face, her blonde locks dancing in time with the curtains behind her. She caught the scent of his aftershave and felt her stomach flip slightly, just like it had that time at the gate. Jack leaned in, Autumn mirrored him. *'Is this really happening?'* she questioned. *'Is he about to kiss me?'* Jack moved his hand up towards her face, pausing briefly before tucking the stray piece hair behind her ear.

"Jack…" Autumn trailed off.

"You'll also need to stay on reception until we find a suitable replacement," Jack finished, delivering his final blow.

He walked past her and back into his office. Embarrassment coloured Autumn's her cheeks; she was thankful Jack had his back to her and couldn't see. She drained the rest of her coffee and set it down on the wall. She couldn't believe that she was, once again, acting like a silly schoolgirl, nor could she believe that she'd misinterpreted Jack's actions yet again. She shook her head as if to dislodge these thoughts. Autumn concentrated on the task in hand and felt more than daunted at the prospect of her new role. It sounded very much to her as though she'd just agreed to take on another job as well as doing her own. She'd been well and truly suckered into this: without even really saying anything she'd managed to agree to do more work in the same amount of time with a pitiful pay increase. Autumn's emotions quickly turned from apprehension to anger. Again Jack had thrown his weight around. She'd often heard examples of this type of thing happening with Jack but had never truly experienced it first-hand – that was, until now. When it came down to it, Autumn realised, Jack Thorne could be a bit of a bully. It was as if the only control he had was at work. Still, as angry as she was she couldn't shake the feeling in the pit of her stomach that she hadn't been entirely repulsed at the thought of his advances and that, really, she had secretly welcomed the thought of Jack leaning in to kiss her.

Coming to her senses she took a step towards Jack's desk. She had no time for this, she needed to keep her old job exactly how it was and no one, not even Jack Thorne could force her to do something she really didn't want to do.

"Actually Jack…" Autumn began, her confidence waning with each syllable uttered.

"Sorry Autumn," Jack said, once again cutting her off. "I need to get on, close the door on your way out," he said, gesturing to the door behind her.

Before she knew it, Autumn was out in the hallway, file in hand, feeling very deflated. It was then it dawned on her. The meeting was first thing tomorrow morning! Autumn usually finished work at five o'clock on the dot but today she would be staying late to make sure everything was in order. It was beginning to look like this pay rise wasn't a rise at all, just Jack covering himself for the additional hours she was going to have to work to manage all her new duties. It was then and there that Autumn decided that, more than ever, she needed to pass her journalism course with exceptional results so that she could go on to get a job that she actually wanted, somewhere where she would be a valued member of the team, somewhere where her boss wouldn't be Jack Thorne. In a perfect world, it would be working for renowned magazine editor, Melissa Abbott.

The rest of the day passed quickly, much to Autumn's relief. Both Rosa and June had popped down to see her at various points in the day, helping to break up the monotony. Rosa was heading off early today. Playing her cards close to her chest, she didn't exactly go into much detail about where she was going, or with who for that matter, but Autumn had a very good idea it was 'diamond bracelet guy.' Rosa must really like him; she'd been even more secretive than usual. One of her favourite colleagues, June, had visited her much later, brandishing a box of chocolate brownies in Autumn's face with a warm grin.

"I saved these for you," June said with a smile.

June was approaching retirement age now, but showed no signs of slowing down. She had worked at Thorne PR in the admin department since the company's inception, which was probably one of the reasons they'd kept her on. However, where she failed at being able to alphabetise files she succeeded in making the world's best baked goods. No one ever complained if a job's file went missing, especially if June had been in the kitchen creating something sugary for the staff at Thorne PR to indulge in. Autumn gobbled down the brownies greedily. She'd skipped lunch and these sweet treats were tiding her over nicely. She and June had chatted for a while, as Autumn loved June's wicked sense of humour. She looked like butter wouldn't melt, was a member of the WI and was always the first to crack a blue joke at staff parties.

Autumn always thought of June as her work mum: she was kind, caring and compassionate, much like her own mother.

Then end of the day drew nearer. *'Just a few minutes until clocking off time,'* Autumn thought thankfully. She shut her computer down, closing down her emails and switched the phones answering service on. The mechanical whirring of her computer ceased and Autumn enjoyed the brief silence that followed.

The silence didn't last long. Jack's voice crackled over the speaker again: his timing couldn't have been better, or worse as the case may be.

"Autumn, I'm leaving now for a golf game. I trust you haven't forgotten about tomorrow's meeting." The phone hung up once more. It wasn't a question, just a statement, posed as a question with the sole intention of reminding Autumn of her place.

Autumn dialled the caterer's number from her mobile phone. Preferring to take the hit on her bill rather than faff around enabling the phone system again, she placed an order for a selection of pastries and fresh fruit for the meeting. *'At least that's one thing I can tick off the list,'* she thought.

An hour later and Autumn was busy setting up the boardroom, moving chairs, setting out water glasses and distributing the relevant documents around the large mahogany table that sat proudly in the centre of the room. She had been instructed to make sure the presentation software was up to date and in good working order. She leant over the boardroom's computer and flicked the on button. Nothing happened. She pressed the button again, harder this time. Still nothing. She sighed exasperatedly. She really didn't have time for this. She wasn't a technical genius and had absolutely no idea which wire was supposed to go where. It looked fine, the bloody thing never moved and never gave anyone any trouble so why was it playing up now?

"For fuck's sake," she muttered irritably under her breath. She had this one last thing to do and just wanted it to be over and done with. Autumn hitched up her skirt slightly and bent over the computer.

Autumn sensed someone enter the room. She straightened up quickly, pulling down her skirt to a respectable level as she did so. It was then that Autumn heard a friendly, but unfamiliar voice behind her.

"Excuse me, I'm looking for Jack Thorne," the voice said, the trace of an accent on her lips. Autumn was sure she could hear a hint of Spanish or maybe Portuguese? Either way the woman's voice was mesmerising. It was beautifully husky with a guttural tone. Autumn turned around, trying to give the impression of professional poise to the visitor, who was, Autumn saw, an extremely attractive woman. The first thing she noticed about the woman was her smooth olive skin, which was accentuated by the fitted white dress she wore. She had a thick, glossy mane of dark hair, which tumbled over her shoulders in soft waves. On her feet she wore skyscraper, nude heels: Autumn didn't need to see the underside of the shoes to know they would have red soles. Her elegant footwear elongated her slender frame, and gave her an impressive air of importance as well as elegance. Her makeup, although understated, was immaculately applied and the only jewellery she wore was a selection of glittering bangles, which adorned her slender wrist. Over her shoulder was a giant, white leather tote bag, which looked out of the box, brand spanking new.

Autumn gathered herself together. This woman was obviously a prospective client, and what had Jack said? She was to be charming towards them. Switching into work mode she turned on a warm smile and extended her hand.

"Autumn Carter," she said in her smooth work voice. This was, however, the first time she'd had to use it without being on the telephone. "I'm afraid Jack's not here at the moment. He's finished for the day and," Autumn checked her watch, "will be teeing off around about now."

The woman faltered slightly but shook Autumn's hand and smiled nonetheless. Autumn marvelled at the beauty which radiated from her. Her teeth were so white and straight, *'Now this is a woman who genuinely does have an A-lister Hollywood smile,'* Autumn thought to herself. As they shook hands, Autumn admired the woman's soft skin. Her long nails were painted a beautiful light grey and had been shaped into perfect ovals.

"He's not here you say?" the woman said in that beautifully accented, low voice. "That's odd. We were supposed to be meet."

"Oh. I'm so sorry," Autumn said, trying to stall for time and wishing she hadn't said Jack was off golfing. Why hadn't she made up some other excuse, anything that sounded more professional than that?

"So you're telling me he's unlikely to return this evening?" the woman went on. "Well, that is disappointing. Still, you're here so it's not an entirely wasted trip." She smiled at Autumn, once again displaying those perfectly white teeth.

"I'm afraid I'm just the receptionist," Autumn replied. She wanted to try and save the situation but she was way out of her depth. When it came to the world of Thorne PR, taking calls and forwarding on emails were her strong points. "I could maybe take a message and have him call you first thing in the morning?" she suggested.

"It looks like you'll be busy first thing in the morning." The woman nodded towards the documents spread out on the boardroom table. "Early meeting, I assume."

"Yes, but we don't want to let you down again. I can assure you Jack's not normally forgetful like this. I don't recall seeing anything in the diary for this evening so I can only assume someone forgot to put it in."

Autumn was scraping the barrel with this excuse. However, it seemed to suffice: the woman didn't say anything further and instead perched herself against the meeting table. She flipped open one of the files and began to leaf through, her bangles chiming together as she did so. Autumn stood there awkwardly for a second, unsure how she should read this.

"Can I get you a drink?" Autumn asked, filling the silence with the first thing she could think of.

"Do you know, that's the best offer I've heard today!" the woman exclaimed, a wry smile on her lips. "A whiskey straight up would go down fabulously."

Not wanting to let the woman down further, Autumn decided it was better not to clarify that she had meant tea or coffee.

"Coming right up." Autumn smiled and backed out of the room somewhat awkwardly.

When she was out of sight, Autumn turned and bolted up the stone staircase to Jack's office, her footsteps echoing throughout her empty workplace. She knocked lightly, more out of habit than anything else, and pushed the door open. Stepping inside, she glanced around quickly, double-checking that the coast was clear. She went over to the drinks cabinet and opened it, carefully selecting the whiskey bottle furthest to the back. She wanted to make sure she chose one that Jack wouldn't miss.

She pulled the bottle out. It clinked noisily on the others around it as she brought it forward. Autumn reasoned that this one couldn't be very nice as it was shoved to the back and was almost full: it looked like Jack had tried a bit, decided he didn't like it and squirrelled it away. From what she could tell Jack loved whiskey, so to only drink a tiny bit then shove the rest to the back of the cabinet must mean this wasn't great. The bottle was quite pretty though: a silver stag head was stuck to the outside of the bottle just above the words Dalmore Constellation. *'Oooh, fancy,'* she said to herself. She popped the cork and gave it a sniff just to make sure it was still okay. At 35 years old she wouldn't be surprised if it hadn't gone off by now. It smelt pretty much like all other whiskeys, so, returning the cork to its rightful place she left Jack's office and headed downstairs to the mysterious client waiting in the boardroom. Autumn poured her a small measure of whiskey and set the bottle down on the table where the woman was still sat. She picked it up and surveyed the bottle.

"You know your stuff," she said, clearly impressed with Autumn's selection. "This one is my absolute favourite." Autumn smiled and took the credit for her lucky guess.

"We aim to please," she said, trying to suppress the smug look she could feel forming on her face.

"Are you not having one?" her new friend asked, raising an eyebrow as well as her glass.

"I shouldn't really. I'm technically still at work," Autumn explained. The woman didn't appear to hear Autumn. Instead she reached over, delicately picking up a water glass and reached for the bottle of whiskey.

"I won't tell if you don't," she said, pouring Autumn a measure which matched her own. "Chin chin," she said, passing Autumn the glass and clinking it with her own before take a sip of the amber liquid. Autumn sipped too. She'd never been a great fan of whiskey but this was delicious. She couldn't for the life of her figure out why Jack wouldn't have liked it.

They sat there for a few moments in relative silence. The sun was beginning to set and was sinking low in the sky. The light in the boardroom had changed and was now a warm, orange glow. Autumn relaxed, the stresses of the day seemed to melt away with each sip that she took. The woman had still not properly introduced herself and Autumn had little idea from which company she came.

"Rough day?" the woman asked, flexing her feet and admiring her presumably expensive heels.

"You could say that," Autumn replied. "I basically got a promotion, which was actually a fancy way of getting me to do more work in less time. I had to stay late to sort the boardroom out for a meeting tomorrow and when I get home tonight I have to read this bloody thing." She tapped the file Jack had given to her.

Autumn went on to explain her predicament, the whiskey giving her a false sense of confidence. She rolled her eyes at various intervals for added drama. The conversation between the two women flowed easily from there. Autumn found her incredibly easy to talk to and felt drawn to her. She exuded a warmth and confidence that was rare. Autumn found herself telling the woman all about Jack, about her boyfriend and her dreams of writing for a highbrow women's magazine. Although, she concluded, it would be hard to find the time to get all her coursework done whilst her boss was making her work extra hard.

"So, basically, your boss is a bit of a tyrant and you're just a poor, underpaid, overworked young lady looking for a bit more of a challenge?" Autumn nodded. "Well, this might be your lucky day then."

The woman leaned down and pulled a solid silver business card holder out of the side pocket of her oversized bag. Autumn regarded how immaculate the bag was, knowing that if she were to ever own a white bag, it would be marked and stained within minutes. The woman took out a business card and inspected it, she pulled a pen from her bag and wrote a number on the back of it. "I've been looking for well organised, open-minded creative to join my company. I need assistance during the events we host," she said. "Now, while I can't promise it'll have much more to do with writing than this job does, I can promise you flexible hours, better pay and way more excitement."

Autumn took the card and inspected it. She'd never been 'head hunted' before.

"I don't know what to say," Autumn began, looking at the card: it was a pearlescent white colour with the words 'Encounters Events' embossed on the front. She turned it over. The woman had, in extremely neat handwriting, written what looked to be her personal mobile number.

"You don't need to say anything," the woman interrupted. Again, she flashed Autumn those pearly whites. "Just keep the card, think about it and if you do decide it's something you want give me a call and we'll go from there."

"Thanks," Autumn said, genuinely grateful.

She placed the card safely inside the breast pocket of her jacket. The day had been a bit of a downer and this had certainly been a welcome distraction, one that had certainly boosted her self-esteem. The woman stood at one of the large windows, surveying the mature grounds that the offices of Thorne PR were set. Without taking her eyes off the gardens she reached over and picked up the bottle of whiskey and poured herself another drink. She turned around and set the bottle at the head of the table.

Autumn liked this lady a lot. She was ballsy, easy to talk to and had an air about her that made Autumn instinctively know that no matter what the situation, the woman in front of her would know exactly what to do. She was self-assured, confident and made Autumn feel more collected just being around her. Autumn could tell that this woman had her shit together; she was exactly the kind of person Autumn had planned for herself to be. They chatted further, and Jack came up more than once.

"Well I must say, your boss certainly can't value you as much as I would," she said.

"You're telling me." Autumn agreed, then feeling a twinge of guilt added. "Still, he's not all bad, I suppose. He could be a lot worse." The woman cast Autumn a downward smile.

"I'm sure he's not all bad," the woman agreed before sliding off the boardroom table and standing up. "Well I'm quite sure I've wasted enough of your time, plus my driver must be positively dying of boredom now." She handed the empty glass back to Autumn who couldn't help but look thoroughly impressed that this woman had a driver.

'*She must be very successful,*' Autumn reasoned.

"I'm so sorry," Autumn said, stopping the woman as she headed out of the door. "I never caught your name."

"It's Celina." The woman said, turning around and facing Autumn, her expression unreadable, "Celina Thorne."

With that Celina turned around and walked out of the door. Autumn stared after her in her wake, mouth agape. She was speechless; still, she couldn't help but admire the glimpses of red she caught on the soles of Celina's heels as she strutted away, leaving the building and heading back home to her husband, Autumn's boss.

Autumn stood there in shock, for a few moments. A wave of dread washed over her as she stared after Celina Thorne. She didn't really know what to do with herself. Feeling a mixture of embarrassment, guilt, worry and remorse Autumn decided there was only one thing for it: she was going home.

Snatching up her bag and car keys she hurriedly left the office. Autumn let the door slam shut behind her. She wanted to flee the scene of the crime as quickly as humanly possible.

CHAPTER 11

"BEN, ARE YOU EVEN LISTENING TO ME?" AUTUMN moaned. She'd been trying to tell Ben the utterly cringe-inducing story of how she'd met Jack's wife. But Ben had only been half-listening.

'I'm well and truly fed up with not being listened to,' Autumn simmered internally. She looked at him for a full minute. He was sat on the arm of the sofa, staring at his phone; he was meant to be reading over a script that he'd been sent last minute, although right now he was tapping away at the screen, with a silly half-cocked smile on his face.

"Ben?" she repeated, more forcefully this time. "You're not reading, you're on Facebook or something, and I can see you typing! I'm probably going to lose my job and you don't even care!" Autumn whined.

Unhelpful thoughts swam around her head. She was so wrapped up in her own drama, she barely noticed Ben re-adjusting himself before resuming whatever conversation he was having on social media that took precedent over Autumn's personal drama. No matter how hard she tried, she couldn't shake the idea that as charming as Celina Thorne had been to her face, deep down she was fuming at Autumn for slagging off her husband, badmouthing his business and... she trailed off.

'Oh God,' she thought. *'Celina won't want anything to do with me now.'* It was this thought that bothered her most, which was wholly odd because she'd only just met the woman.

"Ben?" she said, practically shouting now. She put her hand over the screen of his phone, blocking his view.

"What?" he replied impatiently, pulling the phone away and sliding it into his back pocket. "Babe, I'm sorry but they've made a lot of changes and I just needed to look everything over before I go to bed."

"Go to bed?" she asked reproachfully. "It's not even nine o'clock." Autumn knew Ben's response before the words left his lips.

"I've got to be up early if I want to get to the gym before work, babe," he said, a softer tone to his voice now. He looked up at her and seeing the distress on her features stood up to meet her face to face. "I'm sorry, go on: you were saying…?"

Autumn went on to tell him the whole saga, in detail. Ben listened and nodded in all the right places. When she'd finished he put an arm around her. "If you had offended her, then she would have retracted her job offer, now wouldn't she?" Ben soothed.

Autumn nodded and gave him a kiss on the cheek. Ben was right. Celina hadn't seemed offended; if anything, she'd seemed annoyed with Jack too. He had, after all, forgotten he was meeting her and gone off to play golf instead. Autumn felt better about the whole situation. She still didn't know what to do about the job, though. She liked the idea of working for an events company. It sounded way more glamorous than her current job title of receptionist-cum-dogsbody.

"You shouldn't take the job," Ben offered. "With any luck, you'll pass your course soon. Then you'll want to find a writing job, won't you? So, if you leave Thorne PR and go and work for this party planner then by my calculation you'll be handing your notice in even before your probation is up."

Ben was right, of course; he always was. Taking on a new job now would be like jumping from the frying pan into the fire. She already had enough on as it was without having to learn the ropes at a new business in an industry that she knew nothing about. He gave Autumn a big squeeze, then released her, sat back down on the arm of the sofa and pulled his phone back out of his pocket. Autumn decided she couldn't think on an empty stomach so headed into the kitchen.

"You hungry, babe?" she called over her shoulder to Ben.

"Hmmm, not really," he answered. "Don't bother doing me anything, I shouldn't eat before bed anyway." Autumn bent down and opened the fridge door. *'Not a lot to choose from in here,'* she thought hungrily, her stomach growling in anticipation. There was nothing for it, she was definitely going to be ordering a pizza.

"Double pepperoni, extra cheese and an extra topping of mushrooms please." Autumn placed her order over the phone. "Are you sure you don't want anything, Ben?" she asked, covering the phone's speaker as she did. There was no answer from Ben. She peered round to see into the living room, he wasn't there. She strained her ears, trying to decipher his location. She could hear the sound of running water again. He was quite clearly in the shower and Autumn knew would be straight into bed afterwards.

'Oh well, more for me I guess,' she thought to herself. No more than twenty minutes later and Autumn was handing fifteen pounds in cash over to the delivery man and telling him to keep the change. She slumped down on one of the cool, cream leather sofas, pizza box resting on her lap, and looked around. The silence was deafening. Ben had finished in the shower. She'd heard the water go off and the creak of

the floorboards as he climbed into bed. Autumn didn't feel happy. She'd had a stressful day at work and now she felt, more than ever, that Ben just didn't have enough time for her. She opened the box and inhaled, the smell of her favourite pizza hitting her nostrils and causing her stomach to rumble again. She tore off a slice and watched the melting cheese drip down. She lifted it high in the air and caught the errant cheese in her mouth, it was hot and burnt her instantly.

"Shit!" she exclaimed, spitting the hot topping out into a napkin. She ran into the kitchen quickly and poured herself a large glass of milk, downing it in one. She enjoyed the feeling of marginal relief as the ice-cold liquid cooled and soothed her mouth.

She padded back into living room, suddenly pausing at the foot of the stairs. Autumn could hear something, or someone, in the house. She froze for a second, trying to determine where the noise was coming from. She craned her neck, tilting her head at the same time. The voice was hushed and so faint Autumn wasn't sure if it wasn't all in her head. But there it was again: no louder than a whisper, but it was definitely there, coming from somewhere inside the house. She listened again, and then it dawned on her. Ben, who was too tired to have a conversation with her, was on the phone. A strange, creeping sensation overtook Autumn. Something wasn't right. Ben was acting odd and had been hot and cold with her for a while now and no matter how many times he put it down to work stresses or something else which easily explained the change in his behaviour, Autumn couldn't shake the feeling that there was something he wasn't telling her. Thinking quickly, she grabbed the TV remote and pressed the 'on' button. The TV buzzed into life: a late night chat show was on. Autumn turned up the volume and used the cover of the sound to sneak upstairs. Carefully she crept up the first few steps, her heart thudding against her chest. Autumn worried that it would become so loud Ben would hear it over the sound of the TV. She could feel it pounding against her chest.

Autumn found herself outside their bedroom door, which had been shut firmly. She leaned against it, pressing her ear to the hard surface. Ben's voice was muffled, he was definitely trying very hard to go undetected. She still couldn't make out his words. Not quite sure what to do she reached out her hand and placed it on the door handle. It rested there: Autumn felt like she wasn't in control of her own body, her pulse quickened and she had to hold her other hand over her mouth to keep from breathing too noisily. Autumn didn't know what to do, she trusted Ben – but if that were true, why would she be sneaking around trying to spy on him? She removed her hand, scolding herself for acting so irrationally. She needed someone to talk to, and she knew just the person, Autumn turned on her heel and as silently as she had come returned back downstairs.

"He's just always on the phone," Autumn moaned in hushed tones to David, clutching her mobile phone so hard her knuckles were starting to whiten.

"Oh hon," he replied, his voice sounding distant, "it was always going to be hard. You guys even sat down and talked it through before he took the job. He was so considerate, so you can't blame him now everything he said might happen has happened."

"I know you're right, but it's still so difficult, I feel like I'm going crazy. Like just now, he told me he needed to get to bed. He disappears without saying goodnight and then I hear him talking on the phone all secretively."

"I don't know what to say," David said, an air of resignation in his voice. "Have you spoken to your friend at work? It sounds like you need a girl's perspective on this. I'm basically useless."

"You are not," Autumn said, her voice creeping up slightly in volume. "I tried Rosa before you, but her phone's off. It went straight to voice-mail and I didn't feel like confessing my relationship woes to an answering machine."

"Maybe she's on the phone to that new guy you told me about?" David suggested helpfully.

"Yeh maybe," Autumn replied. She didn't allow her mind to wander to Rosa and her mystery man happily chatting on the phone together. She felt utterly down on love at the moment. "Sorry David, I'm boring you. I think I just need to chill out, or maybe…" she trailed off.

"I know you want me to dig now," David said knowingly, "so go on then, or maybe what?"

"Well. I could do a little digging of my own. Look, I know something's going on. I do. I can feel it. He's not been straight with me for days, probably weeks now and, as his girlfriend don't I deserve to know what's going on?" she finished defiantly.

"Well you could," David began, "but it's a slippery slope, Autumn. Sneaking about in his private affairs means you don't trust him. If you don't trust him why are you with him?"

"I do trust him, I just need to know what's going on. It's driving me mad," she retorted, still half-whispering. Autumn couldn't think of anything worse than Ben hearing about her DIY espionage plans. She sighed and started on another slice of pizza.

"OK, whatever you say, hon. I just think it's a recipe for disaster. I mean, say you do find something, what are you going to do? You'll have to tell him how you know and then you look like the bad guy; and probably even worse still, what happens when you don't find anything? Which I'm sure will be the case. You've breached his trust, you're going to feel horribly guilty, you'll probably end up confessing what you've done and then you really will have problems in your relationship. You're better off just talking to him if you have issues."

"I've tried that," Autumn said bluntly. "You're just not getting it, ugh!" She exhaled irritably. "Look it's not just that. Work's been... challenging." Autumn was beginning to get even more annoyed now. She'd phoned David for rock solid support; she needed him to be on her side.

'Damn Rosa for being on the phone,' she thought angrily to herself. She resolved to go and see her at her desk, first thing in the morning; she'd go in a bit early and sneak in a little tête-à-tête with Rosa before that meeting began. She knew she'd have to time it just right. If Jack saw her before the meeting, he might have other plans for her. If Celina had spilled the beans, he might even want to fire her. Maybe she should go straight to his office and make her excuses before he came to her? Maybe she'd just leave it? Autumn figured that if Celina had told Jack everything she'd said, then she would have at least had an abrupt email requesting her in his office the second she walked through the door the next day. No, she reasoned she would go and see Rosa if Jack had found out, he'd be coming to see her anyway. Autumn couldn't shake the feeling that Jack didn't wholly deserve an apology. After all, as Ben had pointed out, this was far from her forever job, so maybe she could stand to hold her ground a little.

"Autumn? You still there?" David questioned. Autumn had gone silent on him as she pondered over everything that was grating on her.

"Sorry David, look I'm going to have to go. It's getting late." She bade him a not so fond farewell and hung up, deciding that from now on, any and all men problems would have to go through Rosa first. David was right about one thing at least. She needed a female perspective, and Rosa would know exactly what to do.

Autumn sat in her living room in silence, mulling over her conversation with David whilst eating her pizza. She had hoped to leave a couple of slices for lunch the following day, but before she knew it the whole thing was gone

Autumn was up and ready for work a full hour earlier than usual. She'd had a good night's sleep, felt well rested and ready for the day ahead. Even though she was early herself, she was no match for Ben who'd pulled her into him before the sun had even made an appearance. He'd given her a big squeeze, a kiss on the nape of the neck and left their home to go to the gym. Autumn hadn't responded to Ben's affections, she had pretended to be fast asleep. She still wasn't sure what she'd heard the previous night, what it meant or how she truly felt about it. When Ben had gone in the shower she had tried to get into his phone again to check the caller ID but that bloody passcode had stopped her in her tracks, again. Autumn was unable to go back to sleep after Ben had left: she tossed and turned but it was no use, she gave up and got up.

She stepped into the shower: the warm water beat down on her, seemingly washing away the tension she had felt previously. She got out, dried herself and got dressed in record time. She had chosen what she felt was her most professional outfit: a fitted pencil dress she'd not yet had the courage to wear and a pair of high heels that she usually reserved for nights out. She had been so impressed with Celina's style that she'd decided to try and adopt it as her own. She'd even teased her hair into loose waves in a bid to recreate the powerful, sultry yet sophisticated style that Celina Thorne had. Thinking of Celina her stomach dropped slightly, as if she was just about to do the first loop on a particularly scary roller coaster. Had Celina told Jack what she'd said? That she had robbed whiskey from his office? That she'd badmouthed both him and the company he'd worked so hard to build? Shaking the thoughts out of her head, Autumn decided that what would be, would be. She gave herself one final look in the mirror and headed downstairs and out the door.

The drive was quiet, so Autumn made a mental note to leave this early more often. She was pulling up at the familiar metal gates of Thorne PR before she knew it. She scooped her work keys out of her bag with ease and scanned the fob whilst walking through the gate at the same time in one fluid, easy motion. As she walked to her desk she flipped on the light switch. The reception lit up instantly. She leaned over and flicked the switch that redirected the telephone system from voice-mail back to its normal order. Then she dropped her bag and all of its contents under her desk before heading upstairs to see Rosa.

As she had predicted Rosa was at her desk, and already working, her nose buried in a ton of printing samples. She looked up when she heard footsteps approaching and smiled.

"Grab us a tea from the machine will you?" Rosa said when she saw that it was Autumn. Autumn obliged and got herself a coffee at the same time. She preferred the coffee from the staff lounge's new machine but she'd be damned if she was going back downstairs for it.

"You're in early," Rosa said in surprise, looking at her watch. Autumn followed her eyeline and caught sight of that beautiful bracelet once more. She couldn't believe she wore it to work, it looked as though it would have set her mystery man back a few hundred pounds easily. If that bracelet belonged to Autumn she would only wear it on special occasions. This time when she saw it she didn't feel curious about who gifted it to Rosa or happiness that her friend might have found her perfect match. She felt a bit hollow. She couldn't remember when Ben had last given her a gift even close to that. The last time he'd given her anything was on her birthday. He'd handed over a bubble bath set with an apologetic look. He has said that he was sorry it wasn't much but that he was saving hard for something extra special. That had been months ago, and even though they had had that wonderful day together she hadn't even had so much as a bunch of flowers since then. Autumn was no fool, she knew he wasn't saving for anything. He just preferred spending his money on expensive gym memberships and fancy restaurants with his famous new friends. Autumn wasn't jealous by a long shot – well, not of the friends anyway. She had no interest in celebrity; that world just didn't excite her. Sure, she liked a trashy magazine every now and then – who didn't? – but that was about as far as it went. She sipped at her coffee pensively, trying to find the right words to explain to Rosa what had happened last night.

"Okay," she took a deep breath. "I'm just going to come straight out and say it. It's about Ben." Rosa stiffened and set her tea down. Her hands lay in her lap, her fingers gently stroking the bracelet she wore.

"Go on," she said. "What's happened?" Her voice was terse, worried for her friend. They never seemed to have any relationship problems and the idea that all was not what it appeared to be was disconcerting to Rosa.

"I'm pretty sure Ben is cheating on me. Well if he isn't, the intent is certainly there. I saw a text on his phone a little while back. My mum told me not to be crazy about it but last night he said he needed to go to bed early but I heard him on the phone, talking really quietly like he didn't want to be discovered."

She eyed Rosa expectantly, fully supposing her reaction to be one of outrage and contempt. Rosa picked up her tea and took a long sip.

"Did you hear what he said?" she asked. Autumn shook her head and took another sip from her cup. The two women went quiet in contemplation. "He's not cheating on you Autumn. He just isn't," Rosa said after some consideration. "You guys are great together," she added softly.

"You barely know him," Autumn retorted, her voice laced with a little more malice than it should have been. Rosa hadn't done anything wrong and was just trying to offer her friend some comforting words, but flat denial was going to do little to help. Autumn knew that she shouldn't be taking her feelings out on her, yet she couldn't help it. She found herself saying, "Hell, *I* barely know him at the moment. He's just so secretive, well when he's actually there. It's like I'm going out with a different person."

"Why didn't you speak to me before?" Rosa questioned, her tone quieter now she had been verbally berated for believing the good in Ben.

"I spoke to my mum, then to David last night," Autumn replied. "I did try and call you but you were on the phone, for ages…" she added.

Rosa didn't say anything, the silence was palpable, Autumn had not envisioned their conversation being like this. In her mind's eye, she'd seen them Ben-bashing, with Rosa offering her unconditional support instantly. She shouldn't be taking Ben's side. She was *her* friend after all, not his.

Autumn could see that Rosa was keen to get back on with her work. Rosa started rearranging the printing samples on her desk, her delicate fingers examining each one in turn. As she ran her fingertips over the third sample her bike horn message tone went off loudly, interrupting the quiet calm of the office. Alerted to the fact that Rosa had an impending message, Autumn made her excuses. She hastily thanked her friend for listening and said her goodbyes before turning on her heel to leave. Rosa's phone went off twice more before she descended the stairs to the boardroom.

'Too busy in her own love life to bother with mine,' she thought bitterly.

Autumn walked into the boardroom to see Jack leaning over the projector unit at the back of the room.

'Damn, I never fixed that,' she thought to herself. He turned around at the sound of the door opening behind him.

"Ah, Autumn," he said, "just the girl I wanted."

Autumn stiffened. This was it, the moment she found out just how bad her punishment would be. She braced herself, ready for a dressing down at best and a firing at worst.

"Well," Jack said, crossing his arms over his chest. Autumn clocked his biceps: had he been working out? He looked good. *'What is it with all the men I know suddenly hitting the gym?'* she wondered. She braced herself. Jack took a breath. This was it, the moment of truth.

"The projector was playing up this morning but not to worry. It's all sorted and good to go, plus the food arrived earlier, the caterers set it out. Good choice on the pastries, by the way," he added.

Autumn exhaled and smiled broadly, trying not to show just how relieved she was. She couldn't believe her luck. Celina had said nothing. Maybe she couldn't remember after the whiskey, maybe she was just a cool woman who didn't really care that Autumn had issues with her boss – after all, she reasoned, who didn't? As the wave of relief ebbed away her mind turned back to the task in hand. She was making her debut as Jack's assistant and she didn't even have so much as a notebook. Calmly she asked Jack if there was anything else he needed. When he said that there wasn't she nipped out of the boardroom to grab a notepad and a pen. She could hear the hubbub in the office coffee lounge and knew that the potential clients would be finishing their drinks and heading over any second. Grabbing the items she needed from the stationery cabinet, she hurried back into the boardroom. As she pushed the door open Jack turned around. To Autumn's horror she saw that in his hands he held the remainder of the whiskey she'd robbed from his office the previous evening, a look of disbelief on his face.

"I assume you know something about this, Autumn?" he asked, his tone clipped and stiff.

Autumn didn't know exactly how to play this. She decided to say she'd fancied a tipple and leave the fact that Celina had been there out of it. After all, if she hadn't mentioned it, why should Autumn? She didn't want to get in the way of their relationship in any way, shape or form.

"I just fancied a tipple," Autumn said nonchalantly, hoping her casual tone would help diffuse the tension that was now so apparent.

"You fancied a tipple?" Jack repeated, raising an eyebrow incredulously: "You fancied a tipple!"

"I'm, I'm sorry Jack, it was late and your office was open. I'll pay for it if that's the problem?" she offered.

"Aside from the fact that you took liberties Autumn, you helped yourself to a nine-thousand-pound bottle of thirty-five-year-old whiskey. Whiskey that I was saving – whiskey that was a gift!" he hissed. Jack was at boiling point now, with each word his face became more and more puce. Autumn stood there agog: nine thousand pounds? That couldn't be right surely. Who would spend that amount?

"I, err, I'm sorry," she stumbled.

There was nothing more she could say. Right now she'd happily take an ear bashing for what she'd said to Celina the previous evening over what was happening now. Jack fumed, visibly swelling with rage. Autumn felt scared now. It was the angriest she'd ever seen anyone be without resorting to physical violence. She took a step backwards, wanting to be as far away from him as she could be.

"Jack, I'm sorry. I just didn't think," she said, trying to mask the distress in her voice.

"You never do, do you? You're fucking unbelievable Autumn. Such a selfish bitch!" he spat nastily, then halted, suddenly realising what he'd just said. His face flushed with regret as the door to the boardroom opened and in with the noise came seven other people, all smiling, suited and booted and ready for the meeting. Jack stared at them, then at Autumn. Collecting himself quickly he removed his suit jacket. Obviously his outburst had made him a little hot because as he did so Autumn was treated to the sight of newly forming sweat stains under his armpits.

"Ladies, gentlemen," Jack announced in a professional and welcoming fashion, all traces of anger disappearing almost instantly. "Please help yourself to refreshments and take your seats as soon as you're ready."

He gestured to the neatly laid out breakfast food and settled himself at the head of the table, placing the whiskey on the floor next to him out of sight as he sat down. Autumn wanted the ground to open up and swallow her whole, once again feeling like she couldn't do anything right at the moment. It was like she took one step forward followed by two steps back at every turn. Everything felt like it was on a downward spiral and there was nothing she could do about it.

Jack was able to quickly switch between the whiskey-loving psychopath Autumn had been forced to deal with and a calm and collected professional, eager to impress a gaggle of potential clients. As far as Autumn could tell the meeting went well. However it had taken most of the morning and she felt her stomach rumble: she realised she hadn't eaten at all today. The telling off she'd received had numbed her appetite and even when it had returned she hadn't dared take anything for fear of getting on the wrong side of Jack again. During the meeting, Autumn had kept her head down and made detailed notes of everything that was said. Including that Mr Colman's favourite wine was Malbec, just like hers, and that he nearly always enjoyed it with a piece of Argentinian steak. She also noted that Mrs Victoria Chan, of Chan Homes Limited, had three sons in attendance at Wentwoods boys' school. An establishment that cost a pretty penny and that had turned out many a successful businessman and politician. Autumn hoped against hope that these notes would go some way to fixing her dwindling relationship with her boss. He barely looked at her throughout the entire meeting and didn't talk to her at all. In fact, no one did. Autumn had never felt more invisible. The only time anyone had acknowledged her presence was when Mr Colman had turned around to pass her his empty plate, which she dutifully took and placed on the side. She felt more like a handmaid than glamorous personal assistant – and to make matters worse, her shoes were beginning to pinch. The last part of the meeting had really dragged, so Autumn checked her watch. She was keen for Jack to wrap things up so she could grab some lunch and potentially have another chat with Rosa. She still felt dissatisfied with how things had gone earlier. In fact, she felt dissatisfied with things on the whole. Her outlook was very bleak as she internally surveyed everything that was going on in her life.

Just when it seemed like the meeting was going to go on for the rest of the day, Jack called time and the esteemed guests began to collect their belongings and leave the offices of Thorne PR. As their numbers diminished, Autumn was surprised to find that she was struggling to hold back tears. Her eyes stung hotly and she quickly grabbed a nearby napkin and pressed it to her face, dearly hoping Jack was still so annoyed he wouldn't look at her. Autumn felt a presence next to her, which was then confirmed by a hand on her shoulder. She looked up from the napkin to see Jack there, a look of concern – or was it guilt? – etched on his features. Not only was he now looking at her, he was offering comfort, and this didn't make sense. She opened her mouth to speak but Jack shushed her.

"I'm sorry for snapping, Autumn," he said. "I was just caught off guard. I'm under a lot of pressure, at home. I shouldn't have spoken to you like that. It was wrong and unprofessional and I hope we can get past it. Look, I probably shouldn't be telling you this, you know as your boss but I've not had the easiest time of things lately. I'm stressed and I shouldn't have taken it out on you."

"It's not that," Autumn sniffed, barely able to hold herself together. "I mean, not *just* that," she corrected when she saw Jack's brow furrow. She went on to tell Jack everything, the words fell out of her easily: it felt good to sound off to an impartial ear. When she had finished, she found that her tears had dried. She breathed a sigh of relief, realising for the first time that things could be a whole lot worse.

"I wasn't aware you had a boyfriend. You never mentioned it, you know, before," Jack said, referring to the time they'd shared whiskey over jazz music. He seemed to have a sudden sense of vulnerability. He was talking to her for the first time like an equal.

"Anyway," Autumn interjected, "enough about me. What's going on with you then?" She tried to sound jovial, like this was nothing more than two friends having a catch up. Jack didn't appear to appreciate this and looked at her as if she'd overstepped the mark. He opened his mouth to say so but then appeared to think better of it and closed it again.

"Oh it's nothing, just old people stuff. It's hard work, you know, keeping a wife happy, working all the time, seeing people constantly but feeling a bit lonely. But I guess that's the risk you take when you trade in a social life for work," he said.

"Jesus," Autumn said, exhaling at the same time. "Well, if that's what happens when you get old," she said playfully, "then count me out."

Jack couldn't help but crack a smile.

"Right then, back to the grindstone," he said, standing up and brushing the creases out of his trousers. "No rest for the wicked and all that. By the way Autumn," he said, "you look very nice today."

With that he patted Autumn on the head awkwardly and took his leave, once again managing to make her feel like a little girl, the charade of being equals now clearly over.

CHAPTER 12

THE LONG SUMMER DAYS WERE DRAWING TO A close and the leaves were beginning to fall from the trees, waving goodbye to the summer. Autumn smiled and waved out of the kitchen window at Ben who was diligently clearing up the first flurry that had made their way onto their back garden patio. He smiled back and blew her a kiss, which she caught in an over-the-top, cheesy manner. He laughed and set back to work stuffing the leaves he had raked into a large bin liner.

Autumn watched as he worked. He had a faint sheen of perspiration gleaming on his forehead; she watched him, admiring his physique and noting with particular appreciation how his biceps flexed each and every time he bent down to scoop up the next set of leaves. She watched him work until he was done, pausing every now and then to sip at her wine. Okay, so it was the middle of the day, but it was Sunday after all and she hadn't had a drink all week. She'd been diligently working and revising. Once Ben had bagged up the last lot of leaves he stood up, stretching and wiping his brow. The faint sheen of perspiration was now full-on sweat, which glistened in the sunlight. Autumn grabbed a beer out of the fridge and took it outside to him.

"A little something for the worker?" she asked, cheekily offering him the ice-cold beer. He nodded enthusiastically and took it off her, downing the first half in one go. He let out a long satisfied breath as he took the bottle away from his lips, running the cool glass against his forehead in an attempt to take the edge off the heat. He perched against the patio table and kicked a chair out for Autumn, gesturing with his free hand that she should sit.

"What should we do for the rest of today?" she asked lazily, resting her head on his lap. Autumn inhaled his raw, musky scent. He wasn't wearing any aftershave but smelt incredible nonetheless. The last few weeks had been odd. Autumn had been up and down emotionally. Ben had changed, there was no doubt about that, but his behaviour was becoming more consistent, which is what Autumn realised she had missed. She would just have to adjust to their new dynamic. Autumn couldn't hold it against him; all his dreams were coming true and it was up to her to make sure that they stayed strong as a couple throughout this entire process. Things were changing. Ben's character was a small, but staple cog in the machine that was *The Edge*. So much so that he'd now got three times the amount of followers on social media than he had just three months ago and offers of other work were starting to come in. Autumn realised that from now on, Ben would only get busier and busier, so instead of dwelling on how terrible things were when he was absent, she should be concentrating on herself, getting her coursework done and cherishing the time they did have together. Things at work were fine, her job had become busier too. She was finding it hard to sneak in stolen gossip sessions with Rosa and she barely saw June anymore, although she still found little parcels of baked goodies on her desk from time to time.

"Maybe we could go to the park or something?" Autumn suggested. "We could ask Rosa, and maybe she'll bring that guy she's been so secretive about, seeing as she's my best friend and I still don't know the first thing about him." She could tell immediately that Ben wasn't keen on this idea as he tensed and squirmed beneath her.

"I was thinking something just the two of us," he said, gently moving Autumn's head from his lap. She looked up at him, Ben had an unmistakeable glint in his eye.

"Oh really?" Autumn enticed, "What exactly were you thinking, Mr Wood?"

She reached out towards him, pulling at his waistband. He lifted himself up off the patio table allowing her to slide both his shorts and underwear down in one fluid movement. Ben leant back, his arms locked supporting himself as Autumn took his quickly stiffening erection in her mouth. He gasped at the warm wetness that enveloped him, edging his hips forward gently, encouraging her to take his entire length. She did so without question. Ben was fully erect now, Autumn could feel his girth stretching her lips; she widened her mouth, eager to please and envelope him in his entirety. As she sucked the intensity increased as she became hungry for his release. She reached between his legs, encouraging him to spread them, and cupped his balls in one hand. She squeezed gently, enjoying the feeling of him writhing under the attention. She continued, her grip tightening and loosening rhythmically each time she got to the tip of his manhood. She sucked the end of it greedily, feeling him shift his weight as she did so.

Autumn knew Ben inside and out and could tell that he didn't have long left. The thought of him climaxing spurred her on, she pulled away from him and spat on her hand. Taking him firmly she worked on him with sure, definite strokes; her pace quickened as she took one of his testicles in her mouth and sucked on it gently, enjoying the loud moan of pleasure that escaped Ben's lips. Her other hand was between his legs now, her fingertips deftly stroking the patch of skin below the base of his shaft. This was enough to send him over the edge: just before the point of climax Autumn took him once more in her mouth, enveloping him in a warm oral embrace and coaxed the orgasm out of him. He came hard: hot seminal fluid shot into her mouth. She swallowed quickly but could not retain it all, it seeped out and down his shaft. He bucked and thrust into her one last final time, in an effort to prolong his pleasure.

Once Ben was still Autumn stood up, her hand wiping at the corners of her mouth. If Ben had been sweaty before he was positively drenched now, and his hair clung to his face, little beads of sweat dripping into his eyes. He smiled and wiped his forehead with the back of his hand.

"Ahhh," he exhaled loudly. Ben looked at her, a cheeky yet smug look on his face. "You're amazing," he said as he pulled her in for a kiss, pulling away from her quickly the second their lips met. "Ewww!" he exclaimed, "you've got me, literally, all over your face."

"And whose fault is that?" Autumn said, play-punching him in the arm before turning and walking back into the house. "Why don't you go and get a shower?" she asked. "We can go out for an early dinner if you like."

Ben agreed eagerly. The work in the garden plus the blow job had taken a lot out of him and he was now positively starving. Doing exactly as he'd been instructed, he headed back inside.

"Don't you dare go through there in those filthy clothes," she admonished, holding out her hand. "Pass them here and I'll get them in the wash."

"They're just my work clothes, babe," Ben contested but Autumn was having none of it; she shook her head, her hand remaining outstretched. He stripped and dropped the clothes in a big, sweaty bundle into her arms before running upstairs totally naked, his hand cupped over his private parts. Autumn opened up the washing machine and threw Ben's clothes in with half a load that was already in there. Just before the machine door slammed shut she caught it, pulled out Ben's shorts and patted them down just as she had done before. There was a crumpled tissue in the back pocket, along with a few loose coins and his tattered old wallet, khaki green with burgundy stitching. Autumn still couldn't believe he preferred it to the one that she had bought for him. Ben didn't even look after it; it was covered in stains from only God knows what.

'Maybe it could do with going through the wash as well,' she thought. Opening it she emptied the contents out onto the worktop and shoved the now empty wallet and shorts back into the machine and turned it on. As the door clicked shut and it whirred into life, she began second-naturedly going through the wallet's contents. There was a passport picture of herself: she smiled as she reflected on the person she'd been when this picture had been taken. It was a couple of years old. She was much younger and fresh-faced; back then Autumn didn't have a care in the world. There were some crumpled up receipts and his bankcards and a few pounds' worth of loose change. Autumn scooped the contents up and took them to Ben's office. They'd converted the small box room into an office-cum-study, somewhere Ben would have a quiet place to learn his lines. Being a freelance actor he also had to do his own taxes, and that included sorting out all his receipts. He had a big tall metal filing cabinet in the corner of the room. The bottom drawer was reserved for all of his expenses. She opened it and was surprised to see how organised Ben was. Each category had its own separate file. She opened up each receipt in turn and deciphered which category it fit into. The first few were easy: she opened up

the envelope marked 'entertainment'. Basically any time Ben had a drink with a fellow actor, he put it through his books – after all, he needed to maintain a good working relationship with these people. There were a few for 'travel' and one for 'appearance'. Autumn grinned when she learnt that Ben had visited a beauty salon for a facial.

'He kept that one quiet,' she mused. Autumn opened the next receipt up and frowned. It read five hundred pounds and was from the most expensive jewellers in town, 'John Cusson'. It was dated a few weeks ago. Autumn racked her brains: Ben hadn't told her about any extravagant purchases. Nor had she been given an expensive piece of jewellery as a present.

"Babe? What are you doing?" Ben's voice said from behind her. She turned to see him leaning against the door frame, his muscular arms crossed over his chest, a look of concern on his face.

"Nothing," she answered quickly, shoving the receipt in the drawer and closing it quickly. "Just putting your receipts away, and I've washed that pitiful excuse for a wallet you have," she explained.

"I've heard it all now," he grinned. "Who in their right mind washes a wallet?"

Autumn didn't reply, she mustered a half-smile and squeezed past him. Her heart was beating hard against her chest. What had he bought and who the hell was it for? She needed to know more, but how? This was surely just one more brick in the wall of deceit Ben was building between them: late night phone calls, disappearing for long periods of time, putting passwords on everything he owned. She now couldn't use his laptop, phone or tablet. All of it led her to believe there was something going on, something that she definitely wouldn't like.

"Where are we going to go?" Ben asked, entering the bedroom and pulling open his wardrobe doors.

"I'm not feeling well," Autumn said, slumping down on the bed, holding her hands to her face in a bid to hide her expression.

"Oh no, what's brought this on?" Ben asked, genuine concern in his voice. He pulled a crisp white T-shirt over his head and stepped into a pair of faded blue jeans. Walking over to the bed as he did them up, he placed a tentative hand on her shoulder. Autumn shuddered inside; she wanted to scream, to demand he tell her exactly what had been going on these past few weeks. Had she just been making excuses for him? Was the truth plain to see? Or, if she vocalised this to her friends and family, would they tell her that she was crazy? She could hear them now, telling her how great Ben was and that she should trust him. How could you trust someone who had been so secretive for so long? This wasn't a case of getting used to a different lifestyle, it was a case of getting used to a different person.

"I think I'm getting a migraine, maybe I should just go to bed for a bit," Autumn replied dully.

"Okay well, if you're sure," Ben said, removing his hand from her shoulder and putting it in his pocket. He pulled out his phone and scanned the screen quickly. A small smile formed on his lips.

"I've got to nip out for a bit, babe. My mum needs me to do something. You'll be alright for a few hours, won't you?"

He waited for a reply, but Autumn offered nothing. Instead she rubbed her temples, moving her fingers in a slow circular motion, her eyes lowered to the floor. She could feel frustrated and confused tears bubbling, threatening to burst to the surface. She fought them off, knowing that if she cried, Ben would stay. She wasn't ready to have any sort of conversation, or to give him the opportunity to lie to her. She had decided she was going to do some digging and she could think of only one person she wanted to help her.

Once Ben had gone she sent a text to Rosa asking her to come over. Rosa replied almost instantly saying she wouldn't be able to make it, as she was planning on seeing her new guy. Autumn felt a twinge of jealousy and wondered if she was ever actually going to meet this mystery man.

Ben had left and the house was still. Autumn went downstairs. She was in autopilot, hardly able to concentrate on anything. She knew that if she did start snooping she might find out something that she really didn't like. Still, she carried on regardless, going through drawers and cupboards, pulling out anything she thought could hold even the tiniest bit of information as to what was going on.

An hour went by. Autumn was losing steam: there was literally nothing to point to any wrongdoing. Her house phone rang. It was the third time since she'd begun her mission. Whoever was trying to get hold of her wasn't giving up. She snatched up the receiver and briskly said hello to the determined caller.

"Hi sweetheart," crooned the unmistakable voice of Mrs Wood. "Is my darling son there?"

"He's at yours, isn't he?" Autumn said, as her heart skipped a beat. She clutched the receiver tightly, awaiting the answer.

"No angel. I thought he was at home today. Is he working? Have I got it wrong again?" asked Ben's mum with a chuckle. "I can never seem to get the hang of his new schedule. I've tried him on his mobile but it just rings and rings."

"He's nipped out," Autumn lied quickly. "I'll get him to call you when he's back." She hung up the phone.

So, he wasn't at his mum's. She decided to call his phone for herself. She dialled his number from the house phone, making sure to include 1-4-1 at the beginning in order to conceal her identity. Ben answered on the third ring: he had put on his best professional voice, clearly expecting this to be a work call. Autumn was silent for a minute.

"Where are you?" she mustered.

"Just at my mum's, babe," he began, going on to tell her, in detail, the chores his mum had saved up for him, his improvisational skills shining. Autumn listened. The background noise didn't sound like that of his mum's quiet semi-detached property. She pulled out her mobile phone and quickly typed out a message to Rosa: she needed backup and she needed it now. Rosa would just have to abandon her new man, after all her best friend needed her. She pressed 'send' and went to hang up on Ben; his story was getting ridiculous now. Just before she pulled the phone away from her ear she heard the unmistakable sound of a loud, obnoxious, old-fashioned bike horn message tone. Autumn dropped the receiver and sank to the floor as her knees gave way.

CHAPTER 13

THE BOTTOM WAS DROPPING OUT OF AUTUMN'S world. How could she have been so stupid? The truth was right in front of her the whole time. She felt sick. All those times she'd expressed doubts, concerned over Ben's actions, and her friends and family had waved those uncertainties away, always believing that Ben was a good guy and that Autumn was over-reacting. What was it her mother had said? "You've not been betrayed or hurt in anyway, and until you have a bit more than a three-worded text message, then it's simply not worth giving yourself a headache over." Well now she did have a bit more than a three-worded text message and she had way more than just a headache.

Her thoughts turned to Rosa, her friend Rosa, the person she'd confided in for all this time. How long had this been going on for? How many times had Rosa sat opposite her, laughing and joking, acting all coy about her new man when what she meant was *her* man? Rage bubbled inside Autumn now as she thought of the bracelet. The very bracelet from John Cusson. "The most expensive jeweller in town," Rosa had bragged. The mere memory of those words made Autumn shudder.

It was only now that the receipt she had found made perfect sense. Autumn had hoped against hope that she'd been mistaken when she'd found it. The suspicion she had felt had been overridden by the idea that maybe Ben had bought her something fantastic and was waiting for the right time to give it to her. But no, it was for Rosa.

'That fucking bitch!' Autumn exploded inside, remembering the pathetic bath bomb set she'd received from Ben for her birthday and his pitiful excuses. Well she couldn't accuse him of lying now, he *was* saving up for something special – the only problem was that it wasn't anything special for *her*. How could he? How could he throw all that they had away? Autumn struggled to recall a time when she'd noticed Ben and Rosa getting close; she racked her brains trying to recount a time when they'd spent any time together at all, when this whole sordid mess could have started. Betrayal stung at Autumn's heart and tore at her chest. Waves of nausea washed over her as more and more heart-breaking incidents started clicking into place. She could now explain his sudden interest in improving his physique, not because he was on telly, but because he had a new woman to impress. The secrecy with his phone suddenly made sense.

'That fucking passcode,' she fumed. Autumn stood up and slammed the phone back in its cradle. She felt sick as she thought about having sex with Ben whilst he was having sex with Rosa. How could Rosa stoop so low? Autumn felt hot, salty tears begin to pour from her eyes. The fat droplets streaked down her face.

Her mind was racing; her mobile phone started to vibrate in her hand. Looking down she saw Ben's name flash up through her cracked screen. Accompanying it was the photo of them sat happily enjoying champagne at Leonard's, the fabulous restaurant Ben had taken her to. Now she realised that all of that was just for show, affection born from guilt. The attention he had lavished upon her that day had been punctuated by 'work emails'... Autumn scoffed again at her stupidity. He had been texting Rosa. Her stomach flipped, as she reversed her thinking, remembering with horror the amount of times over the last few weeks she'd heard that horrible, grating vintage bike horn going off in Rosa's bag or pocket. Were all of those messages from Ben? Autumn shook her head violently, clawing at her forehead with her fingertips in an effort to dislodge these vile thoughts. She no longer cared about the ins and outs of what had happened. She needed to get out. She needed to escape.

Autumn was amazed at how quickly she was able to pack up her things. Half of her was pleased whilst the other half was saddened at the fact that all of her time spent making a home for the two of them added up to just one hour of packing: two suitcases of household items, three pieces of furniture and four black bags of clothes. All of which could be packed, albeit snugly, into her little red car. As she worked, she had rung David. He was, bless him, almost as devastated as she was. David had only met Rosa a handful of times as they ran in very different circles, but he'd warmed to her instantly and his relationship with Ben had always been friendly enough. David had encouraged Autumn to stay, to talk things out with Ben and to find out what was really going on. He just couldn't believe that Autumn's best friend and her boyfriend would betray her like this. Autumn had told David that the time for talking had been and gone. Ben had had plenty of opportunities to be honest with her. They'd sat down and talked things through several times before, any of which would have been a perfect opportunity to either tell her the truth so they could work things out or break up so he could be with Rosa. The bottom line was that Ben was a coward. She could see this now, and she realised that his new job had changed him: all of his behavioural changes had coincided with him getting his part on *The Edge*. She wasn't going to wait around so Ben could lie to her, yet again.

Autumn stood in the doorway surveying what had once been her happy home. She blinked back a set of fresh tears, determined to be strong about this. Autumn's practical nature made this easier for her than perhaps it should have been. Every fibre in her body fought against leaving, the devil on her shoulder tempting her back, to forgive Ben, to allow him back into her life and just chalk the whole thing up to weakness. Maybe if he promised never to do anything like this again they would be alright. But Autumn knew better, she didn't want that kind of relationship. Their trust hadn't just been broken, it had been shattered. No, the only way forward was to leave all this behind. She knew she would never speak to Ben again: hearing his voice would be too hard. She needed to stay strong and her best chance of that was to cut him out of her life for good. She sighed. Her life lay before her in tatters. Not only had she lost her boyfriend, she had also lost her best friend. She would never forgive Rosa. She was disappointed in Ben immeasurably but her feelings towards Rosa were different. She despised her. Hatred bubbled inside her so strongly she had to brace herself against the door frame. She had been used; Rosa had never been her friend, not really. She had kept her friends close but her enemies closer.

Autumn's hand gripped the wooden frame harder. Her face blanched; the cocktail of emotions she was experiencing made her feel more light-headed than any actual cocktail ever could. Betrayal, misery, gut-wrenching sadness and utter disgust washed over her as the gravity of her situation took hold. If she left now, truly left now, never to speak to either of them again then that would be it, there would be no way back for any of them. If she stayed, well, how would she ever be able to look at herself in the mirror again? How would she be able to face her family and David? How would she ever be able to respect herself? Autumn knew she was doing the right thing; the easy thing would be to stay, to patch things up but she knew she deserved better. The door clicked shut behind her, the heavy Yale lock clicking loudly. That sound signified the end, and Autumn got in her car and drove away, not glancing once in the rear-view mirror.

'Keep looking forward Autumn. Don't look back,' she instructed herself, her foot pressing more firmly on the accelerator as she drove away and into her future.

Autumn was all over the place, figuratively and literally. As her emotions swerved so did the car. Several angry car horns sounded; she didn't care though. She just wanted to see her mum and dad as soon as possible. She had much bigger things to worry about than the highway code.

She overtook a sporty Mercedes. The driver, a middle-aged man in his fifties, was travelling well in excess of the speed limit. He looked over to Autumn, clearly in disbelief that not only was he being over taken by a young woman, but that the young woman in question was driving a little, red Fiesta that was, in no uncertain terms, past its best. Autumn wiped another tear away from her cheek as she pulled back in, perhaps a little sooner than she should have. The man behind sounded his horn twice; she didn't even glance back at him and instead her eyes, which were unfocused from the free-flowing tears, were firmly fixed on the road in front of her.

Approaching the exit for her parents' village, she sped up, the road sign indicating she was almost there spurring her on. It was another ten minutes or so to her parents' house. Her bedroom had remained practically untouched since she'd moved out at eighteen years of age. Autumn couldn't wait to feel that reassuring welcoming feeling that only being back at home with your mum and dad could bring. The car shook slightly as she tried to coax another ten miles an hour out of it, the poor thing already incredibly taxed. A lorry was up ahead and she wanted to get past it before the road became too winding. Autumn drifted onto the other side of the road. An oncoming car blared its horn at her. She swerved back in behind the lorry, her heart pounding, and without thinking, she beeped back and stuck her middle finger high in the air, calling the driver an assortment of colourful insults as they went past. Autumn clutched the steering wheel aggressively, her bleary eyes glaring in the rear-view mirror at the other car; the car that had almost killed her sailed off into the distance.

The sound of a police siren shook her out of her funk. She put her foot on the brake and pulled in slightly to let it past. The police car didn't overtake, instead its lights flashed and persuaded her to pull over. Autumn didn't do anything for a moment: this was quite literally the last thing she needed right now. She glanced back at the police car, catching sight of her tear-stained, puffy face in the rear-view mirror. With a long exhalation, she hit her indicator, slowed down and pulled to a stop at the side of the road, her heart hammering against her chest as she watched the policeman get out of his car and walk over to hers. Autumn would have guessed he was in his early thirties. He was a tall man with broad shoulders and a commanding manner. Autumn steadied herself, gave her face one last wipe with the back of her hand, wound her window down and for some inexplicable reason gave the approaching officer an overly large, toothy smile.

"Is there a problem officer?" she said, in a falsely sweet voice that she instantly regretted. The policeman, who was rolling up his sleeves, surveyed her apprehensively. He wore aviator sunglasses, which he pulled down to reveal extremely blue eyes. Autumn was surprised to see this, as the man that stood before her had dark skin and hair that was almost black.

"Do you know how fast you were going back there miss?" he asked, taking a step back and looking at the car. Autumn genuinely didn't know how fast she had been going, she hadn't once checked her speed on the drive to her parents' house.

"No, sorry," she squeaked, suddenly very aware that she could be in quite a lot of trouble. "I'm just going to my parents' house," she concluded, as if by way of explanation.

"What's your name please?" he asked, disregarding her previous comment.

"Autumn," she said, "it's Autumn Carter, sir."

"Well Miss Carter, you probably don't need me to tell you that you were driving extremely dangerously there. You committed three minor offences that I could see, including speeding, tailgating and improper lane use," the police officer said, his tone serious. "I'm going to need to see your licence, please."

Autumn scrabbled in the passenger footwell for her bag, retrieving it with all the grace of a baby elephant. It got caught under the seat as she pulled it up, spilling half the contents onto the floor. Her old green purse, however, remained safely inside the bag. She opened it up and pulled out her driving licence, wincing at the awful photo gracing the front of it. Her hands were shaking as she handed it over, but the police officer took it from her without saying a word. He turned it over in his hands to examine it and after a few elongated moments handed it back to her. He stood there for a moment, looking at Autumn. She could feel her lip begin to tremble and her eyes begin to sting. She didn't want to cry in front of him. He was a perfect stranger and, besides, he'd probably think she was trying to manipulate him into letting her off which would do her no favours at all.

"Am I okay to go then?" Autumn asked, managing to regain control of herself and feeling that the silence had gone on long enough.

"Not yet, I'm going to issue you with a warning this time. I can see you're in some sort of distress. I highly advise you to calm down, though; driving in a state like this is dangerous and you could cause serious harm to yourself or others," he said, an authoritative air to his voice. Autumn nodded in agreement, slipping into that familiar feeling of reprimanded schoolgirl.

"Thank you," Autumn said with genuine appreciation. "I've had such a shitty day. I've just found out that my boyfriend's been sleeping with my best friend," she added – stopping dead in her tracks. She hadn't meant to say that, it had just kind of slipped out. The police officer stared at her, obviously taken aback by the sudden over-share of personal information.

"Well I'm sorry to hear that," he said awkwardly. "Drive safely now and you have a nice day."

The police officer stood there and watched her pull away. Autumn made sure she did everything by the book, repeating the mantra 'mirror, signal, manoeuvre' over and over again in her head. She took another twenty minutes to get to her parents' house, driving well within the speed limit the entire way.

Autumn pulled up the vast driveway to her parents' house. The trees that lined it had begun to shed their leaves, leaving the driveway feeling exposed and bare. A horrible sinking feeling set deep within her, a sense of foreboding so great that she almost turned the car around and drove home. Except, Autumn knew that the place that she and Ben had shared wasn't her home anymore, nor would it be, ever again. She had made her decision and she was going to stick to it. The house loomed into view, the red brick complementing the warm amber of the autumn sky. She pressed on and eased the car to a standstill in front of the house, the gravel crunching underneath the wheels as she stopped. As if conjured by some spell the second the ignition was turned off, her mum appeared out of the front doorway and bustled outside. Making a beeline for the driver's side, she opened the car door with a fervent tug.

"What on earth has happened?" she cried. "I've had Ben on the phone. He's been ringing non-stop saying you've taken your things and you're not answering your phone to him. Oh darling, whatever it is, just go back. He'll forgive you, he's said as much."

Autumn stared at her mum in disbelief, barely being able to believe the absolute cheek of it all. "*He'll* forgive *me*?" she exclaimed incredulously. "*He'll* forgive *me*?" Gobsmacked, Autumn climbed out of the car and shook her head. "Mum, he's been cheating on me, categorically fucking someone else," she added bluntly.

The words cut into her mother like a knife. Sarah recoiled, almost losing her footing in the process. Her expression was one of shock. "Surely not?" she questioned, her usual jovial tone sombre now. Autumn nodded sadly: as much as Ben had hurt her, she didn't want to see her parents hurt on her behalf.

Sarah looked at her daughter. Seeing the utter devastation on Autumn's face, Sarah knew that what she was saying was true. Without saying another word Sarah put her arms around her daughter and hugged her tightly. The contact from her mother, the loving, warm and safe contact, made Autumn cry. She sobbed onto her mum's shoulder heartily.

"How could he do this Mum?" she wailed. "And with Rosa, of all people, my best friend," she sniffed loudly. Her mum gripped her tighter: this new piece of information was the final nail in the coffin.

"Oh darling!" Sarah Carter wailed. "What a horrible boy. Come inside angel." She ushered her daughter into the house. Autumn kicked off her shoes just as the house phone began to ring again. Autumn looked at her mum quickly, a look of horror and hurt on her face.

"Don't answer it please. I never want to speak to him again," she said, a resolute tone to her voice.

"We'll block his number, darling. He won't be able to get through to you here and you can stay as long as you want to, you know that. Don't worry sweetheart, your dad and I will look after you." Sarah Carter gave her daughter another squeeze as she said this, her heart breaking for her little girl.

They went into the living room. Sarah settled her daughter on the sofa and disappeared into the kitchen, reappearing with two large glasses of white wine. Autumn raised an eyebrow: only her mother would immediately combat heartache with a good glass of wine.

"It'll do you well to get this down you. It'll be good for the shock," she said knowingly. Autumn didn't think it would be good for anything other than making her even more weepy than she already was, but nonetheless she took the glass from her mum and sipped gratefully.

"You don't have to tell me what happened," her mum said solemnly. "You didn't, catch them, you know, at it?" she asked.

"No Mum," Autumn said glumly, "but I may as well have. They've been seeing each other for weeks, maybe months behind my back. All those late nights, gym sessions, they were all for her."

Sarah looked aghast. "What an absolute bastard," her mum said bitterly, adding a few choice words about what she thought of Rosa at the same time.

"This isn't helping, Mum," Autumn told her mother. "I just don't want to talk about it. There's nothing to say really. It's happened now and I need to get on with things. All my stuff's in the car, would you help me bring it in?"

"Your father can do that when he gets back. He's going to be so upset, darling. He thought you and Ben were such a good couple."

"We *were*," Autumn said, before adding ruefully, "past tense there Mum."

Autumn set her glass of wine down. She really didn't feel like drinking. She needed to decide what she was going to do. She certainly wasn't going back to Thorne PR, that much was certain. She hadn't liked the job anyway, and Rosa had been one of the only saving graces about it. Her blood boiled at the thought of Rosa, so smug about it all. Laughing at her all the time behind her back, texting her boyfriend right in front of her. Rosa Dawson was one selfish, fucking bitch and if Autumn ever saw her again she'd seriously regret ever going near Ben. Autumn's blood boiled, her cheeks flushed as she felt fresh tears prick her eyes. How could they do this to her? Her world had been shattered, and they were probably relieved that she knew. Autumn could only assume that they were now happy that they could be together without sneaking around. But what if they didn't stay together? What if it had only been a bit of fun and everything was ruined for nothing? Autumn couldn't help questions like these from plaguing her mind; she just couldn't believe she hadn't seen it sooner.

Autumn yawned. She was absolutely shattered; emotional turmoil had really taken it out of her. She looked at her watch.

It was approaching 9 p.m., the Sunday sun had set and it was dark outside.

"I think I'm just going to go to bed," she told her mum, getting up from the sofa and stretching. Her body ached all over; she felt as though she'd been beaten up. Autumn yawned again, exhaustion starting to get the better of her. "I'm sorry, Mum, thanks for letting me stay. I just really need a good night's sleep."

"Of course you do, darling, you've had a nasty shock. You go up, do let me know if you need anything, though," her mum said, a warm but sad smile on her face.

Autumn bade her mum goodnight and went upstairs to her safe, familiar bedroom. She was exhausted, both physically and emotionally and fell asleep quickly. Autumn did not enjoy the peaceful night's sleep that she needed but instead tossed and turned throughout the night, unable to shake the thoughts of Ben and Rosa together. She awoke at regular intervals throughout the night, each time enjoying a peaceful few seconds of blissful ignorance before crashing back to reality.

It was a little after ten the next morning when her mum bustled in through the door of her old bedroom, a tray in her hands laden with croissants, jam, toast and a cup of steaming hot coffee. Autumn rubbed her eyes blearily as her mum opened the curtains with vigour.

"Morning sleepyhead," she cooed. "I wasn't sure what you'd want so I brought you a selection," she said, setting the tray down on the end of the bed.

Autumn sat up and pulled the tray towards her. The last thing she felt like doing was eating, but with her mum's concerned gaze raining down on her, she had little choice. Selecting a triangle of toast, she delicately nibbled the corner and ran her hand through her messy hair.

"Was it all a bad dream?" she asked humourlessly. She looked up to her mum, who with tight lips shook her head.

"I'm afraid not sweetheart," she said. "Dad's already emptied your car. We've put most of it in the garage for storage but your clothes and anything else we thought you might need are in the hall ready to come up." Autumn smiled. Her parents really were so lovely.

"Has Ben tried calling again?" she asked, trying to sound indifferent.

"No darling, he hasn't. Your dad's already put his number down as a nuisance caller so if he tries again he'll just get the busy tone," Sarah explained to her daughter, who in turn nodded her head in approval.

"Any word from Rosa?" Sarah asked tentatively.

"I haven't looked at my phone since yesterday afternoon," Autumn admitted, "and to be honest, I'm not entirely sure where it is." Autumn had decided during one of her sleepless episodes that she was going to get a new phone and change her number. Rather than waste her money repairing her phone's cracked screen she was going to invest in a new one, something new and shiny and not broken. Autumn was sick of trying to mend broken things. After a moment's silence Sarah Carter sat down on the edge of the bed and looked at her daughter.

"You'll be alright, you know," she said soothingly.

Autumn knew she was right. She wasn't the first person to be cheated on and she wouldn't be the last. But at the moment, while the pain was raw, she felt far from alright.

"So, what are you going to do today?" her mum asked in an effort to change the conversation to something a little more positive. "Moping in your room won't help matters."

Autumn quietly agreed. Chewing thoughtfully on her toast, she thought about all the unpacking she had to do, but that wouldn't take too long and she had an entire day to fill.

"I'm going to prepare for my finals," she said in a matter-of-fact kind of way. "They'll be here before I know it and I'll be damned if I'm going to fail because of *him*." She spat the last word out bitterly.

"That's my girl." Sarah nodded her approval and placed a hand on Autumn's shoulder. She bent down and gently kissed the top of her head before leaving the room.

Autumn pulled the breakfast tray closer towards her and inspected its offerings. The tray, an old wooden thing that had been in her family since she was a little girl, was discoloured, probably from years of tea and toast spillages. Even though it was such a simple thing, it made her feel safe and reminded her of happier times, and right now Autumn needed all the happy thoughts she could muster.

CHAPTER 14

DEAR MR THORNE,

I'm afraid I won't be able to come into work for the foreseeable. I've contracted a sickness bug and feel terrible.

Hope to be back soon.

Autumn Carter.

Autumn hit the send button and closed her laptop, feeling a twinge of guilt at the barefaced lie she had just told. She was glad that it was now socially acceptable to 'ring in sick' over email. She'd been with her parents for over a week now and as yet hadn't made contact with her work despite numerous emails from both Jack and the HR department. She knew she couldn't fake an illness forever, but right now, she didn't have much choice.

Her new phone vibrated next to her. It was David messaging to make sure she was okay. David had been absolutely horrified when he had heard the news and like the fabulous friend he was had been in constant contact with Autumn every day to make sure she was alright. He and Gregg had even been over to visit her at her parents' house, both marvelling at the interior design of the place even before asking how Autumn was doing. Gregg, who had extended his stay, had been particularly caring towards her. He enveloped Autumn in just as big a bear hug as David had.

Having them over had been extremely cathartic, and she'd talked it through with them both. They offered a sympathetic ear, advice and tough love when it was needed. She felt as though she'd gained a fantastic confidant in Gregg; just like David, he knew exactly what to say and when. The pair of them together were her personal agony uncles and she was extremely grateful for them. They'd even gone into town to collect a new phone for her, bringing it with them and helping her to set it up on their arrival. Autumn asked them to block both Ben and Rosa's numbers. She didn't want to do it herself, feeling that even seeing their names written down would be too much to bear.

They'd stayed for hours and enjoyed Mrs Carter's fine hospitality, even staying for dinner when she absolutely insisted that they must.

"Your mum is an utter dream," Gregg had said to her, his southern American drawl music to Autumn's ears. She couldn't help but agree: her mum had been an absolute rock – especially when Ben had turned up unannounced. Her frosty reception and outright lie that Autumn wasn't home were Oscar-worthy, and when Ben had tried to talk, she had cut him off immediately and slammed the door in his face. Ben left, red-faced, with his tail between his legs. Autumn had stolen a glance at him out of the window. To be fair to him, he looked upset – distraught, even. Autumn smiled maliciously. She was glad that this was proving to be hard on him. She revelled in the idea that he might be suffering. Ben Wood deserved everything he got. She wasn't going to waste an ounce of energy feeling sorry for the bastard.

Rosa had been a different story, which had surprised Autumn. She had expected an outpouring of regret, she'd expected flowers, presents, letters, the lot. When Autumn had eventually tracked her phone down it had shown an abundance of calls from Rosa and several voice-mails, none of which Autumn listened to. There was also a wealth of text messages that had been sent. At first Rosa had protested her innocence; Autumn flicked through the messages, not taking any of them in. However, she couldn't help but notice the very last one as it was so short it fit onto just one line.

'Be like this then. I'm not going to lose any sleep over it.'

Autumn had been so incensed by this that she'd thrown the phone with all her might onto the floor. It had smashed into several pieces; not quite feeling satisfied, Autumn had then stamped on it for good measure. Afterwards she broke down in tears and swept the mess up and threw the phone into the bin. Since then she had been a hermit to the outside world. She hadn't even switched on the TV, instead preferring to study, determined that out of this devastating situation something good would come.

The following week David had bumped into Ben in town, who had told him they had split up; he had, however, remained extremely tight-lipped on the 'whys' and 'wherefores' and instead insisted that David *mind his own damn business*. By all accounts he had been rude and by David's own admission, a bit of a dick. Autumn couldn't believe how Ben's true colours had come to light. He had always seemed so amiable before all this. She hadn't heard or seen anything of Ben or Rosa since the day after she had found out. Autumn reasoned that they both must have overcome any guilt they had felt pretty quickly and be enjoying their relationship now everything was out in the open.

She had mourned the loss of her romantic relationship and the loss of her friend. But as the people she loved most in the world rallied around her offering her unconditional love and support, she began to realise that her world neither began nor ended with Ben Wood or Rosa Dawson. Her world as it stood now was only just beginning. This prospect excited Autumn, albeit with a little apprehension. She could do anything and she could go anywhere. She realised with relish that she could be anything she wanted to be.

She still wanted to be a writer, but why stop at women's magazines? Why not the only women's magazine she cared about, *Wow* magazine? It wasn't a complete pipe dream, and after all, she had nothing else to focus on now. Or perhaps she could get a job on *The Edge* and write Ben a lovely, painful, long-winded death. She had chuckled at this thought, liking the idea immediately but knowing that in her heart of hearts scriptwriting was not what she wanted to do. She felt like she was no longer restricted by the cosy little lifestyle she had created with Ben, she felt a new lease of life burn inside her; a thirst for excitement swelled within as she contemplated all the possibilities that lay before her.

CHAPTER 15

AUTUMN SIGHED LOUDLY. THE HOUSE PHONE WAS ringing yet again. It was the fourth time that day, and with both of her parents at work, Autumn was fed up of traipsing up and down the curved staircase just so someone could offer her money back on a loan that she'd never taken out or compensation for an accident that she'd never had. Dutifully she put down the armful of clean washing and ironing her mum had done for her and went to answer the phone.

"Hello, Carter residence," she answered, still unable to shake the professional receptionist tone her voice automatically took on whenever she answered a phone that wasn't her mobile.

"Autumn?" the voice on the end of the line questioned, sounding relieved.

"Yes," Autumn answered uncertainly, "who is this?"

"It's Jack Thorne, you know, your boss," Jack said. Autumn stiffened, she hadn't recognised his voice at all. What on earth was he doing calling her parents' house and how had he gotten hold of their number? As if able to read her mind Jack told her that he'd been through her personal file in HR. This number was listed as an emergency contact.

"I can explain Jack. I'm really unwell," Autumn offered, although resigning to the fact that Jack probably wouldn't believe her now.

"Autumn, look, we either need a doctor's note from you now or for you to come in," he paused. "I know your exams are coming up; if you're struggling with the workload perhaps we can look at changing your hours?"

"It's not that," Autumn cut in. "It's, well, I can't really say. It's personal."

"I'm sorry Autumn but that just won't do now; like I said before, either a doctor's note or you come in. Otherwise we'll have no choice other than to let you go."

This was something Autumn desperately didn't want. Being fired was not something you wanted on your CV, especially when you'd soon be looking for the first job to start off your career. No potential employer would value someone who couldn't even hold down a part-time job. She paused, unsure how to handle the situation. She decided that honesty was the best policy and told Jack exactly what she was going through. Her story was met with a silence; she waited with bated breath.

"I'm so sorry Autumn," Jack offered after a few agonising moments. "Why don't you just come in tomorrow morning, early, before anyone else arrives and we can discuss your options? I'm sure we can work this out."

Autumn didn't have much choice, she couldn't hide behind her emails anymore. Knowing this, she begrudgingly agreed. Maybe if she explained to him in more detail and he saw how upset she was he'd be lenient, let her keep her job and make it so Rosa was never allowed to even look at her. Maybe she could persuade Jack to fire Rosa instead. After all, she and Jack had developed a bit of a bond over the last few months and Autumn thought that maybe, if fortune favoured her, she could appeal to his softer side. She was painfully aware that this was wishful thinking but hoped against hope anyway.

She hung up the phone after saying goodbye to Jack. A tight knot formed in her stomach. She literally had no clue what she was going to say to Jack. He hadn't sounded mad at her, more concerned if anything. Still, the knot in her stomach didn't loosen, instead it constricted with a sense of foreboding that made Autumn feel sick. She went into the kitchen and poured herself a big glass of white wine.

'The only way to handle this situation is to get hammered,' she thought to herself with a wry smile before drinking deeply. The crisp floral taste of the wine invaded her senses as she began to, for the moment anyway, leave her troubles behind. Taking the glass, and the rest of the bottle, upstairs with her, she decided that she'd enjoy her last day of freedom by having some much needed 'me time'. Autumn knew exactly what she was looking for, a small black box with a gold ribbon tying it shut. It took a while, but eventually she found it at the bottom of one of her overnight bags. Box in hand she went over to her bedroom door and closed it quietly before heading over to the window and drawing the blind. Sitting cross-legged on the bed she opened the box, her secret, one that she had kept from Ben the entire time they were together and not for any other reason that she enjoyed having something that was solely for her. It gleamed at her as she lifted it out, examining it briefly in the dimly lit room before reclining back onto the bed. She pulled at the waistband of her jeans and underwear and slid them down in one fervent movement.

Autumn took another sip of wine and carefully placed the glass down on her bedside table and picked up her new phone. She put on some music. For one, it helped get her in the mood and the second reason, well, it helped mask any noise that she might make. Even though she was in the house alone she still didn't want to risk being overheard, even by the cat.

Autumn twisted the base of the object she held in her hand: its curved chrome form buzzed into life, sending waves of anticipation through her. She lay back down, pulled off her top and spread her legs, the warmth between them already starting to spread.

She held her breath in anticipation, knowing that the pleasure she was about to experience would be far from prolonged and passionate but would fulfil her most visceral urges.

She passed the toy over her nipples, lingering there, allowing herself to enjoy the deep vibrations fully. After a few moments and feeling like she had waited long enough she traced the toy down her midsection, moving it in sumptuous spiral movements before gently resting it against her most sensitive spot. She shuddered as the rumbling vibrations washed over her, feeling the pent-up emotional torment she had experienced begin to ease. The stress seemed to seep out of every pore, giving way to a delectable bliss. Autumn moved the tip of the toy from her clitoris and ran it around the outer edge of her most intimate area, feeling her sanctum swell with expectant pleasure. She could feel herself beginning to get wet; this only spurred her on, her movements becoming more rapid and desperate as she stepped closer to the sweet release she was so desperate for. She made herself wait, encircling her sweetest area over and over again, allowing just the briefest pause over her most sensitive part. She moaned as the delicious sensations washed over her. She ached internally; her body was desperate for more, contracting frantically, searching for the intense stimulation that would send her over the edge. Finally, she succumbed and plunged the toy deep inside her. She let out a husky cry, her body quivering under the attentions of her vibrator. She used her other hand to work her clitoris, feverishly strumming at it repeatedly, eagerly urging herself on. Within moments she was climaxing: the vibrator had done its job beautifully. She clenched around it, feeling the vibrator's tremor throughout her entire being. She shook uncontrollably as she came, her hand tensing up as she did so, gripping the toy fiercely.

Once the waves of pleasure had subsided she pulled the silver C-shaped toy out of her and switched it off. She lay there for a few moments panting, with the music still playing softly in the background. The toy, still wet from her climactic peak, lay on her stomach, rising and falling in time with her breathing.

Autumn lay there in a post-orgasmic haze before swinging her legs over the side of the bed. She sat there for a moment, before re-dressing herself, all the while drinking her wine and singing softly along with the background music. Autumn surveyed her room: she had only half-unpacked her belongings and her mother was beginning to lose patience with the state of her bedroom. It hadn't been redecorated since she was a teenager. The dusky pink walls were dated now, but at the time she'd been at the forefront of teenage interiors. All of her school friends had loved her bedroom: the twinkling fairy lights over the headboard and the mirrored wardrobes had made it the perfect setting for many girly sleepovers. She smiled as she remembered one particular sleepover where the theme had been makeovers. They'd each taken it in turn to be each other's stylists, doing their hair and makeup in front of the big mirrors. Afterwards they'd treated Autumn's bewildered parents to a fashion show. She smiled to herself; she hadn't thought about that evening in years.

She sighed and returned her vibrator to its box, stowing it secretly under a pile of old magazines in her bedside drawers. She unpacked again and moved onto her work wardrobe, which had lain in a bin bag at the foot of her bed for the entirety of her stay at The Barings. With a grunt, she hauled the over-packed bag onto the bed, wincing slightly as it strained underneath the weight of the bag's contents. Autumn unpacked the clothes one by one: each item could do with an iron but Autumn really couldn't be bothered. She'd do that at a later date.

"Ewww," Autumn said in disgust, recoiling her hand quickly. Something had exploded in the bag and covered her clothes. Her hand was now coated in a thick gelatinous goo. She wiped it on her already covered clothes and reasoned that next time she packed she'd put all of her toiletries in a separate container. She drained the last of her glass, feeling a tipsy cloud settling over her.

Autumn dragged her soiled clothes downstairs and took them to the laundry room, patting each item down and throwing it in the machine. She pulled out her work jacket, a smart, fitted black jacket that seemed to go with everything. She delved in the pockets and retrieved a crumpled tissue, a small piece of card and a chocolate wrapper she must have sneaked whilst at her desk. She popped them on the side and shoved the jacket in the machine. As she bent over to close the door, she gasped. The card she had taken out was a business card and it belonged to Celina Thorne. She had clean forgotten all about Celina and her job offer since she'd found out about Ben and Rosa. How could she possibly have forgotten? This solved all of her problems. She would phone Celina and go and work for her. It was perfect and for a moment she contemplated this exciting opportunity. Autumn was keen to start anew and what was better to go with her new single status than a job planning parties? Hell, she might even meet someone there.

Autumn grabbed at the little white and silver card and she held it tight, feeling as if the tighter she held it the better the chances of moving on were. She bolted upstairs, poured herself another glass of wine – her second of the day – and picked up her phone. She dialled the telephone number on the front of the card with trembling hands; she needed this phone call to go well. She suddenly had an inexplicable urge to hang up the phone before it connected. After all, if she didn't make the call it couldn't go badly. She went to hang up – but she'd procrastinated for too long. The phone rang once, then again and again.

'Too late,' she thought to herself. Celina wasn't the type of woman to leave a missed call unreturned, even if she didn't know the number that had called her. The phone continued to ring and Autumn's mind raced. What if she'd left it too late? It had been a fair while since Celina had handed her that card. What if she'd already filled the position. What if it went to voice-mail? What would she say?

"Hello?" Celina's smooth tone sounded down the phone, interrupting Autumn's train of thought, Autumn opened her mouth to speak, but no words came out. "Hello?" repeated Celina, a little annoyance lacing her voice now at the thought that this might be a prank call.

"Sorry, is that Celina?" Autumn asked hesitantly, wanting to make sure she'd definitely got the right number.

"It is, and who may I ask is this?" Celina said, her voice commanding and assured.

Autumn explained herself, once again opening up to Celina easily. She didn't know where to stop: she told Celina about Ben, about her work situation with Rosa; she told her pretty much everything. Autumn was rambling now, over-sharing, but she couldn't help it and Celina didn't stop her. Talking to someone not directly involved in her situation felt really good. The expulsion of emotion felt cleansing and she revelled in the weightlessness that followed. Autumn seemed to gain confidence and power from merely having contact with Celina; she couldn't explain why but the woman had such an effect on her that she felt like an entirely different person.

"Well Autumn, I had hoped I'd be hearing from you sooner. I thought you were hedging your bets with my husband? But it's a case of better late than never I guess," Celina said. Autumn blushed on the other end of the phone, thankful that Celina couldn't see her. Seemingly sensing Autumn's embarrassment Celina went on, "No need to be embarrassed, any woman would have done the same in your shoes."

"I wasn't hedging my bets," Autumn retorted. "I've been sick."

"Oh yes, a broken heart is a serious condition. It's not something that should be taken lightly. Let me guess, did the doctor prescribe your parents, enough alcohol to see your liver off for good and plenty of tissues to wipe away the tears?" Celina said. Autumn couldn't tell if she was joking, or mocking her. She fell silent, not entirely sure how best to respond; she was, after all, stood in her parents' house, where she had indeed done her fair share of crying and was halfway though her second glass of wine that day.

"I'm joking, my lovely," Celina said when Autumn didn't respond. "I'll tell you what. Why don't you come for some work experience this weekend? I have a big event on and it'd be good for you to see all the action as it happens, warts and all. It'll help you understand the business and our clients a little more."

"So I have the job?" Autumn asked excitedly.

"Well, you might want to see if it's the kind of job you'd want first. I trust you've visited our website?" Celina asked. "This industry isn't as vanilla as you might think."

"I think I can handle going to parties for a living," Autumn said jovially, a smug smile forming on her lips. Autumn had indeed been on the site, but you needed a membership number to access anything other than the home page, which she didn't have. But, if the homepage was anything to go by, she knew all she needed to know about the company already: people with lots of money went to hang out with other people with lots of money. She was already excited at the prospect of high society mingling, especially if there was a pay packet involved. "What should I wear?" she asked excitedly.

"They're not just parties, Autumn; my clients have very specific tastes, they expect a lot from every single event, and they're big. We see a lot of people, all of whom are wealthy, and attractive," she added. "The dress code is strictly black tie, or 'full length and fabulous' as I like to call it. So, I'll need you in formal wear," Celina said, "and Autumn, don't come with any pre-ordained ideas. This might not be what you're entirely expecting. I don't want you to feel uncomfortable."

"I won't," Autumn said defiantly. "There's only one problem, I don't really have a, well, a posh dress." She trailed off. Shame flushed at her cheeks; she didn't want to appear childlike to Celina.

"Don't worry about that, I wasn't expecting you to have a ball gown at the ready," Celina said in a knowing way. "I'll send a car for you next Saturday at 4 p.m., you can come to the office and I'll lend you something of mine. I have more dresses than Oscar de la Renta," she laughed.

Autumn joined in, although not entirely getting the joke. She gave Celina her parents' address, and after a short conversation about pay, they said goodbye and hung up. Autumn stood there, the phone still pressed to her ear. She was smiling. She was going to earn almost twice the amount of money she was paid at Thorne PR and she was quite literally going to get to attend swanky parties for a living. She couldn't wait to tell David. He'd be so jealous, and now all she had to do was tell Jack she wouldn't be coming back to work. She would do it tomorrow in their meeting; she should do it face to face. She'd agreed to meet him early on in an attempt to avoid seeing Rosa. Autumn bubbled with bitterness and she thought of her.

'No, don't let her spoil anything else for you. Don't give the bitch the satisfaction,' she instructed herself, giving herself an internal slap on the wrist. She was excited and nothing and no one could take that away from her; to top it all off she was even going to be attending the event in one of Celina's designer dresses. She just hoped that it would fit her. Celina was lithe and slim and Autumn – she eyed her reflection in the full-length mirror – was not.

The rest of the day went by in a blur, as she couldn't stop clock-watching. She wished her parents would return home from their respective jobs so she could tell them her good news. She'd tried to get hold of David but he wasn't answering. She had even called his house phone. He wasn't there. Gregg was, though; they'd had a pleasant chat. Gregg had seemed eager to get off the phone. He was obviously in the middle of something important. She hadn't told him about her new job as she didn't want to run the risk of him telling David before she had a chance to. She wanted to be the one to give David her good news. She did talk to Gregg about his stay in the UK, how he was finding it, what his plans long-term were and when he would be off to see his mum. Autumn could listen to Gregg talk for days: his voice was like velvet, his smooth American accent hadn't lost its novelty yet. Eventually Gregg had managed to make his excuses and get off the phone, leaving Autumn feeling a little put out.

Hanging up the phone she wondered whether or not Gregg actually liked her. He was always pleasant enough, well very friendly actually, but he hadn't want to talk to her just then. He'd seemed shifty to her, and Autumn wondered if maybe

Gregg was seeing someone else too and just like Ben was sneaking around. Maybe he needed the phone free to plan an illicit encounter with his new man?

Autumn scolded herself. She couldn't let Ben make her paranoid about every other man on the planet, especially when the man in question was a good guy, who made her friend very happy – not forgetting he flew halfway around the world, uprooted his life and left his friends behind to be with him. Autumn shook her head, unable to fight the depressing feeling that at one point Ben would have done all those things for her.

As Autumn had predicted, her parents were thrilled for her. She waited until they were both home so she could tell them together, not wanting one to feel less important that the other. Her father insisted they go out for a celebratory meal and drinks.

"It looks like you've had enough to drink already," her mum said, eyeing the bottle of wine with two-thirds of the contents gone. "I see you've already been celebrating."

Sarah Carter didn't look overly impressed with her daughter. She had been saving that particular bottle of wine for the approaching weekend. The Carters were due to be entertaining guests and Sarah hadn't banked on her daughter swigging the supplies before the night itself.

"Actually, I was drowning my sorrows. I've got to go into work tomorrow morning. I thought I was going to have to beg for my job but now I don't have to. Instead I'll be handing my notice in," Autumn smiled smugly. "Now where should we go for dinner? Anywhere but Leonard's," she said decisively, answering her own question. "I never want to go back to the place again."

"But it's the nicest place in town," her dad said, and Autumn could sense he was disappointed. "Where are we going to go now?" he added in a childlike manner.

"Don't be ridiculous Richard, there are lots of fabulous places," Sarah retorted shortly. She reeled off a list of a dozen places she deemed just as good as Leonard's and stood there, waiting for her husband to choose. Richard didn't seem convinced, though, and urged his daughter to reconsider Leonard's. Autumn stood her ground. She genuinely never wanted to step foot in that place again. Eventually, and with much persuasion, they settled on dinner at E.C.H.D., a steak-house and wine bar that none of them had tried yet. As her mum booked the table, Autumn tried to call David again, and much to her relief, this time he answered.

"Autumn, my gorgeous girl! How are you?" David exclaimed. He seemed very joyful. "I have some fabulous news," he said without waiting for Autumn's answer.

"Me too!" she chimed in excitedly. "You go first though." She wanted the good news first and her better news second.

"Gregg and I are engaged! He asked me when I got back this evening. He'd laid out a rose petal trail with cute little notes and when I reached the end he was stood there, with a bottle of champagne and said we were celebrating. Well I was super-confused, I thought maybe he was buying a gym here or something, but no. When I asked what, he said, and I quote, 'We're celebrating us, you've made me the happiest man ever, you accept me and love me and I couldn't ask for more.' I was nearly in tears at this point, then he pulled out a box – he's even bought a ring, Autumn! It's a simple band with a diamond inset, very Gregg, very classy. Anyway, through tears I said yes! We popped the bubbly and have been celebrating ever since. I'm going to get married, babe!" David reeled off his tale enthusiastically, clearly elated with his new relationship status. "So, that's me, your turn now."

"Well, it's nothing next to that!" screamed Autumn, obviously over the moon with David's news. "I got a new job with Jack's wife."

"Oh the foxy one?" Asked David.

"I never said that," Autumn blushed, "but yes, the foxy one." David screamed down the phone so loudly Autumn had to pull it away from her ear. She smiled: even with news as big as a proposal David was still able to put that to the back of his mind and be pleased for his friend. He was so unselfish and caring; it was the thing Autumn treasured about him most.

"Well, do you want to come over for a glass of fizz?" he asked. "Gregg bought a whole case of Laurent-Perrier, he's got good taste."

"Of course he does, he's marrying you," Autumn chuckled. Just as she did, her mum walked past and gave her a little smile.

"What's all the screaming about?" she asked nosily, looking at Autumn in a way that suggested she might be able to reach into her mind and find out.

"David's getting married!" Autumn answered. "He's asked me round for some champagne," she added, hoping her mum would drive her; there was no way she could get behind the wheel of a car safely after two large glasses of wine.

"Oh that's wonderful," she raised her voice. "Congratulations my sweetheart!" she shouted down the phone. "Do join us at E.C.H.D.'s later, we've got a table booked at 8 p.m., I'll phone back and make it for five people. Don't say no, I won't hear of it. Let us treat you to a slap up, celebratory meal!"

"Ahhh, tell your mum thanks," David said politely. He asked Gregg if he wanted to go, covering the receiver as he did so. Autumn still heard every word. Gregg, being the beautifully perfect human that he was, graciously accepted. Autumn heard him say something about thank you flowers for her mum. He was so thoughtful. She was so unbelievably happy that David had met him and so pleased that they were engaged. David deserved his happy ever after. But there was another feeling creeping in next to her happiness, threatening to boot it out and consume her whole. *Jealousy*. Autumn realised was burgeoning inside her. How was it fair that David was now engaged and she was single? Where was *her* happy ever after? She pushed these thoughts to the back of her mind, determined not to let her subconscious ruin this moment.

"Great, so we'll meet you there at eight," Autumn finalised. David agreed and thanked her again. She congratulated him once more and then hung up, wondering if David had noted the dip in sincerity in her voice. She hoped not.

'Sort yourself out and don't be so bloody selfish, he's your best friend!' she scolded herself. Still, she couldn't help feeling that little twinge of envy every time she thought of David being engaged. It just wasn't fair. Pushing those thoughts away she ascended the stairs to get ready, realising that since she'd been staying with her parents she hadn't worn any clothes that didn't have an elastic waistband or a zip up front.

E.C.H.D. was busy, and it was clear to see why the place was so popular. It was modern, minimalist and ever so stylish. The attractive host checked them in and took their coats. Autumn looked around in an effort to catch a glimpse of David and Gregg, but they hadn't arrived yet. She checked her watch: it was 7.45, they'd be here any minute now, she reasoned. Their table wasn't quite ready so they were shown to the bar where Richard ordered a bottle of champagne, four glasses and a Coke.

Richard Carter had hardly ever touched alcohol, for no particular reason other than he just always seemed to fancy a water, a tea or some other non-alcoholic beverage instead. Autumn smiled at her straight-laced dad, watching him as he sipped on his Coke before handing the bottle in its ice bucket over to his wife who dutifully and expertly poured them both a glass of the fizzing golden liquid without spilling a drop. Autumn took hers eagerly and took a sip: it was icy cold and very refreshing. Taking another drink, she caught her mother's eye.

"Not so fast darling, we haven't even toasted your new job yet," Sarah said to her daughter.

"Ah, so we've remembered, have we?" Autumn countered. "Haven't forgotten in all the engagement excitement?"

"Oh, don't be so childish," her mother chided. "You'll have plenty of jobs in your lifetime, David will only get married once. My God, Autumn, not everything's about you, you know." Autumn knew her mum was right but still, she couldn't help feeling as though her thunder had been well and truly stolen.

"Okay, well here's to our wonderful daughter and her wonderful new job," Richard interjected, not wanting there to be an altercation before they'd even sat down. He raised his glass and clinked it gently against Autumn's and then his wife's. They in turn clinked their glasses: the toast had worked and both women resumed normal service.

Autumn was in the middle of telling them about how excited she was about her first event when David and Gregg walked through the door. Even though Autumn had her back to them, she knew they were approaching due to the majority of the women falling silent and looking over in Gregg's direction. He was after all, a very beautiful man. Gregg was dressed smartly in a black suit, matching tie and crisp white shirt, looking very dapper. David too was in a suit, only his was a pale pink colour; he'd followed Gregg's lead and teamed it with a crisp white shirt, only instead of a smart black tie he's opted for a multi-coloured bow-tie. David sneaked around her and planted a big, wet kiss on her cheek. Turning to see who the culprit was, she burst into a huge grin when she saw them both there. David had his left hand outstretched showcasing his beautiful, subtle and very elegant engagement ring. Autumn instinctively took his hand and examined it.

"Cartier?" she questioned, extremely impressed with Gregg's choice. David nodded, his hand still held out, examining it proudly himself. Autumn had never seen him so happy. He positively glowed. Gregg came up beside her and put his arm around David affectionately. Autumn couldn't help but smile; their happiness, it seemed, was infectious.

"I was just telling Mum and Dad about my new job," she announced, clearly wanting to stay on the subject of her.

"We've heard enough about that, Autumn," her mum said dismissively, visibly gleeful that David and Gregg had joined them and eager to find out all about the proposal. Sarah Carter was a sucker for love. She'd seen every romantic film going and loved a soppy story. "I bought my hanky in preparation," she said. Winking, she pulled out a lavender coloured handkerchief from her bosom and pretended to dab her eyes. Autumn cringed; sometimes her mum could be so embarrassing.

It was then that the *maître d'* informed them that their table was ready. Gregg insisted on assisting Sarah, taking her gently by the arm and escorting her through the dining room to their table. Unbeknown to them, originally they had been squeezed onto a small table, in a dull corner of the room but once Sarah had phoned ahead and increased their party size due to there being an engagement they'd been upgraded to what Autumn assumed was the best table in the house. It stood higher than the rest on an elevated platform; a huge crystal chandelier floated above them, bathing the table in a warm, shimmering light. Several votive candles adorned the table top, making the elegant stemware and gleaming cutlery glint attractively. David pulled out Autumn's chair for her and she sat down. Surveying the party she felt, auspiciously, like there was no place she'd rather be and with no other people. She was blessed that her nearest had come together to join her in celebrating her new job, and the engagement of course. *'We can't forget the engagement now can we?'* A bitter little voice harassed her within. She took another sip of champagne in an effort to drown it out and proposed a toast instead.

"To David, Gregg and one long and happy marriage," she said sweetly, smiling at each member of the table in turn. They all raised their glasses and clinked. Overhearing the toast the table nearest to theirs raised their glasses as well. Before she knew it, her private little toast had almost the entire restaurant raising their glasses amongst congratulatory cries of adulation. David and Gregg grinned and, somewhat self-consciously, raised their glasses and nodded their thanks.

"Well that wasn't embarrassing," David chuckled. "I hope this doesn't mean we have to invite them all to the wedding," he said in mock-horror, clapping his hand to his face. The engagement ring twinkled handsomely in the candlelight. They all chuckled at this.

"Well that's a point," Sarah said. "When is the big day? Are you going to have it here or should we all be saving for a trip to the States?"

"Sarah!" Richard admonished. "That's rather presumptuous of you. Pay no attention to her, boys, she's just pulling your legs."

Gregg smiled and told them they'd be getting married just as soon as David's extravagant plans would allow. The ceremony would be over here in the UK and of course they'd be invited. Sarah Carter positively swelled with delight; being deemed important enough to warrant an invitation sat very well with her. They ate, talked and drank the night away hardly straying off the topic of the wedding. Autumn joined in for the most part but couldn't shake the bitter feeling of resentment mounting inside her. She was of course, happy for David; her feelings didn't really have a great deal to do with him, it was more about her and what she no longer had. She mourned her relationship, and even though for the most part she was positive and looking forward to her future, she couldn't help dwelling on what could have been.

She was brought back to the table by a sudden realisation that everyone had stopped talking. The abrupt hush that had fallen caused Autumn to look up. Every single one of their faces looked solemn, and Sarah Carter glared over her daughter's shoulder, her face contorted with anger. Richard put a hand on his wife's arm in an attempt to calm her. She flinched and continued to stare.

"What's everyone looking at?" Autumn questioned, somewhat amused by their strange expressions. Turning around, she tried to catch a glimpse of whatever had stolen everyone's attention. Autumn's breath caught in her throat, as standing at the bar was Ben. With her heart beating rapidly she turned back around to the table and mustered a determined smile.

"Ignore him, don't let him ruin our night, I honestly couldn't care less that he's here." She mustered a half-smile. "Just, don't look at him. Mum, I said don't look at him." She reprimanded her mother who was still glaring aggressively in Ben's direction. "Mum!" Sarah Carter had begun to get up from her seat, much to Autumn's horror.

"Do not go over there!" Autumn commanded. "I don't need you fighting my battles, just leave it. He'd not seen us and we can just ignore him if he does." Autumn said with a little more force. Sarah hovered, half out of her seat, not sure whether to obey or defend her daughter. "Stop it, he's all the way over there and we're here." Autumn kept her voice cool and collected. The last thing she wanted was an argument at the table over Ben Wood. Sarah settled back down, she seethed in her seat but finally came around to Autumn's way of thinking. She gave him one last death stare, unbeknownst to him, and then returned her attention to their group.

"You're right, darling," she cooed, "nothing's going to spoil David and Gregg's big night." She smiled at the pair and clocking Autumn's less than impressed expression added, "and your job too, sweetheart."

Again, an unsettling feeling of jealousy pricked at Autumn; why was she the afterthought here? Her celebratory meal had been hijacked and her cheating, lying, bastard of an ex-boyfriend was drinking happily mere feet away from her. She took a deep breath and, once again, pushed those feelings to the side. Ben was not going to ruin anything else for her and she needed to get over this petty 'stolen thunder' thing, as it was childish and silly. David had always been her rock, especially in the last few weeks. She needed to put this behind her and get over it.

They chatted happily for the rest of the meal, continuing their conversation about David and Gregg's forthcoming nuptials. Dessert had been and gone and they were now nursing the last of their drinks. Autumn had had a lovely time all in all, and she hadn't given Ben a second look, she was proud of herself. She hadn't even glanced in his general direction when she'd used the bathroom just after their main course, in fact she hadn't even thought about him once during the course of the meal. When her mind had strayed from the conversation it had strayed to Celina: Autumn couldn't wait to hand her notice in at Thorne PR and get working planning glamorous parties.

"Ask her now," Gregg interrupted the conversation, nudging David gently to catch his attention. "You've had all night and you still haven't done it yet," he chided his fiancé.

"Ask me what?" Autumn asked suspiciously. "What is it, D?" David looked at her and cleared his throat, smoothing down his shirt as he did so.

"There's no easy way to do this," he took a deep breath. "Would you, Autumn Carter, light of my life, do me the honour of agreeing to be my best woman?"

Autumn let out a little squeal of delight and nodded her head fervently. She had a lump in her throat as she felt happy tears forming.

"Yes! Yes, yes yes yes yes!" she spluttered, nodding her head enthusiastically, a big grin spread across her face. Standing up she leant over and gave David a huge kiss, hugging him fiercely over the table. She couldn't believe he'd asked her to be such a huge part of their big day. Happy tears rolled down her cheeks, which she wiped away with her napkin. This was without a doubt the best thing that could have happened to her: all negative thoughts flew from her mind, replaced completely by happy excited ones. She beamed and continued to do so for the rest of the night. Even as she got ready for bed she was smiling, so very happy with the outcome of the evening.

She drifted off to sleep quickly. Her full stomach and tipsy state meant that she slept like a baby. In the excitement of all of it she completely forgot to set an alarm for the next day. Jack and Thorne PR never even entered her mind.

CHAPTER 16

JACK THORNE LOOKED AT HIS WATCH; IT WAS quarter to eight in the morning. He had been waiting for Autumn for almost half an hour. He had tried the mobile number he had for her, and an automated voice on the other end of the line told him that the number was no longer recognised. He reclined in his chair and looked at the ceiling impatiently. Jack didn't like to be kept waiting, especially when he had come in early on his day off, just so he could talk to a staff member about her problems.

'What am I doing?' Jack thought to himself. He knew this wasn't normal behaviour from a boss. Autumn was different though, special somehow. She seemed to need looking after and Jack couldn't help but feel like he should be the one to do it. He felt an affection towards Autumn akin to that of close friends, which was crazy. He barely knew her outside of the office – hell, he hadn't even known about her boyfriend. But nonetheless, Jack knew that he wanted Autumn to remain working for him. He enjoyed their working relationship and up until recently having her around made things easy for him. Still, regardless of the reason, her tardiness put his back up, no matter how much he liked the girl.

Autumn opened a bleary eye. She paused for a moment, taking a minute to fully assess the intensity of her hangover. She was pleasantly surprised. Apart from a slightly fuzzy head she felt fine. She could smell bacon cooking downstairs, and her stomach rumbled at the thought of one of her mum's world-class bacon sandwiches: rich, hearty wholemeal bread, best back bacon from the farm shop and a ton of homemade tomato ketchup. Her stomach rumbled again, and she rolled over and stretched a hand to the floor to retrieve her phone. No calls, no surprise but she did have a text message from David.

'Good luck today hon. We'll be thinking of you. D xxx.'

"Good luck?" she questioned aloud, asking no one but herself. "Good luck for what?" She shrugged, guessing the message must have been for someone else. Getting out of bed she dressed in a pair of faded grey jeans and a white vest top.

"Morning sleepyhead," Richard said, giving his sleepy-looking daughter a loving kiss on the top of the head as she sat down at the kitchen table. "What's the plan for today then? When's your meeting?"

"What meeting?" Autumn said as she gratefully took a cup of coffee from her mum, taking a sip then wincing as she realised it was far too hot to drink yet, so setting it down on the glass coaster in front of her. She didn't need her dad to clarify: it dawned on her in one horrible crashing thought.

'Shit,' she thought to herself, glancing at the clock and realising it was over an hour after she said she'd be there, *'Jack's going to be so mad.'* She shot up from the table, grabbed her car keys and slipped on a pair of sandals that she had left by the front door.

Once again Autumn found herself driving at breakneck speed. She didn't have Jack's number and felt that an email would just be insulting. Her best bet was to apologise in person. She pulled up to the offices of Thorne PR in record time. Thankfully her fob was still in her bag, so she buzzed herself in and instead of turning to her desk she went straight on, up the stairs and to Jack's office.

"Autumn?" she heard an intrepid voice say from behind her. "We need to talk."

Autumn froze on the spot. She hadn't banked on seeing Rosa, in fact she'd plain forgotten about her. She wasn't mad anymore. She felt sorry for her. She pitied a woman so callous and heartless she would stoop so low as to steal her friend's boyfriend.

"No, we don't," Autumn said forcefully. She didn't turn around, she stared fixedly on the step in front of her. Steadying herself, she took a deep breath and carried on up the stairs, leaving Rosa in her wake.

"For fuck's sake Autumn, I'm not sleeping with Ben!" Rosa screamed up the stairs after her. Autumn ignored her.

'Liar!' she thought to herself, anger bubbling inside her. It would be marginally less offensive if Rosa had just apologised, begged for her forgiveness, tried in some way to justify her actions, but no. The selfish, thoughtless cow who had been her friend hadn't even offered that – worse, in fact, she had continued to deny it. Autumn was about to be the bigger person, but the insulting behaviour Rosa had just demonstrated caused her to turn around. Glaring down the steps at her nemesis she calmly and coolly stared at Rosa. She seemed, to Autumn, much uglier now. The lies and betrayal were showing on her face, and she looked tired and downtrodden. Autumn smiled smugly, knowing that although she looked scruffy, it was only her clothes that made it so.

"Looking good," Autumn said sarcastically. "I can see what Ben saw in you." Rosa sighed and walked up the steps to Autumn. She was half-smiling, and Autumn couldn't believe the nerve of her. Rosa stretched out a hand to place on Autumn's shoulder. Usually this would be seen as caring and compassionate but to Autumn it was manipulative. The diamond tennis bracelet glinted again, mocking her by reminding Autumn of their betrayal. It was like a red rag to a bull: all the memories came crashing down on her. The bracelet glinted again, taunting her.

'How dare she still have that on,' Autumn raged. She leaned back to avoid Rosa's outstretched, hopeful hand. Bringing her own hand forward she shoved her away. Rosa wobbled and lost her footing; she reached out for Autumn, her hands coming forward whilst the rest of her fell back. Autumn instinctively regretted her action and lunged forward to grab Rosa, catching her expensive, tailored blouse but nothing else. The fine fabric slipped through her fingers and Rosa was gone, crashing backwards down the staircase, crying out in pain as she collided with the hard stone steps. Her arms flailed, trying desperately to grab hold of something, of anything, but every time she came close to saving herself, she failed.

Rosa blacked out as her head struck the bottom step, and she lay there in a crumpled heap. Completely unaware of the alarmed crowd gathering around her, she didn't hear the panic-stricken cries nor did she know that Autumn had turned around and continued up the stairs, not giving Rosa a second glance.

"Autumn?" Jack was stood at the top of the stairs. "How could you?" he asked, his usually jovial expression replaced by one of utter horror. He glared at Autumn intensely.

"I, I didn't do anything," Autumn started. "She fell, and I was, I was coming to get help." Autumn stammered, looking up at Jack. He looked down the stairs, past Autumn to the scene below.

"Someone call an ambulance!" he bellowed down to the gathering crowd as he ran down the stairs to his employee. June was bending over Rosa's unconscious body with two fingers pressed to her throat. She looked at her pleadingly, willing her to be okay.

"There's a pulse," she said, relieved, "but it's weak. She needs to see a doctor immediately." June pushed some of the thick, glossy hair out of Rosa's face. Behind her someone was calling for an ambulance. Jack pulled out his phone, it was with a heavy heart that he punched the number nine in three times.

"Ambulance and Police please," he said, "I want to report an assault." Jack turned away from Rosa to see Autumn disappearing out of the door. He walked purposefully after her, determined to get some answers from her. As he did so he gave his name and the address of Thorne PR before hanging up and bursting into a sprint after Autumn.

"Jack, it was an accident," Autumn said truthfully.

"I saw the whole thing, Autumn. You shoved her and you know you did." Autumn began to protest but Jack raised a hand to silence her. "Look, the police have been called. You need to stay and explain what happened. I can't have ex-employees coming in and attacking my staff."

"Ex?" Autumn questioned. Jack nodded, he'd spoken to his wife who, of course, had told him that Autumn was going to work for her instead. He didn't need his first-class honours degree to put two and two together.

"Well you were going to hand your notice in anyway, and aside from that, Autumn…" He took a deep breath and continued, "You haven't been in work for a long time, with no explanation. Working here isn't optional, and it's not up to you to decide if you feel like coming into work or not. You can't just swan in and out as and when you like, regardless of what's happening in your personal life. I think it's best for all involved if you left, as of today. I had really hoped we'd be able to work something out, and I was even going to transfer

Rosa to our other office. But now, well, after what I've just seen, I don't want you here."

Autumn was gobsmacked. She thought Jack knew her better than that. She would never had intentionally physically hurt someone, even if that someone had done irreparable damage like Rosa had.

"I'm not listening to this," she lashed out angrily. "You can't speak to me like that. You have no idea what I've been through because of her."

"So, you thought you'd just push her down the stairs? Autumn, you can't behave like that! You could have killed her. Hell, you don't know what damage you've caused. God, Autumn! It's like I don't even know who you are anymore!" he exclaimed. Anger and exasperation dripped from every word.

Autumn stared at him, dumbfounded he just wasn't getting it. She hadn't pushed Rosa, certainly not on purpose, and certainly not with the intention of physically hurting her. She shook her head at him, gutted that he couldn't see things from her perspective. She turned around and walked off, vaguely aware of the whispers growing louder.

"What the fuck are you lot looking at?" she spat at the baying crowd.

The words were alien to her. These had been, up until moments ago, her friends, her colleagues, the people she saw almost every day. The whispers stopped as all eyes looked at her. June was still crouching next to Rosa holding her. She shook her head sadly, June looked crestfallen: this, more than anything, crushed Autumn. Even June, who had been more of a mother figure to her than anything else, thought she was capable of this. Something inside Autumn snapped, she shot them all a scathing look, then ignoring the cries of protest from Jack behind her walked out of the building.

"Fuck you Jack!" she shouted without turning around. "Fuck you all!" Autumn got in her car and sped off without giving Jack or Thorne PR another thought. She couldn't shake the niggling feeling that the Autumn of old certainly wouldn't have believed Rosa got what she deserved, but this new Autumn, the one that from now on would be thinking about number one, not only didn't give a shit; if anything, she thought bitterly, she was glad it had happened.

Well, that was it. Autumn and Thorne PR would never meet again. She had left a handful of personal items in her desk drawer but nothing that she wanted so badly that she'd go back there for. Autumn thought of Rosa: on the one hand she hoped there was no lasting damage, but on the other, well, if she were brutally honest, she didn't really care if there was. Autumn realised that her hands were trembling a bit as she drove. She steadied herself and gripped the wheel a little tighter, taking a deep breath and exhaling slowly as she did so. Perhaps the earlier episode had affected her a little deeper than she'd imagined. She took another breath and pressed on, keen to get back to her parents' house and forget this entire day ever happened. She pressed harder on the accelerator, increasing her speed as the need to get home and feel safe and secure swelled inside her.

"Darling, whatever's wrong now?" her mum said, an exasperated air in her voice. Autumn didn't say anything, but instead flung her arms around her mum and hugged her tight. "Autumn? What is it? You're scaring me," Sarah said, her tone taking on a more serious note now.

"Rosa fell down the stairs at work and everyone at work thinks that I pushed her," Autumn wailed, although the tears that she had been expecting to shed never came, her eyes remained dry and stony-looking.

"Is she hurt?" her mum questioned. "Why do they think you did it?"

"I don't know. I just don't know," Autumn rebuffed, not appreciating the accusatory tone her mum seemed to have. "We were both on the stairs and she just fell when I tried to get her off me."

Sarah Carter had no choice but to believe her daughter, but she couldn't help but wonder if maybe Autumn had had a little more to do with the fall than she was letting on. She scolded herself internally for doubting; it was a mother's duty to stand by her kids and whatever the outcome of this was she would definitely be standing by Autumn. The poor girl had had a rotten run of luck, and it was only natural she would act out in some way, Sarah theorized. She stroked Autumn's hair and gave her a kiss on the top of the head.

"Don't worry, darling, it'll be fine. Why don't we go and finish unpacking your room? Come on, I'll do all the work and you can tell me where everything goes," she suggested, taking her daughter by the hand and encouraging her up the stairs. She hoped Autumn would agree. Sarah was an easy-going kind of woman, but the half-unpacked mess in Autumn's old room was driving her to the brink of insanity.

Autumn had clean forgotten all about Rosa and her run-in with Jack by the time there was a loud knock at the door. She looked at her watch: the rose gold face told her that it was getting on for 5 p.m. She scratched her head, wondering, *"Who could be at the door now?"*

"You're not expecting anyone are you, Mum? Dad didn't forget his keys or something did he?" she asked, getting up from the bed and easing her feet into her favourite fluffy slippers.

"No, your father's not due home until much later. It's Parent Teacher evening at school today. Why they have them on a Friday is beyond me. I bet he's about ready to rip his hair out by now," she joked.

Autumn got up to go and answer the door. She padded downstairs, stretching to see if she could make out who it was through the glass panel. She couldn't decipher a face and could only see a vague bright yellow blur. She immediately thought it must be David in one of his outlandish outfits. Autumn swung the door open, a smile on her face, ready to greet her friend. Instead of David standing there was a man she vaguely recognised but couldn't place. She looked into his piercing blue eyes. He wore a serious expression and was exceptionally handsome; however, his fine features didn't shine as brightly as they could have, due to his grave countenance. She looked him up and down and instantly knew where she knew him from the second she clocked his clothing. Her stomach did a flip and she swallowed hard, bringing her eyes back up to meet his.

"Autumn Carter?" the man asked, not a trace of the pleasant understanding tone he'd used with her when he'd stopped her for reckless driving. She nodded, dropping her gaze again, she stared at the floor in front of her, wishing it would open up and swallow her whole.

"Who is it, darling?" called her mum from upstairs. Her voice got louder with every word and Autumn knew she was in descent, keen to see who the unexpected visitor was.

"No one, Mum. It's nothing," Autumn called over her shoulder. She then turned to the police office and whispered urgently, "Look, this isn't a good time. Could you come back tomorrow?" The officer's expression didn't change; however, Autumn thought she saw a ghost of a smirk dancing behind his eyes and a subtle raise of an eyebrow.

"I'm afraid not Miss Carter. Now, if I could come in? I just need to ask you some questions in relation to an incident concerning one Rosa Dawson. You are aware of the incident in question, Miss Carter?" he asked her, not taking his eyes off her for a moment.

Realising that it was a lost cause, Autumn stepped out of the way and gestured for the officer to enter. Her mum had appeared in the hallway looking concerned.

"Is everything alright?" she probed the police officer with her eyes, hoping for some sort of assurance from him. He merely stated that he needed to speak to Autumn and asked where was the best place to do that within their house. Sarah Carter ushered them into the sitting room and lingered for a moment, not wanting to leave her daughter without backup. However, Autumn assured her that she would be fine and instead suggested that perhaps her mum could make them a drink. Sarah dutifully obliged and switching into perfect hostess mode eagerly took their drink orders. The officer raised an eyebrow at this request but didn't say anything; instead he took out a small notepad and pen from his bright yellow jacket pocket.

"Autumn, my name's Jake Sentori, and I'm the officer they've assigned to this case. Earlier today we received a call from your ex-employer, Jack Thorne, notifying us of an incident at your former place of work." Autumn nodded. She knew all of this and didn't need telling again. Sensing her impatience, Officer Sentori pressed on. "I know you're keen to get this over and done with and so am I. I should have clocked off around the time I was knocking on your door," he said dolefully. He went on to ask Autumn to recount her version of events which Autumn did, feeling that the key element to this story was the fact that Rosa had been sleeping with her boyfriend, which in turn had caused them to break up. Jake Sentori nodded his head.

“I am aware of your personal circumstances Miss Carter,” he said, referring to their chat on the day that he’d stopped her.

Autumn flushed. She didn’t want to seem like a bitter ex-girlfriend to him, but she couldn’t help it. If Ben and Rosa hadn’t done what they’d did, then none of this would ever have happened and he needed to know that. Autumn didn’t know why she felt so strongly about what this man thought of her, maybe it was because she couldn’t bear for one more person to think that she was the bad guy in all of this, or maybe it was because he was just so damn handsome.

Sarah Carter re-entered the room, the drinks sat neatly atop the old wooden tray. She set it down on the glass coffee table between the pair and without saying a word, took her leave, giving her daughter a meaningful look as she went. Officer Sentori continued eyeing Autumn up as she reached for her wine and drank deeply. Her hand shook a little so she gripped the glass tighter, not wanting to give the impression that she had anything to be nervous about; she had, after all, done nothing wrong.

“So, what is it you want me to say?” Autumn said finally, refusing to make eye contact once again and instead favouring the contents of her glass. She watched as the wine washed around the inside as she gently tipped it from side to side.

“I’d like to hear your version of events. Rosa Dawson was unconscious still when she left the ambulance so we couldn’t speak to her. However, we took detailed statements from Mr Thorne and from a June Breslin. I believe she’s a work colleague of yours also?”

“That’s right, only Jack isn’t a colleague. He was my boss,” Autumn offered, trying to be helpful and keep the tone of her voice calm, although she was beginning to bubble with anger inside.

"Well, they've told me their version of events," Jake was cut short.

"But they're lying!" she exploded, unable to keep a lid on it anymore. "This is ridiculous. It was an accident! They weren't there, they didn't see what happened!" she exclaimed in frustration. This was so unfair; it was everyone else's word against hers and no one else had even properly seen what had happened between her and Rosa. She flushed again but this time not out of embarrassment but pure anger. The officer raised a hand to diffuse the situation.

"I simply want your side of the story, Autumn," he said calmly. Autumn looked at him for the first time since they'd sat down together. There was something about him saying her name that made her sit up and pay attention. She bristled slightly, still irritated that she was even having to give a statement at all, irritated that Jack would think this of her and that there were others too, people who knew her well, who would even consider that she was capable of shoving someone down a flight of stairs in cold blood. She sipped her drink, taking a moment to collect herself.

"Okay," Autumn conceded. There was only one way this was going to be over quickly and that would be by her co-operating as much as she could. She retold the entire tale, making sure to emphasise fully how she had tried to catch Rosa but that her silk shirt had slipped straight through her outstretched fingers. She told him in detail how she had watched as Rosa fell, unable to do anything, neglecting to mention that, for a brief instance she had felt a fleeting second of smug happiness that it had happened, but when she saw the severity of the fall, that feeling had given way to absolute horror and regret.

When she had finished telling her side of events, she was surprised to find that a tear had rolled down her cheek. She wiped at it with the back of her sleeve, unable to allow herself to feel sorry for the woman that had ruined her life. All the while she was talking Officer Sentori scribbled in his notepad, occasionally stopping to sip on his coffee or to ask for clarification on certain points. He wanted to know at which point on the staircase had Autumn stopped and turned to face Rosa and why she had left after the accident. He questioned her about her angry outburst, since Autumn had neglected to disclose this information, again afraid that the handsome officer would think ill of her. Acting as if it had merely slipped her mind, she downplayed it, insisting that it was just a result of everyone ganging up on her and hoping for sympathy rather than doubt from him.

When Officer Sentori seemed satisfied with everything he flipped his notepad shut and placed both the pen and pad back in his front pocket. He stood up and brushed down his trousers before standing to full height. Autumn took a moment to appreciate his fine physique. He was tall, broad and muscular, his dark hair tousled messily atop his head. He ran his fingers through it and exhaled.

"Thank you, Miss Carter. That'll be all. We'll be back in touch if there's anything further that we need," he said with a finality in his voice that Autumn didn't like very much.

"Already?" she asked hastily, forgetting the reason he had come in the first place. "Stay for a drink at least? We've got wine if you'd like?" she suggested. For the first time that night, Officer Jake Sentori smiled at her. Autumn felt her stomach tighten, he was handsome, that much was definite, but with a smile he was absolutely heavenly. His straight white teeth gleamed attractively and she found herself mirroring his expression.

"I'm afraid I can't." But noticing Autumn's crestfallen expression he said, "It wouldn't be appropriate."

She nodded, appreciating how forward she must seem to him and cringing at herself. He wasn't going to want to stay for a drink, this was a work matter, and she'd just given a statement on why she'd allegedly pushed someone down a staircase – hardly the actions of someone who was girlfriend material. Psycho girlfriend material, maybe, but somehow, she didn't think that would be his thing. Anyway, he was bound to believe everyone else, and why wouldn't he? They were all saying the same thing; this, teamed with the fact that Rosa had stolen her boyfriend, didn't exactly put her in a favourable light. Officer Sentori thanked Autumn for her time and made his way to the front door on his way out. He thanked Mrs Carter for her fine hospitality and bade them both a goodnight.

Autumn watched him go, deeply regretting coming on to him like that. What had she been thinking? She scorned herself for being so stupid. Even if the circumstances had been completely different, if he hadn't thought she was a danger to others, either in a car or on a flight of stairs, he would hardly go for someone like her. He was on another level, in a position of authority and obviously took his work very seriously. He was, also, probably not single. She was currently unemployed and, at the moment, definitely not looking her best. She made a mental side note to try and cut down on booze and sweet treats. To top it all off she was being investigated for committing actual bodily harm. Autumn realised that she couldn't be less attractive to someone such as Officer Jake Sentori.

She sighed: it was looking to Autumn like she might be on the singles' market for a while to come yet.

CHAPTER 17

"DARLING, THERE'S A CAR OUTSIDE FOR YOU!" Sarah Carter squealed upstairs with excitement when she clocked the cream Mercedes pulling up the drive and coming to a standstill outside her home. Sarah couldn't believe it, her daughter had a driver and was now attending high society parties for a living. It was all very glamorous and fashionable. Sarah bristled with excitement, partly for her daughter but more at the idea of the triumph she'd feel at telling all her friends and neighbours what Autumn now did for a living. This would be the shining jewel in the crown that was her social life. After all, being a partly retired part-time librarian meant that she needed to live vicariously through her daughter. "Autumn, he's waiting!" she shrieked, excitement now giving way to impatience. She didn't want her daughter holding anyone up or being late on her first day. She heard Autumn's bedroom door close and footsteps coming down the stairs.

Autumn appeared, fresh-faced and eager to get going. She couldn't wait to see Celina's offices. She imagined a big, modern building, elegant in design and bustling with busy and important people. She imagined seating arrangements strewn about and guest lists tacked on walls with photographs of Britain's elite next to their name, job title and an interesting fact about them. She wondered what her role as PA to the

CEO would be like, and what it would entail. She'd seen *The Devil Wears Prada* and hoped it wasn't going to be like that, although if it was she'd know exactly how to handle the situation. She mentally thanked Anne Hathaway and Meryl Streep as she gave her mum a quick kiss on the cheek and headed out the door to the waiting car.

"I'll take your bag, miss," the smartly dressed and kind looking middle-aged man said. "I'll be your driver for today. Hendricks," he said, holding out a hand. Autumn stared at him for a second, confused: she wasn't entirely sure what 'Hendricks' meant exactly. Was he offering her a drink? But it was only four in the afternoon – not that that had ever stopped her before. His hand hovered there, awaiting hers. She shook it vigorously and mocked herself for being so stupid. Hendricks was his name!

"Autumn," she said, copying his friendly but business-like tone, then added for effect, "Autumn Carter."

"Well Miss Carter, let me take that for you."

He took the bag from her with one hand and opened the back passenger side door for her with the other. Autumn got in, impressed with the entire set up. Hendricks was a pale guy with watery blue eyes and soft, but permanently etched, smile lines around his eyes that made Autumn put him at around the fifty-five age mark. The car she had been sent was a brand new Mercedes. It boasted blackout privacy windows. Cream on the outside and cream on the in, it had a buttery soft leather interior finished with Celina's initials embroidered in a calligraphic font on the headrests; the thread she'd chosen for the embroidery was a deep burgundy colour which went superbly well with the car. Autumn was hugely impressed. If this was the car she sent for her PA, then just imagine what the car she drove around in must be like.

Hendricks pulled a smart black cap on top of his head, which hid his thinning mousy brown hair and shielded his eyes from the bright sunlight. He switched on the ignition and slowly pulled away from The Barings, driving with expert care down the winding drive. Autumn turned around and looked out of the back window to see her mum hanging out of the doorway, waving her daughter off with a huge, proud smile on her face.

They drove for the first few minutes in relative silence. The only noise audible over the low hum of the engine was the soft jazz music Hendricks had chosen playing in the background. Autumn, feeling slightly self-conscious, took out her mobile phone from her pocket and quickly took a picture of herself in the back of the car, making sure she posed right next to the personalised headrest and that she got as much of the luxurious car in the picture as possible. It didn't go unnoticed by Hendricks, who glanced in the mirror and smiled to himself. It was nice to have someone to drive around who wasn't used to the opulent lifestyle and appreciated the sumptuous glamour of it all. Autumn typed out a brief message to David. He'd texted her earlier that day wishing her good luck, and she replied with the picture she had just taken and a winking face, accompanied with the words: 'I don't think I'll need it.' Maybe a little self-assured, she thought, but reasoned that it was better to be confident than not.

The drive wasn't a short one, and Autumn soon found herself a little bored, even with her fabulous surroundings. There were only so many times she could marvel at the in-built television, the fancy lighting system or the beautiful interior. She had tried making conversation with Hendricks, and although friendly and polite, he was hardly forthcoming with information about his employer. Autumn had asked a lot of questions, mainly about Celina and the business – after all, other than it being an events company she didn't know much about it. She hadn't been able to find out anything online. There was a website, but you had to have a membership to access it, a membership that cost money, money that Autumn didn't have. Hendricks had remained suspiciously tight-lipped about both. Autumn could only assume that he just didn't know anything, and he was masking his ignorance under the guise of confidentiality. After all, how likely would it be that someone like Celina Thorne would discuss her business in any depth with her driver?

After what seemed like an eternity Hendricks pulled off the main road and not long after approached an imposing-looking, large, metal gate. It reminded her of the gate at Thorne PR so much so that she had to glance around just to make sure Hendricks hadn't mistakenly taken her there instead. Thankfully, they weren't outside her old workplace. The gates were mightily similar, though: *'Perhaps it was buy one get one free,'* she thought to herself. They waited there a moment before the gates opened, seemingly of their own accord. Hendricks slowly eased the car in and stopped it a little way past the gate. Autumn peered out the front window and couldn't see anything that remotely looked like an office in sight. They appeared to be in a small, walled, overgrown garden, nothing but shrubs and bushes to either side of them.

There was a metallic groan and a creak from below. Autumn was surprised to find herself in descent; the floor seemed to be sinking, taking the car with it. Slightly panicked Autumn shot out her hand and grabbed the armrest tightly, unsure of what exactly was going on. The greenery disappeared above them as they sank further and further into the ground. Soon they were engulfed in complete darkness, still slowly descending deeper and deeper. The only source of light came from her mobile phone, which was resting in her lap. She glanced down to see a reply from David. It consisted of just one word: 'Jealous'.

The car's sinking platform stopped almost as suddenly as it had started. Hendricks rolled forward. Autumn could see they were in some sort of underground car park. It was bright white with silver metal strips denoting each parking space. It was hands down the swankiest car park Autumn had ever seen. Hendricks pulled into a space opposite a large set of metal doors. Autumn sat there for a moment, unsure as to what was expected of her. Should she wait for Hendricks to open the door? Would it be rude to just get out herself? Or would he think her an expectant diva if she just sat there waiting for him to act? He opened the door for her and stepped aside, smiling as he did so.

"Here we are, Miss Carter. If you just take those doors to the entrance, someone will be there to meet you," Hendricks said, nodding towards the ominous doors. He handed Autumn the bag she'd brought with her and got back into the car, closing the door firmly behind him.

Autumn turned around to face the large, foreboding metal doors that separated her from the potential of a new and glamorous job, working alongside a woman that she admired wholly. Autumn not only thought Celina an exquisitely beautiful woman, but also a savvy, intelligent and confident businessperson. Celina Thorne really did have it all and Autumn wanted that for herself. With this in mind, Autumn started for the door, and reached it quickly, her heart beginning to beat faster – she couldn't believe how nervous she was.

She stopped and surveyed the doors, looking for some sort of button to open them. There was nothing. The only thing that stood out was a shiny black square, about the size of a piece of paper. She leaned in closer to inspect it, her heart felt like it would burst through her chest. This place was a complete mystery, one she was hesitant to unravel. There was nothing obvious that she should press and no written instructions for her to follow. She turned around, hoping Hendricks would be on hand to offer some help, but he wasn't. The cream Mercedes had left already, and she had been so busy trying to figure out the seemingly impenetrable door system in front of her that she hadn't notice the sleek car leave. Autumn sighed and looked at her phone. She didn't have any signal down here, not even one measly bar to call for help with. She prodded the black panel, her hand shaking slightly. She didn't want to be late or look stupid and not being able to work a simple entry system would mean that she would be both. She had left a greasy finger mark on the panel's spotless surface; she rubbed at it with the sleeve of her hoodie in an attempt to clean the mark off. The last thing she wanted was to ruin something before she'd even set foot in the building.

She looked at her watch. It was almost 5 p.m. now, and she had to be dressed and ready for the party in a little over two hours; that was plenty of time. Her shower, dress, makeup and hair routine was down to a fine art, so all she'd need to do was pick out one of Celina's fabulous dresses, slip it on and she'd be good to go. As she rubbed at the panel, it lit up, and a keypad emerged in bright white light. The screen instructed her to enter her membership number.

"Membership number?" she questioned out loud, scratching her head, searching for any memory of Celina giving her a number to use.

"Your membership number can be found on the back of your membership card." The machine said in an eerily good impersonation of a human. "If you have forgotten your card or it has been damaged or defaced, please press the speaker button to be connected to a host." Autumn pressed the lit-up button that most resembled a speaker. There was a brief pause before a voice she didn't recognise spoke.

"Welcome to Encounters. I'm sorry but our event will begin at 7.30 this evening. If you would like to come back later, we can admit you then. For a reminder of your membership number, please may I take your surname?" the voice said in a silky smooth professional tone that Autumn had used herself on more than one occasion.

"Actually, I'm here for Celina," Autumn said, unsure of herself. "My name's Autumn, Autumn Carter. I think she's expecting me." There was a pause on the other end and Autumn could hear papers shuffling.

"One moment please," the voice said.

After a short while there was a loud clunk and the doors slid into life, sweeping gracefully to each side. Autumn expected this to be a lift: they'd travelled down so deeply into the car park that it only stood to reason that now she'd need to go up. She was astounded to see that behind the doors there was a room, clinically but elegantly decorated in white and gold with a small, hotel reception-style desk, a plush looking sofa to one side and a large modern-art painting of two men in a romantic embrace, hung on the wall opposite. It was as if she'd stepped into the world's smallest art gallery. Autumn walked in, past the sofa and towards the desk.

"Hello?" she said uncertainly, unsure if she was the only person in the room or not.

"You must be Autumn," a voice said from behind the desk. Autumn peered over the desk's privacy screen and saw a petite brunette woman, with skin so pale it was almost translucent. "Celina is expecting you. If you'd like to go up she'll be waiting for you. Just one thing. You'll need to leave your phone with me. No phones or cameras are allowed past this point, unless you're staff." Autumn begrudgingly obliged, handing over her phone and noting with some disdain that she wasn't quite classed as staff yet.

She looked around. On one side of the desk was a door. She hadn't noticed it at first since it had no frame. It was built flush with the wall and was decorated the same as the walls. At first glance it was completely hidden: the only thing that gave the door away was the large golden door knob protruding from it. Autumn went towards the door. Hand outstretched she grasped the knob and turned, opening up a room filled with clothes hangers. Confused, she turned to the receptionist. Her face asked the question for her.

"That's the cloakroom," the woman said, clearly amused. "The entrance to Encounters is over there." She gestured to the painting.

Autumn was dumbfounded. This whole experience so far had been like something out of a spy movie. She was utterly intrigued; this place was well and truly shrouded in mystery. She walked over to the painting, unable to take her eyes of the explicit scene before her. The two men in the painting were naked, their bodies entwined becoming one. The embrace had been painted in such a way that their bodies tastefully concealed one another's modesty. The two men, one blond, the other brunette, were sharing a deep and loving kiss. Their lips pressed firmly against one another; both of them had their eyes closed in ecstasy. Autumn was lost for a second in the painting. It was intricately done, and she could see each individual brushstroke. She marvelled as they swirled and danced in front of her eyes. She jumped back; the painting jolted to the side in one quick, fluid and silent motion. It shocked her beyond belief. Heart racing, she peered inside. Behind the painting was the lift she'd been expecting earlier. It was mirrored from floor to ceiling and it was lit by many small vintage light bulbs suspended from thin semi-transparent wires, giving the illusion of them floating in mid-air.

The lift climbed upwards. It moved slowly, so slowly in fact that Autumn wasn't entirely sure that it was moving at all. Eventually it came to halt and the doors opened onto a scene that took Autumn's breath away. The sight was spectacular. Before her was a beautiful, antique ballroom. Its expanse stretched out almost endlessly ahead of her, the walls were covered in old, mercury tainted mirrors and underfoot was a darkly stained wooden floor, topped with a large, ornate, gold rug in the centre of the room, beautifully made from what Autumn could only assume was fine silk. On top of the rug stood an oval-shaped table adorned with a huge and very impressive display of white calla lilies; hundreds of them made up an incredibly striking and very elegant arrangement. Autumn cast her eyes upwards. The ceiling was domed slightly, the curve amplifying the sounds of her footsteps as she walked in further. From the centre of the ceiling, hanging directly above the rug, table and lilies, was an enormous chandelier. It sparkled invitingly as she walked further into the room, her footsteps echoing, painfully aware that she was disturbing her serene soundless surroundings with her clumsy footfalls.

"What do you think?" Celina asked, appearing from an archway towards the back of the room. While Autumn had been attempting to tread lightly Celina strutted through the room; the sound of her stilettos resonated throughout. Autumn walked towards Celina, who was, once again, impeccably dressed. She wore black fitted trousers and a cream chiffon blouse that was slashed to the waist showcasing her perfect cleavage and svelte mid-section. She strutted over to Autumn and embraced her in a sincere hug.

"Welcome to Encounters," she said warmly. "Let's get you all kitted out. Follow me," she initiated, before turning on her heel and walking back through the archway from where she had emerged.

Autumn hurried after her, clutching her bag under her arm and being careful not to collide with any of the boxes that had been stacked neatly on the floor next to the archway.

"I thought there would be more people than this," Autumn stated in a matter-of-fact tone. "You know, setting up and whatnot."

"We run a well-oiled machine here, Autumn. Bar staff and our hosts arrive just thirty minutes before our guests. You'll meet Leonardo soon. He sorts most other things for me; he's an angel, nothing is ever too much trouble. I also take it upon myself to decorate as and when it's needed."

"So, if the events run themselves, why do you need an assistant?" Autumn asked, hoping she didn't sound rude or ungrateful.

"Clever girl," Celina asserted. She stopped walking and turned to face Autumn. Placing one hand on her shoulder, she lowered her voice. "I need help vetting our guests, making sure we have the right kind of people here and, once the event is in full swing..." She raised an eyebrow at Autumn. "I'll need someone, similar to myself, to interact with the guests, make sure their every whim is catered for; you'll need to leave no stone unturned. Our guests' utmost satisfaction is the key to this business," Celina explained.

She pressed on, walking them further into the depths of the building. The hallways were just as opulent as the room she'd first entered. Autumn got the impression that the building was old, and that the offices of Encounters Events were set in an long-standing mansion of some kind. Everything about it was ostentatious and elegant, from the mirrored walls of the ballroom to the hallways connecting all the rooms together. Autumn noticed that on every door they passed there was a hinged, removable panel, at roughly eye level, and beneath each panel was what looked like an antique coat hook. It took every ounce of energy Autumn had not to let her inquisitive nature take over and have a look inside one of the rooms. She imagined there would be plenty of time for getting to know the ins and outs of the business later, and that included the building itself.

Celina turned off down an adjacent corridor and Autumn followed obediently. She stopped at a large oak door. There was another shiny black panel to the right of the door, much like there had been in the car park. Celina placed her hand onto the pad and the door clicked open. Autumn thought she couldn't be any more impressed with the place, but how wrong she was. This was Celina's personal office by the looks of it – every bit as elegant and well-appointed as the rest of the building. It was tastefully decorated in what Autumn was now coming to know was Celina's favourite colour palette of creams and golds, often finished off with a touch of deepest, darkest burgundy. To one side there were built-in, open wardrobes packed with sweeping long dresses, shoes from only the finest designers and jewellery that dripped from inbuilt, jointed wooden hands that had been painted cream and arranged to look like they were offering the jewels to whoever happened to be standing in front of them. There was a full-length mirror encased in a beautifully ornate, French rococo frame that Autumn just adored. A tiny pang niggled inside of her as she remembered her own mirror, very similar to this one, that had been in the hallway of the home she had shared with Ben.

Shaking the thought away she swiftly returned her mind to the task in hand. She turned to Celina, her mouth open slightly, struggling to find right words.

"Take your pick." Celina offered casually. "Whatever you want is yours." Autumn continued to stare: she was expecting, at best, Celina to produce a nice but old dress she no longer cared for, but no, Autumn Carter had *carte blanche* over a collection of dresses that probably cost the same as she would earn in her lifetime. She looked though and overwhelmed noted the designers amongst her collection. Wang, Valentino, McQueen, Dior – the list was endless.

"Any one I like?" Autumn asked, unsure as to what the trap was here. But there was none: Celina nodded and echoed Autumn. She sat down on the crisp white sofa and crossed her legs.

"Try that one on," she insisted the second Autumn's hand touched a blood red, satin dress. Autumn pulled the dress out and held it against herself, surveying her reflection in the mirror. She could never get away with wearing this: it had a plunging neckline and low cut back. It was fitted with a mermaid-style train; it was the kind of dress you would see on the red carpet, not on Autumn Carter.

"Oh, I don't think I could pull this off," Autumn began but was stopped immediately by Celina, who had come up behind her. Peering over Autumn's shoulder at the reflection in the mirror, she reached around her from behind and smoothed at the luxurious fabric of the dress.

"I think this one is perfect," she said finally, her eyes never leaving Autumn's reflection. "Now just for shoes and some jewellery."

"I'll need a little bit of time to put some makeup on," Autumn confessed apologetically.

"You'll do no such thing. Martin will see to you before you get changed."

Autumn glanced at Celina. Who the hell was Martin? Celina walked over and pressed a button on her desk. The voice from the strange mini art gallery waiting area crackled into the room.

"Yes, Mrs Thorne?" it said.

"Can you send through Martin please. Have him hurry," she said, glancing at her watch. "I don't want to run behind schedule."

A few moments later there was a knock at the door. Celina opened it and greeted the man with hugs and kisses. Autumn could tell they were old friends.

"Martin!" she exclaimed. It reminded Autumn of how she herself greeted David. "Here she is. I'm thinking vampy, smoky and sexy. Wouldn't you agree?"

Autumn felt slightly uncomfortable now as a perfect stranger plus a woman she barely knew looked her up and down. Martin took a strand of her hair and twirled it around in his fingers.

"Teamed with a loose up do?" he suggested, dropping the hair and returning his measured gaze to the rest of Autumn.

"Perfect," Celina agreed. "I'll leave you to it, don't be longer than an hour. She still needs to be shown the ropes." With that Celina walked over to the wardrobe and begin pawing through the dresses herself, occasionally asking Autumn what she thought. Autumn was of no use: each and every dress Celina pulled out was utterly gorgeous. Autumn couldn't see how Celina would look anything less than perfection. Martin was a laugh a minute, a charmingly witty man with a killer sense of humour. He was a makeup artist to the stars and didn't mind telling you about it. He dropped names left, right and centre and, even though celebrity culture wasn't exactly

Autumn's mastermind topic of choice she was still suitably awestruck as the makeup artist reeled off A-lister after A-lister.

"So how come you're lowering your standards with me?" Autumn asked him self-deprecatingly. Celina rolled her eyes in the background. She wasn't one for false modesty.

"Don't be ridiculous," she reprimanded Autumn. "Martin is a friend and he'll do anyone's hair and makeup. Providing the money is right, of course." Martin took on a look of mock offence.

"Please," he exclaimed in a super-theatrical voice. "I only ever work with the best, and actually I'll have you know, I've worked with a lot of girls like you," he said, stopping short when Celina gave him a chastising look.

He finished Autumn's smoky eye makeup with a melodramatic flick of his wrist and ran his fingers through the loose ends of her blonde hair. Autumn grinned, she was actually having the best time. She hadn't been fussed over like this in her entire life. She was being treated like a rock star and as if Celina had read her mind she was handed a glass of something sparkling. She took a sip, and the crisp tawny liquid was both refreshing and invigorating.

"Dom Perignon, vintage." Celina emphasised the last word, purposefully studying her new employee's reaction. Autumn put on an expression of what she hoped conveyed both knowledge and gratitude.

The hour went by in a blur. Autumn had another glass of champagne whilst Martin finished arranging her hair in a beautiful, romantic up do. Autumn stared at herself in the mirror: even she had to admit it, Martin had done an incredible job, and she almost looked like a different person. Her hair and makeup was flawless – Celina's instructions had been followed precisely. Autumn had had her reservations at the beginning; she wasn't one for overly heavy makeup. She couldn't believe her reflection: she looked, dare she say it, sexy. Celina spun the chair round and looked at her, she held her hands out and helped Autumn to her feet.

"Thank you, Martin, she looks wonderful."

Martin agreed wholeheartedly and gave both women a very Hollywood double kiss, one on each cheek, before heading for the door. Celina opened it for him and as he left, promised that his fee would be paid immediately. She closed the door and turned around to Autumn, beaming and clapping her hands slowly.

"You look so good, positively gorgeous," she murmured. Autumn radiated a beautiful confidence that as of yet, Celina hadn't witnessed. "Right, before we get you dressed I need to know if you're planning on staying with us."

Autumn couldn't think of anything else she'd rather be doing with her time and nodded enthusiastically.

"I think I'm going to love it here," she said thankfully.

Celina walked to her desk and pulled out a piece of paper and handed it to Autumn. "You have a three-month trial here, starting today. We pay a lump sum at the end of that period regardless of if you choose to stay or leave. Any commission you make will be paid the week after the event. Does that sound good? If you need time to look over the contract, that's fine. However, I'm eager to know if you're committed or not now."

She rested a hand in a caring way on Autumn's shoulder. Autumn didn't need asking twice. When she would receive the pay was a bit of a bummer, but she could stay with her parents. She'd be there over Christmas anyway and would get paid before the new year, plus she'd earn six months' worth of money in terms of her previous job. Then she'd be able to move out and move on. Plus, she could earn commission.

Probably by selling tickets to the events. She grabbed the pen from Celina and scribbled her signature on the bottom of the page.

"Right then," Celina smiled and placed the newly signed contract safely in her desk drawer, "let's get you dressed."

She took Autumn's hand and led her back to the open wardrobe, carefully taking the red dress off the hanger and handing it to Autumn. Autumn looked around. She hadn't noticed a changing area before but surely in a place like this there must be one, perhaps behind another hidden door. There wasn't: she turned back towards Celina, a question in her look.

"Don't be shy," Celina instructed. "You can change here."

Autumn stood there, a little shocked: she barely knew this woman and now she was expected to strip in front of her. Celina sat down on the white sofa, her eyes remained fixed on Autumn as she did so. Autumn shifted her weight from one foot to the other, unsure of whether to obey or not.

"Go on," Celina encouraged. "I don't mind at all."

Autumn laid the dress over the back of Celina's office chair and began tugging at the waistband of her jeans. She slipped them down past her thighs, over her knees and stepped out of them. Celina's eyes lingered on Autumn and she shifted in her seat, her delicate hands resting in her lap. Next Autumn unzipped her hoodie and shrugged it off, letting it fall down next to her discarded jeans. She stood there, in her black pants and white vest top. Neither woman said anything. Autumn wasn't wearing anything underneath the vest top, this much was obvious. Her nipples were erect, pressing hard against the fabric. Celina stared at the young woman's chest; her face was deadpan, giving nothing away. Autumn grabbed the ball gown and stepped into it, pulling it up over herself in a quick motion. She pulled it up and over her ample bosom. Once she was certain the dress was secure and wouldn't slip down, she began to remove the vest she still wore. She shimmied underneath the dress, removing her top in a move that nearly all teenage girls master in the PE changing rooms at school. She then slipped her arms through the capped chiffon sleeves and did the small zip up at the bottom of her back. She stared at her reflection in the full-length mirror before her. She positively dazzled, the dress fitted surprisingly well; almost as if it had been made with her in mind. It was the tiniest bit on the snug side. Autumn's eyes focused on her crotch: the pants she had chosen were not the skimpiest and the lace pattern was more than visible through the delicate satin fabric of the dress. She smoothed at it with her hands trying to improve the appearance but it was no good. She'd just have to manage with a visible pant line all evening. With any luck the lights would be dim enough so that no one would notice.

Celina's hands were on her before she had time to turn around.

"Here, let me help," she said in an almost sterile fashion.

Celina hitched the dress up to Autumn's waist in one swift motion. Autumn could do little but watch what was happening in the reflection of the ornate mirror. Once the dress was over her waist Celina knelt down and hooked her fingers underneath the waistband of Autumn's briefs and pulled them down. She was naked from the midriff down now and felt vulnerable, exposed but also extremely alive. Autumn watched in the mirror as her new boss re-dressed her. Celina bit her lip and pulled her hands away. She seemed to be fighting the urge to take this further. She stood up, now face to face with Autumn. Celina gave her a self-assured smile and turned towards the neatly organised shoe racks.

"Now which pair would look best?" She phrased the question to no one in particular, and after a quick look at her extraordinary collection she picked out a pair of gold strappy Louboutins and handed them to Autumn.

Autumn stared at her. Had that all been in her imagination, was Celina just super body confident and therefore thought everyone else was the same? Or had there been an air of flirtation there?

"These should fit," she said commandingly.

Her words broke Autumn's train of thought. She took the shoes and slipped them on: they were perfect, the shoes could never have been worn before. They looked, and felt, brand new. She experienced an odd sensation as she surveyed her final appearance. What on earth had just happened? Celina had, well, acted inappropriately. Autumn didn't know what to think, she hadn't stopped her, she'd just stood there and let it happen. In fact, the more she thought about it maybe she'd encouraged it to happen. Making a big deal of her VPL had only served to entice Celina. Autumn could feel some kind of chemistry between the two of them, as she had done from the moment she'd met the olive-skinned beauty. Never, though, had she thought that that chemistry might be a sexual one.

CHAPTER 18

AUTUMN AND CELINA WALKED BRISKLY BACK DOWN to the ballroom, the sound of their heels deadened by the sumptuous carpet that lay underfoot. Celina had opted for a backless little black dress; it hugged her curves and left little to the imagination. Underneath she wore no underwear. Autumn knew this because Celina had chosen to brazenly change right in front of her. Autumn had averted her eyes but couldn't help stealing glances through the mirror. Social nakedness seemed to be normal for Celina. She had continued to chat to Autumn as if she'd been doing nothing more than filing her nails. Autumn could tell that his woman was a force to be reckoned with: she seemed to be confident in every single aspect of life, business-wise, socially and sexually. Her makeup had been redone and her hair twisted into an elegant chignon, secured with a sparkling diamond clip.

They entered the grand ballroom. The change in the room was palpable. The compact bar in the corner was now staffed with two barmen. They looked so similar they could have been twins, and they were dressed smartly in white shirts, black trousers and bow ties with burgundy braces. Either side of the bar stood a pair of waitresses. They wore the same clothes as the men but slightly more tailored, giving the look an altogether more feminine feel. The waitresses carried an ornate silver tray each. The trays looked to be as old as the building itself – *'Perhaps an original feature?'* Autumn thought to herself when she noticed the tarnished edges. Atop each tray were glasses of champagne and neatly arranged, elegant looking canapés. Each drink was served in a fine-cut crystal champagne saucer. The women stood, stock still, staring forward, as did the barmen. None of them looked at either of the two women as they strode past.

A small man with a microphone headset on dashed over to them. His face was red and he was dressed very casually for the event. Autumn scowled at him internally: did he not know what tonight was? How important the evening would be? What the dress code was? She looked at Celina, sure that she would reprimand him for his shoddy appearance. She did not, instead the two engaged in an urgent-sounding but hushed conversation. Autumn couldn't make out what they were saying but understood from the pair's body language that whatever was going on, couldn't be good. Celina broke away from the man as Autumn approached.

"Everything alright?" Autumn asked, desperate to be part of the exclusivity that Celina seemed to have with everyone but herself.

"All fine," Celina said curtly. "That's Leonardo," she nodded as a small, friendly looking man wearing a grey cap gave her a wink before skidding off around a corner, through an archway and out of sight. "He's, let's say, the glue that holds these events together. He never attends, merely makes sure everything is in place."

"I thought you did that?" Autumn questioned, then seeing Celina's raised eyebrows added quickly, "I mean, I just thought you did everything, that's all." Celina didn't miss a beat.

"Autumn, tonight we're expecting 106 guests, mainly singles but some couples. They will all arrive within the space of fifteen minutes. No one is permitted into the building before, or after, the allotted time. All of our guests are extremely wealthy – do you know that this event has a three-thousand-pound price tag, per person? Yes, we only entertain the very *crème de la crème* of society. They have come from all over to attend tonight's event and expect a very high level of personal service. Some of them have, well let's say, demanding tastes. My role, is, as always, to welcome guests, entertain them, make sure they feel completely at home with every element of the proceedings. I'm a constant presence reminding them that all is well."

Autumn nodded, although in her mind she did wonder if Celina appreciated that what she seemed to be saying sounded like her job consisted of making sure Daddy Warbucks had whatever caviare he liked best.

Three loud chimes interrupted them, and Autumn quickly came to realise that this must signal the start of the evening. Within a matter of minutes, people were pouring out of the lift in the corner of the ballroom. They must have been very used to the grandeur of it all because not one person stopped to admire what was in front of them. Some people headed over to the bar, mainly men whose tastes were a little harder than the champagne that was on offer. It seemed that all men of a certain position in life liked whiskey. The waiting staff seemed to effortlessly drift throughout the swelling crowd, returning to the bar only when the last glass had been taken from their tray. None of them spoke, they simply extended the tray towards whichever guest was in front of them, in an unspoken but clearly understood gesture of service.

One of the servers sidled up to Autumn. She took a glass of champagne and sipped at it. She'd never drunk from a champagne saucer before and some spilled over the side; it narrowly missed her dress, landing on the floor next to her. The waitress bent down nimbly, the tray balanced on the fingertips of her left hand and using her right wiped the spot on the floor where the champagne had spilt in one graceful and effortless motion, standing up the second her cloth left the floor. If Autumn had blinked at that precise point, she would have missed it.

"How are you enjoying it so far?" Celina asked. Autumn had to strain to hear her over the combination of music and the general hubbub of the crowd.

"It's absolutely amazing," Autumn exclaimed, raising her voice slightly to compete with the surrounding noise. Celina placed her hand on the small of Autumn's back and leaned in closer to her. Autumn could smell the older woman's perfume, a deep, musky scented fragrance that filled her nostrils.

"You haven't seen anything yet," Celina said, smiling knowingly. Autumn felt her stomach somersault at the words: what could possibly top this? She was surrounded by some of the richest, most attractive men and women that she'd ever seen in her life, dressed to the nines in outfits that before today she would never even have dreamt of wearing and to top it all off, getting paid for the pleasure. Autumn looked at Celina searchingly, hoping for some clue as to what could mean but none was offered.

'I guess I'll just have to wait and see,' she thought to herself. The first hour flew by, Autumn's belly began to rumble: in all the excitement of earlier she'd forgotten to eat. The handful of canapés she'd had really weren't enough so when a good-looking gentlemen struck up conversation with her she was pleased to find out that there would be a dinner.

"Have you seen a copy of the menu?" he asked Autumn. She said that she had not but was ravenous. He nodded in agreement, "Me too, I do hope there's something a little more exotic this time, last time there wasn't really anything to my taste."

Autumn, feeling partly responsible now she was part of the team apologised to the man and promised she would make the organisers aware of his needs. This seemed to do the trick; the man appeared to swell with importance and thanked Autumn before flagging down one of the waiting staff and grabbing a handful of the bite-sized goat's cheese tartlets. He asked Autumn what she did at the event and Autumn told him that it was her job to fulfil the needs of the guests, no matter how exotic they might be. She put special emphasis on her personal and professional relationship with Celina; by the end of it he would have been forgiven for thinking they'd been best friends and business partners for years. Autumn felt a little underhanded practically lying to her new friend, but she'd once overheard the phrase 'fake it till you make it' and that was precisely what she intended to do. The man seemed suitably impressed.

"So, you've been in this game a while then?" he asked.

Autumn took an overly long sip of champagne to prevent herself from having to give an answer but gave a small nod which seemed to satisfy him.

"Well, it's been a pleasure making your acquaintance," he said, "but I really should find a copy of that menu. I'm ravenous too, if you get what I mean." He gave Autumn a grin and walked off.

'Of course, I know what he means,' she thought to herself. *'I'm not an idiot.'* Autumn watched him descend into the crowd. It looked like something out of an old Hollywood movie: so many people, all dressed in fabulous outfits, the men in dinner jackets and bow ties and the women in all manner of stunning gowns. Autumn felt very privileged to be a part of it although wondered if every event was this easy; it wasn't exactly back-breaking work. Autumn caught sight of Celina, swan-like, gliding through the crowd, greeting as many as she

could as if they were old friends. She stopped several times to pay the women compliments or to flirt a little with the men. Autumn followed her lead and made her way out from the sidelines and into the action: it was time to ensure that all the guests were 'well catered for', as Celina had put it.

After a while Autumn found her mind wandering. She was enjoying herself but all anyone seemed to be able to talk about was how excited they were to see the menu, and after the fifth person to say this to her she decided to take matters into her own hands. The guests seemed ready for their food. She strode over to Celina and took her by the arm, excusing her from the two couples she had been talking to.

"I think it's time we let the guests decide what they're having to eat. They're getting hungry and lots of them haven't even seen the menu, plus, I don't know if you're aware, but I don't think the dining hall has even been set up," she said, a little more authoritatively than perhaps her position should have allowed. She didn't want to panic Celina but things needed to move quickly if they were going to cater for all these people.

"There's no food here Autumn. We only provide light bites in the form of canapés, plus our guests haven't come here to eat," Celina said, a look of mild amusement on her face.

"Then what have they paid for?" Autumn asked, feeling completely clueless. Celina stared at her in disbelief.

"You *did* look at our website before you called me, didn't you?" she asked, pulling Autumn away from the throngs of people and into a quieter hallway. The two women walked through the corridors talking in hushed tones as they meandered deeper into the warren like building. Autumn looked at Celina, not understanding what she was going on about. She'd been on the website, of course, but surely Celina didn't expect Autumn to sign up just so she could flick through online galleries of rich people at a ball.

"I did, but only the bits I could see without signing up," she confessed not really understanding why this was so important.

"I wrote my membership number on the back of the card I gave you, so that you could access the website. I thought that would have been obvious," Celina explained. She looked concerned now but also annoyed. She stood there with her hands on her hips looking at Autumn for an answer.

"I didn't know that," Autumn rebuffed. "Does it really matter? We've got hungry guests and we've slinked off to talk about the website."

Celina gave Autumn a pleading look. "If you had used that number Autumn, you would know what you've gotten yourself into."

Autumn was confused. What on earth was Celina talking about? She was acting really strangely. Autumn wondered if maybe Celina should have hired an assistant sooner; the stress of planning and entertaining at these events was clearly affecting her.

"Celina, let's just get these menus out, okay? It'll all be fine. I'm here to take some of the burden," Autumn offered kindly. Celina grabbed her hand.

"Look in here," she instructed.

She flipped down one of the hinged wooden panels on a nearby door. Autumn peered in. She could see what looked to be a masseuse's table in a clinical white room and nothing else. She looked at Celina, even more confused now. Celina walked to the next doorway and flipped the viewing panel down, then to the next door and the next one. Autumn walked after her, peering into each room as she went. There was a room full of giant teddies, a dingy cellar, what looked to be a plush hotel room and, could Autumn have seen the last one correctly? She did a double take – a morgue? Stainless steel benches and human sized drawers, it was an exact replica of the kind of morgues you'd see on a crime television show.

"I really don't understand; are these sets?" Autumn asked.

"In a way, yes. We cater for the wealthy, Autumn, we cater for them in a way that no other events company does. We fulfil their sexual fantasies discreetly."

The revelation hit Autumn like a tonne of bricks. She hadn't even for a moment thought that these events had anything to do with sex. No one had even mentioned the word, and as for sexual fantasies, these people were pretty messed up if a morgue and giant teddies came into that category.

"But what's the menu then?" she asked, not entirely sure if she wanted to hear the answer.

"Well, we have an entrée, the main course and the dessert. They're people, Autumn, people who want to satisfy someone else's predilections, regardless of what that is. We open the floor up to bids, much like an auction and the highest bidder gets to own whichever course they buy for the evening. The money is split between myself and the course. I take seventy percent, and their commission is thirty."

Autumn's mouth dropped to the floor.

"This is a sex slavery ring?" she asked, appalled.

"Not at all. The 'courses' apply online, and we get hundreds of applicants each year but we only pick three per event. They get a fee for their time, most of them fantasise about belonging to another person, so in a way they get to fulfil their fantasy as well as fulfilling someone else's. At the end of the night, they take their money, if they want it. They do have the option to donate it to a sexual awareness charity I'm involved with. Some people feel that taking the money amounts to prostitution while others just take the money and run. Pardon the expression. Oh, and most importantly, everyone here, and

I mean everyone, is responsible for their own sexual health. Condoms are provided and we require all guests to have a medical all-clear as well."

Autumn still couldn't quite get her head round this.

"Am I meant to be involved with that?" she asked sheepishly.

"Well, not if you don't want to. Sometimes I might join in if the mood takes me and sometimes I just liaise and make new acquaintances."

"Join in? So, if you don't win a course you just have sex with whoever you like?" she asked incredulously.

"That's pretty much the gist of it," Celina said. "The people who place the highest bids, or 'diners' as we call them, get to choose their room first and any spare are then opened up to the rest of the guests. The doors remain closed for privacy, but if an individual, couple or group don't mind sharing their experience, they leave the viewing panel open. If they're open to others joining in, they hang one of those on the hook on the door."

She pointed down the hall to a rectangular console table. Autumn walked over to the table and surveyed it. On top of the table stood a decorative silver bowl; inside were several large coloured tokens, either burgundy, white or gold. Autumn picked one out to take a closer look. It was made from wood and elegantly carved with a scene from what surely had to be the *Karma Sutra* on it. Other than that it gave nothing away. Engraved at the top of each coin was simply the word 'Encounters'.

"The burgundy one means you're open to men joining in, the white is an invitation for women only and if you hang a gold one on the door, then really anything goes: men, women and anyone in between. If there's no coin on the door, but the panel is open, you're allowed to watch. If it's shut, that means it's a firm 'keep out'," Celina explained, slightly amused at Autumn's shocked expression. It was one thing to be bombarded with information on your first day but when the information was this kind, well, Celina could quite understand why Autumn's face looked like it did. Still, she couldn't help but feel that Autumn deserved everything she got right now. She had been quite clear about Autumn doing some research on the company before she agreed to this event.

"So, what happens if the panel is closed but there's a token on the door?" she asked, hardly believing that the high society event she was at was basically a posh sex party.

"Then you take a chance. The only rule is you absolutely have to adhere to whatever fantasy you walk into. As I've said many times, our clients have specific tastes, so it's important that nothing and nobody brings them back to reality. You have to work with whatever they do or say," Celina said, with a finality that meant Autumn knew the conversation was over and it was back to work – well, this extremely weird version of work anyway.

"What if I want to try something new but I don't like it?" Autumn asked, hardly imagining that people just went along with any old thing. These people were successful, wealthy and good looking. They weren't idiots; if they weren't into something Autumn was pretty sure they'd say so and put an end to it.

"We have a safe phrase. If you want to leave for any reason, you do so by saying, 'I think that's the door, I won't be a moment,' or words to that effect. Then quietly gather yourself and leave. Not everyone engages in the sexual side; some people just come for the drinks and company. The mere idea of what could be going on in these rooms is excitement in itself." Celina turned around and began to make her way back to the party but turned to face Autumn before they disappeared back the way they came.

"Please take a few minutes to think about this. If this is too much for you, Autumn, please don't feel obligated to stay. I won't hold it against you."

Autumn stood still for a moment. She had two choices: she could slip out down the nearby fire escape and this would be a hilarious anecdote she'd be telling for years to come; or she could follow Celina and see where the night took her. As Celina disappeared around the corner Autumn thought about her family and friends. What would they say if they found out? But how could they? None of them were likely to spend three thousand on a sex party and she might actually learn something, plus she didn't have to join in after all. Maybe this was just the thing she needed, somewhere where she could let loose. She wasn't obligated and no one was forcing her into anything.

Her stomach rumbled noisily: she was so hungry now. But what should she do? If only there was a sign. At that precise moment, a loud gong sounded in the ballroom, a hush fell over the crowd and Celina's voice rang out.

"Ladies and gentlemen, please charge your glasses. Dinner is about to be served."

There was an almighty roar from the crowd. It seemed that they were all rather hungry too. Curiosity got the better of Autumn. She wanted, if nothing else, just to see what all the fuss was about, at least that's what she told herself as she re-entered the ballroom, careful not to bump into the tall table laden with champagne ready for the winning bidders and their 'course'.

Autumn turned to retrace her steps back to the ballroom, but after a few wrong turns she was a bit lost. She noticed a plush deep red curtain had been drawn. She could hear commotion the other side and assumed that somehow, she'd found her way back. Autumn pushed the heavy curtain to one side and struggled through. She blinked, unable to see anything but a brilliant white light. Putting a hand to her eyes she squinted.

'What the –' she thought to herself. The crowd was facing her, and as she looked around, her eyes adjusted to the new brightness. It was a spotlight on her: she was on the stage.

"Five thousand," a voice bellowed from the crowd.

Autumn, now panicking, looked around frantically for Celina but she couldn't see her. There was an unusual pause in proceedings, the crowd murmuring and whispering their disapproval. Where was Celina to rally the event along? Autumn felt a hand on her shoulder and she was pulled back through the curtain.

"What are you doing?" Leonardo hissed. He was still in his casual clothes; in this crowd he'd stand out like a sore thumb.

"I could ask you the same thing," Autumn admonished. She smoothed down her dress and stood to her full height in an attempt at imitating Celina's authoritative stance. "You're not meant to be here," she finished.

"I'm always here," Leonardo explained without hesitation, throwing his hands up in a wild gesture. "I'm just not a part of this." He pointed at the baying crowd through the curtain. "Our first course hasn't shown up, and I was on my way to forewarn Celina. My headset doesn't work from down in reception, and I heard her start as I came up and realised I was too late. Then I heard someone start the bidding. I thought somehow the first course had made their way up here by themselves. I couldn't believe it when I saw it was you! It's going to be really hard to convince them to forgo the first course now," he sighed. "Especially when they think you're on offer," he said in an appreciative tone, eyeing Autumn up as he did so.

Autumn felt strangely proud of herself. Leonardo obviously thought she looked good, and from the reaction of the crowd so did they. She grabbed one of the champagne saucers and, throwing her head back downed it in one. She'd made up her mind. She was doing it.

"See you on the other side," she said to Leonard confidently as she strode back through the curtain, another champagne glass in her hand. As she stepped out on stage, she caught a glimpse of Celina, urgently talking on her headset, the auction's microphone held away from her mouth. She knew Leonardo was telling her that she was in. An excitement buzzed throughout her now, her heart raced as she strained her eyes and looked out towards the crowd, wondering who would bid on her, and for how much.

"We apologise for that interruption ladies and gentlemen, we can now continue with dinner as planned." Celina's voice floated effortlessly through the air. "I believe we have a starting bid of five thousand? Any increase on five thousand?"

There was a momentary pause. Autumn thought that perhaps no one else was going to bid on her. The crowd exploded into life, cries of thousands echoed in Autumn's head, the amount increased quickly from five to fifteen thousand.

"Turn around!" someone yelled at her from the floor. She did so to appreciative cheers; the crowd loved her and she happily lapped up every second of it.

"Twenty-five thousand," a strong resolute voice echoed through the crowd. It eased the frenzied crowd. A calmness fell over them as they looked to see who had made the extravagant offer.

"Any improvements on twenty-five thousand pounds?" Celina's voice drifted over the speakers. There was no reply. "Going once, going twice, sold to the gentleman in navy."

She gestured to some distant point in the crowd, and Autumn peered excitedly but couldn't see her bidder. The crowd began to swell then ebb as guests moved to let the mysterious man through, the throng parted and Autumn's fate for the night was revealed.

She was impressed. He was taller and broader than most of the men there and younger than most of them too. He had neat blonde hair and cut a fine figure in the obviously expensive suit that he wore. The man reached the front of the platform and climbed up the steps at the side and joined Autumn centre stage. He took her hand and turned around, leading her through the curtain to the fantasy rooms.

He didn't say anything as they walked. Autumn was unsure how to react. Was she supposed to be friendly, sultry or quiet and submissive? She didn't know so thought it best to just follow his lead. They paused at the bowl of tokens: he peered inside then decided against it and pressed on. Autumn breathed a sigh of relief. She was feeling adventurous but not *that* adventurous.

They stopped about two-thirds of the way down the hall. The handsome stranger hesitated between two doors, peering into each one in turn. He made his mind up and chose the door to the left, number seventeen, and opened it confidently. Autumn stepped in. The room was dimly lit and it was much cooler in there than it had been in the hallway. From what she could see it was the antithesis of the rest of the place: the grandeur and opulence had been replaced with stark concrete walls; a fairly large but old wooden table stood in the centre of the room with matching wooden chairs surrounding it. Autumn counted six in all. At the back of the industrial-feeling room next to a metal cupboard built into the wall was a set of shelves with various objects on them. The door shut firmly behind them. Autumn turned and saw that the man had dropped the door's wooden panel and knew instinctively that no matter what happened, should they wish to, anyone would be able to see. He pressed his hand to a familiar looking, shiny black panel by the door; it lit up and he tapped on the screen lightly. The blue light emitted from the panel didn't make the room look any better, in fact in all honesty it looked even more industrial than it had before. Autumn could now make out a set of coat hooks varying in height screwed to one of the walls and faint multi-coloured splashes on the table of what looked to be candle wax.

"Drinks?" he asked. Autumn nodded, glad that the silence had finally been broken. He tapped the panel lightly once more and the blue light faded to nothingness. Autumn felt a shiver run over her; other than the satin dress she had nothing else to keep her warm.

"Take your clothes off," he instructed calmly.

Autumn was taken aback by the formality of it all. He was business-like about the whole affair, so hesitantly, she unzipped the dress and let it fall down to her feet, surprising herself with just how okay she was with all of this. Here she was, totally naked, about to engage in whatever this man, whom she had never met before, wanted. Rather than feeling apprehension, she felt excited, and she could feel herself getting turned on at the thought of what could lie ahead.

A bell chimed in the far corner. Autumn turned her head to where the noise had come from: the metal doors on the far wall were a dumb waiter. The man walked over and opened it. Inside were a bottle of whiskey, a bottle of champagne, an ice bucket, two burning candles and the appropriate glasses, all served on one of those beautiful antique silver trays. He poured Autumn a large measure of whiskey and dropped several cubes of ice in it. He strode over to her, making the distance in just three strides. She held her hand out to accept the drink, but he batted it away. She took a step backwards, and she was up against the wall now. The man leaned over her, and his hand above her rested against the cold concrete wall. Autumn shuddered as her skin made contact with the cold surface. The man was leaning in closer now: Autumn could smell his aftershave, it engulfed her senses, it was a rich, sensual smell. He brought the whiskey glass up to her lips and allowed her to drink. She did so, never breaking eye contact.

"Say thank you," he instructed, taking a sip of the whiskey himself.

"Thank you," Autumn repeated, glancing down now and shifting her weight from side to side. He took another sip of the cold, burning liquor and let an ice cube wash into his mouth. He bent his head towards her breasts and took one in his mouth. Autumn jumped when his ice-cold lips connected with the sensitive skin of her nipple. He sucked on it gently, using his tongue to push the ice cube firmly against the hardening pink bud. Autumn closed her eyes, shutting out any other stimulus: she was committed to enjoying this experience.

"What should I call you?" she asked breathlessly, pushing her chest outwards, encouraging him to suck harder. He pulled away and looked at her. His eyes bore into her. He drained the rest of the glass then reached out a hand and held her face, squeezing her cheeks slightly. Intuitively she parted her lips; he leaned forward and spat a mouthful of whiskey into her mouth, releasing her face as he did so.

"Sir," was all he said. He offered nothing else. Instead, he took her hands and held them over her head. She felt one of the coat hooks she'd seen earlier and grabbed it. He turned around and pulled a box from one of the shelves and tipped it out onto the table. Autumn couldn't quite make out what the objects were but she bristled with excitement anyway.

He came back over to her, a long dark rope in his hands. He reached up and secured it around her wrists, making sure to incorporate the hook as well. She pulled at the restraint, testing the strength of the ropes. With one tug, she knew that this was certainly not the first time he'd done this. She was well and truly restrained. She struggled against the ropes but he stopped her by placing a hand firmly over hers. He gave her a look that effortlessly instructed her to desist, and she became still, eagerly awaiting what was in store. The man surveyed her, appreciating her naked form. Autumn could see a bulge in his trousers. She reached a foot out to explore further. He once again batted her away.

"*I* do the touching," he said, returning to the table and picking up an object Autumn wasn't familiar with. She knew it was a sex toy, that much was clear. It was shaped like a bowling pin, the lower part black and the head of it a tarnished chrome colour. He knelt down and parted her legs a little too wide for comfort; her arms stretched with the movement and she let out a little whimper. He looked at her and silenced her with his hand.

"You do not come until I say so," he said, looking up at her.

Autumn nodded. He flicked a switch on the toy. It buzzed into life, deep rumbling vibrations that Autumn could feel even before it made contact with her. He rubbed the head of the toy up the insides of her legs, pausing every now and then to take a step back and admire his handiwork. Her being aroused was all that he needed; he set back to work, slowly increasing the intensity of the vibrations. He never once touched her most sensitive area, he continued to skip over that part whenever he reached the top. Autumn was desperate now for some sort of release: every time he came near her she tried to reposition her body in order to get as low as possible, hoping that this time he'd allow her even the briefest amount of delicious contact. He did not. Instead, he switched the toy off and set it down by her feet. She still wore the gold strappy heels given to her by Celina. Taking one finger he lightly pressed it against her clitoris. The anticipation that had built within her threatened to burst out in the form of a spectacular climax. She shuddered as he pressed harder, barely moving his finger at all. She couldn't believe that this simple action had brought her so close to the edge. He pressed harder now, his finger sliding from side to side as she became wetter and wetter under his attentions. He felt her jerk under his touch and removed his hand.

"You will not come until I say so," he repeated commandingly.

"Yes, sir." Autumn responded, frustration mounting within her at being denied her release. She squirmed against her restraints; they were beginning to dig in now. Noting her discomfort he stood up. She was sure he was going to tighten them but instead he released her and commanded her over to the table. She went over to it and perched on the edge. He opened her legs wide and buried his head in her wetness. She leant back allowing him easier access. He licked and sucked insatiably, taking it in turns to focus his attentions firstly on her clitoris and then the soft lips enveloping her throbbing centre. He delved his tongue inside her with an expertise that made her scream with delight. She leaned backwards and arched her back, writhing in pleasure as he skilfully probed her inner folds with his skilful tongue.

"Please can I come?" she begged, fearing that she would anyway with or without his permission. He pulled away and looked at her, lazily inserting his fingers inside her and stroking the heart of her pleasure. After a moment of watching her struggle he nodded.

"Come for me now," he ordered, moving his fingers faster, pressing his thumb against her swollen pearl and moving it in a delectable circular motion. Autumn threw her head back and cried out, a deep husky cry she didn't recognise as her own. The following instant she was racked with waves of exquisite pleasure as he continued to strum, elongating her gratification. She felt her wetness splash on her feet, the result of an astoundingly dominant orgasm. She didn't care; the sensations washing over her were unlike anything she'd ever felt before, powerful and all-consuming. The stranger never took his eyes off her. He watched intently as the orgasm broke over her and devoured the sight in exultation.

Once she had stopped shaking, he stood up, undoing his belt as he did so. He undressed and Autumn watched. He had a well-built, toned body that looked more athletic than muscular. She watched as he folded his clothes and arranged them neatly on one of the wooden chairs, coiling his belt up into a near circle and placing it on top. He stood there completely naked now. Autumn let her eyes trail down his body; his thick, throbbing manhood bulged invitingly. Autumn wanted it inside her more than anything: to feel that driving into her wetness was all she could focus on. Learning her lesson, she did not reach out for it, and instead, let him bring it to her. He did so, watching her intent eyes greedily taking in the sight in front of her. She was still resting against the edge of the table. As the orgasm subsided the cold began to creep in; she shivered slightly, her flushed pink skin showing the tell-tale signs in the form of goose bumps. The man pulled her closer towards him. His skin was warm to the touch, and she pressed herself into him as he pushed his leg between her thighs. She mounted it and gyrated slowly back and forth, enjoying this new form of stimulation. He cupped the soft mounds of her breasts, squeezing them gently to start with then increasing the pressure gradually. She winced when he pinched her nipples; he squeezed firmly and pulled them away from her body, all the while watching her intently.

"Don't pull away from me," he ordered, repeating the action for a second and third time and watching her struggle with the fine line that was drawn between pleasure and pain.

His cock pulsed, its veins bulging and eager for its own release. In one swift and effortless motion, he picked her up and held her at waist height. She spread her legs and instinctively wrapped them around his torso. Their faces were barely an inch apart and Autumn could taste the whiskey on his breath. He kissed her, a hard, forceful kiss, which she loyally returned. As their mouths connected and tongues probed one another's Autumn felt an incredible sense of empowerment. She had made this happen – it was she who was controlling him. He thought he was in charge, but in reality it was her. Autumn realised that all of his pleasure, his passion and his desire, relied solely on her. She was fulfilling his fantasy.

"Please, sir," she begged, "I want to come for you."

This was all the encouragement he needed. He grabbed a foil packet from a metal bowl on the shelf with one hand. The other held onto her tightly. He opened it expertly and unrolled the protection down the entire length of his solid shaft. Autumn was impressed. The man effortlessly lowered her down onto him. She gasped as the head of his penis stretched her to capacity, driving its way inside her. Autumn could feel her body resisting but he surged on relentlessly. He eased her down further, closing his eyes in ecstasy as her tightness wrapped around him. She slid down the length of his cock easily; she was still soaking wet from the powerful orgasm he had inflicted on her earlier. His strong arms lifted her up and down in time with his own thrusts. Each time he delved back inside her she gasped, unbelieving that the feeling could be so intense. She felt him tense and thought that it wouldn't be long before he was enjoying his own sexual emancipation. Instead he lifted her off completely and set her back down. His cock glistened with her juices.

"Kneel down," he instructed, and she did so without question, knowing exactly what he wanted of her. She knelt down on the threadbare, burgundy patterned rug and looked up at him. He placed his hand around her face again, and once again she found herself opening her mouth under his physical instruction. His other hand was around the base of his member; he bought it forward to her, instructing her to open wider, which she did. He probed the inside of her lips with the head of his erection, Autumn strained to accommodate his huge girth: he watched her struggle with satisfaction.

"Wider," he said. She tried but was helpless to comply with his instruction. In vain she tried to offer an alternative: she roamed her tongue over his protuberant glans and sucked hungrily on the tip. He gave her a disapproving look. "If you don't do it, you'll have to be punished," he said with an indifference that thrilled Autumn. A rolling sensation of delight washed over her as she felt her essence throb with anticipation.

The man pulled himself free from Autumn; dissatisfied, he stepped away from her and pulled her to her feet. Turning her around he bent her over the table. He positioned himself at the entrance to her wanting sex, pushing himself in. She inhaled a lungful of the cold air; he felt, if it were possible, even bigger than he had done before. He eased himself inside her, pausing every now and then to enjoy the view he had. He loved seeing her stretched so tightly around his member.

He glistened as he pulled himself out of her, admiring the way her folds welcomed him each time he pushed himself back in. She arched her back but he pushed her down. Gripping her waist with both hands as he quickened his pace, he slammed into her, forcing her to bang against the table with each frantic thrust. He reached over and grabbed something from the table, Autumn didn't see what but if what he'd done to her earlier was anything to go by she was definitely going to like it.

"Close your eyes and open your mouth," he instructed she obeyed instantly. She had come to revel in the dynamic of this relationship; never before had she been dominated. It somehow felt incredibly liberating to be at the mercy of someone else. He pushed the object inside her mouth, smaller than his cock but big enough to make her gag when he pushed it in further; it felt firm and smooth against her tongue. He pulled it out, a trail of saliva still linking her and the toy. The man put his hand on the small of her back and eased her further down, forcing her backside higher in the air. He pressed the tip of the toy between her buttocks, she impulsively shied away but his hold on her was firm and she remained put. He pressed the tip against her anus and held it there for a moment, Autumn assumed he was gauging her reaction. Celina's safe phrase echoed in her mind. Should she say someone was at the door and she'd be back in a minute?

No, she decided, this experience had been sexually redemptive. Even though she didn't know the man inside her, she trusted completely that his only goal was her pleasure. She pushed back a little, feeling the tip of the toy begin to penetrate her. She paused: she had never done this before and it was certainly proving to be more of a challenge than she had assumed. He rocked his hips back and forth, causing her innermost warmth to convulse around the stranger's length.

He pushed the toy a little further inside her. She steadied her breathing; now this really was right on the line between pleasure and pain. One moment she wanted it all, she wanted him to force the damn thing inside her, and the next she wanted out. He felt her hesitate and relented for a moment, allowing her body to become accustomed to the new sensations. She took a deep breath and began easing herself backwards again. She felt an enormous stretching sensation: for an instant she thought she was sure she was going to tear, but almost as suddenly as it had started it gave way to intense pleasure as the bulbous body of the toy tapered off into a narrow neck and the last inch slid inside her easily. It was held firmly in place by her clenching muscles and pressed on every single pleasure point inside her. The plug combined with his mammoth organ pushed her to the very limits of sexual hedonism. She bucked wildly; the man struggled to hold her in place but quickly regained control. He had both hands on her hips now, roughly plunging himself into her over and over again, desperately chasing his own satisfying end.

"Please can I come, sir?" she cried loudly, as he hunched himself over her.

"Yes," he grunted.

She could feel his sweat dripping onto the small of her back, his grip tightened and his movements became more erratic. Each time he pushed himself inside her the plug seemed to swell, it intruded further with each thrust of the man's hips. He grabbed a vibrator from the table. It was a long thin, black toy with no stand out features. He deftly switched it on with one hand. The motor rumbled into life and he held it underneath her pressing it against her swollen nub thus allowing the vibrations to run wildly over both of them. It slipped around, making Autumn gasp with delight each time it came into contact with her. She was so close now;

she pushed back against him, he took the hint and ploughed into her harder than ever. The orgasm surged through her like a dam breaking, it seized hold of her and took control. She fell against the table and let out a long guttural cry of satisfaction. This was all he needed, her immense pleasure pushed him over the edge. She felt his hands constrict tightly around her waist as he convulsed, the produce of his lust spurted out of him violently; as the orgasm surged through him he jerked a couple of times, before coming to a halt. His breathing was heavy, he took in deep lungfuls of breath after breath as he slowly came back to reality.

He pulled out of her and gave her a playful slap on the backside. Autumn laughed awkwardly; she was completely unsure what to do next. Celina had told her the ins and outs of what happened during and how to get out of it if you decided it wasn't for you, but not what to do afterwards. Autumn decided that the best course of action was to just do what any normal woman would do in her situation, get dressed, thank the man and leave. She picked up the red dress from the floor and inspected it in the dim light. It appeared to be fine, a little crumpled but not damaged in anyway. She stepped into it and pulled it up, she slipped her arms through the capped sleeves and was surprised to find that the man had his hands on the zip and was doing it up for her.

"I'm a gentleman really," he said cheekily. "Thanks for making my first time so enjoyable."

Autumn giggled and felt instantly at ease with him. She liked the fact that they'd lost their Encounters virginity together. What they had just done was against the social norm, but somehow it had felt so natural. He was fully dressed now, except for his cuff-links, which he decided to put in his pocket. He rolled up his sleeves and gave Autumn a business-like kiss on the cheek before opening the door. The light in the hallway seemed so bright compared to that in the fantasy room they had occupied for – Autumn she looked at her watch: it had lasted two hours. She was shocked, barely able to believe that much time has passed. She looked up from her watch. The man she'd just spent most of the evening with had rounded the corner and was now completely out of sight.

'*Gentleman indeed,*' she mused as she made her own way back, unaccompanied, to the ballroom.

CHAPTER 19

AUTUMN AWOKE THE FOLLOWING MORNING feeling like a new woman. The party the previous evening had been an eye-opener. She had no idea places like that even existed. Afterwards she and Celina had discussed the night's events; both women had been surprised at how the evening had developed. Celina had been worried that Autumn would be filled with regret, but had been pleasantly surprised when Autumn had been so pleased with the proceedings. Autumn revelled in the fact that she was now a fully-fledged member of the team, and she would be joining Martin, Leonardo and Celina, plus the six waiting staff that she now knew were called Liz, Jen, Kate, Rhiannon, Matthew and Robert. She would have to make a concerted effort to remember their names, since the parties only took place once every month and even then, she would really only be working with Celina and Leonardo. Autumn dozed; her head was dully thudding.

'Too much champagne and not enough food,' she thought to herself, remembering the confusion over menus and smiling. How could it be that a mere matter of hours ago she was a sweet, naïve young lady? The encounter with her blond mystery man had opened her up to a whole new world.

There was a knock at the door; the brass doorknocker echoed loudly through the halls. Autumn's bedroom door was ajar, meaning she heard the knock much louder than she wanted to. She heard her mother bustle to answer it and the familiar sound of her name being shrilly called up the stairs.

"Autumn! It's for you," Sarah shouted, elongating the last word for added emphasis. Autumn grabbed her watch from her bedside table and looked at the time. She'd had barely six hours of sleep, nowhere near enough for someone like her. She dragged herself out of bed, pulled on a black vest top and a pair of faded blue jeans and an elastic band for her bedhead mane. She padded down the stairs tying her blonde hair up in a high ponytail as she went and marvelling at how long it had gotten, seemingly overnight. She entered the living room and ground to a halt. It was the policeman investigating the case against her. In all the excitement, she had totally forgotten about Rosa, lying in a hospital bed somewhere, battered and bruised from a fall that she knew was not her fault.

"Hi Officer…" she paused, struggling to recall his name.

"Sentori," he finished for her. "Officer Jake Sentori." Autumn nodded and sat down hesitantly, perching on the end of the sofa anxiously. And fiddled with her hair.

"Are you going to arrest me?" Autumn asked a little naïvely. She couldn't think of any other reason why he'd be here. She'd told him everything that had happened, the truth. What more was there? Rosa had either come around and pointed the finger squarely in her direction, or – Autumn gulped – had Rosa died? Was he here to tell her that the injuries she'd sustained were too great and she'd passed away? In which case, she'd definitely be under arrest. After all, everyone else in the office swore blind that Rosa had been pushed. Autumn began to perspire and her breathing became shallow as her heartbeat quickened.

"No, you're not under arrest," Officer Sentori smiled and Autumn relaxed a little.

"Is she alright then?" Autumn asked. Even though Rosa had betrayed her and there was absolutely no going back for their friendship, she didn't want her dead or even hurt, really. Autumn just never wanted to see her again.

"Rosa was sedated whilst they ran some tests, everything came back normal thankfully. They brought her round yesterday evening at which point we spoke to her and she told us what had happened. Her version of events correlates with your own. She isn't pressing charges. I'm just here to tell you the good news."

Autumn breathed a huge sigh of relief. She was so pleased that this mess could be put behind her now and that Rosa had told the truth. *'It was the least she could do after what she did to me,'* Autumn thought angrily; now that she knew Rosa was okay it was fine to resume her normal disdain towards her. Officer Sentori got up and smoothed his trousers down. Once again Autumn found herself admiring his fine form.

"Would you like a coffee?" she asked casually, scraping her long hair back into a high ponytail and securing it with an elastic band from around her wrist.

"I shouldn't really," he said. It was never a good idea to get involved with the general public. Jake liked to keep things strictly professional when he was out on the beat. He didn't know why but it seemed that he was always rejecting the advances of women he spoke to, regardless of age or background. In the last month he'd rebuffed an old woman who thought she'd had one of her antique figurines stolen – turned out she'd put it in the back of her wardrobe for safe keeping and forgotten all about it – and a middle-aged housewife who, at the time of propositioning him, had been in handcuffs after being arrested on suspicion of murdering her wealthy husband. Now it was Autumn's turn to receive a flat no. Granted, she was more his age, and he couldn't deny she was very pretty, maybe under different circumstances they could have gone out, but when you got down to the bones of it, she was pretty messed up. To him, Autumn was probably looking for a rebound from the ex-boyfriend who had cheated on her with her best friend, who had then mysteriously fallen down the stairs in her company. No, Jake Sentori decided that he'd treat the young woman in front of him just like any other person he met whilst he was working. Plus she seemed to be a bit of a party girl. She'd been drinking the last time they had met and from the looks of it now she was hung over.

He bid her a stiff farewell. She leant in to give him a kiss on the cheek but stopped herself before she embarrassed herself further. It didn't go unnoticed; Jake was already leaning back in an attempt to politely avoid any kind of contact with her.

"Bye then and thank you," Autumn bitterly called after him as he went. Rejection wasn't a feeling she cared all that much for.

'His loss,' she thought as she watched him climb into his police car and drive off. She turned around to see both of her parents standing in the hallway with their eyes set on their daughter, eager to find out what had happened.

"It's fine," Autumn snapped exasperatedly before her parents had even said anything. "I'm off the hook. I'm going back to bed." She stomped off past her parents and upstairs, making sure she shut the bedroom door firmly behind her. Back downstairs her mum rolled her eyes.

"Teenagers," she said sarcastically.

"If only that was a valid excuse nowadays," Richard said dejectedly. "I don't know what's gotten into her recently. You don't know if you're coming or going with her. One moment she's fine, then the next she's, well, like a stroppy teenager." He sighed.

"She's going through a hard time," Sarah said, not wanting to make excuses for her daughter but doing so anyway.

"*Was*," Richard corrected his wife. "She was going through a hard time, but she's moved on now, and she's got a new job. She hasn't mentioned Ben in ages and wouldn't have mentioned Rosa had all this business not happened. She's on thin ice, Sarah; it's our home and our rules. There's really no reason for her to stay here much longer. I don't know about you but I'm getting a little sick of playing butler to her."

Sarah nodded. She loved her daughter dearly but Autumn had regressed back into child mode whilst she'd been at home. Her parents did everything, including her washing and ironing. She came and went as she pleased, rolling in at all hours and never telling them exactly what she was doing. She'd developed an attitude that didn't sit well with either of her parents, who resented the fact that she could go from sweet to snappy in all of five seconds.

"You're right Richard," Sarah agreed. "I'll have a word with her. Chances are she's as fed up as we are and that's why she's being difficult," she reasoned. "Anyway, on to something a little more fun." She grabbed her husband's hand playfully and all but dragged him into the kitchen, where on the table lay several lists, a couple of cookery books and a pot of tea for two.

"What's all this?" Richard asked suspiciously, eyeing up the paper that, now he was closer, he could see it was a list of names.

"Let's have a party!" Sarah exclaimed excitedly. "Oh come on, darling, please. It was so much fun last year. We really should put on something fantastic again."

Richard inspected the list. "But Sarah, there's more than double the amount of people than we had last year on here," he said with uncertainty. Richard was a happy, social man but only in very small circles. The thought of hosting a party for more than fifty people in his home quite frankly put him on edge. Sarah saw the trepidation on his face as he inspected the list, so she poured him a cup of tea and handed it to him, as if tea was a magic tonic for social anxiety.

"I know what you're thinking…" she pre-empted. "Too many people. I'll have a cull." She picked up the list and the pen that was on top of it and started crossing names out. Richard took a sip of tea then the pen off her and sighed. He had learnt by now that Sarah didn't do anything by half, he may as well just say okay now and have it over and done with. She'd find a way to up the numbers somehow. He could just imagine her saying, "Oh but Richard, I could hardly invite the Halls without inviting the Cohens, and if I invite the Cohens then you know that I simply must invite the Buttons. It'd just be rude otherwise." He smiled, loving the feeling he got from knowing that he knew his wife better than anyone else on the planet.

"It's okay, let's invite whoever you want. It'll be fabulous. When shall we have it?" he asked, trying to mirror his wife's enthusiasm.

"Well. I was thinking the first weekend in December. You know, it'd be fabulous if we could kick off the Christmas season!"

Richard looked at the calendar on the wall behind him. He flipped the page over and counted the weeks.

"Do you think you've got time to organise this in six weeks?" he asked, raising an eyebrow at his wife and wondering how she'd find the time to plan a party, work and maintain her home and social life, both of which she loved in equal measure.

"Of course!" she squealed with happiness. "And now we have an events co-ordinator in the family, we'll be doubly fine, plus it can double as a celebratory party. Autumn's finals are the week before. It couldn't be more perfect!" she said smugly, still basking in the glow of her daughter's new job title and prospective success in her exams. Richard gave his wife a squeeze and kissed her tenderly. She returned the kiss and hugged him back, truly thankful that she had such a wonderful husband.

"Right," she said authoritatively, picking up the list once more and scrutinising it. "Hand me that pen, darling. I forgot to include Heather Webber from work! I can't very well invite Charlotte and Sabrina without inviting Heather, now can I?"

"Absolutely not," Richard exclaimed in mock-horror. "We can't have that." The playful sarcasm was lost on Sarah as she furiously scribbled down the additional name, then for good measure adding a couple more. Richard shook his head; his wife really was one of a kind.

CHAPTER 20

OVER THE NEXT FEW WEEKS CELINA AND AUTUMN became practically inseparable. They hung out most days at the office, planning in precise detail the ins and outs of the next event. Autumn had started to view Celina as her new best friend, because they got on like a house on fire. Autumn had put her coursework to the back of her mind and instead concentrated her efforts on impressing Celina. Her final exam and deadline date were looming but she was having way too much fun and, besides, she loved her new job and could happily see herself continuing even after her finals.

Autumn's main role was to vet potential guests. They had to have a certain income or net worth and she was really enjoying deciding if people were good enough or not. Passing judgement over the wealthy and fabulous was fun: placing a millionaire on the 'no' pile gave her a smug sense of satisfaction and importance. Prospective guests needed to submit three untouched photographs of themselves as well as fill out an extensive form that asked some pretty personal questions. Autumn loved the voyeuristic nature of the job; delving into the private lives of the rich and magnificent was something she could get used to. Celina hadn't been lying when she said they had guests from all over: Italian businessmen, debauched celebrities from over the pond and even some of the landed gentry put their names forward. There really were no upper limits to the type of person who wanted to attend one of their events.

"Do we get much repeat business?" Autumn asked Celina one day, curious as she couldn't remember seeing many recurring names on the list.

"Lots," Celina contradicted. "Once they've been accepted they get a membership number." She gave Autumn a look. "Then as long as they pay their entry a minimum of twenty-four hours before the event, they just use that number to come in."

"What happens if they don't pay?" Autumn asked as she perused a fresh batch of applicants.

"Then their number is locked out and they have to reapply," Celina explained.

Autumn gave a small nod to show she understood and continued with her work.

In the weeks following her first event, she had really gotten to grips with how everything worked. She was expected to be able to do everything, from ensuring the fantasy rooms were cleaned and hygienic, to keeping the bar fully stocked. Celina had final say on the guest list; Autumn was amazed to find out that many guests waited months and months for acceptance into an event.

"We don't want the place overcrowded and there's a strict 'one in one out' policy we adhere to. Exclusivity is key," Celina had clarified.

The building where the events took place was like a maze: hallways lined with fantasy rooms either side stretched from the ballroom, which was the epicentre of each event. Through a side door after the fantasy rooms and down another hallway were the offices. Autumn had been given her own space plus a budget to decorate it how she liked. She'd chosen to imitate Celina's style and had it painted white; she'd adorned the small room with gold accessories and, in a final nod to Celina's style, she'd added a luxurious, circular burgundy rug made from angora wool. Autumn dug her toes into the plush floor covering as she sat at her desk. She still was in the habit of kicking off her heels every time she sat down at a desk.

Autumn had grown close to Celina quickly and at times Autumn was convinced that Celina looked at her as more than just a work colleague, maybe even more than just a friend. She even had to remind herself on several occasions that Celina was married, plus she wasn't gay. Still, Autumn couldn't shake the feeling that this wasn't just sociable banter between two friends. Sometimes Celina pulled rank, which Autumn found hard to swallow. Striking the balance between employee and friend wasn't particularly easy to do with someone like Celina Thorne. Autumn leaned back in her chair and took a picture of her office as she reclined. Now it was finished she wanted David to see it. She didn't want to stereotype but David had a fabulous eye for interior design; he'd simply love her office, she was sure of it. She sent the picture and before she could even set her phone down it began ringing in her hand,

'Wow, he must really like it.' She thought to herself smugly. She looked at the screen. It wasn't David at all but rather her mother.

"What is it Mum?" Autumn asked abruptly, rearranging some paperwork on her desk importantly and feeling slightly put out at this sudden disturbance.

"Darling, I'm just ordering the catering for our Christmas party. Do you think one or two vegetarian options for the buffet?"

Autumn sighed, she really didn't have time for this.

"I don't know Mum," she answered distractedly as she came across Thomas J. Herschel's application for December's event. The guest list had been finalised for this month's event but he could be Autumn's Christmas treat. He was a stunning black guy, absolutely gorgeous with soulful dark eyes and rippling muscles that were visible even beneath his expensive suit – not quite expensive enough, though, when she noted his salary. Autumn ran her finger over his photograph: would it be terribly bad form for her to say yes to a person with not quite enough money just because he looked like a wanton sex god? Her mum coughed, bringing her back to the conversation with a bump.

"Just get whatever you think, sorry I've got to go. I'm just going into a meeting. Bye Mum."

She hung up the phone. She saw that while her mum had been boring her with party food David had replied to her message.

'Love, love, LOVE!' was all that the message said. Autumn smiled to herself proudly: she really had landed on her feet. Her mind wandered to those she'd left behind, she wondered how Ben would feel if she knew what she did for a living now, and, if they had still been friends, what Rosa's face would have been like when she told her. Although upon reflection, without the two of them deceiving her none of this would have happened.

'In a way, I guess I should thank them,' Autumn mused before dismissing the idea as ridiculous. Her phone vibrated in her hand. She looked down: another message from David.

'Are you free next Sunday for wedding shopping? Kingsman are opening the entire store, just for me! Gregg pulled some strings, So excited!' it said. Autumn responded automatically that of course she was free. She was so excited for the pair of them that she didn't feel even one pang of jealousy. Or at least that's what she told herself. Still, she was having fun and if she wanted to date someone she would be dating someone. She cast her mind back to the dishy police officer.

She had thought about him several times since he'd told her she wouldn't be going to prison anytime soon. He had been kind to her, and there was something about him that Autumn found instantly appealing and it wasn't entirely down to the fact that he was drop-dead gorgeous. But that ship had sailed.

'Onwards and upwards,' she thought to herself. She set her phone down on the desk and began typing up the monthly newsletter Celina had dictated to her earlier that day. Each month they sent out a newsletter by email to all the guests on the list for the forthcoming event. It went out the Monday before the event and specified dress code, times and any other important information. Autumn was looking forward to seeing the menu for the event. After being the first course herself at the previous party she was keen to see who the next meal would consist of. There was a knock at her door, and she looked up to see Leonardo standing there, as usual wearing his casual uniform of jeans, jumper and peaked cap.

"Everything going alright?" he asked casually, glancing at the room's new décor. "I like what you done with the place, Celina," he said.

Autumn glared at him. "We just happen to have the same taste," she countered indifferently, as if his comment meant nothing to her. But inside she was blushing: was it that obvious?

"If you say so, hon," Leonardo quipped with a smile. "I'm done now, so I'll see you Saturday for the event?" he asked.

"Why won't I see you tomorrow?" Autumn asked.

"You've got the rest of the week off, haven't you?" Leonardo questioned, a look of confusion on his face: how could anyone forget booking time off work? "You should know, you booked it off!" he finished.

Now it was Autumn's turn to be confused. Had she booked the rest of the week off? She couldn't think why, or what for.

Autumn looked at him puzzled, then picked up her phone and checked her work calendar, week starting twenty-fifth of November. Leonardo was right: she'd booked the twenty-sixth, seventh and eighth off. But why?

"Fuck!" she blurted out loudly, startling Leonardo with the sheer volume of her voice. He looked affronted at her use of language. He didn't care for swearing, or any type of vulgar behaviour. He was surprisingly prudish and how he managed to work for Encounters remained a mystery to all who knew him. "I've got to go," she cried, grabbing wildly for her belongings and hastily slipping her shoes back on. She ran out of the door leaving Leonardo staring after her, totally perplexed by her sudden outburst. She ran through the maze-like building, descending down to the car park as quickly as she could, given the sluggish lift systems that the Encounters Events' building employed.

Autumn drove off in a blind panic. How on earth had she forgotten, how could she have been so occupied with sex-crazed rich people that she forgot about the one thing she'd been working towards for so long? She had her final exam this coming Friday. Her deadline for her coursework was the same day. Autumn's heart raced. She'd thought many times how she could just give it all up and work at Encounters for the rest of her life, but when genuinely faced with the prospect of failing she knew that she just couldn't let that happen. The thought of not having the opportunity to go into journalism made her feel sick, but she'd been so preoccupied with so many other things – Ben, Rosa, the accident, her new job and David's engagement – that her own dreams had taken a back seat, so much so that she'd clean forgotten about them. How could she be so stupid? How could she have allowed this to happen? Why hadn't her parents reminded her?

She drove faster now, foot pressed firmly to the floor, the speedometer creeping up on her little red car. She swerved round a tight corner and headed for the motorway. She needed to get back home as fast as humanly possible. As she approached the motorway she passed the spot where she'd been pulled over by Officer Sentori, and she instinctively applied the brakes and her speed dropped to well within the legal requirement. She looked up and saw, parked on the other side of the road, a police car waiting for offending passing motorists. She slowed right down and stared into the car. Sure enough, sat behind the wheel was Jake, staring out into the oncoming traffic. He looked just a handsome as he ever had, well, from what Autumn could see, which granted wasn't a lot. She could just about make out those piercing blue eyes and that was enough for her. She passed him, her eyes flicking to the rear-view mirror, desperate to prolong seeing him.

Autumn's concentration was broken by a sudden jolt: she had slowed down so much to catch a glimpse of Jake that the car behind her hadn't noticed and had driven right into the back of her. Autumn yelped as the seatbelt constricted, she strained against it as she was harshly propelled forwards and then whipped backwards as her car came to a halt. Her neck cracked loudly as the car shunted to a standstill. Autumn sat there, hardly believing the day she'd had. It had all started out so well. She raised a hand to her neck, which was now extremely sore. It felt horribly bruised already. She groaned in pain, dreading to think what it would be like in days to come. She gingerly opened the driver's side door and unfastening her seatbelt carefully eased herself out. The driver behind was already surveying the damage.

"Are you okay?" he asked, both panic and concern in his voice. He looked at the young woman he'd just hit and felt extremely guilty. He'd taken his eyes off the road for just a second and by the time looked up it had been too late. Autumn nodded, not entirely sure her mouth would be able to form words yet; she was in shock.

She looked at the two vehicles. The accident had felt like there should be a lot more damage than this. His BMW was practically untouched. A small dent to the driver's side bumper which looked like it could be tapped out with a toffee hammer was all the damage his car had sustained. Her car, however, had come off a little worse. Autumn's poor little car now had a split bumper and dented paintwork, not to mention a few deep-looking scratches. It was superficial damage, of course: the car was still drivable, but it did look a mess.

"I'm so sorry," the man went on, "here, let me give you my details."

Autumn slumped against her car and waited for the man to return, watching as rubber-necked drivers slowed down to pass them. She stared at the at the road in a muddled haze and looked up when she heard distant, but heavy imminent footsteps. She was expecting to see the guy that hit her returning with his insurance information. The pain in her neck shot through her like lightning as she did so and she winced, drawing in a deep lungful of breath in an attempt to breathe through the pain.

"Autumn!" a familiar male voice called. She turned to see who was approaching.

'Well I guess it's not all bad,' Autumn thought to herself as she saw Jake Sentori running up to her. He was slightly out of breath from his sprint to get to her quickly.

"I recognised your car. Are you okay, do you need an ambulance?"

She shook her head. She just had whiplash and needed painkillers, there was nothing that a doctor could do for her that she couldn't do for herself. Besides, she really needed to get home, her future depended on it. Pain shot through her again as she raised her head to look at Jake. The driver of the other car walked over to them apprehensively.

"Look officer, I've apologised. I'll pay for the damage. There's really no need…" he trailed off.

"It's okay. I'm just checking that everyone's alright," Jake interrupted, placing a hand on Autumn's shoulder. "You wait here and sort out your insurance details out, and I'll drive your car off the road to somewhere a little safer then come back and take you home."

Autumn looked at him gratefully. "Thank you," she said croakily, the adrenaline was subsiding now and starting to give way to shocked tears. Jake gave her a thin smile before he got into her car. She turned to the other driver and took the piece of paper in which he'd written his details on.

"Again, I am really sorry," the man said apologetically. "These things don't usually happen to me. I'm normally an exceptionally careful driver." He went on to relay his driving credentials to Autumn but she wasn't listening, her mind was racing, trying to make sense of the day's events. The man realised his words were falling on deaf ears.

"Well if you're sure you're okay I need to be getting off."

He backed up towards his car eyeing her awkwardly; he'd caused the accident and now he was leaving. Autumn didn't look at him again. She stared straight ahead, only vaguely aware of him leaving and joining the other traffic on the road.

Jake returned. He'd been gone barely ten minutes but it had felt like much longer. Autumn had stood there feeling very sorry for herself. He returned with her car keys, her bag and a scarf he had found on the back seat.

“Here,” he said wrapping the scarf around her neck several times, “this will give you a bit of support. I really think you should go to hospital, Autumn, just to get checked out.”

“I’m okay, really,” she said, pulling away from him. The scarf tight around her neck immediately took her back to her first ever Encounters experience. “I really need to get home.”

He took the hint and helped her over to the stationary police car. He led her by the arm, but she drew away; she wasn’t an invalid, after all.

The drive back was uneventful. Conversation was stiff at first; Autumn really didn’t feel like having a friendly chat. She wanted to down some painkillers, have a soak and then go to bed so she could spend the next three days revising and finishing coursework in time for Friday. The scarf neck brace Jake had made worked surprisingly well; as long as she didn’t move her head suddenly she didn’t feel too bad at all. Jake asked her question after question, wanting to keep her alert for the longest time possible. He didn’t care if he came across nosy or annoying, since his only concern was making sure Autumn was alright. By the end of the drive Autumn had warmed to him even more. He was an all-round nice guy. He’d wanted to work for the police since he was a little boy, and Autumn admired him for following his dreams. The conversation began to run dry around the time they were approaching The Barings.

“Here we are,” Jake announced as they pulled up to Autumn’s family home. Miguel the gardener was sweeping up the very last of the fallen leaves and stopped to stare as the police car came to a halt outside the house.

Sarah Carter was enjoying a rare day off and some much needed ‘me time’ when she heard the car outside. She got up and removed the slices of cucumber from her eyes, and she hesitated before popping them into her mouth and devouring them in one go.

"Who could this be?" she questioned out loud before peering out of the window. Her heart fell when she saw her daughter arriving in a police car. What the hell had she done now? Sarah's blood instantly boiled. She couldn't take much more of this: what on earth was happening to her daughter? She bolted to the front door and flung it open, preparing for all-out war with the hellish young woman her daughter was becoming.

"What have you done now?" she began haughtily. She stopped dead in her tracks when she saw the officer helping Autumn out of the car. She was moving very slowly and stiffly, Sarah saw the scarf wrapped around her neck and couldn't for the life of her figure out why. Sure, it was getting cooler now winter was approaching, but it wasn't that cold yet.

"Mrs Carter?" began Officer Sentori. "I'm afraid your daughter's been in a bit of an accident."

Sarah ran over to her daughter to assist her, feeling terrible for doubting her so strongly.

"Oh you poor thing!" she wailed. "What happened? Are you alright?" she continued, fussing over Autumn and rearranging the scarf. Autumn smiled a small and tired smile.

"I'm fine Mum, just a bit of a sore neck. Officer Sentori was luckily there to move my car and bring me home," she explained, looking gratefully at Jake again.

"I think we're past formalities now," he grinned. "Just call me Jake."

Autumn nodded her acknowledgement and winced. The pain, although reduced by her DIY scarf support, hadn't quelled completely. Sarah took her daughter into the living room, informing Jake that she would only be a moment. She settled Autumn down on the sofa, plying her with every type of painkiller they had in the house. Autumn took them all without saying a word and rested back into the comfortable cushions behind her. Sarah returned to the hallway to join the police officer. She closed the living room door behind her, leaving Autumn recuperating on the couch.

"What happened?" she asked in hushed tones. Jake told her what he had occurred – neglecting to mention the fact that he had quite clearly seen Autumn slowing down to get a good look at himself. Jake had seen her out of the corner of his eye, but not wanting to give her the wrong idea, he had done his best to ignore her. Just when he thought she'd driven off, he'd heard a crash and knew instantly what had happened. Sarah listened intently, managing to hold her tongue until he was finished.

"You should have taken her to hospital," she admonished, trying not to sound too ungrateful for his assistance or like she was reprimanding the Officer.

"She doesn't want to go. She's got to revise and thinks a good night's sleep and painkillers will do the trick. I spoke to her in the car, and I don't think she's suffering from a concussion but if you're worried, you should take her regardless of how she feels," he replied in his defence.

Sarah mulled this over. Her daughter was a tough cookie. Whilst at primary school she'd fallen out of a tree and broken her leg; the teacher didn't notice straight away as Autumn had carried on playing, hobbling around saying it just hurt a bit. By the end of the day it had doubled in size, and she had been in a cast for weeks afterwards. Sarah had always marvelled at the strength her daughter seemed to have, both physical and emotional.

CHAPTER 21

OVER THE COURSE OF THE NEXT THREE DAYS Autumn wrote, revised and planned like she had never done before. She worked hard every day from the moment she woke up until the sun set. The only exception to the rule had been when David had come to visit her. He'd popped over with bridal magazines under one arm and a fruit basket under the other, wearing a bright orange T-shirt with the words 'Drama Queen' emblazoned across the chest. He'd stayed only for a couple of hours, and Autumn felt like David's company was way better for her health than any of the painkillers she was on. He was positively overflowing with excitement about his wedding to Gregg. He had so many ideas, and from the sound of it his wedding was going to be bigger and flashier than all of Kim Kardashian's weddings combined. She listened intently and was glad of the distraction.

When David had come to leave, he'd given her gentle hug, being careful not to cause her further injury. There had been a lull in the conversation at one point and Autumn thought about telling David about her new job. Every time he'd asked about it she'd brushed him off by saying, *"Honestly, it's nothing exciting,"* or *"It's really mainly paperwork."* One of which wasn't wholly a lie. This was the time, she thought. Taking a deep breath, she told him everything, enjoying the look of shock on his face. She watched with interest as he became more and more in awe of her with every new revelation. When she had finished, she sat back happily and looked at David closely.

'Bless him, he's so impressed he's completely lost for words,' she mused.

"Are you kidding?" he asked abruptly, his voice completely flat. His lip was curled upwards in a look of abhorrence.

Autumn was too involved with her story to notice. "Nope, every word of it's true," she bragged, although a little of the joviality had gone from her voice. David went quiet again, clearly thinking hard. His mouth moved; it looked as though he was chewing on his words, deciding whether to swallow them, or spit them out. He chose the latter.

"So, you're a prostitute," he asserted without inflection. The statement got Autumn's back up, and she bristled with annoyance.

"No," Autumn said defiantly, irritated with herself at how she'd misread her friend's reaction.

"You've just told me that some rich guy bid twenty-five thousand pounds so he could have sex with you and you kept the money. You were paid for sex. Autumn, that's prostitution."

She shook her head, wincing slightly. The painkillers worked well but didn't eradicate the discomfort completely.

"Well, I only got thirty percent of that," Autumn said defensively.

"That's still," he paused for a moment, "seven and a half thousand pounds, Autumn. Christ, what have your parents said?"

"I haven't exactly told them. They know the clean bits and I just kind of glossed over the rest. I mean, come on David, I'm hardly going to tell them the truth! Besides, it's just a means to an end until I get a journalism job. Oh God D, please don't tell them!" she begged, when she saw the look on his face. Autumn was annoyed that he couldn't just be happy for her but at the same time wanted to keep him onside so her secret remained just that.

He sat there silently, contemplating his options. He didn't like this at all. Autumn was better than this, and she was being used at that place. She was just a pretty face to draw the punters in, he was sure of it. She'd get used and abused by the sounds of it, and even someone as strong as Autumn would find that hard to get through.

"I can't pretend to be okay with this, Autumn. I won't say anything to your parents, but I won't lie for you either. If they ask me, I will tell them the truth," he said decidedly.

Autumn couldn't argue; she was hardly in a position to, as she liked that job and wanted to keep it. She felt empowered by it. It was well paid and she wasn't *a prostitute* no matter how David dressed it up. In the short month or so she'd already made enough to pay off her credit card bills and splash out on some lavish clothes and take herself on a nice holiday. Or at least she would have, when she got paid. She was becoming more financially, personally and sexually independent. In Autumn's mind, this was nothing but a good thing; she was proud of her newly-found independence and thought David should be proud of her too.

They sat there awkwardly for a few moments. Autumn looked into her tea cup with fascination. Pretending there was something worth staring at in there was far less work than making conversation with David.

"Don't forget," he said as he turned to leave, "we're meeting 10 a.m. under the clock tower in town. That is, if you're still up for Sunday's wedding trip. Maybe we grab a coffee first and plan our strategy?"

"Sounds like a great idea!" Autumn said softly. "I wouldn't miss it for the world."

"Are you sure you'll be fit enough?" he asked, pushing the thought of Autumn in that seedy place to the back of his mind and replacing it with thoughts of his upcoming nuptials.

"Honestly, it's not that bad. I'll be fine by then, I'm sure of it," she insisted. "That's if you still want me to come?"

David rolled his eyes.

"*I'm* supposed to be the drama queen," he said, pointing to his chest. "Of course I want you there, you're still my Autumn," he said kindly. "Just promise me you'll reconsider this new career path before it's too late?"

Autumn gave a small nod but didn't look him in the eye; for the sake of keeping David sweet she pretended that that was an option. She made a mental note not to share any more Encounters stories with him from now on. She had assumed, wrongly, that he would have been more open-minded than this.

"Exactly what I wanted to hear, thank you," he said, making for his car.

Autumn stood in the doorway as he walked over to a brand spanking new, sleek, blue sports car.

"Err, excuse me! What is that?" she demanded, pointing to the shiny new car.

"Oh, this old thing?" David said in mock confusion. "It's just a little engagement present from Gregg." He paused, waiting for Autumn's reaction.

"Oh my God, D!" she cried, her eyes wide with a combination of jealousy and admiration. "It's beautiful, you lucky boy. Wow, I had no idea he was, you know, mega rich," she finished, not sure whether that was offensive or not.

"I know, I didn't really either. I mean I knew he was not exactly poor. I can't believe my luck, he's so effing handsome and so effing lovely and now I find out that he's also effing rich!" David laughed with glee. He wasn't shallow at all, and Autumn knew he'd love Gregg even if he didn't have two penny pieces to rub together, but this was clearly the icing on the cake for him.

"So, everything we've just talked about, you're actually going to have?" she asked, gobsmacked, referring to the lavish wedding ceremony he'd just depicted. Autumn thought she had been humouring him, believing that there was no way he'd actually be releasing doves and having a 24-piece gospel choir to serenade them down the aisle. Nor had she believed that he would be holding the wedding at Stopton Park, the most beautiful manor house and estate for miles around. There it was again, that little pang of jealousy, only this time it was a big pang and instead of being able to ignore it she let it get the better of her.

"Wow David, well it sounds like it'll be really classy, such tasteful choices," she said sarcastically, giving him a nasty smile that he didn't deserve.

She closed the door on him coldly. Her cheeks were flushed, partly with anger and partly with embarrassment. Why had she said that? What a mean thing to say. After a moment, she calmed herself and opened the door to apologise, but David was already gone, disappearing down the driveway in his new sports car. She pushed the feelings of guilt down, deep within her and went back to her revision. She didn't have time for this nonsense.

Friday came around far too quickly. Her alarm sounded and begrudgingly she dragged herself out of bed. Time seemed to move faster today, and it seemed like she had only just got up when she looked at her watch and realised that it was now or never. She tested her neck on the side of the bed, slowly moving her head from side to side. It didn't feel too bad today. She'd been on a steady dose of strong painkillers since the accident and they'd certainly taken the edge off. After washing, dressing and gulping down a quick bowl of cereal, she got her things together and made to leave her parents' home. Sarah and Richard Carter waved their daughter off amongst cries of "Good luck sweetheart," and "We know you can do it!" Autumn rolled her eyes and cringed inside. Why were her parents so cheesy nowadays?

She drove to the examination hall and dropped her final articles in at the entrance. An adjudicator showed her to her seat and seemingly seconds later a buzzer sounded indicating the examination was now in progress. Autumn opened the paper and scanned the questions, drawing a blank on every single one. She closed her eyes and took a deep breath. Maybe her parents were right, maybe she could do it. She looked at the examination paper again; no, she definitely couldn't. Hesitantly she picked up her pen and began to write, cursing the fact she'd chosen a creative course with an examination at the end of it. Why did she always bite off more than she could chew?

Autumn tried to concentrate – why was the damn clock so loud? It seemed to get noisier with each and every tick until all she could hear was the roar of the second hand. The buzzer sounded again and it was over. Autumn had finished the exam. The adjudicator walked briskly up and down the aisles, snatching the examination papers from each desk and whisking them away for marking.

'That's it then, there's nothing else I can do now,' she thought glumly. All the bluster about how unimportant the exam was now she had her Encounters job had been just that, bluster. No matter what she told other people, she couldn't hide from herself. Autumn would be bitterly disappointed if she failed this course. If only she'd taken something less taxing... She

was now convinced that her initial ambition was going to turn out to be her downfall.

CHAPTER 22

"HOW WAS IT?" SARAH ASKED THE SECOND AUTUMN came through the door. Her face fell the second she laid eyes on her. Autumn was quite clearly drunk. After the exam Autumn had stopped off at E.C.H.D. and drowned her sorrows with wine. Her car had been towed the day after the accident, the cost of repairs turning out to be more than the car was worth. It had been scrapped, but Autumn rationalised that with the money she'd earn at Encounters she would be able to buy a something that would blow David's new car out of the water in no time at all, but until then it was trains and taxis all the way. She glared at her mother who was stood with a bottle of champagne in her hand, cork popped, ready to pour. Her dad, who held the champagne flutes, was smiling broadly; the smile, however, waned the instant he saw the state his daughter was in.

"Autumn," he scolded, "I think you've taken the celebrations too far."

"Celebrations?" Autumn ridiculed, "Celebrations? What is there to celebrate? I failed. God! Why are you guys like this?"

Autumn pushed past them and stomped up the stairs. She didn't have time for this. They were so nosy and presumptuous. She slammed her bedroom door behind her, the sound echoing through the house as she slumped down on her bed. Her eyes burned as tears threatening to spill down her face.

She took a deep breath in an attempt to draw them back in, but it was no good. She sat on the edge of her childhood bed and silently let the tears run down her face. She cried for the loss of her career, the loss of her relationship, her friends and family and also the loss of herself.

She shook her head violently in the hope that these vile thoughts would be dislodged and lost in the deepest recesses of her mind, but it was no use. Wiping her eyes with the back of her sleeve she forced herself to think about the positives and be grateful for the good things in her life. She was at unease with herself and she didn't know why; the feeling unnerved her. She quickly steadied herself, resolving to power through. She was just having a wobble, a moment of weakness, that was all. But she couldn't shake the uncomfortable and unbalancing feeling that she didn't much like her own company, and yet she couldn't stand to be in anyone else's. She couldn't pinpoint the sensation exactly and she found it unsettling. There was only one person who made her feel truly alive right now. Everything and everyone else paled into comparison. She needed Celina. Autumn pulled out her phone,

'Ugh, a message from David.' She swiped past it. She'd reply to him later if she had the time. Right now, she needed to speak to Celina, her boss and her friend, the only person who knew Autumn on a whole other level. The phone rang and rang; Celina didn't have a voice-mail service by the sounds of it. After a minute or two the phone went dead and cut off. Autumn pulled it away from her ear and stared at it. Irritated, she dialled Celina's number again. The same thing happened. She tried once more for luck, just as she was about to hang up an exasperated voice answered.

"Is this important, Autumn?" Celina said.

"I, just wanted to tell you about my exam," she said hesitantly, taken aback by the abruptness of Celina's tone. There was no reply, Autumn could hear the tapping of a keyboard in the background. "But, if it's not a good time…" she trailed off.

"Autumn, going forward can we just keep to the rule that unless it has something directly to do with Encounters we'll leave it for out-of-hours conversation?"

Autumn felt abashed. Celina had pulled rank again and she didn't like it. Besides, they never had any out-of-hours conversations. They spoke pretty much only in the office and they barely spoke at the event. Celina was always too busy schmoozing with the guests. Autumn thought back to the times they had spent together, and it dawned on her that she knew very little about Celina. She didn't think they'd had a real conversation in the entire time they'd known one another. Autumn had offered several nuggets of information about herself. Celina knew all about the breakdown of her relationship, and she knew about Autumn's dreams of becoming a writer. In fact Celina had a veritable feast of knowledge about Autumn, yet Autumn knew almost nothing about Celina. Sure, she knew her dress sense was impeccable, that she had a flair for interior design and that she spoke Portuguese fluently, although she had overheard this, rather than witnessed it.

"Autumn? Are you still there?" Celina asked impatiently. "Look, if there's nothing I can help you with I need to go, since you did your little disappearing act it's been left to me to keep things together."

"I'm so sorry, I left you a message, and I thought you were okay with it. I'll see you tomorrow for the event, though?" Autumn said, justifying her absence. Celina made a guttural noise of acknowledgement down the phone and bid Autumn an almost frosty farewell before hanging up.

"What a bitch," Autumn said out loud to herself, the words slipping out before she could stop them. Maybe Celina was just having a bad day, she reasoned, but that little voice wormed its way to the front of her mind: maybe this was just Celina all along and you were so desperate to *'better yourself,'* you ignored what she's really like. Autumn chose to disregard her thoughts. She suddenly had an unsettled feeling in the pit of her stomach but forced herself to overlook it. She was, after all, having the time of her life. She was just a bit tipsy still and irritated by how badly her exam had gone. Her parents hadn't helped matters – what were they thinking, dumbly waiting for her with celebration champagne of all things?

There was a light knock at the door. Autumn ignored it, hoping the person on the other side would get the hint. They didn't: the knock came again, louder this time.

"What?" Autumn bellowed through the door. Her mum's face appeared as the door opened a crack, a look of concern – or was it anger? – on her face. Autumn wasn't quite sure, nor did she really care. She scowled at her mother and busied herself on her phone. She was randomly tapping away on the calculator but her mum didn't need to know that, she just really wanted to be left alone at the moment.

"Autumn, we need to talk," Sarah said sternly. Autumn continued to stare at her phone screen stubbornly, willing her mum to get the hint and leave her alone. Sarah didn't leave, though, and instead advanced into the room, looming over Autumn in a way that told her that this confrontation was inevitable. Autumn looked up from her phone and looked at her mum. She was dressed in pale pink jumper and cream trousers; around her neck she wore the pearl necklace Autumn had bought for her when she'd turned forty. That was some time ago now and the necklace still looked as good as the day she'd bought it. That had come from John Cusson the jewellers too, Autumn thought, a bitter taste rising in her mouth.

"What do you want?" she said churlishly, flipping her long blonde hair over one shoulder and inspecting her nails in a way that reeked of teenage attitude.

"I want to talk to you about that," Sarah said, more bluntly now. She was too long in the tooth to be beaten down by this angry caricature of her daughter. She stepped further into the room, the champagne bottle still in her hand.

"What?" Autumn asked, a little confused now. Had her mum lost it? What the hell was she referring to?

"You and this horrible attitude you've developed." She set the bottle down on Autumn's desk and raised a hand when her daughter tried to interrupt her. "Let me finish. Your father and I are sick of it. One minute you're perfectly pleasant and the next we're dealing with a selfish little madam, who drinks too much, eats too little and seems to have some weird superiority complex that quite frankly doesn't suit her."

Autumn stood up, drawing herself to her full height, she swelled with anger, her lip curled up in a rancid snarl, she looked her mother up and down.

"What?" she spat. "Superiority complex? It's not a complex Mum, it's a twenty-four carat, solid gold fact. You and Dad just can't handle the fact that I'm not a pathetic little crying mess anymore. You don't like my independence and probably wish I was still sobbing on the sofa whilst you and Dad could fuss and feel validated."

Sarah looked at her daughter, completely shocked. No one had ever spoken to her like this before, let alone her daughter.

"Well if that's how you feel maybe it's best if you find somewhere else to live. You know, being completely independent now and all that. We think it's best for us all if you move out, Autumn, any time before the weekend. We don't want you spoiling our Christmas party," she cautioned, an air of resignation in her voice.

"Christmas party?" Autumn demanded. "It's the first I've heard of it. By the way, thanks for the invite," she scoffed derisively.

"It's not the first you've heard of it at all," Sarah said calmly. "I've tried speaking to you about it, involving you, but you're always too busy."

Autumn rolled her eyes dramatically. "Oh poor you," she mocked.

Sarah Carter gave her daughter a hurt look. "We love you, Autumn, but we just think you need some time to find yourself again and you can't do that here."

She walked out of the room, leaving Autumn feeling infuriated. She couldn't believe the nerve of her parents. How dare they kick her out! Well, she wasn't going to stay where she wasn't wanted. She'd find somewhere else, maybe she'd stay with Celina for a bit, maybe she'd put herself forward as another 'course' and use the money as a deposit for a nice flat somewhere. Her mum had left the champagne, and Autumn grabbed for it and gulped a few mouthfuls down straight out the bottle. She winced as she threw her head back to accommodate the golden liquid; her neck still wasn't quite right after the accident.

Autumn blinked against the fading sunlight and reached for her watch, which she'd left, as usual, on her bedside table. It was cluttered and she had to rummage around a while before her hand clasped over the cold rose gold metal face of the delicate timepiece that her grandmother had given to her many years ago. In the process, she managed to knock over the half empty bottle of champagne, and the remainder of its contents spilled out onto the carpet. Autumn groaned, and swung her legs out of bed, leaning forward to rescue the fallen bottle and grimaced at the dull ache that was clawing at her head. On the floor a large dark, wet patch had already formed. Autumn scooped up a towel that she'd left on the floor the previous morning and threw it over the spilt liquid.

'That should do it,' she assured herself before climbing back into bed. She just needed another hour or so to sleep off her headache.

Autumn slept until after midday, and she would have slept longer had her mother not woken her up with the vacuum cleaner. She seemed to be purposefully going over the spot outside Autumn's room over and over again. The cleaner was sarcastically loud and its angry drone threatened to bring her headache back to full force. She scrunched up her eyes and buried her head under her duvet.

"For fuck's sake Mum! You've got to be joking!" she bellowed, throwing herself out of bed and whipping the door open. It seemed the rage and disdain hadn't ebbed away during the course of the night. It had merely lain dormant underneath the surface, awaiting the slightest trigger to come back, larger and even more unreasonable than before.

She was surprised to see her dad in the hallway. He was wearing a floral apron with bright yellow marigold gloves hanging out of the front pocket, and he had on top of his head an old-fashioned pair of chunky headphones and was bopping away as he ran the vacuum cleaner of the carpet half dancing and mouthing the words to whatever song he was listening to. He looked ridiculous. There would have been a time where Autumn would have found this endearing; perhaps she'd have joined in with her dad's middle-aged man-dance and they would have laughed and joked together. But not today, today Autumn found him pathetic. A grown man being bullied by his wife, forced to do the housework when they both knew they had more than enough money for a cleaner. It was pitiful. She looked at her father with distaste. As he bent down to turn the cleaner off he caught sight of her out of the corner of his eye and jumped.

"Bloody hell Autumn, I almost had a heart attack," he said in a jolly way that almost broke the ice encasing Autumn's heart. She surveyed him coolly; any affection she had for her parents had been quelled when her mother had all but kicked her out of their house. Recalling their conversation from the previous night, she felt bile bubble inside her. She held her father's gaze and watched with malice as his face fell, twisting from a half-smile into something far gloomier.

"Pity," she replied dispassionately before turning and heading back into her bedroom. Once inside she closed the door behind her, calmly. It shut with a finality that told her that the time was now. She had absolutely no intention of staying where she wasn't wanted. She packed a bag, telling herself that for now she only needed the essentials and a few bits for the next Encounters event. She needed to remain focused on that... Autumn felt very strongly that she needed her head in the game and no matter how hard her parents, or anyone else, tried, she wouldn't let Encounters get ruined too.

Autumn waited for the taxi at the end of the driveway. She exchanged awkward goodbyes with her parents. She'd tried to avoid them but her mum, being the eagle-eyed woman she was, had spotted her before she could head out of the door. They'd said that she didn't have to leave right then and there. Autumn had told them that she was fine and would be staying with Celina. She was certain that she would have a big enough home, probably some huge ten-bedroomed affair with waiting staff and a swimming pool. Her taxi pulled up next to her.

"Miss Carter?" the driver questioned once he'd rolled the window down. Autumn nodded and got in. "So where are we going?" he asked casually, raising his hand to the dashboard to enter the details into his sat nav.

"Could you just make your way towards the north side of town, please? I can show you the way once we're closer," Autumn instructed politely, a false cheerfulness in her tone. The driver pulled away, and just as she'd done with the home she'd shared with Ben, she didn't allow herself to look back. She stared straight ahead, fixedly on the road in front of them. She would direct the driver towards Encounters' offices. Celina was bound to be there by now preparing for tonight's event, and if she wasn't, Leonardo would definitely be there, scurrying around, doing Celina's bidding like the good boy that he was.

Autumn instructed the driver to stop a few hundred metres away from where she really needed to be. She would walk the rest. She needed a bit of fresh air to clear her head, both from the headache, which granted was now receding, but also from the unpleasantness with her family. She tapped her number into the panel next to the wrought iron gate that so reminded her of the entrance to Thorne PR, and as she did so she spared a thought for Jack. She'd never heard Celina speak of him. In fact, if she didn't know they were married she would think Celina free and single. Hadn't she told her that when the mood strikes she dabbles with guests? Surely Jack couldn't be happy with that? Did he even know? She felt a pang of sadness for him. She was sure he wouldn't know what Celina got up to; he wasn't the type of man to put up with something like that.

She didn't care much either way, since Jack had turned on her when Rosa had her accident. He rounded on her like a lion would on a wounded animal. He showed no faith in her – and after all, what did it matter if he knew or not? His business wasn't hers, and all she cared about now was making Encounters even more fabulous for Celina.

The gate opened and she stepped into the small, walled, overgrown garden and prepared for the drop. It came after a few moments and she slowly descended into the clinical car park. She strutted over to the lift, the shiny black panel glinted at her invitingly as she walked. She marvelled at how much she'd changed in barely a month. The last time she came here for an event she had been unsure of herself, nervous and terrified of making a bad impression. She recalled how she'd struggled with the lift, how the entry system had baffled her and then, once the night had got underway, how she'd misinterpreted pretty much everything. She pitied that woman, naïve and foolish.

She was a far improved version of herself now. She no longer suffered fools gladly and knew what she wanted, and tonight she wanted to let go. She needed to forget everything. She would have no barriers tonight and would certainly make sure that every single guest had every need met. She boarded the lift and after a few moments found herself in the little art gallery-like reception. The painting of the two men entwined in a passionate embrace now made much more sense to her. There was no one on reception yet, so she leaned over the desk and pressed the button to call the lift. The painting door slid open and she climbed inside. Once upstairs she walked briskly to her office. She had followed Celina's lead and kept her clothes for events in there. Hers, however, were hung on a white coat rack rather than displayed, as Celina's were in a huge, impressive open wardrobe.

She had decided that she would make it a tradition to go without underwear to every event. Looking back, she felt that being naked aside from a beautiful dress was one of the reasons she'd felt so liberated that night, and she was looking forward to recreating the feeling. She knocked on Celina's door as she passed but there was no answer.

'That's odd,' Autumn thought. Celina was nearly always here. Perhaps she'd taken a day off and forgot to tell her. Giving up after knocking again and then again, she made her way to her own office. She sat down in her comfortably padded swivel chair, switched on her computer and opened up the surveillance system. This was used to make sure all the rooms were set up and in good order. There were no cameras in the fantasy rooms, only in the hallways connecting them. The cleaning team were finishing up, the flowers had been arranged in the centre of the ballroom, calla lilies as usual, and both Matthew and Robert were already there stocking up the bar. They hadn't changed into their uniforms yet and instead wore just tracksuit bottoms. Autumn eyed them both. They had lean, dancers' bodies and were both so handsome that they could have been models. She wondered why they settled for bar work. Perhaps the street cred of working at an event such as Encounters was reward enough? They probably bragged to all their friends about what went on here, plus the tips they must get from the wealthy guests must be considerable as well, she reasoned.

Autumn looked at her watch, or rather looked at her wrist. She moaned, annoyed with herself. She'd left her watch on her bedside table. She remembered setting it back down when she'd knocked that stupid bottle of champagne over. Autumn cursed loudly. She loved that watch and wouldn't be able to go and get it back any time soon.

Over the next couple of hours Autumn made sure that any and all loose ends were tied up. She strode through the building inspecting the fantasy rooms, hesitating when she approached room seventeen. She opened the door and inspected the room just like she had done all the others, only this time she took her time. Her stomach flipped as she remembered the strong and masterful way the blonde stranger had controlled her, how he'd made her come so hard she'd almost collapsed and how, afterwards, she'd found out that it had been the first time for them both. She smiled, half at the memory and half at the prospect of repeating the proceedings tonight. She felt the inner recesses of herself wrench with anticipation. A knock at the door startled her.

"Can I come in?" Martin said through the crack in the door. Autumn looked up.

"What are you doing here?" she asked, surprised to see him.

"Your hair and makeup…" he replied with a cheeky smile, "unless you want to do it yourself?" He raised an eyebrow at her, almost by way of a challenge.

"Ha, no you're alright. I didn't expect for you to do it again, though. How much do I owe you?" she said, reaching down for her purse.

"Put your money away, hon. I'm on a retainer. Celina's all done so I thought I'd see if you needed sorting too."

"Celina's here?" Autumn questioned, feeling affronted and wondering why she hadn't answered the door to her earlier. She'd let Autumn run around making sure everything was perfect for tonight's event like some sort of dogsbody while she enjoyed a pamper session. Martin seemed to read her mind so gently reminded her that it was Celina's business after all and she was entitled to do exactly as she pleased. Autumn gave a curt nod. She knew he was right but she felt more like partners than employee and employer.

"Anyway," he went on. "Are we beautifying you or not?" Autumn smiled.

"Yes, please," she accepted, reprimanding herself for her little internal temper tantrum. She had it so good here and needed to keep that in mind and not get above her station, no matter that Celina was her friend.

Martin spent less time on her than he had the previous month; however, she was still superbly happy with the end result and didn't want to appear ungrateful. This time her hair was down, teased into loose waves that fell around her face, framing it beautifully. Autumn noticed how her face shape had changed over the past few weeks. She had lost weight, that much was certain: her new job had kept her so busy, and without the constant supply of June's home-baked goods and the rich, calorie-laden, foamy coffees of Thorne PR's staff lounge, the few extra pounds she had been carrying had dropped off. Her face was better chiselled now, and her waist more nipped in. She did a little three-quarter turn, admiring herself in the mirror in front of her. Martin gave a dramatic eye roll.

"I know, I know, you look fabulous, darling. Now give me a kiss, I've got to scoot. See you in a couple of weeks."

"Couple of weeks?" Autumn asked dumbly. As far as she knew each event took place the last weekend of every month, not every fortnight.

"Yes. We have our Christmas event mid-December. Why don't you know that? We can't have it too close to Christmas day. The carol doesn't exactly go *'seven swingers swinging'* after all," he said, singing the last bit to the tune of "The First Day of Christmas".

"I suppose the last weekend would be too close to Christmas and New Year for most people," Autumn said rationally. Martin nodded his agreement.

"We tried it one year, had practically no one turn up. Celina was so pissed off she swore never again. So, from then on it's always been mid-December." He paused. "Now give papa bear a kiss, I really have got to dash."

Autumn obliged and gave him a peck on each cheek. He bid her a farewell with a dramatic flourish of his hand and with that was out of the door and gone. Autumn stood for a second dumbfounded, annoyed that something as important as having a mere two weeks to prepare for the next event hadn't been mentioned to her before. She vowed to bring it up with Celina the second she saw her. She would be working every hour God sent at this rate. How on earth would she find the time to do it? The last thing she wanted was to let Celina down, so she took a deep breath. She would do it, even if it killed her. She looked at the clock on her desk. She needed to get a move on herself; chatting to Martin had taken up any spare time she had. She felt a pang of excitement as she turned to the coat rack in the corner of the room. She closed the door and began to slip on her new gown.

Autumn surveyed herself in the mirror. If anything, she liked how she looked even more than last time. She had chosen an emerald green dress. It was fitted around the bust and had a full length, chiffon skirt with a full thigh high split in it. Celina had insisted she keep the shoes after Autumn had told her about how she'd most probably defiled them at the hands of the blonde stranger. After cleaning them up they were good as new, and she'd chosen to wear them again, loving how glamorous yet comfortable they were. She thrust her foot forward, her slim but shapely leg protruding though the split in the dress, to examine the shoes. They went perfectly. Her outfit was less sexy than last time but she somehow felt more striking, more ladylike and more elegant. She pulled her hair over her shoulders and ran her fingers through delicately. She turned around and was surprised to see Celina stood in the doorway, watching her. She wore the same lustful expression she had the last time Autumn had dressed in front of her.

"You look incredible," Celina said. Autumn returned the compliment. Celina had opted for a more dramatic gown this time around; it had a full skirt made from ruched silk and was a stunning pale grey. The bodice was beaded with tiny crystals. Her hair was up in an elegant bun. Autumn admired the glint of the diamond earrings hanging from her lobes, so long they almost touched her collarbone. Autumn blushed a little under Celina's attention. She felt like a schoolgirl getting much coveted praise from her favourite teacher.

"Thanks," she said, "so do you."

Celina moved in front of Autumn to admire her own reflection; she turned to take in the view from the back. Autumn watched as Celina gave herself an appreciative once-over before taking Autumn by the hand and leading her outside.

"Celina, there's something I need to speak to you about," Autumn said quickly. "It's important."

"Is it about the event?" Celina asked, concerned.

"No, nothing like that, everything's fine for tonight," she answered quickly, not wanting Celina to think she was incapable of doing her job. "It's just that…" she stopped when she was abruptly interrupted.

"Autumn. Let me stop you," Celina admonished. "I thought I made myself perfectly clear, work talk only."

Autumn gazed after her as Celina marched out of the room. All she had wanted was a place to crash for a few days, and they were friends after all. Maybe she needed to wait until after tonight. Celina did seem to get pretty heated up in the days preceding an event.

They had around ten minutes until the guest began to flood in. The lights had been dimmed in preparation. Autumn studied her reflection in the mercury mirrored wall of the ballroom; she moved her head, still slightly stiff from her accident but almost entirely better now. She caught sight of Matthew and Robert watching her in the reflection and she gave them a little wave from across the room. The female waitresses were taking their places either side of the bar. Autumn realised that unlike last time she hadn't had a drop to drink. Maybe it was because she was far more confident this time around or maybe it was because she was starting to get a bit sick of champagne. She walked over to the bar and inspected their offerings. It was limited: champagne on tap, white or red wine and a very small selection of spirits. She ordered a glass of red, and Robert poured her the drink and handed it to her. She took a long, satisfying drink and took her place next to Celina who already had a glass of champagne in her hand.

"Don't you ever get sick of champagne?" Autumn asked, realising that other than the whiskey Celina had drunk when they first met she'd only ever seen her sip on champagne.

"No. Never," Celina replied jovially. Her mood had changed dramatically; no longer was she short and snappy with Autumn, she was now like a kid before Christmas, excitedly waiting for the flocks of moneyed, upper-class guests with open and liberal, albeit secretive, sexual tastes. She rested a dainty hand on Autumn's bare shoulder and gave it a little squeeze.

"Any minute now," Celina said eagerly. "I don't know about you, Autumn, but this month has been stressful and I'm very much looking forward to a release." Autumn couldn't agree more; she felt exactly the same way.

"What about Jack?" Autumn asked abruptly, the words spilling out of her mouth before she had chance to stop them. She knew from the moment she'd uttered them that it was a mistake to mention her husband. Celina's face contorted, she turned to Autumn brusquely, removing her hand and placing it on her hip.

"Jack and I, not that it's any of your business, Autumn, have an agreement. We subscribe to an open relationship. He's married to his work, as I am to mine. He prefers the thrill of the golf course and scoring a client over making love to a woman. I, on the other hand, love sex. It's why I started this company. Our lifestyles and polar opposite predilections mean that we rarely have time for intimacies. So, we have an understanding. I play the role of doting wife whenever he needs me to. It makes him feel like a big man to have me play the part of dutiful servant in front of his family. In return, I can do whatever, whenever, in my own time," she explained. Autumn paused: that didn't make any sense.

"Why are you together then?" Autumn couldn't help herself, she knew that Celina was a notoriously private person but to be with someone who from the sound of it you barely like, let alone love, was crazy. Celina lowered her eyes; for the first time since Autumn had known her she looked vulnerable.

"I need my marriage to stay in this country." She replied flatly. Her accent, which Autumn had become accustomed to, seemed stronger with these words. Autumn didn't have time to reply as the guests were pouring in. They made their way either to the bar, the canapés or to Celina, wanting to be one of the first to shake the hand of the woman who had organised this fabulous event.

Autumn glanced around the room. It was just as amazing as it had been last time, even more so now she knew exactly what the night could bring. She caught the eye of a man with jet black hair and stubble from across the room standing at the bar; he gave her a look that couldn't have been clearer. Autumn didn't want to miss her chance so started to make her way over to him at once. She recognised him from the applications but couldn't remember his name. She hesitated when she saw a scarlet-haired woman, lithe and athletic-looking, sidling up beside him, her hand snaked around his neck as she planted a passionate kiss on his lips. He returned the kiss, maintaining eye contact with Autumn the entire time. They broke away and she followed his gaze, running her eyes appreciatively over Autumn. The woman returned her attention to the man, giving him a small nod of acceptance before leaving him alone at the bar. He beckoned Autumn over, and she noticed the glint of a gold wedding band around his finger.

"Drink?" he asked, when she had arrived next to him. Autumn, not wanting to fall into a submissive role immediately, ordered herself a double whiskey on the rocks. A droplet of the amber liquor had spilled when the drink had been poured and was now streaking its way down the side of the glass. Autumn lifted it to her lips and licked the side of the glass, enjoying the warmth of the liquid on her tongue. The man devoured the scene and took a step closer to her. His breath was warm on the nape of her neck. His desire was palpable, he wanted her and she was going to let him have what he wanted.

"Would you like to join me and my friend later?" he asked. Autumn was surprised to hear him speak with a soft Irish accent, and the sound thrilled her. She'd always had a thing for the Irish ever since Colin Farrell had burst onto the Hollywood scene. The icing on the cake was that the man in front of her didn't look too dissimilar from her celebrity crush.

"Your friend?" Autumn asked, glancing down at his wedding ring.

"My wife's not here. I come to these events alone." He explained, "She's fine with it, not much of a party girl I'm afraid. I met her on the way up and since she's in a similar situation to me, we thought we'd join forces."

Autumn looked at him, trying to hide her astonishment. This morning she'd known of no one who was in an 'open' relationship and now, in the space of mere minutes she knew of three couples who chose that way of life.

'Maybe they're onto something,' Autumn mused. She looked at the man, then decidedly stuck out her hand.

"Autumn Carter," she said.

He took her hand, but instead of shaking it brought it up to his mouth, and administered a soft kiss. Autumn felt herself ache inside at the touch of his lips on her skin.

"So, what do you think?" he asked. "You interested?"

Autumn thought about it for a second: she'd never been with a woman before. She'd enjoyed the moments of flirtation between her and Celina, but she'd convinced herself that it was purely the positive attention that she'd enjoyed. She mulled it over. It was only sex after all, and what happened in Encounters stayed in Encounters. It was a judgement-free zone; if the worst happened and she found that it just wasn't for her she could always utter the magic words: "Someone's at the door," and leave.

"I'm in," Autumn confirmed before downing the rest of her drink. She ordered another one and made to leave. "Find me after the courses," she murmured over her shoulder. Securing an experience for the evening made her feel twice as confident now. She was untouchable. She watched as Celina made her way from person to person and from group to group, stopping to chat and flirt where necessary. She wondered how long Celina would do this. She couldn't do it forever and in a few years she would be the oldest here. Would her strict policies on guests extend to herself when the time came? Somehow Autumn didn't think so.

Autumn swayed in time with the soft music; the whiskey was warming and she felt the familiar tipsy haze beginning to creep over her. Two other people in quick succession approached her; Autumn didn't feel an attraction to either of them and politely declined. She positively gagged at the last man who, although good looking, had a creepy air about him that Autumn didn't like. Celina appeared next to her.

"I see you're proving to be very popular," she said enviously. "I thought you might be. The guests have always loved a young, hot blonde to play with."

Autumn smiled awkwardly. She was more than just a plaything to draw in fresh punters. She had more value than that to bring to Encounters.

"Err, thanks," she mustered as politely as she could. She didn't want to irritate Celina again by saying the wrong thing or sounding ungrateful.

Celina sipped on her champagne. The glass lingered on her lips as she surveyed the room proudly. The menus had been handed out this time around, a mistake Celina was not keen to repeat, although it had ended happily enough last time and she didn't have too many regrets about it. Without the mix-up, Autumn wouldn't have been dragged backstage for an emergency explanation and she wouldn't have stumbled on stage at precisely the right time. She also wouldn't have set a record for the highest amount of money any course had ever made.

The thought of the money warmed Celina's heart. She knew from the moment she'd clapped eyes on Autumn in her husband's office that she'd make a fantastic addition to her PA collection. As long as she got what she needed, which she always did, there were plenty of heartbroken young things desperate to rebel and find themselves. The deal was always sealed by the money, always.

The gong sounded stridently in the ballroom and the first course entered the stage. It was a young man in his mid-twenties. He wore black jeans and a pale yellow top. He stood with his chest inflated self-assuredly. Autumn could tell that this guy was more than just confident, he was extremely comfortable with what was going on. This probably wasn't his first time in Encounters.

The bidding began. Celina chaired the auction as usual, rallying the guests who, although raucous and vocal were nowhere near the baying mob they had been when Autumn herself had stood on that stage. The first course made the princely sum of seven and a half thousand pounds.

'Pitiful.' Autumn heckled within; she had practically made that amount from her percentage alone.

The main course was next. A chubby girl who couldn't have been older than twenty-one appeared. Autumn felt more pity: surely she'd attract even less attention. The bidding started again. Autumn couldn't have been more wrong. The crowd loved the girl. She flirted with them and hitched up her skirt to show a little more leg. She ran her hands over her body to accentuate her curves and played with her hair in a cutesy fashion. She made twice as much as the previous course and strutted off to the fantasy rooms with the man who had won her, where he would choose her fate. Finally, the last course appeared. Autumn was, in all honesty, getting bored now. The procedure seemed to be pretty monotonous, but the crowd, however, clearly disagreed. They were like hungry dogs fighting over scraps of meat, belligerent and quarrelsome if things didn't go their way. The last course made a solid ten thousand pounds and followed the winning bidder behind the curtain emulating the actions of the previous two courses.

The music started up again and the crowd calmed, although they were considerably more riled up than they had been before the auction. The behaviour of the guests in the ballroom was pretty normal from what Autumn could tell, aside from some obvious flirting and propositions being made. People behaved as they would at most high-class social occasions: they danced, drank, chatted and occasionally stopped to help themselves to canapés when the waitresses walked by. Autumn had finished her second drink by now and wanted a third. She couldn't be bothered to push her way through the throngs of people to get to the bar for another whiskey so beckoned one of the waitresses over. She didn't even try to remember her name. She thanked her politely and took two saucers of champagne, drinking the first quickly and setting the glass down on a nearby table before starting on the second. She felt a hand on the small of her back and turned to see the Irish man and his red-headed friend.

"Shall we choose a room?" the woman suggested. Her voice was soft and sultry. She was well spoken and had an air of grace about her that gave Autumn the impression that she came from old money. She moved with an exceptional elegance and poise that Autumn envied and almost certainly would not be able to replicate. The man guided Autumn to another branch of fantasy rooms through an ornate archway. The rooms behind the stage were reserved for bidders only; they were able to take their pick and use as many of the rooms as they liked, knowing that they would only be joined if they'd denoted that wish with the presence of a token on their door. Autumn allowed herself to be directed whilst the woman with the red hair flanked him on the opposite side, entwining her arm with his.

"Any preference?" he asked his companion. Clearly both of them had been here before.

"Something luxurious," she said decidedly. "I want sumptuous interiors and eight-hundred thread count Egyptian cotton."

He nodded, impressed with her choice. He opened the panel of a few of the doors, leaving the two women stood in the hallway. Before long they were being beckoned over. Autumn realised upon entry that she didn't know either of their names.

"I'm Autumn," she reintroduced herself, hoping the man didn't notice the repetition of information.

"I know," said the man, sliding a white token over the hook on the door before opening it. "I'm Blaine and as I mentioned before my glamorous assistant here is Genevieve," he said grabbing Genevieve's buttocks and giving them a squeeze. Genevieve giggled furtively then, narrowing her eyes slightly placed a hand on Blaine's crotch and gripped his manhood firmly.

"I'm here for her remember, so you can look, but don't touch unless I say so."

These words sent shivers down Autumn's spine. Genevieve was here for her? She felt incredibly wanted: her sexual state heightened without even the slightest touch.

The room they were in was exactly what Genevieve had wanted – Autumn got the feeling that what Genevieve wanted, she generally got. The space was an exercise in luxury, decorated with sumptuous draped fabrics and a huge four-poster bed with several plush feather stuffed cushions for added indulgence. A large velvet chaise longue stood proudly in the corner of the room. On it laid two blindfolds, a satin sash and a large feather tickler, which resembled an old-fashioned ostrich duster. She picked up one of the blindfolds and examined it before setting it back down on the chaise for later use. This room was a stark contrast to the one she'd been in last time; the two rooms couldn't be more different. The hard concrete surfaces she'd experienced in the other room had bruised her knees to the point where they'd only just faded a month later; still, she hadn't complained at the time.

Blaine retrieved drinks from the dumb waiter. Autumn quickly came to realise that these were a feature in all the rooms and must be part of the ticket price. He handed her another whiskey, which she sipped at. Autumn had lost count of the number of drinks that she'd had now; she was feeling confident and was determined to enjoy this new experience as fully as possible. Genevieve and Blaine casually sipped their drinks, neither uttering a word. Autumn watched, intrigued as to who was going to make the first move. The air was thick with sexual energy, but once Genevieve had finished her drink, she stood up from the edge of the bed where she had been sitting and ran her fingertips over the plush material that was draped over the rich mahogany frame. She straddled Blaine, pulling up her barely there, nude silk dress in order to spread her legs wide enough. She ran her fingers through his hair seductively. She shifted on his lap and over her shoulder beckoned Autumn to join them.

'This is it,' Autumn thought excitedly as she walked over to the couple and deftly picked up a blindfold and satin sash as she went. Just watching them had turned her on.

She could feel the wetness developing between her legs already. The couple resumed kissing as she sat on the bed, a little unsure as to where she would fit into this. She had thought after all that Genevieve was solely interested in her, however looking at them now she wasn't entirely convinced that was true. As if reading her mind Genevieve broke their kiss. She pushed Blaine down on the bed and climbed over him, stalking her way towards Autumn, a look of pure lust on her feminine features. The two women were face to face now: Autumn could almost taste Genevieve's breath on her face, and it was sweet and warm. The lights had been dimmed and soft music was now playing. Genevieve leaned in and tentatively kissed Autumn who returned the affection. The feeling, so different from kissing a man, was more sensual. The kiss was far gentler and more arousing than Autumn had expected. Her pulse quickened as the kiss intensified, Genevieve placed a hand delicately on the small of Autumn's back and guided her in closer. Their kisses became more urgent; their lips pressed firmly against each other, Genevieve's tongue probing the depths of Autumn's mouth. Her hands moved upwards to tease Autumn's breasts, she pulled at the material of her dress, desperate to release the pert mounds beneath. Autumn helped slide the dress down to her waist. Her nipples were already hard, standing to attention in anticipation of Genevieve's touch. Genevieve grabbed at them greedily. Her fingers brushed Autumn's hard pink buds and she twisted them lightly between her fingers, rolling them around, basking in the delectable pinch she was inflicting on Autumn.

Autumn let her head fall back and let out a small moan. She gasped when she felt fingers between her legs. They were not Genevieve's – hers were still caressing Autumn's breasts, alternating between cupping them with the entirety of her palm and skilfully pinching her tender nipples. The hands parting her thighs were Blaine's. Autumn looked down and saw that he was naked; his muscular physique was a mouth-watering sight. His hands were strong and rugged, they found the split in her dress and entered, expertly locating her most sensitive spot. It was his turn to gasp now as he realised she wore no barrier. He took a second to enjoy her wetness before pushing his fingers inside her. Autumn lay back a little, wanting him to enter her deeper. Genevieve read her mind and released her breasts. She pulled the dress up and off, revealing Autumn's beautiful nakedness. Autumn opened her legs further and

Blaine leaned in, taking her soft lips into his mouth: insatiably he sucked, transferring his attention between them and her engorged pearl. She throbbed with anticipation as she felt his tongue snake over her most sensitive area. More and more of her juices flowed out and coated his lips as he worked diligently to deliver her to the precipice of fulfilment. Genevieve seemed to like the look of this. She gave Autumn's nipples one last pinch and joined Blaine, kneeling between their plaything's legs. She nibbled up and down Autumn's inner thighs, her hands masturbating Blaine's thickly veined member at the same time. His shaft pulsated at Genevieve's touch, and she skilfully split her attention equally between her two partners until wanting her own release. She stepped out of her dress, and climbed back onto the bed. Genevieve straddled Autumn's face. She looked down at her.

"Make me come," Genevieve commanded, a rough edge to her soft voice. Autumn obeyed and grabbed at Genevieve's thighs, pulling her down, eager to taste the glistening wetness that was offered to her. Genevieve obliged and lowered herself onto Autumn's outstretched tongue.

Autumn had never felt more alive: electricity coursed through her veins. The fact that she had never done this before didn't enter her thoughts. She tentatively explored Genevieve's inner recesses and relished the boost to her ego as Genevieve squirmed and moaned with pleasure. Blaine wanted his own release now and pulled his head from between Autumn's delicious sanctum. He stroked his almighty erection and squeezed it at the base on each downward stroke, lapping up the scene in front of him. He entered Autumn easily, pushing into her aching centre in one dominant movement. Blaine placed his hands on Genevieve's shoulders and used her as leverage to delve in and out of Autumn as deeply as he could. Autumn raised her hips in time to meet his every stroke, all the while continuing her assault on Genevieve's silken slit. Strands of Genevieve's pleasure ran down her thighs as she rode Autumn's face, groaning in ecstasy, on the threshold of climax. Genevieve leant towards Blaine. He moved forwards to meet her, his fingers outstretched, searching for her pale upturned nipples. He began circling them with the tips of his fingers. He pulled Genevieve closer to him, turning her face to meet his. Blaine kissed her passionately, his tongue savouring her sweet taste.

It was Genevieve who broke the kiss. She extricated herself and knelt at the side of the bed surveying the scene in front of her. Autumn's face glinted with the residue of her pleasure; Genevieve moved towards Autumn and licked her face, tasting her own nectar and savouring the sweet, honey-like flavour. She held Autumn's face in her hands and inspected it: the girl certainly was very pretty. She was impressed with Blaine's choice and showed her appreciation by showering Autumn with soft fluttering kisses. Autumn closed her eyes and stretched her arms out in bliss.

Genevieve got to her feet and turned her back on the two. Blaine, when presented with Genevieve's pert behind, a behind that he wasn't allowed to touch unless instructed to, became even harder. He thrust more desperately into Autumn. Genevieve placed a hand on each buttock and spread herself wide.

"Dive in Blaine, the water's fine," she purred enticingly. Blaine didn't need telling twice: he pulled her up onto the bed. Genevieve straddled Autumn on all fours; the two women's faces were now inches apart. Genevieve's backside was pulled up higher and Blaine bent his head to meet it, burying his face between her cheeks. He flicked his tongue over her taut hole, probing when he felt it give a little. Genevieve gasped as he did so and pushed back into his face, eager for more. She took one of Autumn's pert nipples in her mouth and began to suck, gently nibbling on it. Autumn arched her back, enjoying this but missing the frantic thrusts from Blaine, which had all but stopped since he'd become distracted. She pulled herself out from underneath Genevieve, Blaine's erection slid out of her. She picked up the blindfold and looked at it, feeling the sleek material between her fingers.

"Put it on," Genevieve demanded, still on all fours. "Get on the rug, on your hands and knees and put it on."

Autumn did exactly as she was told, climbing quickly, eager to see what new experience lay ahead of her. Autumn kneeled there, on all fours with the blindfold on. The noises Blaine had been making whilst he tongued Genevieve's tight ass had stopped and she could hear them whispering, making their plan. The anticipation was almost too much. Autumn was in a deep state of longing; the entrance to her sex pulsated and throbbed with anticipation, she could feel herself aching to be taken. She reached a hand underneath her and delicately strummed her swollen jewel, slowly rotating her hips as she did so. Being blindfolded heightened her other senses, she felt more sensitive and receptive to her own touch than ever before.

She felt movement underneath: someone had slid beneath her. She reached out a hand and felt a large, stiff erection. It was Blaine. He grabbed Autumn by the hips; she arched her back slightly, giving him better access, and he pulled her down onto his iron-hard cock, driving her down on him with such a force that it took her breath away. Behind her Genevieve stirred and Autumn felt movement behind her. Genevieve's hand pressed gently against the back of her neck. She encouraged Autumn's head downwards, flattening her against Blaine's rugged body. Her face pressed against his chest.

Genevieve's other hand played with Blaine's balls, gently squeezing and tugging them as he impaled Autumn on his solid shaft. Autumn was totally restricted, the blindfold still impeding her vision. Blaine held her hands behind her back in a vice-like grip, thrusting upwards, plunging in and out of her masterfully. Genevieve pressed down on her neck harder still. She was completely at their mercy and she loved it.

"I'm going to fuck you now, Autumn," Genevieve directed, her sultry voice taking on a commanding edge. Autumn nodded under Genevieve's hand. She felt Blaine leave her and a large, baton-shaped object gently part her soft folds. It was girthy and cool, so she wriggled in order to accommodate it better, but Genevieve's other hand was now on the small of her back, pressing down commandingly and restricting her movements even further. Autumn wondered how on earth Genevieve was managing to insert the toy; she had both her hands occupied holding Autumn down. The object plunged into her, demanding her full attention and surging throughout her every inch. It slid in and out of her with the rhythmic force that only came with the thrust of hips. Had another man joined them? It was impossible: Blaine had put a white token on the door, not gold or burgundy.

Genevieve bent lower and grazed Autumn's back with her soft, full lips. Her silk-like red hair trailed over Autumn and sent a shiver down her spine. Genevieve was thrusting in and out of her. Autumn wiggled a hand free and Blaine loosened his grip, allowing her a small amount of freedom. She reached backward, desperate to solve the mystery. Genevieve was wearing a supple leather pant-like harness and protruding from the centre and penetrating Autumn was a huge, baton-like penis. Autumn felt the base of it as it pumped in and out of her, her fingers barely able to wrap around its thick, wet shaft. She pulled her hand away, her fingertips coated thickly with the essence of her excitement. It clicked: Genevieve was wearing a strap-on. Autumn felt the thrill of taboo surging through her, as she was once again being completely dominated – somehow this time it felt different.

Blaine's lips were on hers now. With his free hand, he rubbed his shaft, his stride hastening with each and every stroke. His tongue danced in her mouth and he bit her bottom lip gently. Autumn extended her hand, and Blaine sucked on her fingers greedily. To him, she tasted exquisitely sweet. He was getting impatient now, desperate almost. Vying for his own release he pulled Autumn forward. Genevieve realised what he was doing and allowed it to happen, knowing that she had had the majority of the fun so far. The dildo slid out of Autumn and she sat down hard on Blaine's eager cock. His hips arched, desiring her immediately. Autumn heard the pop of press-studs and the heavy dildo Genevieve had been wearing fell to the floor along with the harness. She reached over and pulled Autumn's blindfold off, throwing it on the floor alongside the harness. She was once again completely naked.

Autumn gyrated her hips; Blaine's penis was not as big as the toy Genevieve had used but it had a delectable curve to it that rubbed deliciously against her innermost pleasure point. Genevieve nimbly straddled Blaine, making sure to face Autumn as she did so. She lowered herself onto his face: his mouth connected with her neatly shaved, soft lips. He explored them deftly with his tongue, indulging in the silken wetness she had presented to him. He had Autumn riding his dick – she was young and tight and felt incredible, and she was so wet he could feel her essence dripping onto his thighs – and he had Genevieve riding his face. The two women leaned forward to share a deeply passionate kiss, their hands entwined in one another's hair, creating a perfect triangle of debauchery. Blaine could feel himself approaching climax. He pulled Autumn down hard and thrust deeper inside of her, exploding into her with an intensity that shook him to his core. He cried out, the sound muffled but obvious. His thrusts became less and less powerful. Autumn gyrated still, eager to persuade every last blissful orgasmic wave from him.

Genevieve surveyed Blaine. Once he was still, she pulled Autumn from him and couldn't help but notice the ejaculate dripping down her thighs. Genevieve positioned her on the bed next to Blaine, who reclined in a post-orgasmic stupor, lazily watching the two women. Genevieve climbed between Autumn's legs and began sucking and licking, lapping up every drop of Blaine's cream. Her tongue connected with Autumn's swollen pearl. Autumn gasped loudly and rocked her hips. Genevieve buried her face further and, at the same time inserted two fingers into Autumn, curving them upwards and pressing on her G spot with expert precision. She rubbed at it steadily, applying more and more pressure. Her tongue enslaved Autumn's slick softness. Genevieve flicked it over the nub continuously, working tirelessly to bring the orgasm out of her, all the while stroking Autumn internally and enjoying the feeling of her clenching around those digits.

Autumn began to tremble. Knowing the young woman was close, Genevieve quickened her pace, feverishly swirling her tongue around the quivering bud. Autumn cried out; Blaine had taken one of her nipples in his mouth and bitten down on it gently, but firmly, his hand massaging the area around it. It was too much, this additional stimulation pushed her over the edge. Genevieve felt Autumn's canal spasm and clamp around her fingers, as she began to shake uncontrollably as the orgasm swept over her. Genevieve did not stop, she redoubled her efforts, this time flattening her tongue and pressing it against the entirety of Autumn's sex, slowly dragging it upwards.

Autumn moaned. Her hips bucked against Genevieve's face as she came to the summit of her pleasure. She closed her eyes and allowed the mouth-watering intensity to wash over her. Genevieve pulled away and straightened up. Autumn could see Genevieve's fingers strumming against her own engorged nub now. Autumn ran her eyes over Genevieve. Her pale skin was flushed, reddening further as she approached her own release. After a few moments, Genevieve came, and her head rolled backwards. She opened her mouth, letting out a soft, low moan. She slumped onto the bed panting, her head resting on Autumn's abdomen. Blaine turned to the women and kissed each of them in turn.

"Thank you," he said genuinely. "That was... something else." Autumn stifled a small, smug giggle. Genevieve smiled.

"I'm inclined to agree with you there, darling," she said warmly, before getting up and pouring them all a drink.

Next to the drinks stood a grand-looking gramophone. Genevieve loaded up a record and lowered the needle. Autumn regarded it with surprise. She had totally missed it earlier, obviously too wrapped up in lustful passion. Genevieve strode back, passing Autumn her newly filled glass. She gulped at it thirstily. Mulling over all she'd experienced, she couldn't help but thank Encounters and Celina. They had opened up new doors for Autumn and helped her to break personal boundaries.

The threesome chatted for a few minutes. Autumn was surprised at how quickly the conversation turned to the mundane. Both of her partners were business-minded and their conversation reflected that.

"What should we do now?" she asked a touch impatiently. Last time she had just put her clothes back on and rejoined the party, but this time they were lounging about like old friends, sipping drinks and chatting about nothing in particular. The only difference was that she didn't know many old friends who would be happy to do this completely naked.

After a while the conversation grew stagnant. Genevieve and Blaine had talked business, mainly stocks and shares or anything else to do with money and power. Autumn had joined in as and when she could but for the most part she was out of her depth. So instead of talking, she had continued drinking. She had finished off the drinks Blaine had ordered earlier single-handedly and when the bottle had run dry she decided to make a move and rejoin the rest of the party, reasoning that although Celina had given her blessing to do whatever she wanted, she didn't want to push her luck by being absent for the rest of the night.

Genevieve and Blaine showed no sign of finishing their conversation, so Autumn said the only thing she could think of that would allow her to leave, no questions asked.

"That was great but I think someone's at the door, I'll be back soon," she said.

The two looked at her, a bit put out that she was leaving but neither objected. She stepped into her dress and pulled it up quickly. There was no mirror in the room and Autumn could tell that their session had undone all of Martin's hard work; combing her hair through with her fingertips, all she could do was to hope that that would do the trick and that it didn't look too dishevelled. Autumn made her way to the door, opened it and, casting one last appreciative glance at Genevieve and Blaine, stepped out of the room.

It was cool in the hallway; the frigid air felt nice against her flushed face. Autumn wasn't sure if it was from the sex or the alcohol – maybe, she reasoned, it was both. She strutted back into the ballroom and felt like all eyes were on her. She caught many appreciative glances cast her way and positively swelled with self-assured pride. Celina was nowhere to be seen – probably engaging in a little extra-curricular activity herself, Autumn mused. She realised that she still needed to speak to Celina. After all, when the event ended Autumn was officially homeless. The thought was a sobering one. She set off to find Celina, having no clue which room she might be in, so instead headed straight to her office.

Autumn knocked first. There was no answer so she pushed the door open gently and stepped inside. She flicked the light switch on and blinked into the bright light. Celina wasn't here. Autumn wandered into the room, knowing that she should leave but wanting to stay nonetheless. Autumn sat in Celina's swivel chair and turned gently from left to right. Celina's computer was on: her screen saver was a picture from many years ago of Celina collecting an award and smiling that Hollywood smile from ear to ear. Autumn reclined, imagining herself as the lady of Encounters one day; this office would be hers, those clothes would be hers and *this* – she thought of the business as a whole – would be hers. She stopped rocking in the chair when she noticed a file on Celina's desktop with the name 'PA Analysis'. She leaned forward, unable to help herself. She was the PA and she wanted to know how and why she was being analysed. Clicking on it she sat back, her eyes wide.

There were several folders inside, each with different names on. Her eyes scanned the screen, stopping when she found the file with her name attached. Inside was just one document, it was entitled 'projected earnings' and showed a graph calculating how much money Autumn would make the company. She felt sick: the graph showed last month, this month, and the Christmas event. After that there was nothing but a red cross next to the months that followed. She came out of the file and clicked on the previous name. This girl's income was dated the three months previous to her, the file preceding that one showed another three months of service and so on and so on. Each time the income amount spiked, then trailed off. It looked very much as though Celina kept people on for a few months at a time, used them to earn as much money as she could, then cut the dead weight. Autumn noticed in horror that every single PA had started their time at Encounters as one of the courses. She had been manipulated. Autumn had to ask herself: were the strong feelings of liberation and empowerment she'd been experiencing real? Or was everything here a lie, designed to massage the egos of the super-rich and lull vulnerable girls such as herself into a false sense of belonging? She felt sick. She had placed this job and Celina above everything else in her life. Was she really that easily influenced? She couldn't, or wouldn't, believe it.

Pushing herself away from the desk, she decided that she needed yet another drink. She wanted to speak to Celina now more than ever. Closing the folder, she made her way back to the party, making sure she left everything in the office as it had been when she'd entered.

The gong sounded loudly as Autumn re-entered the ballroom, signalling to that the guests that party time was about to be over and that they should finish whatever or whoever they were doing. Celina was saying farewell to a group that Autumn recognised from last month's event. The men were something to do with motor racing and the women their extra-marital partners. Autumn steadied herself: she needed Celina to let her stay tonight and Celina was an 'I'll scratch your back if you scratch mine' kind of woman. It was now Autumn's turn to do the manipulating. She approached Celina and adopted a flirtatious smile. Wrapping one arm around her she gave her a squeeze.

"How about we take this back to yours?" she suggested. Celina raised an eyebrow. Autumn was clearly not sober.

Tonight would be the perfect time to get to know her a little better.

"I thought you'd never ask," she murmured. "You haven't had enough then? I saw you disappear off with Mr Maguire and I know he has a voracious appetite for young women like you," she said, her hand finding its way between the split in Autumn's dress. "You're still wet," she purred, biting her lip in a suppressive fashion. Autumn pushed her hand away.

"Later. We still have guests," she added, after seeing the affronted look on Celina's face at being rejected. Celina nodded. Her guests were always the most important thing.

Once the ballroom was empty the two women collected their belongings and made to leave. Hendricks was waiting by the lift in the car park for Celina. Autumn couldn't help but note his lack of surprise at her presence. He was silent throughout the drive, only speaking once they pulled over, bidding them goodnight as they got out of the car.

"So, this is where you live?" Autumn asked. Celina nodded and pressed her index finger to a small panel next to an imposing gate. It swung open steadily. Autumn's breath caught in her throat. Celina's wealth seemed to be endless. Before her stood an ultra-modern house seemingly constructed entirely from glass and glowing like a beacon of luxury against the night sky. They walked briskly up a stone path. Small spotlights built into the ground illuminated their way. Autumn wondered if perhaps now she'd see a different side to Celina, a side a bit more human, less obsessed with money, power and sex? She hoped so. Occasionally she thought that she had caught glimpses of the person beneath the mask, plus she knew Jack: he wouldn't be with someone who was cold and calculated through and through.

'Jack!' she thought, panicking slightly. She had forgotten all about him.

“Will anyone else be joining us?” she asked with uncertainty as she stepped through the door, clutching her overnight bag in her arms.

“You mean my husband? Darling Autumn, we haven’t stayed under the same roof in a very long time,” she said without compassion. She pulled a grip out of her hair and, shaking her head, let it fall down loosely around her face. Autumn was surprised. Where did Jack live then, she wondered, hardly believing that this really was a marriage that anyone would enjoy being part of.

“It’s not ‘an arranged’ marriage, if that’s what you’re thinking. It’s a marriage of convenience. He gets to appear one way and I get to stay in the country,” she explained.

“But what way is that?” Autumn asked. She was so confused. Jack, for the most part, was a kind man, he ran his own business and was good looking. Why would he settle for this kind of life?

“Oh Autumn. You can’t possibly be this naïve,” Celina scoffed. “My husband is gay.”

“What?” Autumn laughed. “No, he isn’t. He can’t be.” Autumn thought back to their own encounters. Had all that been in her head as well? She began to question herself in the deepest possible way. Did she know anything about anyone? Her life seemed to be alien to her now: memories distorted or remembered incorrectly, or had they been wrongly interpreted at the time? She just didn’t know.

“I can assure you that he is.” Celina asserted.

“But that’s ridiculous. Why can’t he just be gay, then? No one would care.” Autumn challenged, still not believing that someone would go through all of this just to hide their sexuality.

“His family are deeply religious and very traditional. He adores his parents and I convinced him that it would kill them to find out the truth. Ideally, they would have preferred he marry a nice white girl of their faith; however, they settled for me. Partly because my family are wealthy and funded his business and partly because we are Roman Catholic as a family, and the fact that my father is a well respected member of the church went a really long way with them," she explained. "He knows which side his bread is buttered. I've made him painfully aware what leaving me would mean. A divorce would be bad enough, but for them to find out that he's gay and that he cheats on his poor wife with men? Well, that would destroy his parents; they'd disown him on the spot. He really should have thought it through a little more, but he was in a bad way when I got to him so it was easy to assure him that my plan was the only way. Enough about that." She stopped suddenly before adding, "You know I don't like to talk about my private life."

She poured Autumn a large glass of red wine and handed it to her. Autumn was sobering up now and didn't think another glass of wine was a bright idea. She went to set it down on the counter but Celina caught her hand and raised it back up.

"Drink it. It's good," she said, pushing the glass towards Autumn's lips, encouraging her to drink. Autumn did so. Celina was right. It was a deliciously fruity wine, which danced on her tongue. It didn't take her long to finish the glass. The conversation from then on was torpid and peppered with falsities. Autumn had no intention of sleeping with Celina, she just needed a place to stay. She did however feel that she understood Celina a little more now, the product of an unfortunate coupling between two people who felt, for one reason or another, unable to be themselves with the people who should accept them for who they are and love them unconditionally. Autumn felt bad for Celina but her heart really went out to Jack. How had she been so blind? Her 'Gaydar' was usually spot on. She'd instinctively known David was gay, but that may have been due more to the fact that on the first day she'd met him he'd been wearing a rainbow print T-shirt and handing out flyers for the LGBT Society.

Celina had poured Autumn another glass of wine and Autumn's head was beginning to swim now. She looked at Celina, her olive face fading in and out of focus as Autumn swayed slightly.

"Maybe just a half for you now," Celina said laughing. "I don't want you unconscious."

"You don't want me at all," Autumn said, slurring slightly. "You want to collect me, add me to your assortment of fucked up PAs, make some money out of me then bin me off," she declared, her voice clearer now.

Celina looked at her, gobsmacked. None of them had ever come to that conclusion, she'd always managed to convince them that it was their decision to leave, that they'd 'found themselves'. And remembering Celina as the greatest mentor and lover that they'd ever had.

"No. What makes you say that?" said Celina, false concern etched on her features. Autumn could see straight through it now, even in her advanced state of drunkenness. No longer did she see a beautiful, elegant woman. Now she saw the ugliness inside of her. A selfish woman, who'd exploited a man who, through no fault of his own, found himself in a difficult situation. Under the guise of helping him she'd trapped him, turning a difficult situation into an impossible one. She was disgusted with her.

"I saw the files, Celina," Autumn confessed. "There have been plenty before me and they'll be plenty after me, so don't try and deny it. I'd have a bit more respect for you if you could just tell the truth."

"Respect?" Celina gave a mirthful laugh. "You want to talk about respect? Okay, well how's this? I don't care if you respect me. Do you think I've got here by caring about other people's feelings?" She raised her arms, gesturing to her lavish surroundings. "Get out Autumn, I wouldn't touch you if you were the last woman alive."

Autumn stood shocked. She had nowhere to go and judging by the look on Celina's face she knew it. She had her over a barrel: either Autumn behaved herself, or she was out on the street. Autumn snatched up her bag and quickly headed to the door. A wine glass smashed on the wall next to her head, fragments of glass and residue of wine showered down on her. She shut the door behind her and stood there for a moment with her heart racing. She heard another smash, this time accompanied by Celina screeching, utterly incensed by Autumn's audacity.

"I'll see you Monday, darling! If not, well, you won't see a penny. Terms and conditions, darling, frightfully important that you read them properly." She put on a false high-pitched British accent that turned Autumn's stomach and laughed maliciously. Celina loved the fact Autumn was bound to her.

'The woman is completely unhinged,' Autumn thought to herself as she scurried through the gates. She was still in her ball dress and heels and still clutching her overnight bag. She shivered in the cold night air and pulled her phone out of her pocket. It was approaching 3 a.m., she was drunk and very tired. She phoned the only person she could think of at a time like this: David.

The phone rang and rang before eventually cutting into his voice-mail. She tried him twice more, she didn't leave a message but instead hitched up her dress and began walking. She knew roughly where she was. The drive from Encounters hadn't been more than twenty minutes and most of that had been slow driving through town. She walked; she removed her heels, swapping them for the comfy trainers she had in her overnight bag. The night was cool and she shivered. Pulling out the hoodie and jogging bottoms she'd packed, she pulled them on, breathing a sigh of relief as she felt their warming benefit instantly.

Autumn trudged on and turned down yet another street. She'd left Celina's wealthy neighbourhood, where the houses had been well set back from the road and protected by imposing gates and high fences. The houses now were much further forward, they had no gates or gardens stretching out before them and some of them could do with a lick of paint and a bit of TLC. The street lights highlighted the dilapidated state of some of them. She quickened her pace and turned the corner, relieved to see a brightly lit sign about halfway down the street in front of her. It read '24 hour café'. Autumn could have cried with relief as she all but ran to the sign. She pushed the door open and basked in the warm, comforting smells. She checked her purse – there was a sign on the counter, which read 'cash only'. She tallied the change and worked out that she had a little less than seven pounds. That was plenty of money for a place like this. She ordered a strong black coffee from the girl behind the counter, who looked up from her phone, surprised to see a customer. She put the phone down and set a cup under the machine behind her, pressing the double shot button and taking Autumn's money all within a few seconds. She was clearly keen to get back to the game she had been playing. Autumn took the coffee and settled herself in one of the booths, picking up a dog-eared paper and opening it up as she sat down.

The time was now creeping up to four in the morning. Autumn drank the coffee quickly. It was far from piping hot but it was strong and right now that was all she needed. She leafed through the paper. A huge advert for *The Edge* leaped out at her. She slammed the paper shut and pushed it away from her, her gut wrenching at the thought of Ben again. She thought about calling her parents, begging them to collect her and take her home. She knew they would drop everything and come to her rescue in a heartbeat and she loved them for it, but they'd parted badly. Autumn had behaved terribly towards them. She couldn't face them yet, and certainly not in this state. She took her phone out again: she had six percent power left. This, she thought, would be better used finding the nearest hotel. She kicked herself for not thinking of this sooner – she could be climbing into crisp clean sheets right now.

Autumn located a hotel nearby and downed the last dregs of her barely palatable beverage. The pit stop had actually done her a lot of good. She'd had time to think, to assess her situation. She would be going back to work the following Monday; she wasn't going to let Celina win.

She'd never known a person quite so messed up as Celina – the woman was unreal. The evening had been full of revelations. Jack was gay and in a marriage he didn't want to be in but couldn't get out of. Celina was not who she appeared to be, and was holding Jack to ransom for her own selfish gains. Autumn knew there was nothing she could do about it. She could go and speak to Jack, try and make him see sense. But that would mean running the risk of seeing Rosa, or any of the other people that she used to work with, and she couldn't shake the memory of how they'd looked at her after Rosa's accident.

Autumn checked into the hotel, paying for the room up front on her credit card as the policy dictated, and trudged up the stairs to her room. She climbed into the clean, crisp sheets she'd envisioned. She was asleep before her head even touched the pillow, quickly drifting into an alcohol-induced, coma-like state.

CHAPTER 23

AUTUMN AWOKE FEELING GROGGY, CONFUSED AND disoriented. It took her a few minutes to remember where she was; she enjoyed a few moments of oblivious bliss before the events of the previous night flooded back into her consciousness. She was even more perplexed by what had happened now – even though she had slept on it. Which her mother had always told her helped any difficult situation: "Sleep on it dear, it'll be clearer in the morning."

She hadn't spoken to her parents for what seemed like an eternity now; mind you, she was used to speaking to her mum almost every day so any amount of time was bound to seem long. She pressed the menu button on her phone: no battery and no charger. She fumbled in the depths of her bag. Of course, she hadn't packed one. Why would she have? That would have been the smart, organised thing to do. She cursed under her breath before snatching up the phone on the night-stand and rang down to reception.

"It's your lucky day miss," the receptionist cooed down the phone. "We've got the same phone, so I'll have someone bring it up to you." Autumn thanked her and awaited the life-saving charger. Before long there was a knock at the door. A petite, middle-aged woman stood there, charger in hand, with a kind, sweet smile on her face.

“Here you go, my love,” she said sunnily. “If you could just pop it back down to reception when you’ve finished with it, that’d be grand.”

“Thank you.” Autumn blurted, barely letting the woman finish. The woman gave her a smile and turned to leave. “Sorry, before you go, what time is it please?” Autumn, who was now phoneless as well as watchless, had no clue as to what the time was.

“Oh don’t worry my love, check out isn’t until 1 p.m., you’ve got another hour yet.” She gave Autumn a reassuring smile and walked off.

Autumn closed the door and slumped onto the bed. She smelt of booze, sex and maybe a faint hint of regret. She put her phone on charge and padded into the bathroom. She hadn’t noticed the beautiful slipper bath when she’d stumbled in during the early hours of the morning. She turned the taps and poured in a little of the zesty-smelling bubble bath miniature that had been neatly placed on the side. She cleaned her teeth, staring at her reflection in the small oval bathroom mirror. She looked exhausted, was stressed and felt very alone. Maybe she should just swallow her pride and ring her parents. She narrowed her eyes at her reflection, frowning at the idea of being the one to break first. No, she would get a place sorted to begin with, find a nice little flat somewhere, get herself together and only then would she call her parents. She didn’t want them to think that she was only coming back because she had nowhere else to go.

Autumn climbed into the bath and reclined, allowing the water to wash over her, her ample breasts peaking out of the soapy water every time she took a breath; as she exhaled they sank back below the surface. She soaped herself up and washed her hair. It felt good to be clean as if washing the dirt away somehow washed everything else away as well. Autumn lowered herself in further. Her shoulders became immersed, then her neck – she kept going until her entire body was submerged in the warm bath water. Her long blonde hair looked much darker as it swirled around her in wispy tendrils, floating around her face. She felt like she wanted to stay under there forever. It was safe, silent and comforting under the water, plus even the bitter little voice inside her head refused to talk whilst she was under there. It was exactly where she needed to be.

Autumn pulled herself out of the bath gasping for air. She coughed and spluttered and dragged herself over the side. How could she have almost fallen asleep? The water in her nose had given her an intense headache. She coughed again, then with a concerted effort steadied her breathing and calmed herself down. She climbed out of the bath and sat on the side of it. She reached out for a towel and wrapped it around herself. It reminded her so much of the ones she and Ben had picked out one shopping trip many moons ago just before they'd moved in together.

She dried herself off and pulled on a fresh pair of pants and the same comfy, fleece-lined tracksuit she'd put on in the street the night before. The bath had cleared her head somewhat, but she knew that above all else she needed to find somewhere to live. She picked up her phone, and stared at the screen in confusion. She had twenty-seven missed calls from her mum, dad, David, Gregg plus a couple of numbers she didn't have in her phone. She dialled through to her voicemail. The automated voice told her that she had fifteen new messages, and she listened to the first one, a sleepy sounding David came on the line.

"Hey hon. Sorry I missed you. I was sleeping, obviously, plus you rang me at like 3 a.m.! I'll see you in a bit, gorgeous. Hashtag wedding time!" The voice-mail said jokily.

Autumn froze. It had gone midday, and she was supposed to have met David more than two hours ago for a day of wedding-related fun. How could she have forgotten? In her defence, she had had one hell of a night, but she knew that was no excuse. David was supposed to be her best friend and she should have been there for him. She called him back instantly. The phone barely rang once before a fraught voice answered.

"Autumn. Are you okay? We've been going mad here," David panted down the phone.

"I'm sorry. I'm fine. My phone died and I ended up in a hotel," she began, she paused, not sure of exactly how much to tell David.

"You were out?" he asked bluntly, the tone of his voice changing now from concern to disapproval.

"Well, yeah. We had an event," she explained.

"I know Autumn, but it's supposed to be a job. Fucking some rich snobs, getting wasted and staying out until four in the morning isn't exactly part of the remit, especially if it makes you too hungover the next day to fulfil a promise to a friend!" David said, his voice shaking with rage. "I can't believe you, Autumn. What's happened to you? You're nothing but a self-centred bitch. I can't take it any more, Autumn; I've got bigger things to worry about. So just fuck off and leave me alone. I don't need people like you in my life. Oh and by the way, your parents know. I had no other choice than to tell them. We thought something terrible had happened to you. First you ring over and over again at three in the morning, then you don't show up for something that you shouldn't miss for the world!" He was practically screaming now. Autumn had to hold the handset away from her ear.

Tears pricked at her eyes, a cocktail of emotions spun inside her, and she felt sick. *Her parents knew*. She would have completely lost them now: their little girl, the high-class hooker is how they would see her. She couldn't stand the thought of losing David as well. He was her rock, and she needed him.

"David please..." she began but it was too late. He had put the phone down. The monotonous dead tone sounded in her ear, signifying the flatlining of their friendship. She tried him again and again, but each time all she got was his chirpy voice-mail. It broke her heart hearing it. She couldn't stand the thought of being questioned by her parents. She imagined their saddened faces, and the disgust they would have for her outweighing any concern they might have felt. She opted for a brief text message instead. She put only that she was fine and that she was sorry and finally that she would talk to them soon. She received an almost instant reply. 'OK x.'

Autumn burst into tears. She couldn't go home yet, she needed to do so much. Top of her list was to make things right with David and to sort herself out, which for some reason she couldn't do at home. In the company of her parents she regressed into a stroppy teenager, she didn't know why – she just did. She needed to do this by herself. If she went home, assuming her parents would even open the door to her, she'd only bury her head. From now on she was determined to tackle her life head on.

Autumn caught a cab to the centre of town and paraded up and down the streets looking in every single estate agents window. They were all shut; it was a Sunday afternoon, after all.

"Guess it's going to be another night in a hotel," she sighed. Autumn was about ready to throw the towel in when she spotted someone coming out of 'Moveright', a chain of lettings agents specialising in student accommodation. She sped up her pace and walked in, the little bell above the door tinkling as she entered. A friendly looking young man looked up. Autumn stopped instantly the second their eyes met. He was tall, broad, blonde and extremely good looking. He had also been inside her on her first night at Encounters. She stood with her mouth agape. He was meant to be among the richest people in the country, not working as an estate agent.

"What are you doing here?" Autumn asked, totally bewildered. He beckoned her to sit down, glancing urgently around at the three other people in the room, who, thankfully, all seemed to be engrossed in emails or paperwork.

"I'm being forced to learn the ropes. My dad owns the company and my parents apparently are sick of funding my extravagances," he explained, his blue eyes filling with disdain. "Why are you here? Have you come for money? I don't have any. It's all in a trust fund," he added, suddenly sounding panicked.

"Look," Autumn said, hardly believing that the controlling man from the bondage room was barely more than a moneyed little boy. She saw her chance. "I'm not here for money, up until now I didn't even know your name…" She glanced at his nametag then added with a smile, "Mike, I need somewhere to live." Mike visibly relaxed, he breathed out an audible sigh of relief and began typing on the computer in front of him.

"Okay, Miss…" he trailed off realising he had no idea what Autumn's name was either.

"Carter, Autumn Carter," she said commandingly, surprised at how, in the outside world, their roles had reversed. He nodded politely and continued to type. He asked her several questions, never quite managing to make eye contact. When she had answered them all satisfactorily he turned the screen around to show her the available properties.

"Which ones are available to rent immediately?" she questioned.

"As in now? You want to move in today?" he asked, a look of disbelief on his face. "Well, none of them. We have to do checks, even our own properties need references, plus we need a deposit and that takes at least a couple of days to clear. The soonest I could get you in somewhere would probably be Wednesday next week," he said apologetically.

Autumn looked at him. She was going to play this to her advantage and poor old Mike wasn't going to like it.

"Look Mike. We're going to play this one way. You're going to get me somewhere tonight," she instructed. "You know me," she lowered her voice, "intimately. So, unless you want me to enlighten everyone here on what you like to do with mummy and daddy's money in your spare time then I suggest you just press whatever it is you need on your little computer and give me the keys. I'm not asking for Buckingham Palace, just a nice little one-bed. I don't even care where it is."

Mike looked at her, weighing up his options.

"Okay, well you don't need to be a stone-cold bitch about it. I had you down as a nice girl, you know."

Autumn winced. That was the second time in two hours she'd been called a bitch, both of the self-centred and stone-cold variety. Mike stared at his screen intently, working quickly in order to avoid being blackmailed by Autumn for much longer. He reached into his desk drawer and pulled out a large keyring with many silver keys on it. They jangled loudly, causing one of his colleagues to look up. She saw a deal closing and decided it was best to let the business take care of itself so returned to her task without question. Mike removed a set of keys and handed them to Autumn, along with the rental particulars to the property.

"It's a one-bedroomed flat, a little out of the centre but pretty much everything is within walking distance. You know, all the amenities and that. Plus, there's a bus route on that road." Autumn took the keys and details from him and looked them over, examining her new home with interest. "I will need a deposit though, and references as soon as you can. If they're not sorted by the end of next week you're out."

Autumn nodded her understanding and thanked him. She really was truly grateful for his help, even if it had been forced from him. She was sorry she'd been required to handle the situation like that, but really, there was no other choice.

She walked into the light and airy one-bed. It was smaller than the pictures had made out, but it was clean, warm and had a working television and a comfy double bed. Autumn looked around. It was sparse and definitely needed making more homely. She wouldn't be able to put it off for much longer. She was going to have to go home and get her belongings, which also meant seeing her parents.

Autumn awoke on Monday morning filled with a sense of dread. Today she had to go back to Encounters and face Celina; if she didn't, she could wave goodbye to any chance of being remunerated for her work. She looked around her small flat in the early morning sun. It was starting to look a bit more like home. She'd decorated it with a few bits and pieces from home. The previous evening she'd ventured back to The Barings. She'd caught a taxi and asked the driver to wait outside for her. Her parents had been out, as she had suspected. They usually went out Sunday afternoons. She'd slipped inside and gathered up as much as she could. Fortunately, the homely necessities from the home she'd shared with Ben had never been unpacked so were easy to collect. She bundled her clothes into black bags and this time remembered her phone charger and her precious watch. She loaded up the taxi and off they went. Autumn had noticed bottles of various types of alcohol set out neatly on the dining room table. Her mum always started collecting supplies the week before her parties, but with the amount Autumn had just seen, it looked as though she'd been collecting all year. She'd spent the rest of Sunday setting up her new home. The only thing she'd forgotten was to get her toiletries. She had what Rosa had liked to call a 'stripper shower', which consisted of a lot of face wipes and a spritz of perfume before tying her hair in a messy bun on top of her head. She wasn't going to make a special effort at work anymore; she was going to keep her head down and make sure she gave Celina no reason to withhold her pay and just get on with it. She probably wouldn't have time to lock horns with her now anyway; she had, after all, only got half the time to prepare for the next event as she had grown accustomed to.

'Just two weeks until D Day,' she thought to herself as she fastened her jeans and slipped on her furry winter boots before heading out the door of her new little flat. Even though she'd been living there for less than twenty-four hours it was starting to feel a little like home.

The taxi pulled up to the gates of Encounters. She was so fed up of taking cabs. She needed to get a car sorted and soon. She went through the usual rigmarole of entering the building, tapping in codes onto keypads and climbing through lift doors disguised as erotic art. All of this in the cold light of day seemed so over-the-top, tacky almost. She entered her office and saw that Celina had already been in. The door had been left open and on her desk was an enormous pile of paperwork. She leafed through the first few pages. The entire stack was made up of applicant after applicant; this would take her weeks to get through.

"I hope you don't mind, but I took the liberty of bringing the hopefuls to you, seeing as though you're late," Celina's smooth and calculated voice said. She was asserting her dominance over Autumn early on.

"Not at all," Autumn returned, equally smoothly. "I'll get on it right away," Autumn said, ignoring the latter comment. She was thirty seconds late if that. Celina gave her a cold look up and down, clearly unimpressed with Autumn's attire, then left the room – but only after raising one perfectly shaped eyebrow at her.

Autumn shut the door behind, her heart racing.

'It could have been worse,' she supposed, turning back around to the paperwork and picking up the first applicant. This was painstaking work, thankless work, especially when most of the applicants were, to be politically correct, fucking hideous-looking. It was then Autumn was struck by a genius idea. Celina prided herself on the exclusivity of the events. Only the rich, glamorous and exquisitely gorgeous were allowed in. She loved to be surrounded by these people, as they defined her, and it was being enfolded in fabulousness that made her who she was. Autumn cracked a wry grin and set to work. She knew exactly what Celina's Achilles heel was.

Autumn was so busy that morning that she never had time to make herself even one cup of coffee. It was approaching midday when she eventually succumbed to her rumbling stomach and parched throat. She rang Leonardo's extension.

"Autumn, how are you?" he answered almost instantly.

"Couldn't be better," she declared. "Any chance of some food and a cup of your finest coffee?" she asked. Leonardo always bought her and Celina lunch around this time and Autumn didn't see why today should be unlike any other.

"Sorry hon, no can do. Celina's changed my role somewhat. She said I'm not to do anyone else's fetching or carrying." He sounded proud. Autumn could tell he was happy with his newly elevated status.

'Poor guy, he's got no idea he's just a pawn to her,' Autumn thought sadly. Celina had only *'promoted'* him to get at her.

She knew Autumn was carless so nipping out for lunch wouldn't be an option. She really was a piece of work. This was the first time Leonardo had said no to Autumn and she could tell by the awkward silence between them that he was embarrassed by it. She wouldn't hold it against him, though. She liked Leonardo, despite the fact he was just a glorified lapdog for Celina to boss around. He was laid-back and rarely seemed to get in a flap and was always happy to do anything he could to help – well, used to be happy to do anything he could to help, before Celina got involved. Renewed disdain coursed through Autumn's veins. She willed herself to stay calm. Celina wanted to get under her skin, to force her hand into walking out or doing something rash that would justify her being fired. Either way it would mean no pay-out and no reference.

Autumn marched to the small kitchenette that divided the two offices and made herself a cafetière of strong Colombian coffee, grabbed a mug and strode back into her office, kicking the door shut with her foot on the way in. She sat down on the floor, the pile of papers directly in front of her, and began going through them. She sorted through Joanna O'Hara, the wife of an extremely wealthy financier from London; Mr and Mrs McCarthy, wealthy Irish investors who made their fortune investing in the property market in Dubai; then Lydia P. Nolan. Autumn stared at the woman's picture. She was an actress whose famous director husband was too busy working on his next blockbuster to entertain her. She had been given *carte blanche* at these events and stressed in her application just how important it was that she be given the chance to attend. All of them fit Celina's criteria perfectly, so Autumn collected the three sets of applicants up in hand and placed them firmly in the 'no' pile. She went on like this for most of the day, slowly but surely sifting through the hundreds of hopefuls. Autumn was amazed at how many famous people applied, yet she'd rarely seen any celebrities actually attend an event. Autumn reasoned that this would be a bit much for Celina. She wanted beautiful people but not too beautiful and the women couldn't be too successful. A famous face would take the attention away from her too much. Autumn's yes pile consisted mainly of people who up until now would never have stood a chance. She huffed, inspecting the remaining applicants. The pile seemed to be never-ending. She worked diligently separating the ideal candidates into a separate pile. Celina would insist on going through all successful applicants for final approval. They would then they would get passed on to Leonardo who would put their details on a spreadsheet; he would send that over to Autumn who would in turn send out a mailer inviting them to purchase a ticket.

"Hey hon," she said in a synthetically sweet voice. "All the yesses are done and approved, want to come up and get them?"

"Already?" he asked with a tone of surprise. "I thought it'd be tomorrow at the earliest when I got my hands on those bad boys, I'll pop over in a moment and grab them." Autumn hung up the receiver and smiled to herself. Something told her that this event would be the best one yet.

A few minutes later there was a knock at the door. Autumn looked up and offered a warm, sincere smile. "Here you go," she said, handing over the pile.

"Thanks love," Leonardo said, his arms sagging under the weight of the pile. He rifled through the first couple of pages. "Looks good, think you're getting the hang of this." He gave her a half smile and took his leave. Autumn closed the door behind him and sat at her desk. She reclined in her chair: this event would definitely be one to remember.

CHAPTER 24

THE REST OF THE WEEK DRAGGED BY. THE ATMOSphere at Encounters was at best sterile. At times the tension between the Autumn and Celina was palpable. It was obvious to Leonardo that something was awry, but when he questioned Autumn about it. She just laughed it off as *'stress due to the upcoming event and having no time to plan for it.'*

"You said yourself, Christmas is always the most stressful time around here," she had reminded him when he had brought over the USB drive with the successful applicants' spreadsheet on.

Leonardo, although *'promoted'*, didn't seem to do anything different, other than not be available to help Autumn in any way shape or form. She saw him far less now, which suited her. Autumn had a little surprise up her sleeve, and if she was going to pull this one off, she'd need complete privacy. She picked up the phone and dialled the number she had scrawled on a bit of scrap paper: next to it was the name of a woman, Melissa Abbott.

"I'm sorry, Miss Abbott isn't available today. May I take a message?" the silky-voiced receptionist said down the phone.

"I'd really like to speak to her myself," Autumn replied. "Is there a time later in week where she'd be free?"

The receptionist took a deep breath, obviously used to the high demands of her editor boss. "I'm afraid not. Miss Abbott is very firm on only taking calls from those with an appointment," she explained.

"Well, can I make an appointment then?" Autumn asked, becoming irritated with the receptionist.

"That's not possible I'm afraid," the receptionist said curtly. No explanation was given as to why this was the case. The receptionist was clearly eager to get off the phone.

"So, you're saying that it's basically impossible for me to get through to her?" Autumn argued. "Please, this is something she's definitely going to want to hear. I have the most amazing story," she lowered her voice so as to ensure she wouldn't be overheard. "I work for a company that plans exclusive sex parties for the very wealthy and famous. I'm a writer and want to speak to her about it. Please, if could you just ask her to speak with me? If she says no then – well then I'm not sure what I'll do," Autumn added desperately.

Autumn couldn't believe it: after a brief pause the receptionist decided to put her through.

"Okay," she conceded, "I'll put you through. That does sound like a good story; I'd read it!" There was a loud click and 'hold' music started playing. Autumn took a deep breath: this was it, time to shine.

"Melissa Abbott speaking." The melodious voice of *Wow*'s editor-in-chief chimed down the phone. Autumn was lost for words, she'd never truly expected to be speaking to her idol. She opened her mouth but no words came out. "Hello?" Melissa said, a little agitated now.

"S... Sorry," Autumn stammered; she was sure Melissa would be able to feel her blushing down the phone. "My name's Autumn, Autumn Carter. You won't remember me but you spoke at my University a couple of years ago," she explained, hoping she wasn't rambling too much.

"And you want a job? Well, Autumn Carter, firstly ten out of ten for running the gauntlet that is my receptionist, how did you get past Alexandra?" she asserted, marginally impressed with the young woman's determination. "I'm sorry, I have a meeting to go to, thanks for your call but I'm afraid I can't help you."

"I want to write an article on sex parties for you," Autumn blurted out. If Melissa hung up that would be it, she'd never get back through to her. Alexandra would make sure of it. There was a pause on the other end of the line, Autumn was sure she could hear the click of a ballpoint pen followed by words being scrawled down.

"Autumn Carter, you say?" Melissa asked, racking her brains for some sort of memory of the young woman. "I must confess, I can't remember you. I clearly made an impression on you though?"

"Yes, you did. A massive impression," Autumn replied.

"Tell me a little about this piece then," Melissa encouraged. "I want to know what knowledge you have."

"First-hand knowledge: you don't get more first-hand that what I've got," Autumn said. She had decided that if she was going to do this she was going to do it properly and that meant disclosing absolutely everything. She told Melissa the entire story from start to finish, leaving no detail out. It felt strangely cathartic to unburden herself like this. Melissa remained silent, letting Autumn finish before she spoke.

"Well, that certainly *is* a story. I think it would have to be published in two parts," she said, more to herself than to Autumn. "Okay Miss Carter, you have a journalism degree?"

"Creative writing and media studies," Autumn confessed. "I'm doing a journalism course now though. I've taken my finals and get my results soon," she assured, knowing her university degree wasn't enough and hoped that the addition of her course plus the tenacity of phoning the head of the magazine would put her in good favour with the straight-talking Scot.

"Hmmm," Melissa pondered out loud. "Okay, well have you worked anywhere else in print media?"

"No," Autumn confessed, starting to feeling disheartened.

"Anywhere online?" Melissa asked.

"No," Autumn repeated, her heart sinking further.

"Did you write for your student magazine at all?" Melissa questioned. Autumn remained silent: except for her assignments she hadn't written anything for anyone, ever. This was not going how she had hoped. "Autumn?" Melissa probed when the silence had gone on too long.

"No, I haven't. Look, I know that doesn't look good but up until recently I was a bit all over the place. But I know what I want now, what I really want. You know this is a good story. It's my story, and I've lived it and breathed it. I should be the one to write it," Autumn exclaimed passionately, her voice rising with every word until she was almost shouting.

"You might know what it is you want, but I don't. Tell me Autumn, what exactly is it you're so desperate for?" Melissa asked.

Autumn knew the answer immediately. It had never been clearer to her.

"I want a job, working for you," she said decisively. This answer was met with silence. With each passing second Autumn's hope faded, drifting away like a boat untied from it's mooring.

"Then I have a proposition," Melissa began, breaking the reticence. "You write your article, and if it's good and if you pass your finals to a high standard then you can have your job."

"Really?" Autumn asked, gobsmacked at Melissa's proposal. She clapped a hand to her mouth in disbelief.

"You must pass the exam though, with merit. That's at least seventy percent, Autumn."

Autumn knew what it entailed but felt it prudent not to say so. Instead she accepted the challenge whole-heartedly. She wasn't confident about passing her exam, especially with a grade like that, but she knew she could write not only a good article, but an absolutely fantastic one. She had everything she needed – insider information, first-hand experience and the fire and determination to get out from Celina's grasp and give her the middle finger whilst she was at it. She also wanted to show everyone in her life that although she'd made some bad choices something good could come from them.

She hung the phone up. Melissa had given her a direct number so that she didn't have to repeat trying to get through the practically impenetrable barrier that was her receptionist, again. She was going to use the rest of her time at Encounters to write her article. She felt that it was the perfect way to round off her time there. But that would have to wait. It had gone 5 p.m. and it was Friday. Time to head back to her little flat which was starting to feel a little more like home with each passing day.

Autumn relaxed in front of the sofa. She'd polished off an entire bag of popcorn as well as two mugs of coffee. She was watching a television programme where an engaged couple let a complete stranger plan their wedding. The couple in question reminded her of David and Gregg, and her heart panged. She had phoned and messaged David several times over the last week. He had shunned every single one, and worse than being in a fight was being ignored. If only he would let her talk to him, so that she could explain... She realised, now that contact had been cut, that her behaviour towards him, and pretty much everyone else in her life, had been pretty shitty. She'd been so desperate to be like Celina that she had forgotten to be like Autumn – she'd managed to form some weird hybrid. Occasionally she would show glimpses of the old Autumn, but more and more of Celina's traits had pushed their way through, making her bitchy and short-tempered. It was these traits that had led her to believe that she was better than those who loved her. She needed to make amends and thought she had an idea as to how she was going to do it. She still couldn't help but lay all the blame at Rosa's door; however Autumn looked at her situation, it had all been caused by Rosa stealing Ben from her. She couldn't even think about it without a painful stab in her heart. She still couldn't believe that they could have done that to her. She didn't think she'd ever understand why, or how it had happened. She shook her head violently. She wasn't going to get bogged down in this again, and she wasn't going to sit in watching rubbish telly and feeling sorry for herself. Autumn pulled on a pair of smart jeans, a black top and matching heels, and called a taxi. She was going to go out. After all, a glass of Malbec helped any situation.

"E.C.H.D.'s wine bar," she instructed the driver, after climbing into the back seat. She was taking herself out on a date. She hadn't ever done this before and in the confines of her little flat it had seemed like a fabulous decision. However, now she was on her way, to a presumably packed wine bar, on a Friday night, on her own, it no longer seemed like such a bright idea.

Autumn walked into the surroundings of E.C.H.D. and its décor was every inch as fabulous as the last time she had been in. She glanced over to the table where she, her parents plus David and Gregg had celebrated their engagement. She wondered how the wedding plans were coming along and felt another pang of regret deep within her. She snaked her way through the throng; although busy, E.C.H.D. wasn't over-crowded. They had a strict door policy, and there had been a queue of people waiting outside. They had all groaned when Autumn had strutted to the front and was let in, giving the bouncers the unmistakable impression that she was meeting a group of friends who were already inside. She waited patiently at the bar for her turn and when it came ordered a large glass of red from the bearded bartender. As she reached over to hand him the cash, she felt a hand on hers, an arm reached over her and passed the barkeep a crisp twenty-pound note.

"And one for yourself," a voice said from behind her. She turned around to see who had just paid for her drink.

"Jake." She took a second to recognise him, as he was out of uniform and looked more relaxed than Autumn was used to seeing him. He appeared to have left his stiff demeanour at home along with his uniform.

"I saw you walk in," he admitted. "Are you meeting someone?" he looked around as if expecting somebody to magically appear.

"I'm on a date," she said, then seeing the expression change on Jake's face added, "with myself. Sad, isn't it?" She laughed.

"Not at all, I think it's important to be able to enjoy your own company," Jake said.

They chatted for a while at the bar. Autumn could feel a connection between them; she hoped he felt it too. He was so easy to talk to, plus he'd seen her at her worst and could still give her the time of day. She placed her hand on his arm but Jake pulled away. The brush-off couldn't have been clearer: he was only being polite talking to her. He carried on chatting, ignoring what had happened and told her animatedly about his job, his family and his dog, Max.

"So, what are your plans for the rest of the evening?" she asked, hoping she didn't sound too obvious.

He looked at his watch. They'd been chatting for ages, they got on well and Jake hadn't met a woman he'd felt at ease with for such a long time, but no matter how at ease he felt with her, he couldn't shake the fact that she was bad news.

"Look," he said, leaning closer as if he were about to share a secret with her. "I'm here with my friend. It's his girlfriend's birthday and none of us have met her. He's hired out the space at the back for her. Do you wanna come? You don't have to. I don't want to gate-crash your, um, date." He smiled. The more time she spent with Jake the more she liked him.

"He's hired out E.C.H.D.?" she asked, impressed.

"Yeah, tell me about it. He's in finance and is loaded. So, are you coming or what?" he said, making his way back to the party.

Autumn agreed almost instantly. She picked up her bag and glass of wine and headed to the back with her new friend. Jake opened the door for her and let her walk in first, not being able to help himself admiring her pert behind in those jeans. He reprimanded himself. He just didn't want to see her spend the evening alone, that was all.

"What are you doing here?" a stunned voice said. Autumn looked up: to her horror she was confronted with Rosa. She took a step back. Never in a million years had she expected to see her. She looked good. She was wearing a pretty black dress that was short and showcased her toned, olive-skinned legs perfectly. Her hair had been teased into soft waves that fell in loose shiny curls onto her shoulders. Over her shoulder was a silver sash with the words 'Birthday Girl' emblazoned on it in capital letters. Autumn stumbled; Jake was quick to react, catching her arm. She shook him off belligerently and straightened up.

“Happy birthday,” she said scathingly. “What did Ben get you this time? Diamond earrings to go alongside your bracelet?” She nodded to the diamond tennis bracelet, still wrapped elegantly around Rosa’s wrist. “He should get a loyalty card to that place,” she scoffed.

“What place? Autumn I don’t know what you think but…” She was cut off by Autumn’s shrill, derisive laugh.

“What place? John Cusson! *‘The most expensive jewellers in town,’* remember!” Autumn mocked. She was incensed now. Rage coursed through her veins: even after all this time Rosa still didn’t have the courage or the decency to own up. The least she could do was tell the truth. Autumn felt she deserved that at the very least. Rosa stared at her, totally dumbstruck; to her credit she did a great job of playing the innocent.

“Autumn,” Rosa took a deep breath. “Ben and I –”

At these words Autumn drew her hand back and slapped Rosa square across the face. It was an instinctive reaction and her blow struck with the ferocity of a tightly coiled spring suddenly being released. The force caused Rosa’s to head to snap to the side; her own hand shot up, resting where Autumn had struck. Rosa turned to face her, tears brimming in her eyes, threatening to spill at any moment. A man had come to Rosa’s aid now. He was much older than them, smartly dressed in a dark grey suit, his hair combed back neatly.

“Don’t bring Ben into this, you fucking slut!” Autumn took a step closer to Rosa who instinctively took a step back, she lost her footing and stumbled. The man next to her caught her and glared at Autumn.

“Stop that,” he commanded signalling to the doorman that he needed assistance. “I don’t know who you are but you can’t come here shouting the odds. This is my girlfriend’s party and I have no idea who you are.” He turned his attention to

Jake who was stood redundantly, his eyes wide with disbelief. "Who is this psycho?" the man demanded.

Autumn seethed. So, Rosa hadn't even stayed with Ben; all of it had been for nothing. This guy, clearly Rosa's new victim, deserved to know the truth about her and Autumn was going to revel in enlightening him.

"Your precious girlfriend is a lying bitch. She's cheating, life-ruining scum and you'll get rid if you know what's good for you. She fucked my boyfriend behind my back and still wears the fucking trophy," she spat, pointing to Rosa's wrist. "He bought her that. They lied to me and humiliated me and I'll never forgive them." Her voice started to crack as fresh bolts of pain struck her core.

Autumn felt strong hands take her by the arm. Jake was pulling her away now, eager to suppress the swelling tide of anger that raged before him. He'd made up his mind about Autumn now. He had thought that fate had wanted them to be, throwing them together in ever stranger circumstances. He couldn't ignore it anymore. Nick was right: Autumn was turning out to be a full-blown psychopath. He should have steered well clear of her and not let himself be drawn in.

The doorman had appeared now. He beckoned Autumn over to him, not wanting to cause even more of a scene at a paying customer's party. Autumn knew her time was up. She'd said her piece and felt better for doing so but there was no point carrying on: the last time she'd come close to telling Rosa a few home truths the stupid bitch had fallen down a flight of stairs. Autumn realised how callous that sounded but didn't care. Rosa deserved everything she got. The other guests were staring at her in shock. Autumn suddenly felt very self-conscious and knew it was only a matter of moments before their shock would give way to outrage. The doorman stepped between the two women, arms outstretched.

"Come along, I think it's time you left," he said with authority as he ushered Autumn away from the party. She glanced over her shoulder as she was escorted out: Jake was no where to be seen.

She soon found herself outside, in the street with yet again nowhere to go. She gave the wine bar one last scornful look and turned, holding out her hand to flag down a taxi. Her flat was close but in these heels and in this mood, she'd rather pay the cab fare.

"Autumn!" She heard Rosa's voice behind her; she turned around to see her ex-friend walking purposefully toward her.

'She wants round two.' Autumn thought to herself spitefully. She couldn't be bothered any more: there was nothing Rosa could say that would make this night any worse. Autumn stood there, arms folded wondering what new lies Rosa could possibly concoct.

"Let me speak. Ben and I did not sleep with each other, we didn't kiss and we didn't even hold hands. We did, however, share a hug, a massive happy hug. Do you know why?"

Autumn wavered but continued to stand there, staring at Rosa. *'The woman's deluded,'* she told herself.

"We hugged in celebration, when he chose and paid the deposit for an engagement ring, *for you.* We were talking behind your back, yes, but only ever about you. He was planning to propose to you, *you royal idiot*!"

Autumn's mouth fell open. This had to be more lies, had to be. Not once had this explanation been in any possibly scenario she'd imagined.

"You're lying," she accused, pointing a finger in Rosa's face. Rosa pushed her hand away. A taxi pulled up to the two women, the driver wound his window down.

"You want a cab, miss?" he asked Autumn, who nodded and turned to climb in.

"Ask *him*!" Rosa yelled. Autumn looked up to see the man she could only assume was Rosa's boyfriend running up to them.

"Rosa, come on. I don't want you in another catfight, hasn't she done enough already?" he asked, looking Autumn up and down objectionably and placing a protective hand in front of Rosa.

"Nick, who bought this for me?" Rosa held up her wrist.

"Why does that matter?" he interjected, trying to coerce her back into the building as he shot Autumn another disapproving glance.

"Who bought it for me?" she said, more powerfully this time.

"I did," he sighed. "Why is this important again?" he asked, still failing to see the importance of the question.

"And can you tell Autumn anything about that guy called Ben I kept talking to, remember, when we first started dating?" she probed. Nick looked puzzled for a second and then realisation set in.

"Ah so that's *the* Autumn," he said, grasping who the other woman was in relation to his girlfriend.

"How many people named Autumn do you know?" Rosa chastised. "Nick please, just tell her what I was doing with Ben," she pleaded.

Nick did so: he backed up Rosa's story exactly, even managing to get rough dates and places right. Autumn stood, rooted to the spot in disbelief. She had to see Ben, to see if this were true. She couldn't believe it, wouldn't believe it. If this story was genuine, well, what had everything since been for? Nothing. Autumn felt distraught; pain and confusion consumed her. Why hadn't Ben told her this? If it could be so easily explained, why hadn't he done so? Autumn had so many questions dancing around her head, she felt dizzy and nauseous.

"Look, do you want this cab or not?" the driver said impatiently. Without a word Autumn turned and got in, leaving Rosa and Nick staring after her.

Tears streaked down Rosa's cheeks, leaving silver trails that glinting in the street light. Nick comforted her with a warm hug and a soft kiss on the forehead.

"It's okay, babe," he said reassuringly. "You did nothing wrong. I've been telling you that for months. Come on, let's get you back in and get a drink inside you, you're freezing." He rubbed Rosa's arm and led her back to the bar, apologising to the doormen on his way back in for the disturbance to their venue.

"Seventeen Percival Street," Autumn told the taxi driver, fighting back tears. She had given the address of her old house. She had to see Ben. She couldn't not, especially now she knew the truth. How could she have been so blind, and why hadn't she even once allowed him to speak to her? She'd cut him out of her life so quickly, blocking him on social media, sending his emails to junk and deleting them without so much as reading the subject line. She'd also changed her mobile number almost instantly and made her parents block him from calling their house. She'd made it impossible for him but still, why hadn't he fought for her? If she'd meant as much to him as he had meant to her he should have fought, done anything and everything to win her back. She choked back the tears. She caught the eye of the driver in the rear-view mirror and shot him a look that told him it would be best if he didn't ask questions.

They pulled up and Autumn solemnly handed him a twenty pound note and got out, not waiting for the change. She walked up to the door and knocked, her heart beating faster with ever step. She could hear the television on inside and smiled: Ben always had it turned up so loud. The door creaked open and a woman around Autumn's age answered the door. Autumn leaned back, checking the number on the front of the house to make sure she'd got the right one. She had.

"Hi," the young woman said cheerily. "Can I help you?" She was dressed in comfy casual clothes, her dark blonde hair was atop her head in a messy knot and she wore furry slippers. She was cute, pretty even.

"Hi, is err, is Ben in?" Autumn asked uncertainly, not liking the fact that another woman was in Ben's house late on a Friday night. She strained and tried to peer in through the doorway. The girl narrowed her eyes suspiciously and closed the door a bit.

"Who shall I say it is?" she asked inquisitively, looking Autumn up and down, unsure as to who she was dealing with. If she was a fan of the show then, as Ben had been right to decide to move.

"I'm Autumn," she replied. "I really need to see Ben."

The girl gave Autumn a withering look, her cute and friendly demeanour did a U-turn.

"Well I'm his girlfriend," she shot back, folding her arms across her chest. "You can take it from me, he won't want to see you." She shut the door. Autumn was left on the door step wondering what her next move should be. This just didn't seem right somehow.

'His girlfriend? In their home. That couldn't be.' She banged on the door, calling Ben's name loudly. The couple inside ignored her but Autumn wasn't going to give up. Ben couldn't just throw away what they had. She continued to bang. A neighbour from across the street called out of an upstairs window for her to shut up. She ignored him and carried on

regardless. The door flung open and there, standing in dark grey jogging bottoms and a white vest top, was her Ben. She flung her arms around him, tears re-emerging and falling down her cheeks.

"Oh Ben, I'm so sorry." She kissed his neck and buried her head on his shoulder, desperate for some comfort from him. None was given. He placed his hands firmly on her arms and pushed her away.

"What is it you want, Autumn?" he asked curtly.

Autumn looked taken aback. She couldn't fathom why he wasn't pleased, or at least relieved to see her.

"I finally spoke to Rosa," she began to explain. "I know the truth now."

His new girlfriend had come to join him in the doorway. She'd pulled a blanket around herself. They had quite clearly been enjoying a cosy night in front of the telly before Autumn had disturbed them.

"Is there anywhere we can talk in private?" she asked, eyeing up Ben's supposed new girlfriend.

"No there isn't, Autumn. Just tell me what it is you want."

"To talk. I know everything now." She trailed off. Ben was looking at her indifferently. She didn't like it. There was no emotion there, no fondness, not even anger or frustration, there was nothing but indifference in his bearing. "Why didn't you tell me?" she asked softly.

"I tried, Autumn. I phoned you. I sent messages and emails. I even went to your parents' house to talk to you. You totally cut me out. You didn't care about the truth or about anything I had to say, you were just, so angry." He sighed then added, "You'd already made up your mind."

Autumn couldn't understand. If he truly were innocent surely he would have found a way to explain things to her.

"But you wanted to marry me?" she questioned, blinking back new tears.

Ben blushed slightly, the recollection of his planned proposal seeming like a long-lost memory now. "I did. But how could I marry someone who didn't trust me, who wouldn't even talk to me? It was crazy, Autumn, how you could just sever all ties like that. You destroyed any chance we had, not me."

His new girlfriend, seeing the sadness in Ben's eyes, wrapped her arm around him, in a protective and loving way. It was an innocent and simple gesture that single-handedly told Autumn all she needed to know. She and Ben were done, there was no way back for them now. He had moved on and she couldn't blame him for doing so.

"I really am sorry," she said dejectedly, lowering her eyes to the floor. She was unable to meet his gaze any longer; he saw too much.

"Me too, Autumn. It's for the best, though. Everything happens for a reason."

His girlfriend, no longer seeing Autumn as a threat, retired back into the house, wanting to give them one last moment together to say goodbye.

"I just can't believe it, any of it," she mumbled.

"I can't stay out here all night Autumn, I'm sorry. Look, if there's anything you want, you know, from the house, just take it. I packed a few household bits that got left behind. It's all in the garage if you want the key."

Autumn declined. She didn't think poring over the last surviving remnants of their home was a good idea. As she turned to leave she noticed brown cardboard boxes piled in the hallway, Ben saw her eyeline shift and before she could ask said, "I'm moving, Autumn. Work's picking up and I need to be in the capital," he explained. Autumn could do nothing but nod. She was dumbstruck.

She walked a little way back before hailing another taxi back to her flat. She needed some fresh air and she needed to think. So much had happened in such a short space of time. She was exhausted, both emotionally and physically. All she wanted now was her bed.

Autumn awoke the next day feeling like she'd gone ten rounds with Mike Tyson. She felt battered and bruised and as if the only people in the whole world who would be able to make this any better were her parents. She groaned as she recalled her harsh words to Rosa and worse of all, the slap. To make matters even worse, Jake had witnessed everything. Just when she thought he might like her as well. They'd had a great time at the bar, laughing and joking. But now, well, she knew that ship had sailed. If he hadn't thought she was a car wreck of a woman before last night, then he certainly would now.

Autumn really wanted her mum. Enough time had gone by and she thought that now would be the right time to go and see them, to try and make amends after all she had nothing left to lose. She only hoped that they could see past everything that had happened. Autumn felt vibrations on the pillow next to her. She fumbled for her phone and was relieved to see David's name flashing on her screen.

"Hello," she said down the phone. "I've missed you so much," she added, unable to help herself.

"Hi," he replied bluntly, "I didn't want to ring, but, with it being your parents' party tonight I didn't think it would be good guest behaviour if I went and we were still fighting."

Autumn clapped a hand to her face. She had forgotten all about her parents' annual Christmas shindig. She couldn't believe it was December already. It felt like it was only yesterday that it had been the middle of summer and she had been sitting with her mum in their family garden enjoying the glorious weather, all the while appreciating the garden's new water feature.

"To be honest I'm not sure if I'm going," she said, her voice still a little groggy from sleep. "David, everything's such a mess," she cried.

David couldn't bear to see or hear anyone upset, even if he was mad at the person in question. He listened intently as she reeled off everything that had happened the previous night.

"Oh Autumn," he said when she'd finally finished, "you must feel terrible." Autumn did feel terrible. She felt guilt, sadness and hopelessness all rolled into one, big, horrible emotion that was eating away at her from the inside.

"Have you told your parents?" David asked, genuine concern filling his voice. He had never heard her sound so low, even after she'd broken up with Ben. Autumn clearly realised that the last few months of pain, hurt and upheaval had all been for nothing and this realisation was weighing heavily on her mind.

She shook her head to try and dislodge the unpleasant feeling that seemed to be wedged there.

"I haven't really spoken to them since, you know the night I went MIA," she explained, hoping that bringing that awful night back up wouldn't have a negative effect on the conversation. Luckily for Autumn, once David had chosen to forgive someone he rarely changed his mind.

"I really am sorry, David, you know, about letting you down. You were right. It was a pretty shitty way to behave and I was totally selfish," she confessed, issuing her second genuine apology in twenty-four hours.

"Let's not mention it again," he said. "It's in the past now."

"I wish it was," she said dryly. Autumn told David about her predicament at Encounters, about how if she didn't complete at least three events she wouldn't get paid and how awful Celina really was. She told David what she had done to her personally and to the PAs before her. Finally she told David about Jack and everything Celina had done and continued to do to him.

"Jack's gay?" he asked a soberly. "That's awful for him, I can't imagine having to hide who I really am from everyone around me. That would utterly horrible, absolutely soul-destroying." David finished, his voice sounded thin and strained.

"It is what it is, though," Autumn said. "There's nothing that can be done." The conversation stagnated; Autumn felt bad that David had taken this so personally.

"So tell me," she said, changing the subject. "How are the wedding plans going?"

"Actually, I have news on that front," David said excitement creeping into his voice. "Gregg and I want to do it this year."

"This year? But, there's hardly any of it left!" Autumn exclaimed.

"We've decided to go small-scale. When you didn't turn up last Sunday I phoned Gregg and he came and met me instead. We threw caution and tradition to the wind and bought our suits together. There was so much to choose and so much to think about that we just thought, you know what, we've got the only thing we need to get married, each other. Let's sack everything else off and just do it. I don't need a gospel choir and doves to know that I love him," David said.

It was the sweetest thing Autumn had ever heard. She smiled.

"I think that's a fabulous idea," she said. "So, when's the big day? Assuming I'm still invited?" Autumn wasn't entirely sure if she would be or not.

"Well, that's kind of the thing. It's…" He took a deep breath, "well, it's on a weekday. December the thirteenth."

Autumn sat bolt upright in bed and counted the days on her fingers. "But that's only nine days away," she said in astonishment.

"I know we've booked the registry office and we've hired the back of E.C.H.D's for drinks afterwards. I told you, hon, we're going low key."

Autumn was excited; it was all happening so quickly. She could feel David's exhilaration through the phone.

"I can't wait," she said genuinely: this time she really wouldn't miss it for the world.

Autumn congratulated David once more and said her good-byes. She needed to go and see her parents – she wanted to make things right before their party. Even if she wasn't invited she knew they would have a much better time without the dark cloud of disappointment they felt towards their daughter hanging over them.

Autumn procrastinated for the rest of the day, convincing herself that she needed to start her article for Melissa right that second. She started by bullet pointing her first impressions of Celina. She thought back to that first meeting and how she'd been in total awe of this fantastic woman. She had remembered being captivated by her sheer aura, confidence and charm. Little did she know then what a predatory, destructive force Celina would turn out to be.

Autumn checked her watch: it had just gone 5 p.m., she really needed to make a move. Her parents' parties usually started around the eight o'clock mark, and she wanted to have the air cleared way before then.

Autumn stepped out of the taxi, the driveway was icy so the driver had dropped her off at the bottom. This was fine by Autumn. She reasoned that the short walk would give her a little extra time to plan her apology. She walked up the drive and her family home lit up in front of her festively. Christmas at her family home was on a whole other level. Her parents had always decorated the house on the first of December for as long as she could remember. Twinkling lights adorned the trees that lined the winding driveway and welcomed her invitingly. Autumn breathed in the crisp evening air. It was already dark and there was a definite chill which caused Autumn to pull her coat tighter and quicken her pace. She wanted to get this over with as soon as possible and was dreading seeing her dad. She could handle her mum; she would be the easy part. Her dad however, was a different story. He would just look at her with despondent, doleful eyes that brimmed with disappointment. He'd give her a look that made her feel about an inch big and say nothing.

Autumn knocked on the door. The sound amplified inside the house; she could hear her parents laughing and joking within. They were in the hall, probably up stepladders hanging Christmas bunting on the staircase or something. The thought of that tugged at her heartstrings. She hoped against hope that this meeting would go well, that she'd say the right things and that they'd see how truly sorry she was for all that she'd put them through.

The door opened and Sarah Carter stood in the doorway: her face blanched when she saw her daughter. The two women stood there for a moment, face-to-face, neither saying anything. Autumn opened her mouth to speak but before she could her mum threw her arms around her and embraced her in a huge, all-encompassing hug. Autumn immediately burst into tears. She hadn't expected this at all. The only bodily contact she had envisioned would be a sharp slap around the face if it all got a bit too heated.

"Come in, darling," her mum said, "we need a good catch up. We've been so worried. David has kept us in the loop so we knew you were okay but it's just not the same as actually seeing you."

Autumn nodded. She'd been annoyed with David for outing her to her parents. But after sleeping on it she understood why he had had to tell them the truth. He had thought something terrible had happened to her, he'd woken up to a plethora of missed calls, he'd tried to return them and had only got her voice-mail. Then she'd failed to show up for something she'd told him she wouldn't miss for the world. Had it been the other way around, she would have done exactly the same thing. Really, she should be thankful that she had such a caring friend.

She walked into the house and she could smell the pine of the Christmas tree. Every year ever since she could remember, they'd had a huge pine tree, which stood proudly in the immense hallway. This year was no different. It stood there in its usual place, decorated in traditional Christmas colours adorned with green and red baubles and strings of golden stars. Stood proudly at the very top of it was an ornate angel that had been in her family for generations. Her mum took her by the hand and led her into the living room, which was also decorated exquisitely. Jasper the family cat was sat on the sofa, purring softly to himself. He eyed them warily as they entered, unsure if he was going to be turfed out or not.

"Richard, could you pop the kettle on please?" Sarah asked her husband. He grunted and left the room, casting Autumn a disdainful look as he left. His expression reminded Autumn of Ben's when she'd turned up at their, his house. It had all started with that bloody text message. 'Are you alone?' She remembered it as if it was yesterday. It had been from Rosa, helping Ben to plan his proposal. She'd always kick herself for not recognising her number. Autumn was transported back to that very moment. She had been standing by the washing machine, Ben's phone in her hand and the bottom dropping out of her world. She'd even questioned him about it, and he'd told her he wasn't cheating. Why hadn't she just believed him?

All of that was in the past now. He'd moved on, in fact so had she, but it was still a painful shame nonetheless. Autumn thought that for as long as she lived she would feel that it had been a terrible waste.

Sarah Carter sat her daughter down. Autumn instinctively reached out her hand to give Jasper a scratch behind the ear. Sarah had intended to wait for Richard to come back before questioning Autumn, but she just couldn't hold it in. Keeping her mouth shut never had been one of her strong suits.

"What on earth were you thinking?" she started. Sarah had promised herself she wouldn't get angry. Both she and Richard had felt a wedge between their daughter and the last thing she wanted was to drive that wedge further. Autumn couldn't meet her mother's eyes, she didn't want her seeing all that there was to see. She wished all of this could just blow over and that she wouldn't have to explain herself. She wished above all else, that her dad wouldn't look at her the way he just had ever again.

Richard Carter had walked back into the room; his jolly Christmas jumper did nothing to lighten the mood. He set the tray down on the edge of the coffee table and handed his wife her cup. He took one for himself and sat back, sipping the beverage earnestly. Autumn leaned over and picked up the remaining mug, realising that her father had no intention of handing it to her. She stared into the mug of tea, wholeheartedly wishing that she had something a little stronger to put in it. She felt like she very much needed something to take the edge off the overwrought environment and the impending unpleasant conversation.

"Well," her father said solemnly, "explain yourself."

"Which part?" She asked, genuinely unsure as to where she should start.

"All of it." Her father said unequivocally. He clearly wanted the truth, all of it, no matter how hard it was to hear. Autumn began her story in much the same vein as when she'd divulged her tale to David. She continued to stare into her cup, alternating between looking at that, and looking at the cat. She found it extremely hard to meet either of her parents' eyes. When she was done, she sat back in her chair and breathed a heavy sigh. It was done. A weight felt like it had been lifted from her, like immovable chains had been undone from around her chest.

Her mum had so many questions but her dad remained cold towards her, sporadically fixing her with that contemptuous look. Autumn felt both physically and mentally exhausted. She answered them all, leaving out certain choice parts, namely where she'd had a threesome with an Irish man and a beautiful red-head and that she'd been bought at auction by a mummy's boy property tycoon. No parents needed to know the ins and outs of their child's sex lives.

Autumn finished her tale with a huge, cathartic breath. She looked up. She had, to the best of her ability, been completely honest with them now, so she tried to lighten the conversation by telling them all about Melissa Abbott and her potential offer. It did nothing to break her father's icy temperament. It was a long while before anyone spoke, but eventually her dad broke the silence.

"Well, I don't think we need to know anything else, do we love?" her father said coldly. Autumn could tell he was still deeply unhappy with her. "Your mother and I won't be reading your article either, I get the distinct feeling we've had the PG rated version of your X-rated antics. Still, like it or not, and I don't, we're a family and we'll put on a united front." He turned to his wife who was sitting on the arm of the sofa next to him nodding in agreement.

"Let us give you the money, darling. You can leave that place and never look back," she said.

Autumn pondered the offer. It certainly would be the easiest way out. But she so desperately wanted to be there when Celina's big Christmas event went up in flames. If she were being brutally honest with herself the event still held some appeal. Autumn Carter wasn't quite done with Encounters just yet.

"Thanks Mum, but I need to see it through, for the article and if there's one thing you've taught me it's *once you've started something you better finish it,*" she answered. This was only half-true, but after getting back on speaking terms, no matter how frosty those terms were, she didn't think it wise to tell them that she actually *wanted* to see it through. Sarah looked sadly off into the distance, trying to digest all that had happened when her eyes fell upon the clock on the wall.

"Jesus, Richard, they'll be here soon and we're nowhere near ready," she exclaimed, panic-stricken. It was amazing how her mum could invest the same emotional fervour into a party as she could a traumatic family event. Autumn shot up out of her seat, spooking Jasper who made a run for it and bolted upstairs.

"Okay, what can I do?" Autumn asked.

"Get changed. You look atrocious," her mum answered in all seriousness. She shooed Autumn upstairs. Thankfully some of Autumn's clothes had been left in her room and she managed to cobble together an outfit. She applied some mascara and lip-gloss that she had in the bottom of her bag and headed downstairs to help with the last lot of preparations.

Her dad was still unable to look at her as she helped. He merely grunted when she passed him the champagne flutes and half mumbled at her when she held the step ladder for him.

The doorknocker resounded loudly in the hallway as the first of the guests arrived. Autumn opened the door, a wide smile on her face. It was the Cohens. Autumn opened the door, a wide smile on her face and her arms outstretched, greeting them if they were old friends. If her experience at Encounters had taught her anything, it was how to receive a guest. Mr Cohen brandished a bottle of Pinot Noir in Autumn's direction and thanked her for the invite. Sarah Carter was already on hand with champagne, planting two flutes firmly in their hands the moment they had given Autumn their coats. Guest after guest arrived, all of them greeted in the same cheerful way. David and Gregg came around half an hour later, and David gave Autumn a big hug and she gripped him tightly in return.

"I love you," she whispered in his ear. When he pulled away Autumn was surprised to see that his eyes were glassy, tears threatening to spill at any moment. This fight had really taken its toll on him. David was such a kind person that any kind of ill-will left him feeling really melancholy. Gregg was a little frosty towards Autumn to start with, clearly still wary of her after she had hurt his fiancé so badly. After a while, he warmed to her again. Gregg was a sensible guy and saw no reason to continue being distant toward Autumn when David had clearly moved on. They spent the rest of the night locked deep in conversation. They chatted about wedding plans, Christmas plans and anything else that was a *safe* subject between them. The party was a great success, music played, people danced and several bottles of champagne were popped.

At around eleven o'clock Sarah drunkenly staggered into the living room flourishing a bottle of brandy.

"I think you've had enough," Richard said lovingly, trying to pry the bottle from Sarah's hands. As usual he had stuck to his one drink limit. He'd enjoyed a glass of bubbly with the guests to get the party started and after that had stuck mainly to orange juice. He had spiced things up with a glass of Coke on the rocks at about 10 p.m., though. It was Christmas, after all.

"Never!" she slurred, clutching onto the bottle and taking a swig from it. "Don't be such a spoilsport, Richard. Tell your dad, Autumn."

The rest of the guests joined in, booing Richard as he tried in vain to recover the bottle from his wife. Eventually she relented, opting instead for a glass of half drunk eggnog that she'd found on a nearby coffee table. Autumn caught her dad's eye and smiled at him, enjoying her parent's quasi-argument. She saw her dad's eyes narrow and Autumn felt the blood drain from her face as it dawned on her that her dad was still so angry. She knew it had been a mistake to tell him everything; he probably thought less of her now than he had done to start with. He just didn't want to upset his wife further by continuing the feud.

Autumn could now add that to her lists of regrets, which seemed to be ever-expanding. Her regrets were two-fold: the first was that Jake the handsome police officer had witnessed her total meltdown; and the second, and probably more serious of the two, was the way she'd treated Rosa. Autumn couldn't escape the fact that after all of this Rosa had been shown to be completely innocent Autumn had treated her absolutely appallingly. Autumn vowed to make amends before the end of the year, even if that meant begging on her hands and knees.

CHAPTER 25

BEFORE AUTUMN KNEW IT MONDAY HAD ROLLED around again. She'd spent the majority of Sunday helping her parents clean up from the party, determined to show them she was committed to making amends. Autumn felt a little bit guilty. Her mum had welcomed her back with open arms; yes, she'd been upset and yes she'd been disappointed, but she'd overlooked her feelings in favour of Autumn's. She guessed that's just what you do when you're a parent. Now if only her dad would do the same.

"Right, what do we all want for breakfast?" Sarah had asked on Sunday morning, without even a trace of a hang-over. Autumn had assumed that given the amount of booze her mother had put away, she'd spend most of the day in bed, laid down with an ice pack pressed firmly to her head and gingerly sipping the elixir of life for anyone with a hangover, ice cold Cola. Sarah had made them breakfast, she whistled along to the radio and bopped about happily. They'd eaten bacon sandwiches washed down with plenty of tomato sauce and many cups of coffee.

The weekend had done Autumn good. She felt more at peace now, more ready to tackle Celina and more ready to finish writing the article that would give her a chance at a new life.

Autumn walked into her office at Encounters. Something wasn't quite right. Where were all her decorative bits and bobs? She turned round, jumping as she saw Celina lurking in the doorway, a smug grin on her face.

"I'm sorry to tell you that this week the housekeeping staff are away. I'll need you to clean all of the fantasy rooms from top to bottom and I also need you to sort the bar and catering out. Fabulous news though: Matthew and Robert are moving to the big smoke to start their dancing careers properly. I encouraged them of course, gave them a bit of a bonus to help them on their way; they are so wasted here. So, you'll need to interview new staff and hire someone of the same calibre. Finally, the flowers. Terrible news on that front, our usual supplier is away on holiday so you'll need to hunt around for something equally fabulous. All within the budget by the way, which I've had to cut." Celina smirked as she saw Autumn's face fall with each new order. "Oh, and one last thing, I'm going away for the rest of the week. I've been working so hard lately and Jack thinks I deserve a holiday." She paused and added goadingly, "Well, *I* think I deserve a holiday and, as you know, Jack has no choice in the matter. So, you'll be on your own for the most part. I'll be back Saturday in time for the event."

"That's fine," Autumn replied, trying her best to keep an even tone, "and what about the courses? I assume I'll be doing those too?"

"Leonardo is taking care of those. I'm training him up to tackle the more delicate tasks, so who knows when he'll be needed to step into the breach on a more permanent level?" Celina turned to leave and then added, for her own amusement, "I suppose you're wondering where your décor went? I just felt the little bits you'd chosen, well, they were a bit tacky for Encounters. I've binned them. Don't you feel the room is much more elegant now?" she asked, her tone daring Autumn to challenge her. She really would settle for any excuse now – Celina Thorne wanted Autumn out.

"Much more elegant," Autumn agreed, a sugary, false sense of admiration in her voice. Celina's eyes narrowed, clearly irked by Autumn's indifference. She walked out slamming the door behind her. Autumn smiled as she heard Celina stomping down the hallway, screeching orders through her little black headset as she went.

Autumn sighed. She needed to get on with the article for Melissa, she wanted it done and dusted in time for the event. Autumn decided to dedicate the first half of the week to Encounters. She was, after all, still being paid, in a roundabout way, to do a job. The second half of the week would be spent on the article. She was going to expose Celina for what she truly was, and if she could take down Encounters at the same time then all the better. The fact that Celina was going away was a bonus. Autumn could have a proper snoop in her office now, safe in the knowledge that Celina was off miles away so wouldn't catch her.

The following day Autumn managed to hire two new barmen. Although not as handsome and athletic-looking as Matthew and Robert, they were more than qualified for the job. She'd picked them up on a social media page, students who required little pay and with her budget slashed, this was the perfect solution. She'd phoned round every florist in the area for miles; none of them could fit her in on such short notice. She took a pen and crossed a big black line through the words 'sort florist' on her list. Who needed professional flowers anyway? She would pick up some cheap bunches from the petrol station. As long as each item on the list had been sorted, no matter how poorly, Celina couldn't fire her. *She had this one last event to get through and then she was free*. She quickly totted up how much forgoing the professional floral displays would free up. Autumn smiled: it was more than enough to make the bar a little more exciting. She phoned the caterers and placed their usual order. Autumn drew the line there. The canapés were her evening meal on event nights and she refused to lower herself to ordering sub par food.

Lunchtime came and went. Autumn had once again neglected to bring anything to eat, forgetting that Leonardo was under strict instructions not to do her fetching and carrying. Autumn couldn't help but feel sorry for him; he was totally under Celina's thumb. He did whatever Celina said, no questions asked. Autumn settled herself on the floor. Celina had taken her fancy office chair and replaced it with a chair out of the kitchenette. It was too small and too hard to spend any real time on. The floor was covered in a plush, luxurious carpet so was far comfier. She pulled out her notepad and began adding to her list, writing down anything and everything she thought might be important to include in her article. Leonardo had obviously been instructed to keep watch on her: he burst into her office unannounced several times that day, and he couldn't have made it more obvious. Fortunately, Autumn had seen this coming. In anticipation of this she'd printed out random floral displays and every time he entered unannounced would brandish one at him and ask him what he thought. This seemed to satisfy Leonardo because by the end of the week he had stopped bursting in altogether. Celina had double-locked her office and taken the spare key from the emergency cupboard in the miniature gallery-style reception. She'd even had a glass pane fitted over the black panel so Autumn had absolutely no way of entering.

Autumn tried various methods over the course of the week to get in, including telling Leonardo that she'd left something important in there, but he'd just replied by saying that it didn't matter how important it was, she'd have to get it when Celina got back. Autumn was frustrated: she wanted to get into that office, she needed to find something that would incriminate Celina and set Jack free. Speaking to David and hearing how crestfallen he'd been at the thought Jack not being able to be himself had really struck a chord with Autumn. She wanted to help him, to release him from Celina's clutches. He deserved that much, at least.

Event day came around, as always, far too quickly. Autumn arrived at the offices of Encounters nice and early. She had all but finished the first part of her article. She wondered whether it would be good enough and if it would meet with Melissa's exacting standards or fall short.

Autumn had phoned Martin and instructed him to come in first thing to meet her. Celina's flight didn't land until the afternoon, but he didn't know that. Martin arrived; he was a flamboyant whirlwind of a man, always overflowing with gossip about previous clients. Autumn dreaded to think what he must have said about her to other people. He gave her a kiss on each cheek and a big hug. Autumn pulled away, glad that at least she still had one friend at Encounters. She pushed her hand into her back pocket and produced a photograph which she handed over to Martin who stared at it in disbelief.

"You're sure?" Martin asked, his mouth open and eyes wide. Autumn nodded decidedly and took back the picture of the model with sleek, mid length, dark brown hair. "You're absolutely sure?" he repeated. Autumn nodded again, more fervently this time. "Okay then, sit down, this might take a while."

Autumn sat on the kitchenette chair and wriggled to get comfortable. Martin set to work, a look of dogged determination on his face. Three hours later he was smiling, hair dryer in hand, putting the finishing touches to Autumn's new do. He moved round to face her, smiling.

"Well, I never thought it'd work but I've got to say, I'm super happy with the result." He handed her a mirror, which she held up and gazed into. Her eye's widened with shock, she barely recognised the woman staring back at her. Her once wavy blonde hair was now a sleek, chocolaty brown. Autumn had never once dyed her hair before now. *'Encounters really is a place for firsts,'* she mused. She stood up and held the mirror higher, trying to see her new hair from every possible angle. It was lustrous and shiny and with a fair few inches cut from it now looked incredible healthy and thick. She loved it.

"Now for your makeup," Martin asserted, beckoning her to retake a seat. She respectfully obliged. "Any requests?" he asked.

Autumn shook her head. "I'll leave it in your capable hands," she said.

Martin smiled proudly and set to work: he gave her dramatic eye makeup topped off with a soft winged liner and dark red lips. Autumn studied herself in the mirror and felt a surge of confidence swell within her chest: she was extremely happy with the results. Each time she caught her reflection she did a double-take, not being able to immediately identify the woman looking back. She slipped on her dress, a tight black number that showcased her newly acquired streamlined curves and slipped on her trusty gold heels.

The event was fast approaching and still Celina was nowhere to be seen. Autumn decided to go down to the ballroom and cast her eye over everything just to make sure it was all okay. Autumn strutted down the hallway, catching another glimpse of herself in one of the mirrors. Doing another double-take, she smiled: this was going to take some getting used to.

In the ballroom, everything was going to plan. Leonardo had shown the new boys to their station. It was pretty self-explanatory really, stand behind the bar and pour the drinks. They were unloading crates of beer, cocktail mixers and shot glasses. There wasn't a bottle of champagne in sight. Autumn smiled, remembering the fine wine she'd packed for herself squirrelled away safely in the office. Autumn knew that her revenge might seem petty to some, but she knew it was stuff like this that got under Celina's skin. Autumn had picked two dozen bunches of cheap flowers on her way in, and was now arranging them in the large, cut glass vases of Encounters. The taxi driver had waited for her patiently in the forecourt as she had lingered over three-day-old roses and bunches of inexpensive carnations. She'd opted for the carnations: the bubble gum pink colour would go really nicely in the ballroom. Autumn smirked as she placed the vases around the room.

She strode down to the fantasy rooms. This was one part of the job she had done properly. The guests, after all, did deserve a safe and clean place to fulfil their fantasies. She opened each door in turn and inspected the rooms, taking her time and making sure they were to a high standard. The hot wax room needed some improvement. The candles were practically burnt down to stubs. She made a mental note to flag down Leonardo and have him replace them.

Celina still hadn't arrived when the first of the guests started pouring in. Autumn greeted them with all the warmth and charm of a professional host. Making sure to take the time with as many guests as she could to make them feel special. Many of the women complimented her on her new look; one guest even described it as 'spectacular'. Autumn knew now not to be too overwhelmed by these people. Most of them were there for one thing and one thing only. She overheard a couple of regular guests at the bar, a little dissatisfied at the new drinks menu. The cocktails on offer were the new barmen's specialities: snake bite and sex on the beach, both of which were student favourites. The guests were in the ballroom now; there was no sign of Leonardo, but then again that was nothing new. He avoided the actual event like the plague, afraid his purity would be tainted by the mere proximity to what he viewed as sex-crazed debauchery.

Autumn checked her watch and noticed that Celina was uncharacteristically late. As if the universe had read her mind a loud fanfare sounded and the gong was struck. The deep rumble resonated throughout the ballroom; Autumn looked up and couldn't help but roll her eyes. It was Celina, being escorted in by four bare-chested male models, carrying her in on a baroque sedan chair. It was heavily gilded in gold and cushioned inside by swathes of burgundy velvet, which spilled over the sides like a sumptuous waterfall. They marched through the centre of the room and the crowds parted. Celina waved as the crowd gasped in astonishment. Autumn had to hand it to her; this was one hell of an entrance. They set the sedan chair down and Celina climbed out. Her ball gown was the most extravagant yet: it was raw silk, cream in colour with a fitted bodice and full flowing skirt. She wore matching elbow length gloves and her hair had been constructed into an elaborate design, scaffolded high atop her head. She looked like royalty and lapped up the attention lavished upon her by the guests.

Autumn heard a voice she recognised shouting compliments at Celina over the heads of the others before him. She looked around, trying to find the source of the voice. Chris Lambert stood mere feet from her. She darted behind a female guest with big curly hair; Autumn peered out from behind her, not daring to believe her eyes. It was Chris Lambert,

Thorne PR's single most annoying client. She couldn't risk being seen by him. She trusted her parents and David never to tell a soul about her involvement here, but she certainly didn't want everyone at Thorne PR to find out about it, which they certainly would if Chris discovered her. He was a brash loudmouth who loved showing off. This would be fantastic over-dinner fodder for him.

Autumn ordered a drink from the bar. She decided to go for her university's famous blackcurrant, beer and cider cocktail – that was a 'snakebite'. It was served in a fine cut crystal glass, which made Autumn chuckle: *'A student drink in a millionaire's glass,'* she thought as she sipped on the purple cocktail. The fizzy sweetness was a shock to her system. She hadn't had one of these in forever and the taste immediately took her back. Autumn looked around, satisfied with the event so far. At least half of the guests were too old, not rich or attractive enough or didn't meet at least one other element of Celina's criteria. She kicked herself for not looking through the applicants properly; if she had she would have plonked Chris Lambert firmly in the 'no' pile. The woman he had bought was at least half his age and twice as attractive as someone dating Chris should be. He had obviously booked tonight to try and impress her with his open-minded and sexually explorative ways. Autumn baulked: the thought of Chris having sex turned her stomach. She downed the rest of her drink. She didn't order another. She was done with blasts from the past.

Celina strode over to her smugly.

"I suppose you think you're clever," she said, raising a hand and gesturing towards the room. "Let me see, Leonardo's spreadsheet need a little editing, did it? Or did you just delete the file and start from scratch? Well, you've certainly got one over on me Autumn. Let me see, unattractive guests, common drinks and those hideous carnations? Ah, you wanted to ruin my event, how infantile. Excellent plan sweetheart, I'm livid." She laughed malevolently. "You are nothing, Autumn, and you don't matter. Whatever you do, wherever you go, you'll always be that nervous, chubby blonde, no matter how many boxes of hair dye you get through." She looked Autumn up and down scornfully. "Now, kindly show me the menu you've put together, let's see if you managed to get the courses right for the auction."

Autumn stared agog. This hadn't been part of her remit.

"But you said Leonardo was doing that," she protested.

"Why would Leonardo be doing it?" Celina asked, completely nonplussed. "*That*, my little cherub, was your job; you haven't failed to fulfil your contract, have you?" Her voice was calm and silky now yet still dripping with insincerity.

Autumn could do nothing but stare. She hadn't even got anyone on standby: where was she going to find three people willing to be bought at auction and prepared to do anything their bidders wanted? This would be it; Celina would fire her, then all this would have been for nothing and she wouldn't see a penny of the money owed to her. *'How could I have been so stupid?'* Autumn cursed herself.

"I'll sort it," Autumn said calmly and strutted off towards the offices. The second she was around the corner and out of sight she broke into a run. She had exactly one hour to fulfil a tall order: find three people willing to auction themselves off for sex. She opened the top drawer of the metal filing cabinet in her office and pulled out a thick file. Her best bet was to phone those who had done it before. One course stood out in her head: the overweight girl Autumn had doubted would make a penny but had proven to be very popular. She leafed through and stopped when she found the printout with her picture on. She dialled the number on top of the page and was relieved when the girl answered after just one ring.

Autumn explained the predicament, making sure to tell the girl that she was the first choice on the list. The young woman listened intently on the other end of the phone, then appeared to weigh up her decision. She mulled it over for all of thirty seconds: she was in. Autumn breathed a huge sigh of relief then scribbled her address on a piece of paper.

'One down, two to go,' she thought triumphantly. She would get all three courses signed on, then pass the addresses to Hendricks, he would have to go out and collect them, then return them to their homes later that evening. She leafed through and again saw a familiar face, the guy in the yellow top from the last event stared out at her. She called him: no answer. She set his printout to the side and vowed to keep trying him at a later date. She tried six more people. All of them turned her down. It seemed that for most people this wasn't a decision that could be made at the drop of a hat.

Autumn checked her watch. She had just thirty-five minutes left. She called the next on the list, a reasonably good-looking middle aged man with slightly greying hair and a distinguished air about him. He'd listed the reason for applying as 'money troubles'. Autumn hoped he hadn't won the lottery in the interim. The phone rang twice then connected.

"Hello?" A man's voice answered.

"Hi is that..." She glanced down at the photograph. "Grant?"

The man confirmed his identity. Autumn explained who she was, where she was from and what she wanted, making sure to put extra emphasis on the possible money to be made. The man paused, clearly not one hundred percent sure what his answer would be. Autumn was anxious now. She looked at her watch again: five minutes had passed.

"Okay," he said, "I'll do it."

Autumn breathed a sigh of relief.

"I can't believe I'm doing this!" he exclaimed.

He gave Autumn his address and just like before, she wrote it down. Autumn told the man that a driver would be sent for him shortly hung and up the phone. Both courses lived pretty close but it was still cutting it fine; even if Hendricks left now he would only just be back in time. She dialled the driver's extension number, he answered and she gave him his instructions. He sounded sleepy and Autumn was sure she'd just interrupted a mid-shift nap. There was no time to find a third course. Autumn made the decision then and there. She was going to end things how they'd started.

Autumn stepped out onto the stage to wolf whistles and cries of approval. She heard one guest say, "They saved the best for last, didn't they?" There was a time when this would have fed Autumn's ego, but not now. The two courses preceding her had made decent money. It seemed everyone was in the Christmas spirit. Celina had rallied the crowd expertly, whipping them up into a bidding frenzy in order to squeeze them for every penny she could. The bidding started, Autumn looked into the crowd. In her fever in finding courses she had well and truly forgotten the presence of Chris Lambert. He stood, mouth open, staring at her. Her new hair and heavy makeup hadn't fooled him. She looked at him, pleading for him not to reveal her secret.

"Sold!" Celina cried exuberantly. Autumn's attention was snatched away as she scoured the crowd, trying to see who had won her for the evening. There was movement as the crowd parted to let the bidder through. Autumn examined the horde of people closely; she couldn't make out who was coming forward. She felt a familiar tingle of anticipation. No matter how much she wanted out of this place she couldn't hide from the fact that, sexually, this place had awoken her. A man stepped onto the stage, closely followed by another.

They were both dressed in black; one was tanned, the other much paler. They looked at her, each in turn running his eyes over her body.

'Well, it could have been worse, at least I'll end it with a bang,' Autumn thought, pleased that it hadn't been Chris Lambert who bid on her. The darker of the two men walked past Autumn while the other took her by the arm and led her into the hallway of fantasy rooms. She stopped to collect the wine she had hidden on the way. The men had clearly been here before, and they walked straight to room number twelve. It was about halfway down and was decorated with oak furniture and a large leather sofa with a deep red Indian rug in front of it. Behind the sofa stood a huge set of shelves bursting with what Autumn had come to know as bondage equipment. They walked in. The smaller, darker man took the wine from Autumn's hand and poured her a glass. She took a deep and satisfying drink, thinking she hadn't had nearly enough alcohol for what was about to happen. Still, she was excited, as she'd come to view these experiences as being just that. They were thrilling, exhilarating and extremely satisfying. She had thought she was done with it all, but when she couldn't find a third course, she'd been secretly delighted.

Autumn sat on the sofa, cool against her skin. The men introduced themselves. The taller of the two was Thomas; he was good looking with designer stubble and Autumn would guess several years younger than his counterpart. The other was introduced as Gabriel, a dashing, slightly greying older man who seemed more reserved than Thomas. They were friends who wanted to experience one woman between them. Autumn thought she had heard it all now. They sat talking on the heavy oak chairs. The two men were relaxed which put Autumn at ease; they sipped on the full bodied red wine from Autumn's personal supply and chatted for a while. For the most part it was Autumn who drank from it. The conversation soon turned to sex. They questioned Autumn on her fantasies and what she liked most in the bedroom.

Eventually Thomas made a move. He picked up a length of rope and moved to Autumn, and asked her if it was okay. Autumn nodded submissively. He gently looped it around Autumn's chest and secured her to the chair she was sat on. She stiffened with excitement. These two seemed very experienced and were much older than her. Their combined proficiency was going to mean that Autumn had a truly unforgettable time. Thomas tapped the panel by the door: the room flooded with music. The men stood with their backs to Autumn. The rope cut across her chest, the fabric of her dress straining underneath its rough surface. Gabriel walked up to Autumn with something in his hand that Autumn was unfamiliar with: it was a gag of sorts, and it had leather straps either side of a metal ring. The ring had curved bars on either side. Autumn couldn't fathom what it was, for she had little experience with gags. She knew what they looked like, of course, but this gag was different. She quickly realised that total submission would be her only option. She inspected the gag closely as Gabriel held it before her and tried to imagine what it was going to feel like.

"What is it?" she asked curiously, noticing the curved bars extending from the central ring.

"It's a spider gag, Autumn. Those leggy bits keep your lips and your mouth parted to leave you feeling utterly unprotected. Plus, they make it really difficult for you to escape – I want you reliably restrained while we play with you."

Gabriel held the gag out impatiently and Autumn dutifully opened her mouth. The ring fit neatly behind her teeth; the bars cupped over her cheeks, preventing her from flipping the gag. It was well and truly stuck in place. It held her mouth open, leaving her feeling totally exposed and completely at the mercy of the two men. Gabriel unzipped his trousers and took out his strong erection; a glint of pre-cum could be seen glistening from its tip in the dimly lit room. Autumn began to drool. She couldn't swallow with the gag in place. Thick swathes of saliva dripped down the side of her face. Gabriel tilted her chin towards him and licked her cheek, running his tongue over the bars of the gag as he did so. Thomas moved around to get a better view. He stood there staring, his eyes greedily taking in the sight before him. Autumn's head was at Gabriel's crotch level. He thrust his hips forward and pushed his erection through the ring and into her mouth. His hard on found its way down to the back of her throat; he pushed himself further and further until she could do nothing but gag.

"She's choking on your cock Gabe," Thomas mused from his distanced position. Autumn glanced at him: she could see an enormous bulge in his trousers and was wondering when the taller man would get involved.

Gabriel withdrew himself, his iron hard rod covered in Autumn's saliva. He gave Thomas a smug look.

She shuffled in her chair as Gabriel bent down and pulled her dress up. He was delighted to see that she wore no underwear and was wet with desire. He slapped the inside of her thighs, ordering her to spread her legs wide. She obeyed and looked at Thomas. He had pulled up a chair and was now lazily reclining, rubbing his crotch through the material of his trousers. His dark eyes never left Autumn's body. Gabriel had stripped fully now and was kneeling down. Autumn could see that he had a smattering of dark hair that covered his chest, and she watched his muscular arms flex and contract as he bound her feet to the chair legs. He stood up and loosened the rope around her chest. Autumn took in a big gulp of air, revelling as it hit the back of her throat and inflated her lungs. The relief didn't last long; he pulled her dress over her head and cast it aside. He doubled the rope around her, one strand above and one below her breasts and retied her to the chair.

"Choose me some clamps, Tom," he instructed.

Tom stood up and sauntered over to the shelves. He surveyed their offerings and chose two weighted metal clamps that looked like they'd be more at home in a mechanic's garage. Autumn tensed as her saw him bring them over and pass them to Gabriel.

Gabriel took each clamp in turn and held them over Autumn's nipples, releasing them simultaneously. They were heavy and pulled her nipples downward. She jerked her head down and saw her ample globes stretched under their weight. The clamps offered a delicious pinch, which caused electric pleasure to course through her body.

When he was done, Gabriel stood back to admire his handiwork. The beautiful woman before him was naked, bound and treading that fine line between pleasure and pain. He had total and utter control over her. His cock stiffened further, and it ached to be satisfied. Gabriel picked up another clamp; he bent down and blew on Autumn's glistening folds. She shivered; a wave of anticipation washed over her, which was replaced instantly by a sharp sudden squeeze. She looked down: another clamp, only this time he'd placed it on her clitoris. It had a chain hanging from it and at the very end a jewelled weight. It rested on the seat in front of her.

"This is only half pressure," Gabriel explained. "Each time you disappoint, I will tighten it." Autumn nodded weakly, wondering just how much tighter it could get. She could feel blood rushing to that sensitive area already, she pulsated under the force and throbbed with expectancy. He reached underneath her and pulled something free, the bottom fell out of the chair and it clattered to the floor. The clamp's chain now hung down and pulled on her sensitive nub. The feeling was intense but exquisite; again she found herself walking that fine line between pleasure and pain and loved every single step that she took. The coarse ropes still held her tightly in place, their rough embrace securing her in place, daring her to try and move. Autumn's eyes grew wide as she saw Gabriel drag a black box with a metal arm over to her and positioned it directly underneath her chair.

Thomas passed Gabriel a short but girthy flesh-coloured dildo. Gabriel held it up before kneeling down again. He fixed the dildo to the machine and altered its position.

"We both want to watch you," Gabriel said in a matter-of-fact voice. He drizzled thick lubricant onto the toy's life-like surface and switched the machine on, standing back to witness it at work. The machine started slowly, teasing her. It had barely parted her delicate folds before it pulled itself back. She moaned; this was a machine of torment, it offered her the world, then withdrew the promise almost at once. Hot undulating waves washed over her as she fought not to climax too soon. Thomas bent down and tightened the clitoral clamp, ravenously watching her squirm against the newly heightened sensations. Her eyes rolled back and she moaned again. The gag was making her jaw ache so when Gabriel made to remove it she was awash with relief.

Autumn barely noticed Thomas stand up. He had joined Gabriel in a state of undress. He altered the dial and the machine penetrated her more deeply. It rhythmically pumped in and out of her and seemed to be invading her ever more deeply with each thrust. The two men gazed at her hungrily through lust-filled eyes as they watched her helplessly tied to the chair. It was Gabriel's turn to play God now; copying Thomas's actions he leant down and altered the intensity. He turned the dial sharply and watched as Autumn whimpered and moaned in a pre-orgasmic frenzy. She writhed in ecstasy; every single sensation was delectably intense. Thomas and Gabriel lapped up each cry that escaped her lips. Thomas stepped in closer, he loomed over her and tilted his pelvis forward. Autumn hungrily took his penis in her mouth and sucked on it eagerly. He pushed it deeper, compelling her to take his entire length. She took it in turns to pleasure both men, once again feeling empowered by her submissive role. She was so close to climaxing now; the clamp pulling on her clitoris seemed to be pinching harder, inflicting a delectable arrow to the heart of her ecstasy.

Autumn let her head fall back, her long hair ticked the top of her buttocks; she closed her eyes, wishing more than anything that this moment could be endless. She opened her eyes, but couldn't see. A blindfold had been placed around her head. One of the men tied it tightly around her. She was now in complete darkness.

The machine slowed and finally withdrew and she felt the ropes loosen from around her feet and chest. Strong arms lifted her from the chair that she guessed were Gabriel's. She found herself sat astride one of the men. She was lowered directly onto his immense shaft. It filled her to breaking point; her internal muscles seemed to spasm in order to accommodate his incredible size. The man undid the clamp and freed her throbbing clitoris. The reprieve she felt was heavenly. He pulled her forward and for the first time her lips met his, he kissed her passionately. There was a sense of urgency there. Autumn returned the kiss, their tongues entwined as their lips pressed against one another's. She felt more lubricant being drizzled on her, it fell onto her buttocks and slipped down between her cheeks. The cool, thick liquid was massaged into her anus by nimble fingertips, circling the tight hole. Whoever it was occasionally tempted himself by entering ever so slightly. Autumn gasped every time he came close to invading her. The man underneath would not let her relent, though; he held her head firmly, prolonging their kiss.

"Is this alright?" came Gabriel's voice from behind her as he pushed his erection between her buttocks. The mystery was solved: it was Thomas she sat astride. Autumn flashed back to her first ever session at Encounters, when she had been made to wear a butt plug for the first time. There was no denying it, it had felt incredible and she'd never felt fuller or more satisfied. Autumn nodded her approval, she wanted to replicate that feeling so pushed back, encouraging him to penetrate her. He obliged and pressed forward. The delicate skin parted, allowing him access to her most private area. He drizzled more lubricant, covering his shaft as well as her. Slowly but surely, he pushed inside of her until she had devoured his entire length. She pulled away from Thomas and cried out huskily. The double penetration felt almost too intense to handle. The two men worked in unison, thrusting into her at the same time. Their hips bucked and she writhed under their attention.

Thomas played his trump card. In his hand he held a small, slim vibrator. He turned it on and pushed it down: it connected with her still sensitive and swollen nub and she reared against it, desperate for that sweet release. Gabriel leaned forward and felt her rear tighten around him. He pulled the nipple clamps free in one swift action. Autumn had reached her peak, the sensory overload was too much and she climaxed, shaking and moaning loudly as she did so. Thomas held the vibrator firmly against her, pressing it harder against her as she bucked wildly on top of him, barely able to control herself. The two men quickened their pace, wanting to join her in the exquisite release of climax. In her post-orgasmic bliss, she barely felt them tense inside her. She was lost in her own moment.

They fell in a crumpled pile on top of one another. Autumn was sandwiched between the two men, enjoying the warmth of their skin on hers. Gabriel pulled himself out, panting with the ferocity of what they had just done. Autumn felt him go and momentarily mourned his leaving. She climbed off the table, leaving Thomas lying there and grabbed a tissue from the sanitation station hidden in the corner of the room. She passed the box around and watched as the two men cleaned themselves. Both of them glistened with the sheen that only came from a frantic sex session. She pulled her dress back on, wincing as the fabric brushed her nipples. They were exceptionally sensitive now, and Autumn knew they'd be a reminder of Gabriel and Thomas for a while to come. The two men re-dressed and Autumn noticed them sharing knowing looks. Autumn smiled; *'a subliminal high five,'* she supposed.

"Shall we return to the party?" she asked. The wine was finished and so were they. They nodded; Gabriel expressed a need for a stronger drink and Thomas whole-heartedly agreed. Autumn smiled at the two men and placed her hand on the brass doorknob to leave. It was unusually warm. She hesitated, then, feeling silly, pulled the door open. All three of them stood there, struck dumb as thick dark smoke began to rush in. The sound of an alarm rang in through the open door.

CHAPTER 26

AUTUMN WAS PANICKED: SHE SLAMMED THE DOOR and turned to look at Thomas and Gabriel. Their faces were awash with worry.

"Is, there a… a fire?" Thomas stammered, his voice shaking. Gabriel held onto his arm to steady him. They both stared at Autumn, who nodded. Her mind raced, trying to recall exactly where the emergency exits were. She brushed her hand on the doorknob once more. It felt warmer than before: the fire was clearly creeping closer.

"Okay, we can't stay here," she said commandingly, taking control of the situation. "We have to get out as quickly as we can." The two men seemed to shrink backwards, preferring the sanctity of their little safe haven than the unknown danger beyond.

"Couldn't we just wait it out?" Gabriel asked. "That door's thick; it looks like it'd hold." He motioned to the door hopefully. Autumn stared in disbelief.

"No, we can't stay here," she remonstrated. "Come on, guys, I need you to keep your heads." Autumn had barely known the men for more than an hour but right now they were her lifelines to safety and she was theirs. "Okay, on the count of three I'm going to open the door. Get on your hands and knees. We're going to crawl to the nearest exit." Autumn racked her brains, still not one hundred percent sure she'd be able to find the exit. The two men nodded, both pale in the face now, clearly terrified for themselves and each other.

"Okay," Autumn said, taking a deep breath. Her hand was shaking now, trembling with an uncontrollable fear that was taking over her entire body. She steadied herself: she needed to keep it together, she couldn't die here. "One, two, three." She dove to the ground, joining Thomas and Gabriel. The three of them crawled out. The hallway was in chaos: scantily-clad men and women ran panic-stricken. The hallway was smoky, but not as bad as Autumn had imagined. Autumn called at the guests to follow her, her voice drowned out by panic. Thomas seemed to have found his voice now, he bellowed down the hallway.

"Follow her, she knows how to get out!" he yelled at the top of his lungs before bursting into a coughing fit.

Gabriel beckoned to those closest and the guests that weren't already on the floor followed their lead. Autumn pressed on: she knew if she could just get as many people as she could into the back and through the offices she could get them out alive. The problem everyone else would have was that from the ballroom the only way in and out was through the ridiculous lift system Celina had been hell-bent on installing. She guessed that their guests would probably value their lives more than their privacy in events such as this. She coughed. The smoke was getting more acrid, and she wiped sweat from her face. She could hear the panic rising behind her.

'Breathe Autumn, you can do this,' she repeated to herself over and over again; the mantra calmed her somewhat. She rounded the corner and could just about make out the wooden door with the brass plaque that read 'staff only'. It was one of the doors that led to the offices. She just hoped that through there they'd find safe passage. Autumn was

renewed by a surge of willingness. She crawled forward and pushed the door. It wouldn't open. She braced herself and shoved it harder this time. Still nothing. Thomas broke through the other guests to the front and shoved the door. It gave way and flung open. Autumn felt clean, fresh air rush past her face. The group poured through the doorway, and Autumn fell against the now closed door, breathing heavily. Her chest heaving, her lungs ached and her head pounded.

It was eerily still in the office section of the building. If their lives hadn't been hanging in the balance mere moments before, she'd have found the scene in front of her funny. A woman wearing nothing but a satin nightie, a man in stockings and suspenders and a couple who had quite clearly been mid-coitus as the only thing they wore were worried expressions. They clung to one another in an effort to hide their modesty. Taking pity on them all, Autumn rounded the corner to the offices. She pulled throws off chairs and took them to the fearful guests. They had relaxed a little now they were out of immediate danger and took the shrouds gladly, covering themselves over quickly.

"Right," Autumn said, "we need to call the emergency services immediately..." A portly bear of a man interrupted her.

"But how? We handed all of our phones over when we got here."

Autumn nodded, she had known that was the way since day one but in the panic had forgotten. "I work here. I'll call from the office. Everyone follow me; we need to stay together," she instructed, feeling authority radiate from her. The group followed quickly and quietly, seemingly afraid that any noise might draw the fire closer to them. Autumn picked up the handset from the desk and dialled nine three times. The operator asked which services she needed. Hurriedly she explained their situation. The operator talked her through what she should do: drench towels or sheets in water, wrap them around people and crawl to an exit. Do not stop to collect personal belongings or anything else. Autumn ignored the last piece of advice. She was the only one with a mobile phone, and who knew what other predicaments they might run into? She went for her bag, grabbed it and slung it over her shoulder. There were no towels or sheets here, and she didn't fancy taking a trip back to the fantasy rooms to collect some.

She closed her office door. On the back was an obligatory fire safety diagram. Autumn studied it. The exit was a little further than she had thought, but they were pretty safe here. She was confident they would make it. There was an almighty crash from outside. Autumn ran out and saw that the door separating the offices from the fantasy rooms had collapsed in on itself. Smoke began to seep through. There were screams from some of the guests as they bundled together, hoping that the age-old adage of safety in numbers would hold true for them now.

"Come on, this way," Autumn cried, walking briskly towards the exit. "Don't look back," she instructed hoarsely, her voice straining as she quickened her pace.

The operator had told her not to run: running causes panic, meaning that the chance of injury was far greater. She thought it valid advice so stuck to it. The guests followed her. Their group was about twenty-strong; Autumn hoped she could get them out safely. Before long she saw the exit. It was squirrelled around a corner out of view. Celina had probably thought that the luminous green sign on the door was ugly and should be kept out of sight. Autumn pushed the horizontal bar on the door; it gave way and they spilled out onto a metal spiral staircase bolted precariously on the side of the building. It wobbled and creaked under the weight of so many people, obviously not accustomed to any use. A woman screeched in pain as she lost her footing and fell onto the person below. Thankfully he was sturdier, and by the looks of it, he had a good grip on the railing. He swayed slightly under the unexpected strain but stayed upright. The woman pulled herself off him and continued down the iron steps, hobbling slightly as she went. Autumn stayed inside the building; she wanted to make sure every last guest was out safely before she left herself. Once they were all out and climbing down the metal steps, Autumn went to leave. She thought she heard something coming from the offices.

"Hello?" she called. "Is anyone there?" There was no answer. Autumn strained, listening intently for any sort of movement. She was positive she had heard something, or someone. The smoke was thickening now. It crept towards her, an eerie threatening cloud of acrid smog. She tried to peer through it and called out again, but she couldn't see or hear anything apart from the sounds of approaching sirens.

"Autumn, come on!" A male voice carried over the din – she thought it was Gabriel but in the confusion and panic it could have been anyone. After one last hesitant look she left the Encounters building, making sure the door was closed tightly behind her. She descended the steps carefully, all the while clutching her bag to her chest as if it were her lifejacket.

Fire engines, ambulances and police cars were already pulling up on the street outside. Men and women readied themselves to tackle the blaze. The guests Autumn had ushered out of the building were being wrapped in foil blankets and given oxygen. Autumn coughed; a female fire-fighter came over to her and offered a blanket but Autumn waved it away.

"I'm fine, thanks," she said, a grateful smile on her face. The adrenaline coursing through her veins had made her break out in a sweat; she was more than warm despite the cold night air that circled around her. Autumn looked around. The emergency exit had brought them out onto a side street. The fire-fighters were having difficulty getting to the building itself due to the immense privacy measures Celina had gone through to ensure that the club stayed hidden and exclusive. She could hear them discussing their plan of attack. Autumn heard one of the guests tell an officer that she was in charge. She was approached by two people, a policewoman and from the looks of it the chief of the fire-fighters.

"You own this place?" The policewoman asked, her hands on her hips in an authoritative stance. Autumn shook her head.

"I, I just work here," she replied. "It was actually my last day." The police officer didn't care for this information; she just wanted to know facts that could help them and told Autumn so.

"Anything you can tell us about the building's layout would be really helpful. Do you have any idea where the fire might have started?" the policewoman asked quickly; her tone was urgent now. Autumn knew there must still be people inside. She told them everything she knew, from the complicated entry system to the layout and how many guests had been in attendance. She gave them her membership number for easy access, should they need it: the place really was built like a fortress.

A local news van pulled up alongside the emergency service vehicles. It turned out Channel Seven had caught wind of the incident pretty quickly. A newswoman and her camera operator swarmed upon her. A microphone was pushed into her face.

"Can you tell us how the fire started, miss? How many people are trapped inside? How does it feel to have escaped with your life?" the newswoman fired at her.

Autumn stared at the woman: she was still in shock, she wasn't in a position to be interrogated. None of this was her fault. Autumn burst into uncontrollable tears and turned away, her blackened face crumpling under the weight of what had just happened.

"Well there you have it," the newswoman said, turning to the camera. "One young woman too traumatised even to speak. We'll be back to update you with more details as soon as we can, back to you in the studio."

Autumn wiped at her eyes with the back of her hand, she needed to pull herself together.

She retrieved her phone and handed it to a sobbing woman, desperate to speak to her husband – begging someone, anyone to help. "I need to tell him I'm alright," the woman wailed. She grabbed the phone from Autumn's hand, thanking her over and over again as she dialled a number.

Autumn heard a voice call her name and looked up. Chris Lambert was running over to her, his suit torn, his face smudged with soot. She was so glad to see a familiar face, even if it was Chris's. He embraced her and she hugged him back tightly. Fresh tears pouring from her eyes, he released her. They spoke briefly about what had happened. Chris had led the way from the ballroom, managing to override the lift system with a technical engineer who had attended. Autumn thanked the heavens for her new, less strict admissions policy. Floods of people had spilled out into the car park where Hendricks lay, napping in his car. They woke him up and he let them out, groups of twelve at a time. Chris had waited until every single person was out before leaving and that, in Autumn's eyes made him a hero.

"Do you know how it started?" he asked her, a serious expression on his streaked face.

Autumn shook her head fiercely. She really didn't know; no matter how hard she thought on it, she couldn't fathom how this had happened.

The fire-fighters were in full swing now: having been able to access the building through the external escapes, they got to work quickly and forcefully. Ladders stretched out into the sky; water spurted out in great jets overwhelming the flames, which had been lapping menacingly into the icy night sky. Autumn sighed, then realised the woman had walked off with her phone. She scoured the crowd and spotted her talking to a tall policeman, his back to her. She walked to the woman, passing the fire chief and a subordinate in deep conversation.

"Well, thank God. It looks like the fire was contained just long enough for everyone to escape," the fire chief said, looking skyward, appreciative that his crew were able to battling the dwindling flames.

"I'm sorry to interrupt, but have you still got my phone?" she asked when she finally reached the woman, who was in deep conversation with a tall police officer. She had one hand on her hip and was twirling a lock of her hair seductively around her fingers. Autumn looked up.

"Autumn?" Jake asked, visibly shocked. Had her face not been covered in soot he would have seen the colour drain from it in an instant. She stood there in disbelief, unable to gather her thoughts, let alone assemble them into words. After everything he'd seen with her this must be the cherry on top. "Are you alright?" He asked anxiously. Autumn could do nothing but nod stupidly. She was painfully aware that there was no escaping this situation.

"I, err... I," she exhaled, giving up. She couldn't lie to him. "I work here," she said in a small voice. "Or rather, *worked* here. This was my last day."

"But this is a brothel, right? You're a prostitute?" He questioned incredulously, as though he couldn't believe it. He thought she'd been a receptionist or a PA or something along those lines. Autumn shook her head. She was too tired to explain; besides, he probably wouldn't believe her anyway.

"It's okay, Autumn. You don't have to explain, certainly not to me. Let's just concentrate on making sure you're alright and get you home," he said curtly but not unkindly.

"Thanks, I really am fine though. If I'm not needed, I'll just call a cab. If I ever get my phone back," she half-heartedly quipped.

"I can take you?" he offered, softening slightly. "I'm not technically working today anyway, it was just an all-hands-on-deck kind of situation. I'm sure I'll be able to run you home."

Autumn smiled and thanked him. The fire seemed to be dwindling now, the flames had gone and the black smoke that had been billowing out into the clear night sky was now only appearing in faint, grey breaths. She was sure that there was nothing more she could do. She looked around again for the woman she'd lent her phone to but there was now no sign of her. Autumn decided to leave it. She really couldn't care less about a phone right now. She just wanted to get to bed. She gave Jake her address as he put her in the back of a car and told her to wait there. After a few moments, the driver's door opened.

"You're not Jake?" she said to the man curtly.

"You're right there, little lady. He *wishes* he could have a body like this," the new police officer said, ignoring her abrupt manner and grabbing a handful of his portly mid-section, by way of emphasising their differences. The fine lines around his eyes crinkled as he laughed at his own joke.

Autumn was disappointed. She looked out the window as they set off and saw Jake in deep conversation with an attractive firewoman. He afforded her one last glance as she was driven off before quickly resuming his conversation.

'That's that I guess,' Autumn thought sadly to herself. Perhaps the fact that she worked at a place like Encounters was the final straw. Jake was a good, upstanding man of the law. Autumn was probably the last person he could see himself with. As they pulled away her breath caught in her throat. The fire crew was bringing someone out on a wheeled stretcher, his or her body covered by a black sheet.

'Someone has died,' Autumn thought in absolute shock. She thought everyone was out and that the fire had been contained for long enough for everyone to escape. She'd heard those exact words come out of the fire chief's lips. Autumn strained her head, trying to see if she recognised the body, but it was no use; it was entirely covered. As the policeman backed the car up, Autumn took one last look, just in time to see a hand fall lifelessly by the side of the stretcher: covering it was a soot-stained, long, cream glove.

The policeman dropped Autumn off outside her building. She thanked him and drifted inside. Her body seemed to be in autopilot now; her legs felt heavy, like she was trying to wade through treacle. It was all she could do to put one foot in front of the other. No matter how sluggish her body was it didn't stop her mind from racing.

Celina was dead.

CHAPTER 27

AUTUMN WAS HAULED FROM HER SLUMBER BY A banging at her door. She groggily got out of bed and trudged over; she looked through the spy hole and flung the door open. Her parents stood in the communal hallway, their faces streaked with tears, both red and puffy from crying. All three of them stood in the doorway in an almighty embrace. Her dad, racked with grief, shook uncontrollably as he hugged his daughter.

"Thank God you're alright," Sarah Carter cried through stifled sobs. "Oh Autumn! We saw on the news this morning. Look at you, you're filthy and you look terrible."

Autumn hadn't showered when she'd got in. She hadn't done anything, except to trudge to her bed and collapse on it, still in her little black dress. She managed a wry smile. She'd escaped a fire, managed to save several people and seen her boss die. What did her mum expect her to look like?

"We're so glad you're okay," Richard said, relief flooding his voice. "When I saw you on the news, you just looked so little, so lost. I couldn't protect you."

He broke down again, and Sarah put her arm around him. She felt her husband's pain. She too had felt the absolute feeling of redundancy watching her daughter break down on camera. They had tried ringing but had only been able to get through to a woman named Matilda who had told them of

Autumn's bravery, how she'd remained calm and got them all out alive. Her parents were incredibly proud, and anything they'd felt before the fire was instantly erased. Their daughter was a good person, she was brave and thoughtful and fierce and they loved her for it.

"Come home Autumn. Let us look after you," her mum insisted, looking around at the tiny one-bed their daughter was living in. "You shouldn't be on your own after a trauma like this."

Autumn shook her head. Going back to The Barings was a bad idea, considering what had happened last time.

"We won't take no for an answer," her dad asserted. "We've borrowed a van from the Cohens. They've just moved their son into university. Do you know he's studying economics? Very clever, that young lad."

Autumn cringed at her dad's apparent envy of the Cohen son.

She thought about it. Could she just up and go? She'd barely been in this flat two weeks. Contrary to Mike's warning she still hadn't paid a deposit or supplied him with any references. There just hadn't been time to sort that stuff out. This meant that she could leave, it wouldn't harm anything and she'd never even signed a contract. Poor Mike had been so rushed to get her out of the office that he'd neglected to get her to agree to anything legally. She mulled it over, then the need for a stable environment with her parents overrode her need for independence.

"Okay then, let's do this," she agreed.

Her parents were clearly delighted. Her mum pulled out her own phone now, her fingers typing out a message at breakneck speed.

"Just letting David and Gregg know you're safe," she justified. "They're such a lovely couple. I've said they can use our house after their wedding. We've got eleven guests staying after the evening drinks, including Gregg's mother. She's from Surrey, you know, so I do hope our house is up to her standards," she blabbered.

Autumn was amazed at how her mum could flit between emotions, as barely five minutes ago she'd been an emotional wreck and now she was enthusiastically planning for David and Gregg's big day. Which Autumn realised, with an apprehensive slump, was less than twenty-four hours away.

"OK, we've got a lot to do," her mum said, putting her organisational hat on and pulling black bin bags from the tote bag slung over her shoulder. "Thankfully you don't have a lot. Sorry, love," she apologised after seeing Autumn's affronted expression.

The three of them set to work. They packed things solidly for an hour, Sarah doing the majority of the packing whilst Autumn and her dad carried things up and down the stairs from the flat's front door to the van parked on the street below. Autumn slumped down on the little sofa in the middle of the living room and looked about. Her residence here had been short and sweet. It had done the job and been her port in the storm that had been her life. Now, though, she was ready to sail to calmer seas. She felt mixed emotions about what had happened. She certainly wouldn't miss Celina, but never in a million years would she have wished her dead. Autumn couldn't understand why she had been caught in the fire. Surely she had been in the ballroom with everyone else, so why hadn't she just got out when she had the chance? Autumn now knew it was Celina who she had heard back in the offices. She thought grimly that maybe there had been something in her own office she had deemed worthy to go back for: perhaps money, maybe incriminating files? Whatever it had been, it had cost Celina her life.

'A captain should always go down with her ship,' she thought to herself grimly. The only silver lining would be that Jack would be able to go on with his own life now and be free to be true to himself. Autumn wondered if he would even mourn Celina's loss.

She shook the idea from her head and turned her attention to happier thoughts. She was going home. Her best friend was getting married and she'd still had the chance to work for Melissa Abbott. The hard copy of the article had almost gone up in flames. Autumn glanced at her bag, glad that she'd gone back for it. Deep inside was a USB stick with all her work on, as well as the notes she'd been diligently making since her phone conversation with Melissa, which seemed like so long ago now.

Autumn and her family arrived back at The Barings a short time later; her eyes wide, drinking in the familiar sight of her family home, it once again offering comfort and loving support. She climbed out and feeling utterly exhausted once more excused herself and headed upstairs. Sarah and Richard unpacked the car, placing all the household items back in the garage and dropping the bin bags filled with her clothes outside Autumn's bedroom door, ready for sorting at a later date. Autumn slept for the rest of the day, waking only once to be greeted by her mum who was carrying a tray laden with sandwiches. The two women sat on the bed, and Autumn managed one before nodding back off. Sarah gingerly took the tray away, careful not disturb her daughter who was resting so peacefully.

Autumn awoke with a start. Melissa Abbott had crept into her dreams. She leaned over and grabbed her laptop. It was two in the morning. It might look unprofessional to send the article at this time, but Autumn couldn't wait. She knew she had to do it there and then if she was going to stand any chance of getting a half decent night's sleep. She attached the article entitled 'My Encounter with Encounters' and pressed 'send', hoping against hope that it was good enough for her idol.

The following day the whole house was in pandemonium. It was, after all, David and Gregg's wedding day. All the Carters' house guests had arrived, flights were on time and Gregg's mother's drive from Surrey had gone by easily. She was a small woman who shared Gregg's smooth dark skin tone and striking eyes. It was clear for all to see where Gregg had got his good looks. They spent most of the morning getting ready. Autumn still didn't have a clue what to wear to the wedding: all the fine gowns had gone up in flames, except one. It dawned on her suddenly that the emerald green dress from the second event was still shoved in the bottom of her overnight bag after she had been unceremoniously ejected from Celina's. Autumn scrambled for the bag and retrieved the dress. It had a feint musty smell but looked clean enough. It was nothing some fabric freshener and a good iron wouldn't fix. Autumn tended to her dress quickly, noticing that, as usual, she was running late. Her newly darkened hair was pulled up in an elegant chignon. She had learnt a thing or two from Martin and was now much more adept at hairdos. Her makeup was subtle; just a flick of mascara and a slick of lip-gloss adorned her face. She didn't want it too heavy for the ceremony for fear of it running down her face when it all got a bit too much; she was such a sucker for a happy ending. She'd packed some makeup in her clutch bag and would reapply later if needed.

Her phone rang. The lady she had lent it to, Matilda, had accidentally taken it home with her in the panic. She had brought it around to her parents whilst Autumn had been asleep, once again telling them just how amazing and brave their daughter had been.

"Hello?" Autumn answered the phone, she didn't recognise the number.

"Autumn, it's Melissa Abbott." Autumn's heart leapt into her throat the second she heard the Scottish accent on the line. "I don't know how to say this, but I loved your article, and it was so well-written. I loved its honest, raw qualities. I'd be a fool not to employ you after that."

Autumn managed a small noise in acknowledgement.

"So, let me know the second you've got your diploma. I've got to shoot now, Autumn, and this time I really do have a meeting."

Autumn managed to thank Melissa before she hung up. She was totally bewildered by what had just happened. The shriek from her mother brought her back to reality with a bump.

"Oh no!" Sarah exclaimed as she ushered everyone out to leave for the registry office.

"What is it?" Gregg asked; his southern American drawl sounded strained, panicked even.

"Oh nothing," Sarah backtracked, "you guys get in the cars. I'll just lock up." She shakily picked up her keys which jangled noisily.

Autumn wandered over to her mum. Sarah couldn't hide from her daughter, Autumn always knew when something wasn't right with her.

"What's wrong mum?" She whispered. Autumn had decided not to tell anyone about the job, as she still needed to pass her exams first. Besides, it was David and Gregg's big day and she'd had enough of being selfish. The thunder was theirs and theirs alone today.

"I haven't counted right," she confessed, looking mortified at her error.

"I don't understand. Counted what?" Autumn asked, not comprehending what it was her mother was getting at.

"There isn't enough space in the cars. We're already squeezing in as it is," she admitted.

Autumn racked her brains for a solution. Maybe they could do two trips – if they were quick about it they might make it in time. No, that wouldn't work. She took the key out of her mother's hand.

"You go on ahead. I'll phone for a taxi," Autumn suggested firmly.

"You can't do that, you're a groomsman!" she said, ignoring her daughter's suppressed giggle. "Well, okay then, a 'maidsman' or 'groomswoman', whatever you two are calling it!"

"Seriously Mum, go on. They're all waiting. I need to finish my makeup anyway," she lied.

"Well, I didn't like to say anything, but you do look awfully drained, very washed out. A little bronzer wouldn't go amiss," Sarah said, relieved that her beautiful daughter was going to make a bit more of herself.

"Thanks Mum," Autumn said through gritted teeth. She pushed her mother out of the door and watched her climb into the last remaining car next to her father. Autumn walked inside and phoned a taxi. She knew the damn number off by heart now. She was lucky. It was a mid-afternoon on a Monday so taxis weren't in great demand. She'd only have fifteen minutes to wait. She looked at her watch: that still gave her plenty of time to find get there and find her seat before David walked down the aisle.

She surveyed her reflection in the hall mirror. She didn't look that bad! She actually thought that with the new dark hair she suited the more natural look. The dress looked even more amazing now, as she had teamed it with chunky gold jewellery to give it a more relaxed look, and on her feet she wore the only reminder she still had of her time at Encounters, the gold strappy Louboutins. They'd been with her through thick and thin, although they weren't as pristine now – the souls were scuffed and they were slightly blackened on one of the straps – but that aside, they were in pretty good condition. Every mark on them was a reminder to always look forward and never back.

Her thoughts were interrupted by a knock at the door. Autumn opened it, and it was a delivery driver with a large brown envelope in his hand. He handed it to her and she signed for it, placing it on the antique telephone table by the front door. She picked up her bag and checked that she definitely had packed some tissues. The doorknocker boomed again. She opened the door again.

"Did you forget something?" she asked the postman pleasantly. Only the man stood in front of her wasn't the postman. She did a double take, hardly recognising the man in front of her. It was a very casually dressed Jake Sentori, clad in faded jeans and a chunky knit grey jumper. His dark hair was swept back from his face, his blue eyes staring at her intensely.

"You look amazing," he said almost breathlessly. His eyes fell the full length of her gown.

"I'm going to my friend's wedding," she muttered, completely in shock at the sight of him. She was sure after Saturday's horrible outcome she would never see him again. "Is this about the fire? Do they know what happened?"

"It looks like someone left a lot of candles burning in one of the rooms. They caught on some extremely flammable material and just went like wildfire."

Autumn nodded. Perhaps it had been the room that Leonardo had replenished. '*Maybe he was so keen to do a good job that he put extra candles in?*' Autumn pondered. She figured that she would never know. She cursed herself for not triple-checking everything; maybe if she had this might never have happened. She sighed. As much as she would like to, she couldn't turn back the clock.

"Actually, Autumn." It was his turn to look uncomfortable now. "I'm not here for that. I went to your flat, well to the address you gave on Saturday. But you weren't there, so I ran the address and there's no record of you ever living there."

"It's a long story," Autumn answered truthfully, not seeing how a change of address could land her in trouble, unless Mike had sold her out and she was about to be arrested for blackmail. "I don't live there now. I've moved back home."

"You get about," Jake said, immediately regretting his choice of words. Looking abashed, he averted his gaze.

"Is there something you need to speak to me about?" She asked, still confused as to why he was here. She looked at her watch. Panic was beginning to rise now. Autumn couldn't miss this wedding for anything.

"No, no. It's nothing like that," Jake said. This conversation was going nowhere fast. Autumn glanced at her watch again, hoping Jake would take the hint and either confess why he was here or let her get to the wedding. She looked up and was taken aback: Jake had taken a step closer to her. He stood there, gazing at her intently. He looked as though he were fighting some sort of inward battle, he bit his lip and ran his hand through his hair.

"I think you're amazing," he said quietly.

Her mouth fell open. Had she heard him right?

"You're beautiful, you're interesting and, well, you're downright crazy, but that's what I like about you," he said, a playful half-smile dancing around the corners of his mouth.

Autumn opened her mouth to speak, but no words came out. How could he possibly feel this way? They barely knew each other, and what he did know of her painted her in an extremely unflattering light.

She couldn't deny the attraction she felt towards him. He was good looking there was no doubt about it, but it ran deeper than that. He had a goodness about him that was rare these days. His hand interrupted her train of thought, he'd placed it lightly on her shoulder. She looked up at him: the sunlight catching on his hair made him look almost angelic.

"I've wanted to do this from the second I met you," he said, his voice taking on an authoritative but gentle air. He leaned forward and wrapped his arms around her waist. Autumn's heart beat faster now, she felt it pounding against her chest. She closed her eyes and let him kiss her. As their lips met she felt an explosion of emotion deep within her, a release so sweet it was all she could do not to let it overtake her. The kiss was tender, filled with a warm and deep affection that set her soul alight. Autumn couldn't remember the last time she had been kissed like that. She soared, the feeling lifting her up and elevating her into a higher state of being. She linked her hands behind his neck and pulled him closer, allowing herself to be enveloped by his strong embrace. He pulled away and looked into her eyes, his hand tucking a stray piece of hair behind her ear.

"I want to be with you Autumn. I want to care for you and to protect you. The thought of anyone else being with you devastates me. It's why I couldn't drive you home, I just couldn't deal with it all." Autumn nodded, remembering the connection she too had felt and kicking herself for not being able to see it for what it was.

"I, I don't know what to say," she muttered, she didn't know what to think, all she could do was listen to her heart. "I want to be with you. I'm sure of that now, but I can't think. I don't have time to..." She trailed off as her taxi pulled up the driveway. They had run out of time: Autumn needed to go and she needed to go now. Jake looked over his shoulder.

"I'll take you," he said. "Wherever you're going and for whatever reason, I'll take you there."

Autumn picked up her bag from the telephone table and stopped. The brown envelope she'd signed for was addressed to her. She thought about leaving the envelope – after all, it would still be there when she got back – but she just couldn't. Its mystery captured her: it looked so official and after everything that had happened she just couldn't put off opening it for another time.

"One second," she said to Jake as she opened the envelope and pulled out a pale blue and white certificate. It read, 'Autumn Carter, Journalism Diploma, High Merit'. Her hands started to shake. These were her results. She had passed and she had passed well.

"I passed!" she said, her voice small, hardly daring to believe it. "I passed," she repeated, holding the certificate out for Jake to see. He grinned at her.

"Well done! I've got no idea what you've passed but well done," he joked.

Autumn's initial shock now gave way to sheer joy. She was elated, stunned and deliriously happy. She could not believe she had passed, after everything she had been through.

Autumn couldn't wait to tell her parents, to tell David but most of all to tell Melissa. As excited as she was she knew that her news would have to wait, it was David and Gregg's big day and she'd done enough thunder-stealing as of late. She would save her news, it would be her – and Jake's – secret.

She breathed a huge sigh of relief, steadying herself as she realised that Melissa had liked, no, *loved*, her article. Autumn's pulse quickened as it suddenly dawned on her, she was going to work for her idol. Autumn's hand shook and the certificate wavered as she realised that she was going to write for the best women's magazine out there. The fact that she could put everything behind her filled her with a sense of elation akin to nothing she'd ever felt before. Autumn was unequivocally grateful, she'd been given a second chance and she was going to grab it with both hands.

Jake handed the taxi driver a fifty pound note and told him to keep the change as he apologised for the wasted journey on Autumn's behalf. The cab driver didn't seem at all bothered; it wasn't a waste if he'd earned double the expected fare.

Jake opened the passenger side door of his car and took Autumn by the hand to help her in. She slid into the passenger seat and held her bag tightly. Her hands had stopped shaking now but she still felt a little unsteady. Jake turned the key in the ignition but didn't pull away. Instead he leaned over to Autumn until their faces were barely an inch apart. Autumn closed her eyes and inhaled his scent: a sweet, ambrosial smell that set Autumn's pulse racing. Jake's fingertips brushed her cheek gently and sent an electrifying jolt of anticipation through her. Autumn's stomach flipped as she felt him flood her senses, she welcomed the sweeping embrace that was to come. Their lips met for a second time and the connection was heavenly. A little moan escaped her lips as she found his tongue searching hers. She melted into him, finally letting go of all that had happened. The kiss lasted mere moments but in those moments Autumn felt like she'd found herself. They unwillingly broke apart, both desperate for more but aware that life outside their bubble awaited them.

As they drove off Autumn turned around and watched her family home disappear into the distance. She turned her head and looked at Jake who returned her gaze with a quick glance and a small smile. He returned his attention to the road ahead and Autumn followed suit.

She couldn't explain it, nor did she want to, but she felt with all her heart that she was, for the first time in a long time, facing her future. A smile played around the corners of her mouth, a genuine smile filled with hope and happiness. She felt content, she felt whole – and she liked that feeling very much.